BLOOD ON THE TEES

BLOOD
on the
TEES

JOHN NICHOLSON
Nick Guymer Series
No.12

Published by Head Publishing
Copyright © John Nicholson 2016

Edition edit by Robert Marcum

Printed by CMP UK Ltd

ISBN 978-0-9933817-4-4

http://www.johnnicholsonwriter.com

I have a support network that help me through the process of creating each book.

First in that is Dawn, my love of the last weird and wild 36 years, who not only designs the books, but comes up with great ideas and then leaves me alone to sit writing all day, as long as I cook her meals, do the washing and load the dishwasher.

Thanks also to Robert, my hard-working editor, who came up with a great plot twist in this story and as ever had such an important role in making the book as good as possible.

Big hugs also to my Yorkshire star, Winty, for proofreading this. This whole series has been very influenced by her northern sensibilities. Also thanks to Janet who has been so much help, and Julie at WAEML for her quiet wisdom, and always welcome good vibes.

Cheers also go to my Scottish literary circle of friends Andy Mc, Dan G and Alan M, my vinyl support network who sell me records. Also, Alan T who is always there for me. You are all men of...err...well...err...you are definitely all men...err...well, at least technically.

"The drugs don't work, they just make you worse"

CHAPTER 1

The judge addressed the jury, looking vaguely ludicrous in his wig and gown. Nick took a deep breath and crossed his arms.

'Have you reached a unanimous verdict?' he asked.

The jury spokeswoman, Tina Harris, was tall, middle-aged and dressed in an expensive black-and-red-checked wool jacket and black trousers. Nick thought she looked like the sort of woman who ran an upmarket womenswear shop in Harrogate, with aggressively coiffured hair, lots of makeup and even more snooty disposition.

'No. We have not.'

'In that case, have you reached a majority verdict?'

She nodded. 'Yes. We have.'

'What is that majority?'

'11 to 1.'

The judge noted it down.

'And would you please tell the court what your majority verdict is.'

She cast a quick glance towards the defendant, Glenn Vokes, before speaking. Twenty-five years old, small-framed and with a shaven head, he looked gaunt and had a drawn, yellowing, sickly, almost greasy pallor to his skin. His desperate, sunken grey eyes were pleading for the verdict to go his way, silently imploring her to say 'not guilty'.

He was going to be disappointed.

The jury on which Nick had sat for eight days at Teesside Crown Court in Middlesbrough had found Vokes guilty of the murder of Daniel Ross. The judge had asked them to reach a unanimous verdict if at all possible, but Nick could not accept that the prosecution had proven Vokes's guilt and despite pressure from most of the other jurors, voted not guilty. But even so, an 11 to 1 majority verdict would send Vokes down for a long time.

Sitting in the dock, in the long few seconds before the word came out of Tina Harris's narrow, mean lips, Vokes stared at her in these last moments of at least notional freedom.

'Guilty.'

Vokes's eyes registered both anger and shock at the same time, as though he couldn't really believe it was happening. He glanced from Harris to the judge and then back to the jurors, looking along the line of 12 not-so-wise monkeys. Nick was on the end, furthest away. They had been instructed to be impassive and not have any communication with the defendant, either verbal or by gesture.

'No. No, man...I never killed Danny. Honest I didn't. Not me, like. No. It's not fair, I never did it.' He had his hands on his head now and spun around to the judge and pleaded with the tweedy, bewigged, middle-aged man, who looked like he'd somehow managed to avoid living in the 20th century by being transported to May 2012 from 1851.

'Oh, my god, please sir, don't do this. I'm telling you the truth. I didn't kill him.' He turned to the jury. 'I know I'm nowt to you, I can see why you think I'm guilty, but I am innocent of this. I didn't kill him. I've been set up. I have. I don't know why, but it's true. Please change your mind, please don't ruin my life.' His eyes filled with tears of vivid despair.

He'd found some words at last. When giving evidence he'd been far less articulate and much more glazed over, almost certainly due to being pilled up on something he'd acquired while on remand in Holme House Prison in Stockton. Today he was sober and more clear eyed.

'Silence in court, Mister Vokes,' admonished the judge. 'You've been found guilty of murder by a majority verdict of 11 to just 1. This was a vicious murder carried out with violence and merciless brutality. You stabbed Daniel Ross seven times with little or no provocation.'

'I didn't. I've said all along that I didn't kill him. It's all rubbish. I wasn't even there when Danny died. I didn't even know the man. Why won't anyone believe me?'

Nick knew that last protest was a lie. He did know him. He frequented the block of flats where Ross lived, and he'd been seeing Tracy Berryman, who sometimes stayed with her father in that same block. It was impossible for him not to know Ross. And that had been Vokes's trouble, he'd lied about so many things, to so many people and for so long that the jury just assumed he was lying about his innocence.

But he wasn't.

Nick was 100 per cent sure he wasn't. There was simply no hard evidence and the look in his eyes right now told the truth, whether or not the others on the jury could see it. He doubted they could. To them, people like Vokes - the underclass - were all one and the same person; a sort of subhuman species who they couldn't relate to, and who offended them to their lower middle-class, comfortable core. Though in fairness, there was a lot to be offended by in Vokes and his dissolute life, because he was a thoroughly obnoxious sod. That hadn't helped his case one bit.

The judge spoke impassively. 'Silence, please, Mister Vokes. You are sentenced to 25 years at Her Majesty's pleasure. Due to the seriousness of your offence, parole will not be considered until you have served 16 years of your sentence. Take him down, please.'

An officer stepped forward and took Vokes by the arm. He turned to leave the court, but spun around at the very last moment and shouted across a courtroom that had not heard one single witness speak in his defence for eight whole days.

Now with roaring anger quickly replacing his despair, he yelled at them in his raw, phlegmy, throaty voice. 'Only one of youse bastards got it right. Only one! Thanks mate, whoever you are. The rest of youse - you're fuckin' stuck-up cunts!' He suddenly grew in strength with the rising tide of his anger at this injustice. He tore himself away from the court official, leaned over the dock and screamed at all 12 of the jury members.

'The state of you lot; you think you're so fucking good. Try living my life, then see how you feel about me. You fuckin' idiots!! Well done, well fucking done you fucking arseholes! I'll fucking die in jail and I'll fucking haunt every one of you 11. You fuckers!'

He began kicking violently at the wooden panels, as though trying to destroy the court which had taken away his freedom, then picked up the chair he'd been sitting on and was about to throw it at the judge, when he was pounced on, pulled to the floor and smothered by security officers. He screamed obscenities from underneath several burly men.

It was an impressive and oddly upsetting burst of righteous rage.

Cuffing his hands behind his back, they dragged him up to his feet and wrestled him out of the courtroom, still furiously swearing and cursing.

Nick's stomach churned violently and he had to swallow hard to stop bile rising in his throat. The look on Vokes's face was unbearable to witness. His life was being thrown in the bin for a crime he didn't commit and all because he was a loser, a low life, a nobody; a nobody that no-one cared about, no-one believed in and no-one would miss. It wasn't right and the injustice of it sickened Nick to the pit of his guts. He wanted to reach out to him and apologise, to say he believed him. But he was gone. Down to the cells, never to be seen again.

The judge thanked the jury for their patience and deliberation, then dismissed them. Some were shocked by what they'd just witnessed and exchanged raised-eyebrow looks. Then they stood up and began to file out, their duty done. There was no passing-out ceremony. As soon as the prisoner was sent down, it was all over. Nick handed in his file of notes, left the court and soon stood outside in the warm, late May Middlesbrough sunshine.

He'd never smoked in his life, but now almost felt like it was a good time to start. It had been intense and very stressful in there. The pressure of having a man's freedom in your gift was like nothing he'd ever experienced. Two of his fellow jurors, a pair of respectable, middle-class, middle-aged women from Nunthorpe and Great Ayton, passed by on their way back to their nice, normal lives. They gave him a polite smile and nod. Tina Harris was on her phone. She'd been the worst of them, one of those dictatorial, aloof, snooty people who seem to gain pleasure by looking down her nose at others. Surely in order to make such a judgement, you needed to have understanding, if not empathy, but she had no understanding of the parade of underclass addicts and losers that had come before the court, and nor did she want to. They were all vermin to her and she'd said as much. And, in one way, she was absolutely right. They were vermin, but where Nick differed from Tina Harris was in that he could easily imagine being one of them. Your life falls apart, you turn to drink and drugs to kill the pain, you lose everything you ever had and seek only the company of other people in the same situation. Once you're on the spiral of despair and degradation, it's hard to get off. If you don't think it could ever happen to you, you're just being naïve. There but for the grace of God go all of us. Even the most respectable people can quickly become dissolute.

Nick turned away; he'd had a gut full of her and the rest of them over the last eight days. He'd given it his best shot, had stood up during deliberations and argued that there was insufficient evidence to convict. And that was incontrovertibly true. But they just assumed Vokes was guilty because he was a scumbag who lived a life of physical and moral collapse. And the facts turned out to be a lot less persuasive than inbuilt cultural, economic and societal bigotry. He walked across town to Teesside Magistrates Court, texting Julie as he went.

'It was guilty. Have you given evidence yet?'

She replied immediately. *'As you thought, then. No. Running late. Go to the public gallery, then the lobby once I'm done.'*

He did as he was told, walked in and followed the signs. There was no-one else in the rows of seats reserved for members of the public, so he sat down on a chair at the end of a row. The atmosphere was so different here compared to the court he'd just left. Everything was quiet and respectful, and there was no need for security or police. This was a coroner's court and some sort of doctor or medical man was in the middle of giving evidence about Ruth Small, who had drowned in the River Tees.

Soon, Julie was called to give evidence. She walked in with her usual confident stride. Her yellow-blonde hair, now parted a little to the left of centre and straightened of its usual long, loose curl, fell just past her shoulders. She wore a smart black suit - an old man's suit, which she'd picked up for a few pounds in a charity shop and had refashioned to be close fitting and stylish. She wore it with a buttoned-up white shirt and black boots with a Cuban heel, which clicked on the wooden floor of the court as she entered. On her lapel was a small purple, green and white suffragette brooch, made from amethyst and enamel. It dated from 1910. He'd bought it for her at an antiques fair at Christmas.

He was sitting above and to one side of the court, to avoid her direct eyeline.

As he often did, when he saw her at distance and in quiet isolation, he found himself really fancying her, in that 'phwoarr, check her out!' sort of way, familiar to all men in everyday life. But following directly was a sense of guilt for even thinking such a thing in a sombre location. But then the male libido generally doesn't have a good reputation for being appropriate.

The coroner was David Charlesworth. It was funny seeing him in real life. Nick had spoken to him on the phone in 2006 when his father had died. He had a doom-laden, sombre voice, but the man in the court was, by contrast, bright eyed and fresh faced. Balding and in his late 50s, he smiled nicely at Julie and began to ask her various questions about Small, who had been fished out of the Tees after an apparently successful suicide bid. Bless her. The thought of that sweet release never felt like an especially bad choice to Nick. Not really. Who could blame her? The depressive, on hearing of a suicide, for a fleeting moment feels a small degree of admiration for the deceased, for having escaped this sometimes difficult existence. Though those thoughts also came with a strong pang of guilt.

The coroner's court existed to try and establish why someone had died. Julie had been Ruth Small's support worker at Teesside Women Centre since Christmas, so she was the one called to give account of her background life and emotional state.

She spoke without notes, using what Nick called her London voice; well spoken and crisp, with the only hint of her Teesside accent in the

5

way she drew out the letter 'a' in the middle or end of a word. 'Ruth first came to us on the 15th of December 2011. She was very upset and cried a lot in the initial meeting. She had been drinking and wasn't very coherent. There were clearly some long-standing issues with her husband. They argued over everything and had done for some time, but as far as I could tell, she didn't feel in any physical danger and didn't appear to have been assaulted by him. Because she was very drunk, I encouraged her to come back and see me again when she was more sober. I next saw her on January 13th and then every couple of weeks until three weeks ago, the 5th of May. She was never totally sober, but then a lot of women we see are in some state of intoxication. Sadly, it's how many deal with the abuse they're suffering. We understand that, y'know? We get it.'

'What was her state of mind throughout this period?' asked Charlesworth.

'Very down. At a low ebb. She said she was on antidepressants. She often felt worthless, and felt undermined by her husband, who she described as a bully - not physically, but psychologically. For example, he would belittle her in public. He'd tell her she was stupid in front of other people. He was disparaging about her appearance and would seek to get others to agree with him. He'd say to someone, "Her hair is awful, isn't it?" or "Doesn't she look terrible in that jacket?" He wasn't a nice man, to say the least. He had succeeded in stripping her of self-respect and she had latterly become quite subservient, feeling the abuse was all she deserved. He was an extremely controlling person and deployed the full range of psychological manipulation in order to assert his will over her.'

Charlesworth shook his head a little, brow creased in a frown now.
'Did she want to leave him?'

'She wasn't contemplating that as a course of action when I saw her last.'

Charlesworth frowned again, head cocked to one side.
'I don't understand. If things were so bad, why didn't she just leave?'

Julie jutted her jaw out a little, in exactly the same defiant way her mother did when annoyed. Nick knew why. The 'why doesn't she just leave?' question was the one most frequently asked of victims of domestic abuse, and Julie was tired of having to explain why. She always felt that the question was, at least in part, laying the blame for the abuse on the woman, and not squarely where it belonged, with the abuser.

Patiently, she explained. 'Leaving someone is a big thing to do for a woman in Ruth's position, at her time of life, in her 60s, and with her state of mind. In my view, she had become co-dependent on her husband's abuse for her self-identity. This often happens. He was a bully to her over a long period of time, and she'd come to feel it really was only what she deserved; he'd so robbed her of her ego and self-respect that she didn't have confidence to leave. In fact, she wasn't always sure exactly how abusive his behaviour was, so normalised to it had she become. He'd also threatened to kill himself, if she ever did leave.' She blinked and looked directly at Charlesworth. 'This is also a very commonplace part of abusive controlling behaviour. Like I say, he was something of an expert at breaking her will and keeping her under his thumb.'

'So why did she come to see you, exactly?'

'For support. Mostly to have someone to talk to who wouldn't be judgemental. She felt very alone and isolated.' Julie sighed and glanced up to the gallery, noticing Nick for the first time, but only acknowledging him with a flick of her right eyebrow.

'Did she seem suicidal at any point?'

'She didn't express those feelings as such, but she had issues with alcohol. And when she drank, it made her depression deeper and darker. She told me that.'

'So would I be correct in saying you were not surprised by her death?'

Julie shook her head. 'Death is always shocking. But she was not in a good place in her life, and I know she felt unable to make the lifestyle changes in relation to drinking that she needed to make, in order to help herself get well. She was trapped in her marriage but couldn't see a life outside of it. Not yet, anyway. She may have done in time. At our last meeting, I felt she was very fragile. She was tearful, and I recommended she get medical help as soon as possible. At that time, if she was taken by a notion to kill herself, there was no-one in her life that would care enough to stop her. No-one to protect her from herself. It was very sad. That being said, I didn't feel like she was suicidal. Often when a woman has made up her mind to end it all, and starts to plan it all out, they're quite relieved and, ironically enough, feel happier than they've been for a long time. Ruth was not like that.'

'In your professional experience, was she an exceptional or extreme case?'

Julie sighed, raised her arched eyebrows and cleared her throat.

'The Centre exists as an organisation partly because there are a lot of women like Ruth. Depressed, isolated and psychologically bullied by their partner, and yet psychologically dependent on them, too. They're often misunderstood and berated for not leaving the abuser. They turn to drink and to drugs, or begin overeating, or deploy some other form of self-harm. So Ruth was far from an extreme case - she was typical.'

'Really? Typical?' His tone was ever so slightly incredulous, as though doubting her ability to understand the word *typical*. Nick knew Julie would pick up on that and he knew that Charlesworth was now in for a polite but fierce bollocking. He smiled inwardly, knowing what was about to be said. She raised herself a little on the balls of her feet.

'Absolutely. Abuse of, and disrespect towards women is endemic in our society, so much so that it is entirely normalised and thus, to many people, invisible. A great many don't even see it, or, like yourself, doubt the seriousness, scale and depth of it. I would remind you that we live in a patriarchal society which defines most things through a male perspective; even the abuse of women gets defined this way. This aids the hiding, denial and misunderstanding of such abuse as Ruth suffered. This is not a few weak-minded women, too soppy or hopeless to leave an abusive relationship. It is thousands and thousands and thousands of decent women whose lives are being made a misery by terrible men. In this country, on average, two women are murdered by a current or ex-partner or husband every week. Every. Week. And those deaths are merely at the peak of the enormous mountain of domestic abuse. Frankly, Mr Charlesworth, it's shameful. Were it a disease, it would be considered to be a dangerous epidemic. But it's just women, just 52 per cent of the country, and not so important, it would sometimes seem.'

She gave him her best wide-eyed Hardwick stare, and those crystal-clear sapphire eyes could really bloody well stare. 'Until we start taking the abuse of women seriously, on all levels, the police will keep fishing women like Ruth out of rivers, all over this country and I'll never be short of work. We live in an unequal, unfair society, and that is to the benefit of no-one.'

Nick felt like standing up and applauding. You couldn't beat Julie in an argument at the best of times, but when she was playing at home, talking about something she cared deeply about, she was a force of nature, both fiercely intelligent and passionate. Not for the first or last time, Nick marvelled at how he'd ever ended up married to her. She'd always been out of his league, in every way, and in a moment like this, it was clear she still was.

Charlesworth nodded and gave her a small smile. 'Well spoken. Thank you for your evidence, Ms Wells.'

But she wasn't having that. 'Excuse me, no, I'm not a mizz, whatever that is, I'm Julie Wells. That's my name, you can use that and not some notional - and as it happens, inaccurate - marital status prefix.'

Nick stifled a laugh. That was one thing she absolutely bloody hated. It seemed to speak to the idea of women being the chattels of men, both legally and symbolically. Why can't you just have a name and stick with it through life, no matter what your marital status is?

Charlesworth was nothing if not polite. 'My sincere apologies. Thank you for your evidence, Julie,' he said, looking a bit unsure now, the way so many men do when confronted with a feminist as fierce as Julie. What a woman.

A few minutes later, Nick caught up with her in the lobby area.

'Hey, Jules.'

'Hello, luv.' She pecked him on the cheek, giving him a nice smile and a squeeze of his hand.

'You did well in there. Very articulate, and you really gave it to Charlesworth at the end. Excellent work.'

She raised an eyebrow. 'Mizz Wells, in-bloody-deed. What was all that about? I know he wasn't trying to be horrible, but people like him need to realise we are women first and not a marital status. The fact there is no marital status word for men tells you everything you need to know about the whole stupid thing.'

He put his arm around her shoulder as they walked out in the sunshine.

'I wish I could sum things up so concisely. So, when will he make his decision, do you reckon?'

She looked at her chunky watch with its big bold white numbers on a black background.

'Not long. I was the second to last to give evidence.'

'Was it obviously a suicide, do you think?'

'I really don't know. They didn't tell me anything else about what had happened to her. But I suspect something must be raising doubts or there wouldn't be an inquest at all. Maybe some trauma to the body.'

They sauntered away from the court.

'What's your gut instinct, though?' he asked.

She cleared her throat. 'Her husband, who was actually a copper until retiring last year, was a classic variety of absolute sodding twat.' She said the words as though they really hurt her, wincing and flinching as she spoke. 'He hadn't been violent towards her, but...' she paused, looking at the ground as she did so, thinking. 'That's not to say he didn't just shove her into the water. I mean, he is an absolutely disgusting man. The degree of psychological bullying he employed against her over decades...you have no idea...and I'm sure I only heard a small amount of it.' She paused again and chewed her bottom lip. 'But I have a feeling Ruth wouldn't have fought hard to hang onto life if he *had* pushed her in the river. Death was an option she was ready to embrace if it came along. That's as much as I can say. And I'm fairly sure that he'll rule it as suicide.'

'Poor woman. But I wish suicide wasn't always presented as an entirely negative thing. If her life was as bad as you say, there's no shame, or even any downside to ending it. I mean...fuck it...you didn't ask to be born...you and only you own your life, and if it's done, it's done. I think, in a way, it's brave and even noble.'

She stopped mid-step and hugged him, not saying anything. He buried his face into her neck. It smelled of Calvin Klein's Escape.

'C'mon, let's go and get drink. I could bloody well use one,' he said.

She sighed. 'God, yeah, I want a voddy and tonic the size of my arse.'

He patted her on the backside. 'Bloody hell, I want one much bigger than this, Jules. Owee, let's treat ourselves and go to Beef and Vodka and have a posh drink at their bar. We deserve a bit of posh after all this. I've got a roll of notes in my pocket. Admittedly, it's not a roll of money, just some copies of my trial notes.'

She turned her mouth down and said, 'Oh, is that what that bulge is? How disappointing. I'm not taking you home tonight, then.'

She rubbed the small of his back as they walked along Albert Road, north towards the station.

'So, just as you reckoned, your case was a guilty verdict,' she said. 'You said you thought it was inevitable.' He'd not discussed the case with her in much detail, because the court told them not to. He began to give her a synopsis.

'It was clear from day one that they all thought Vokes had done it, even though there were no reliable witnesses and no evidence to prove he had. Every one of the six people who said they lived there were stoned out their minds on drugs and drink at the time and in court, as well. One was even dismissed for being too out of it. At some point, most of them lied to the police about whether they were there when Danny was killed, or where they really were, and they all changed their story more than once. Half of them didn't know what day of the week it was. One of them asked the judge if he could smoke in court!'

'Ha ha...really? Was he serious?'

'Oh, yeah. He was shaking and in a cold sweat, so they adjourned for 10 minutes so he could go out and have a tab. Eventually, he said he was crashed out on methadone and white cider when the murder happened. Lovely, eh? Then, when the police turned up, they allowed the crime scene to be corrupted by letting a bloke into the flat where the murdered kid lived, just because he said he wanted to pick up an expensive designer tracksuit that he said was his.' He shook his head. 'The whole thing would have been a laughable farce, if it wasn't so serious. The police were totally useless and their stories all contradicted each other in some details. In court, they were all trying to cover their own arses first and foremost, trying to make out they'd not made any mistakes.'

'So the others just thought Vokes looked like a scummy wrong 'un, so convicted him.'

'Totally, yeah. But he wasn't a wrong 'un. Well, hang on; no, actually, he was. But he was just trapped in a shite situation. He'd been to college and dropped out. He was a drunk, a stoner and a pill head, but I don't think he did it and the prosecuting lawyer absolutely could not prove he did. They found the murder weapon in his flat - but it had been bleached and had no trace of anything left on it - and they found a sweatshirt with Ross's blood on in the flat, as well. But as Vokes said, they weren't his. They'd been planted there. There was no evidence it was his sweatshirt - no photo of him wearing it, for example. He swore it wasn't his, and also that someone had told him Ross often had nosebleeds because he snorted so much cocaine. I think someone planted them in his flat, called the police, and they took the path of least resistance. Vokes was sent down on a best guess. We were told by the judge that we had to be sure beyond reasonable doubt that he was guilty...'

'...and you had to have reasonable doubt if witnesses were unreliable and there was no hard evidence that he put the knife in.'

Nick nodded. 'Honest, Jules, he was distraught at getting sent down. I think it only really struck him how serious the whole thing was at that moment. He was such a stoner that he was away with the fairies most of the time. He had that look about him - like he'd messed his brain up with the smoke and the pills and found it hard to focus.'

She shook her head. 'If it's an obvious injustice, maybe he'll get acquitted on appeal.'

'I dunno. I hope so. I felt so sorry for him. I'll tell you something; if he'd been educated middle- class, he'd have got a "not guilty" from those jurors. They just looked at him and thought, "Scumbag. He did it." I mean, he is a scumbag, he is very unlikeable, and he lived a totally dissolute life. He had nothing. He lived in an decrepit flat in Roseworth and had nothing to his name at all. No hope, no future. If I was in his circumstances, I'd be off my face all the time, too. How else would you deal with life? All the nice people of the world look at you as a total shit. But that doesn't mean you are. Being a loser still doesn't make someone a murderer.'

'So who did kill the lad, then?'

'Oh, I'm fairly sure it was Kev Berryman.'

She squinted. 'I can't hold all the names in my mind. Which one was he?'

'He's Tracy Berryman's dad. Tracy and Vokes sometimes slept together. He lives in the Zetland in Flat 1. He's the boss of the place. Apparently, these sorts of blocks always have a boss man. I don't know why. He's the one who knows who comes and goes and he often deals the drugs.'

'Is it always a man?' asked Julie. 'I bet a woman is the boss somewhere. My mam was the unofficial boss of our part of the estate.'

'Yeah, but not like Berryman. He was basically just a chancer who dealt drugs and was top dog by virtue of being a little less fucked up on drugs than the others. He'd also lived there longest. Most, including Danny Ross, drifted through the place. Stayed for a few weeks or months and moved on.'

'Sounds vile.'

'It totally is. The place is a disgrace. Anyway, Berryman's daughter, Tracy, had been having it off with Danny Ross, as well as with Vokes. The prosecution tried to make out that was Vokes's motivation for murder, but that was obviously rubbish. He and Tracy weren't really boyfriend and girlfriend, in the way it's normally meant. They just stayed with each other sometimes, possibly had sex occasionally, but that's all it was and I think she was the same with Danny Ross. They were all occasional drug buddies. She denied being a prostitute in court, but I'm sure she sold sex for drugs and/or money and that was implied by the way she was questioned by the barristers.'

Julie nodded. 'So Vokes and Tracy's relationship was a convenience rather than a romance?'

'Exactly, yeah. Tracy has a one year-old daughter, possibly by one of them.'

'Eh? She doesn't know?'

'No. In court she said she wasn't sure and that it could have been one of several people.'

'So she was deffo a prozzie then, or just very promiscuous?'

'Like I say, that was the implication. Danny and Glenn were both stoned on dope, pills, cheap wine or vodka every day. I'd be amazed if either of them was up to having any sort of sex, most of the time.'

'So who was the lad, Danny, that was murdered? What was his story?'

'We didn't learn much about him, actually. He was just another drifter passing through these wasters' lives. He was in Flat 6 but had only been there for a few weeks.'

'Was he local?'

'His background really wasn't discussed. The rest of the Zet didn't seem to really know him because he was quite new in there. Vokes, in his testimony, said Danny was a big heroin user and that he - and this is what he actually said in court - "was always cunted up and usually had a massive fucking bag of gear up there". He was reprimanded by the judge for his language. But it seemed like Danny was the heaviest drug user there. When they searched the flat, they did find a lot of heroin, dope and valium. The only real insight into Danny's character was from Tracy's evidence. She said he was a clever lad, that drugs had ruined him and that she thought he'd been abused as a boy, though she didn't know for sure. Throughout the whole eight days, the couple of minutes she talked about him was the only time anyone was nice about anyone else. She said something like - I wrote it down but I can't remember it now - something like, life was too painful for him and he had to numb himself with the smack.'

Julie stuck her bottom lip out. 'Aw, poor Danny. God rest his soul. That sounds like they had something with each other. Some sort of understanding.'

'Yeah, it does. I liked her, but she really wasn't well. She was skinny and underweight, and she obviously didn't look after herself very well. I was sitting closest to her and she smelt a bit dirty, y'know? A bit sweaty and cheesy and sort of sour.'

Julie shook her head ruefully. 'We see a lot of young women who are heroin users and they do sometimes stop washing themselves. It robs them of the incentive and self-respect. It's tragic, it really is.'

'But the thing is, she still had a connection to her soul, whereas no-one else from the Zet seemed to. Of course, the rest of the jurors thought she was a total skank. They were so judgemental about her, saying she had no morals and even that she was ugly. I mean, and this really fucking annoyed me, one of the blokes on the jury made a "joke" saying he wouldn't pay to have sex with her, he'd want her to pay him, and the rest of them laughed. Like as though a woman being in a desperate situation was something to laugh at. The sodding twat.' He felt tears well up in his eyes as he said the final three words.

Julie put an arm around his waist and gave him a brief squeeze.

'Why can't people have a little bit of empathy?' she said. 'I despair of some people. How hard is it to imagine life being tough?'

'Those people couldn't do that. Some of them had lived lives that were so easy that it had made them feel full of self-righteous entitlement. Tina Harris and some of the others just made themselves feel good by shaming people whose lives were so obviously worse than theirs.'

He had to stop walking and compose himself. The emotions he'd swallowed down over the eight days, for reasons of public decorum, now boiled up to the surface. He leaned against a red postbox and rubbed the tears from his eyes, head bowed, looking at the dirty pavement.

'Are you alright, luv?' came Julie's voice. She put the flat of her hand to his cheek. He lifted his head to look at her, a couple of tears dribbling down his cheeks.

'Yeah, yeah, I'll get over it. I've got no choice.'

He bowed his head again but she gently forced him to look at her with her hand.

'Listen to me. Right? It's a hard life, don't be ashamed to cry for other people's pain.'

He kissed her forehead, her words only making more tears fall. But he wiped them away, cleared his throat and sucked in some air. Pull yourself together, for god's sake. It was just some scumbag who wouldn't give you the time of day and would have robbed you as soon as look at you.

'It's a terrible burden - deciding on someone's fate,' he said.

She squeezed both of his hands.

'I'm sure you did the right thing, luv. You were true to yourself. That's all anyone can do.'

They walked on.

'So, you think this Berryman bloke was the murderer?' she asked.

'Why would he have done it?'

Nick cleared his throat again. 'I don't really know. Maybe Berryman found Danny with Tracy and, for some reason, probably because he was high on something, got a rage on and killed him. He was stabbed seven times. The knife wounds were made with such force that the knife cracked two of his ribs. Vokes was a skinny-arsed no-mark and I don't think he had the muscle to do that. I think Kev Berryman fitted Glenn Vokes up for it by getting this little toe-rag called Davey Foster to plant the knife and sweatshirt in Vokes's flat. He was the one who turned up just minutes after the police had arrived, saying his tracksuit was in Daniel Ross's flat and he needed to get it, and the cops just let him into the Zet. Bloody ridiculous. He actually had to step over the body to go in!'

Julie looked at him with wide eyes. 'That's terrible, that is. I can't believe they let that happen.'

'Danny was covered in a sheet waiting for the ambulance. The cops tried saying that Ross's flat, or anyone else's flat, wasn't regarded as a crime scene at that time, because he was yet to be identified, but that was ridiculous. Even if it was true, the whole of the Zet was, at the very least, a potential crime scene, and needed securing. In my view the police were either useless or corrupt or both, and Davey Foster was actually given the knife and the sweatshirt by Kevin Berryman. He left the place with a carrier bag which he said in court had the tracksuit in it. Amazingly, the police didn't even check the bag at the time.'

'So this Davey Foster gave evidence as well?'

'Yeah. He was so untrustworthy. One of those people who you're not sure actually knows the difference between truth and lies. It was impossible to tell what, if anything, he said was true, time and again. Foster had beady little druggie eyes and just answered every question as fast as possible, in as few words as possible. He couldn't wait to get out of the court. At one point I wondered if someone was after him. He was looking around nervously and wouldn't look at anyone. His eyes flicked around the room all the time.'

'Sounds like he was speeding.'

He nodded. 'Most of them were on something.' They arrived at the restaurant.

She sighed. 'It's all so horrible, but like I say, you did your best and that's all you can do.' She pushed open one of the heavy, tall glass doors inscribed with the words 'Beef and Vodka'. Inside, it was noisy and every table was taken, even though it was 1.45pm on a Thursday in late May. You had to book a month ahead.

'I'm sorry, we're fully booked,' said the maître d', used to having to turn people away.

'Oh, that's OK, we just want a drink at the bar,' said Nick to the man, whose high cheekbones made him look like a fashion model from a Calvin Klein ad.

'That's all good. Be my guest,' he said, gesturing to the long bar at the back of the room, behind which two women were busy making cocktails for a waitress to take to a table.

Sliding up onto two black wooden stools, Julie ordered them both a double vodka and tonic, selecting an organic Polish brand at random from the long drinks menu comprised only of vodka, a range of mixers, and sparkling and still water.

'Jeff was saying that they're aiming to open one of these in every city north of the M62,' said Nick, looking around the room. 'Along with all the Big Meat restaurants, they'll be rolling in money.'

'It's so weird. All they serve is top-notch, beautifully cooked beef and about 78 different vodkas. I mean, how simple is that? It's posh, but it's also hardcore, so it appeals to all sections of the market - to macho blokes who want to eat half a cow, and boozers who just love strong spirits, but also to fine diners who love obscure cuts of grass-fed organic beef and the vodka from distant parts of the earth. You walk past restaurants with 100 dishes on the menu and they're empty. Here, there's a choice of two starters and mains, no pudding. All you can drink is just vodka or water. Not even tea or coffee. And it's always rammed.'

'It's brilliant and it can't be long before they're copied. They've gone against the whole basic assumption behind restaurants. See, I've got a theory about this.'

She clapped her hands. 'Ooh, have you been thinking about things again? I can't believe that. So unlike you.' She pulled a cross-eyed face and stuck out her tongue.

'You do irony very well. Ha ha.'

'Ah, you keep thinkin', son. So what's your theory?'

He pushed his wedding ring around his finger. 'I'm convinced we're all too choked up with choice. Today we actually want less choice, less to think about and more time to enjoy ourselves. The whole free-market capitalist thing, the whole basis of the economy, in fact, is all about customers wanting ever more choice. But I think that's totally outdated now. It's fundamentally wrong. We've given that a go and it doesn't make you happier. Despite having more stuff and more choice, we've never had so much depression and anxiety. When you've got 48 different olive oils in the supermarket, that's just choice gone insane. Choice makes life harder, not better or easier. And the whole thing about being judged by your possessions is very stressful. Once you step onto that conveyor belt, you're always going to lose. Someone will always have more, bigger, better stuff. Keeping life simple and uncluttered reduces stress and leaves room for love. I really believe that.'

She smiled. 'Well, speaking as a lass who tried and failed at being a London yuppie, I agree.' They raised their glasses and clinked them together. 'Here's to more love. Lord knows, the world needs it.'

He took a large gulp of vodka, just the thought of the drink relaxing him a little. 'Talking of love...well, lust, anyway, you look fantastic in the suit and boots. I didn't get a chance to get a good look at you before you dashed out this morning. I have to confess to getting the mild horn in the coroner's court, but that just felt so wrong, on so many levels.'

She lifted her jaw and looked down her nose at him, rolling her woody laugh from the back of her throat. 'What are you like, you?' She leaned forward and whispered a short but lewd litany of sexual obscenities, followed by a low breathy groan and a lick to the ear, knowing full well what it would do to him.

Nick's heartbeat increased. 'Don't do this to me in public, Jules.'

But she did it again, barely able to stop herself laughing, then sat back, arms folded, a look of amused pity in her eyes.

'Ha ha...eyes like saucers, just like that. You're so easy to seduce with a few choice words. I never knew the like. I swear dirty words get you in a lather quicker than actual naked nudeyness.'

'Of course they do. Words are my thing, aren't they? Always have been. Bloody hell, I'll get arrested for indecency if I stand up now. Is it illegal in Middlesbrough to be in public with a concealed erection, like it is in Missouri or Arkansas, due to weird by-laws?'

'Nah, here it's only illegal if it's *not* concealed, and even then, you might get away with it if the Boro have just won. Ha.' She glanced over his shoulder. 'Oh, hang on, though, you're going to have to stand up in a second or two.'

'I can't. Why?'

'Because Emily has just come out of the back and has spotted us and is coming over.' She whispered in his ear again, telling him exactly what she'd like to do to a certain swollen part of his anatomy and where she'd like him to put it. Oh, Jesus. Why did he have to be wearing such close-fitting pants?

'Hello, you two,' said Emily Davids, trotting across to them. 'To what do we owe this pleasure?'

Julie stood up and gave her a hug. 'We've been in court, Em,' she said. 'Nick's been on a jury and I've been giving evidence to the coroner's court. We needed vodka.' Emily looked surprised.

Nick half stood up, half leaned against the stool, and tried to keep a little bent at the waist in the hope of not revealing too much tumescence. 'You're looking great, Em,' he said, giving her a squeeze around the waist.

She looked from Nick to Julie. 'So do you both. Very smart. All suited and booted.' She looked him up and down. 'Why are you standing so oddly, Nick?' she asked, an amused look in her eyes.

Julie leaned into her ear and told her why. Nick closed his eyes and rubbed his forehead in embarrassment as Emily laughed. He slid back up onto his stool. Bloody thing wouldn't soften. What was wrong with him? The male body was a sodding hostage to fortune; always doing the wrong thing at the wrong time.

'Aw, he's just got a healthy blood pressure system, haven't you, Nicky boy?' Emily said, pushing her tongue between the gap in her front teeth and grinning at him.

'I'm just hoping that a hole opens up and swallows me,' said Nick.

'Well, we've both got holes that could swallow you, Nicky boy, if that's of any use,' said Emily. The two women laughed loudly. Nick covered his face with his hands.

Emily's relationship with chef Mike the Meat had taken them all by surprise when they'd started going out the previous autumn. They seemed to quickly fall head over heels, and by November had become one of those couples who are so in love that they can barely take their eyes off each other. When Mike had suggested she come and work for him, doing marketing and data processing, Jeff had encouraged her. Mike was not only paying three times what he could afford to pay but more importantly, it was clear that she'd found her soulmate. They were crazy about each other, in a way reminded Nick of how he and Julie had been in the first year of their relationship. It was quite sweet, really. After what she'd been through at the hands of Matty Rhodes, and Sean O'Connor and his evil friends, it was nothing she didn't deserve.

She had left her whole rock chick thing behind with that phase of her life, and though she had introduced the idea of the restaurant playing vinyl records on a turntable behind the bar, she was now very much back in computer nerd mode, a place she really felt comfortable. Of course, she was still cheeky and rude, and still loved glam metal, but dressed in a black-and-white lumberjack shirt, loose, faded and torn jeans and a baseball cap, she was now far more at ease, more so than he'd ever known her to be. She seemed to have settled into herself and was inhabiting her own skin for the first time in a long time. It was lovely to see.

'This place is so busy,' said Julie, looking around.

'I know. I'm in spreadsheet hell right now trying to work out exactly why Big Meat and this place are so successful, so we can repeat it in every town. I'm doing complicated equations to match footfall with local population and restaurant turnover. I say "hell" but I'm actually in my element. Gloria came in from Texas last week. She's investing a cool five million in the next expansion phase.'

'Bloody hell!' said Julie, her mouth open wide.

'I know, tell me about it, it's a lot of pressure. It'll be cool, though. The hard bit is finding cooks who are as great as Mike.' She smiled again and bounced on her toes.

'How is he?' said Julie. 'Still got magnificent buttocks?'

Emily put a hand on one hip, and an index finger to her lips in an exaggerated fashion. 'Err, let me think now. Yes, yes...his buttocks are still magnificent.' She leaned forward and whispered something in Julie's ear. Julie opened her eyes wide and laughed.

'Oooh, really? Aren't you the lucky girl? Well, here's to you, both,' said Julie raising her glass.

'So what did you mean, you've been in court?'

Julie briefly explained.

'That's all so tragic. God, the world is an awful place, sometimes,' Emily said, flatly.

'So as a result, we just fancied a bit of a drink-up,' said Nick.

'Well, be my guest. Are you hungry? I can sneak something out for you. How about some carpaccio of beef? It's all grass-fed organic and comes with a herb dressing and these oat biscuits Mike makes. It's melty and lush.'

'God, I'd love that, but we can't afford it. We're pretty skint. We shouldn't really be spending our money on drinking,' said Julie.

'Oh, don't worry, for my fave horny oldies, it's on the house. Have you softened up a bit now, Nick?' She patted him on his thigh.

'The tiger is back in his cage, aye.'

'Aw. Don't worry. He'll not be in there long, if I know Jules,' she said, ruffling the top of his head.

After she'd gone, Nick turned to Julie. 'You know, I never felt happier to see someone properly fall in love.'

'Oh, yeah, totally, and Mike is such a lovely bloke. And, apparently, a very well-endowed gentleman.'

'Is that what she was in your ear about?'

'Indeed. Mike the Meat is an appropriate nickname in more ways than one, it seems.'

'You must be jealous, Jules. She's got access to Mike's ace arse and his other fleshly wonderments.'

'Nah, I've got my own supplier of top-notch, juicy meat, haven't I? Come here.'

They leaned forward and briefly kissed, resting their lips together, tongue tips touching for a mere instant, smiling at each other as they did so. A surge of electric love swept through Nick's synapses. What was this feeling we call love? It wasn't lust. Lust was sometimes a distant family relation of love, but love was this incredible, intangible thing which made you feel profoundly connected to something bigger; like you'd got access to something eternal. And even though you didn't walk around, minute to minute, feeling this thing, there were moments as briefly overwhelming and incredible as an out-of-body experience.

Emotional or spiritual connection to another person, however and whenever it happens, is maybe why humans keep on keeping on. It doesn't matter how long the relationship lasts, be it for one minute, one night, one month, one year, one life, those emotional connections are the jewels in our psychic landscape; the dilithium crystals that power our personal Starship Enterprise of life; the lights in life's darkness.

As Nick pulled back from their kiss, he told himself to hold onto these moments while they lasted and remember them when he was feeling depressed.

'Funny how times change. Emily was always in Jeff's shop and now Guru is there and everything is different,' he said, licking his lips, as though to taste her.

'I love Guru. It's like he's come from a different planet,' said Julie. 'And not a single hair on his whole body. Very exotic.'

'I wish I had alopecia. It would make washing so much easier.'

'Oh, dear, no. Your thingy would look like the last turkey in the butcher's window.'

'Hang on, hang on...if you give me long enough, I should be able to come up with a stuffing-based joke.' He tapped at his forehead with his index finger. '....err...nope, it's not coming.'

'Ha ha, well, that'd be most unlike your turkey, then.' She laughed a little, looked around the room for a few seconds and then let out an involuntary sigh.

'Are you alright?'

She winced a little. 'Oh, I just had a little wave of sadness about Ruth Small. You always think there's something more you could have done to help.' She groaned a little. 'Poor woman. And what an unusual day we've both had. Odd we should both have to be in different courts on the same day. I'm glad your jury duty is done, though.'

'Yeah, me too, though it was actually quite interesting. I just wish the other members of the jury hadn't been stuck up, or stupid, or both. It seems wrong to me that someone's freedom is at the mercy of such people.'

'But how else can you do it, though? Even if you had an IQ test, it wouldn't exclude snobs and bigots.'

'No, I know.' He sighed again. 'I did what I could to try and persuade them he was innocent, or at least I pointed out the lack of proof of his guilt, but they wouldn't have it. It doesn't help that I'm hardly the most persuasive of speakers. I thought again this morning that if Jeff had been there instead of me, he could have charmed them around with his humour and his clever way with words.'

'Yeah, I can imagine that. Jeff is a good mixer.'

'A good mixer?'

'Yeah, you know. He mixes well with people. Doesn't matter if they're rich or poor, posh or common. That's not your forte, is it?'

'No, you can say that again. Jeff has always been like that, going right back to when we were at school. He always managed to prevent both of us getting beaten up by the rough kids just by being funny.'

She smiled and thought about what he'd said. 'I wish I'd known you at school. It's funny that I don't even remember youse two, though I must have seen you most days for a couple of years.'

'Yeah, but you'd have been too young to be in my wank file.'

'Your what?!'

'My wank file.'

'What's that?'

'Basically, it's all the girls at school that you fancy that you'd lie in bed thinking about. You stare at her in school and mentally file her away for later that night.'

She grinned. 'No, you did that. Other boys had dirty magazines and watched X-rated films. Trust you to rely on the images in your mind, instead. That's a very Nick Guymer thing to do.'

He laughed. 'When you were starting first year, we were starting fourth, and I was at Newcastle Poly by the time you got to Stockton sixth-form College. That's why we didn't really intersect, I think.'

'Yeah a first year girl going out with a fourth former would have been a bit odd. My friend Fran went out with a fifth year when we were in the second and we all thought that was basically the same as going out with a 30-year-old bloke! I mean, I think we were all a bit uncomfortable about it, even if we didn't really know why.'

'I knew a lad in fifth year who was obsessed with going out with girls much younger than him. It was very odd and he made me feel really uncomfortable, too, though I couldn't have told you why, either.'

'Hmmm, there was always one or two like that. Probably still is.'

Emily came out of the kitchen with two large, round white plates on which sat the carpaccio of beef, a drizzle of herb dressing, some rocket and long strips of buttered oatcakes, placing them on the bar, along with cutlery.

'There you go. On the house. I can't stop. Lovely to have seen you sexy oldies.' She touched each of them on the back of the head and then skipped back to the kitchen.

They watched her go.

'Bloody hell. Free food! Magic. You know something, this Emily, dressed down in a baggy shirt and loose-fitting old jeans, is much more attractive, sexy even - though I hate that word - than the one in cropped heavy metal t-shirts, make-up and tight jeans,' said Julie. 'Funny, that.'

'Yeah, totally agree. Mind, she's stuck with all the tattoos from those years. A permanent reminder.'

'To see her now, you'd never even know she was covered in them. God, this is delish. The beef just melts in your mouth.'

She was right. It was exquisite. And better still, free. They cleaned their plates within a few minutes. Julie had just taken a drink from her glass when her phone buzzed as a text came in.

'It's from Martha at TW. Ah. The coroner has ruled Ruth Small's death as suicide. She'd asked them to inform her. Well, that's that. End of the case. So sad.'

'You seemed to think it wasn't so clear cut, didn't you?'

'Well, she was very depressed and she had no-one to take care of her if something went wrong with her meds, or if she was taken with a notion to throw herself in the river.'

He nodded and pulled at his stubble. 'Yeah, I was lucky. If I'd been on my own, if you and Jeff hadn't found me on the bridge when you did...'

She interrupted him. '...don't talk about it, luv. We were there and that's the main thing. Everyone needs someone's help at some time in their life, but Ruth just didn't have that. I wonder how her husband, feels about it.'

'He's probably glad. Sounds like he hated her.'

'Yeah. Nasty bit of work.'

'He was a copper, you said. Where did they live?'

'Roseworth, near the library.'

'That's the estate Jeff grew up on.'

'Oh, yeah, of course it is, I'd forgotten that. It's only a 10-minute walk from mam's house.'

'And it's also where Glenn Vokes lived, funnily enough.'

'Huh. Small place, Stockton. Almost all of us live quite near to each other. Remind me where those Zetland flats are, where the lad was murdered.'

'They all call it the Zet. It's a manky two-storey block near Bishopton Road, at the end of Bishopton Lane. It's a dead end, you know, just across from the railway station. Six flats in the block, with a communal entrance that was where Daniel Ross was stabbed - right in the doorway.'

'Oh, god, yeah. I know where you mean. They're desperate, those places.'

'Desperate is the word. Just damp, filthy boxes, really. The council just puts the junkies and wasters in them and leaves them to rot, as far as I can tell. Some just use it as a doss-house. It's no wonder people live like animals when they're treated like animals.'

Julie took a drink and raised an eyebrow.

'I know what you mean, but you can't totally excuse everything just because of that. Plenty of people live in squalid circumstances, but don't end up killing people in a drugged-up rage. You can be poor and still be a decent person, with decent values. You don't have to turn into a low-life scum.'

'That's a bit harsh, Jules. I'm not excusing the worst behaviour, but it's inevitable when you cut off the bottom five per cent of society that they'll just go feral and live in the moment, without a thought as to the consequences of their actions. All people like Vokes have got to look forward to is the next.'

'I know. And I understand. But I also know that there are plenty of people who could do more to help themselves and they choose not to.'

'They choose not to because they've lost all hope of anything getting better, or are mentally unwell.'

She shrugged. 'I understand that, too, but it's not likely to get better when you're sitting in your flat smoking and drinking and swallowing pills, is it? I know you're trying to be sympathetic, but the truth is, some people don't deserve your sympathy. They slob around on the sick, get massively fat and unwell, then claim invalidity and just do as little as possible, apart from having kids that neither parent is in a fit shape physically, mentally or financially to support.'

'What, so only people with money can have kids? That's not right.'

She shook her head. 'That's not what I said, is it? But too many mess their kids up by having them when they're in no fit state to be a good parent. They're just creating another generation of screwed-up wasters. It's just deferred abuse for druggies and wasters to have kids, and then eventually people like us at TW have to pick up the pieces of young lives that are being ruined by the same people you want to feel sorry for. I'm happy to fight for a better life for anyone, whatever their circumstances, but I'm not going to be a soft touch, either. At work, we always empathise with the women who come to us, but there always has to be a line in the sand beyond which you don't go. We can't co-opt into their mindset, we have to see the bigger picture. You're just taking things to the extreme to counterbalance the cold-hearted buggers on the jury.'

He should've known better than to try and win an argument with her. Even if he was right, and he was no longer sure that he was, she was just so good at constructing her arguments that she was impossible to counter. She'd probably have been able to persuade the jury. Also, her default position was to be compassionate, so if she said some people just took the piss, he was prepared to believe it was true.

He ordered them two more drinks of the Polish vodka.

'I was thinking while I was in the court that when I was a teenager, I used to do my pools round in the middle of dark winters, pockets full of money, and I never once had any trouble. I'd go to council estates like Bishopton Court and I'd go down the Avenue, which back then was dark and leafy, with lots of long driveways, perfect for mugging a skinny 16-year-old kid. Those people in the courtroom would have thought nothing of robbing me, taking the pools money and going to buy some vodka and bloody dog valium.'

'Dog valium? What's that? Some sort of street name?' said Julie.

'Nope. Imaginatively, it's actually valium for dogs. They all take it.'

'Getaway with you. They don't,' she said with a dismissive chortle.

'They do, man. Someone robbed a vet's and stole the valium they give dogs. It's rubbish, apparently. You have to take a lot for it to have any effect.'

Julie couldn't help but laugh. 'Dog valium! Ha. That's so stupid. You must know your life's taken a turn for the worse when you have your first hit of dog valium.'

Nick looked across the busy restaurant, the smell of hot beef fat in the air.

'Where did it all go wrong, Jules? We didn't used to have a druggy underclass when we were kids, how come it's endemic to some areas now? The working-class families I knew on Bishopton Court were all house proud, all worked, and they were generous as well. What happened to that working class?'

'They just became lower middle class, but I wouldn't be too rose-tinted glasses about it. A lot of abuse was just better hidden back then. I grew up seeing drunks fighting in the streets, or outside of the Hardwick pub. I came from a broken home. It was a sodding hard life in the 60s and 70s, and especially for women. I really do think things are better now, overall.'

'I suppose so. But at least the fighty drunk men went to work the next day. Blokes like Vokes and his mates just stay in bed until the afternoon and then go in search of drink and drugs, then get high and start fighting amongst themselves, then they pass out and do it all over again the next day. It's like an alternative society that is largely hidden from the nice people. I mean, I knew it was going on, but totally underestimated the sheer mind-numbing miserable existence they've got and also how many of them are really badly drug-damaged. Until you hear eight days of testimony about it, you wouldn't believe how their days are constructed.'

She ran her index finger down the parting in her hair. 'I reckon it's all been caused by three generations of chronic unemployment, the collapse of industry, the falling apart of family life, cheap drugs, irresponsible shagging, and successive governments that either didn't care or didn't understand what was going on. A lot of the old industrial reasons for Teesside existing have all but gone, but the place has yet to invent a new reason to be here.'

'Yeah, and it's hard to see it getting better when you've got this layer at the bottom of the heap who can't break out from it and just bring another generation into the same life. I think some people on the jury saw them all as the same person. They were just "those sort of people".'

She nodded. 'I can understand that, in some ways. But you said Vokes had been to college, though. How come he ended up back here?'

'Drugs. He was chucked off his course at Newcastle University for poor attendance, because he was lying in his room smoking dope. He was mad for it. So he came home and...I dunno how or why...but he got in with some of the Zet residents, the Berrymans, Daniel Ross and a fat bloke who also lived there who they just called Blobby.'

'Blobby? Let me guess, was he big, pink and fat?'

'Very.' Nick took another drink, thinking back to the trial. 'Blobby was a massive piss artist. He was supposed to give evidence on the second day, but he stood in the witness box swaying around, clearly four sheets to the wind at 11 in the morning. The judge dismissed him for being intoxicated and he was told to come back sober the next day.'

'And did he?'

'Yeah. They scheduled him to be first on the stand at 9.30am so there was a chance he'd not have had his first Carlsberg Special. He was more sober, but I could still smell the drink on him from where I was sitting. And he absolutely stank of sweat.'

'Urgh, god, he sounds disgusting.'

'He was like something from medieval times. Just this big dirty oaf. And all he did was say he saw nothing and heard nothing. And that could have been true. It happened in the midafternoon so he'd have been well pissed by then. Or he could have seen everything and was just lying. It was impossible to tell.'

'It's hard to maintain a lie when you're really drunk.'

'And they couldn't. They kept saying different things at different times. It's not even like they were friends, or not what we'd call friends. They didn't even seem affectionate towards each other, except for Tracy towards Danny. In court they all blamed each other for everything. There were petty squabbles all the time about next to nothing. You couldn't trust anything anyone said, partly because they lied so routinely and also because they were off their face so much that their memory was totally unreliable. At least four were on methadone for heroin addiction and they seemed to have been asleep most of the time.'

'Yeah, you said they lied to the police all the time.'

'Oh, yeah.' He waved a hand dismissively. 'They did it by default.'

'But isn't that illegal?'

'I'm sure if we did it, it would be. For example, right, in court, Vokes said that he'd been walking around the streets when Ross was killed, because he'd taken too much speed.'

'What? So he was feeling agitated?'

'Yeah. He took speed to balance out the dog valium...I'm not making this up. I know it sounds like *Carry On Drug Taking*.'

She knitted her light brown eyebrows together. 'I don't understand. What's the point in doing that? Why have a downer if you don't want to feel...well...down?'

'God knows. He'd had about a hundred of the dog valium...'

'...how many? A hundred?! Bloody hell. How don't you die?'

He shook his head and briefly closed his eyes in amazement. 'I know. It's crazy. But he thought they were weak, so he took a lot, but then found they were stronger than he thought, so he took speed to try and get more normal. But he took too much of that, and couldn't sit still. That's what he said in court. Trouble was, when he was arrested, he told the police he was in his flat at the time of the murder and didn't mention any of this about walking around. The prosecution barrister asked him if he was lying now, or was he lying to the police, originally? He said he lied to the police. When asked why, he just said well, that's what you do, everyone lies to the police. And to him, that was reason enough. Later, he was caught out lying again, by pretending he didn't really know Danny Ross, when he obviously did know him.'

'But that's perjury, isn't it?'

'I thought so, but it was as if the law didn't apply to them. Some of it was him trying to be clever and muddy the waters, but mostly it was just that he was too stoned to think straight, or he was brain damaged from the drugs. It's as though none of them could see more than a few seconds into the future and didn't realise they'll get caught out contradicting themselves, and even if they do realise, they simply don't care. They have nothing invested in their life at all, and when you've nothing to lose, not even your self-respect, whatever you do or don't do doesn't matter at all.'

27

She shook her head. 'That's shocking, that is. I can see now why you've been so exhausted every night after a day in court.'

'The thing is, though, I'm sure he was telling the truth about trying to walk off the speed.'

She cocked her head to one side. 'Why's that?'

'Because that story fitted his life perfectly and he never deviated from it in court. Not once. Every other account of his movements varied in detail each time he told it, but that one never did and that must be because it's easier to remember the truth than a lie. And it was totally part of his lifestyle. You know what druggies are like, they love nothing better than to talk about the drugs they've taken. He was like that in court. It was his specialist subject. When he was talking about drugs, he became his most animated.'

'Was he sober in court?'

'It was hard to tell. He turned up most days looking glassy-eyed, but that was his default look after so long on the dope, anyway. Same with the rest of them. Mostly I think they hung out together because they were all as bad as each other. When all your associates are messed up, there's no-one judging *you* for being messed up.'

'The jury obviously judged him...'

'Well, unfortunately for him, he was pitiful, but not at all sympathetic. No-one spoke up for him. Not a family member, not a friend, no-one. He was a nothing, a nobody, and he knew it. That was the worse thing about it, really. He sat there every day knowing he was being flushed down life's toilet, but was unable to stop it happening. And now he's going to spend at least 16 years in jail and probably up to 25. And I'm sure he's an innocent man. I think he was off his nut, just as he said at the time, walking around on his own. But no-one came forward to say they saw him, and the police said on day one that he wasn't on any CCTV camera footage, which he would have been if he'd walked the route he said he'd walked, so he was thought by most of the jury to be lying from the start. I think everyone was happy for him to take the rap and put it all to bed, so they could get on with swallowing dog valium and drinking white cider and Special Brew. I think the police knew they'd let the crime scene be corrupted, so they wanted a quick conviction to get it all locked down. Berryman was less wasted than the rest and Vokes was the most messed up, after Danny, and he had no alibi and no friends and thus was the easiest to set up. He was no match for Berryman and his street smarts.'

'But that means the police are corrupt. Sending an innocent man to jail is shocking, I don't care how much of a low life he is, and it also means the actual guilty person gets away with it. So there's a murderer walking free just because the police want to hide their incompetence.'

'That's not a surprise, though, is it? We know Mandy Beale well enough to know she'll bend and break rules to get a result. I'm not saying she colluded on this, but I'm sure she's aware the police sometimes stitch a story together for their own convenience. So yeah, by virtue of being incompetent and then trying to cover their tracks, they were some kind of corrupt. The officers that gave evidence were all hopeless and frankly, a bit thick. The two on the scene had slightly differing stories, which contradicted each other. The pathologist was the only one with any brains and the rest of the police seemed to vaguely dislike her, almost because of that. They referred to her in that slightly contemptuous way thick kids would talk about clever kids, at school. Like being educated was somehow a weakness.'

'Aye, well, anti-intellectualism is always a popular riff to play in Britain. I never knew why being clever and educated was so uncool. If you wanted to work and get on, you were looked down on by the cool kids.'

'That's so true. Though by the time I got to sixth form less so.'

'I loved sixth form. It felt so grown up compared to school and we didn't have to wear a uniform. And all the nasty bastards had left. Funny thing was, by the time I was ready to go to uni, all the kids who had been cool at school were all either starting dead-end jobs, on the dole or up the duff. Didn't look so cool then.'

Nick finished his drink. 'Vokes actually turned up at the Zet a couple of hours later, hoping to buy more drugs. That's when the police arrested him. By then they'd raided his flat and found the knife and sweatshirt.'

'Why did they raid his flat? What made them suspicious of him above anyone else?'

'George Dunne, the senior investigating officer, just said Vokes was a name suggested to them when they put their ear to the ground.'

'So they went and asked people in the Zet or other criminals and they all said Vokes is crazy, it'll probably be him?'

'Something like that. I was less than convinced. It all seemed too easy. Like it was all set up from the start to make sure he was arrested.'

'Christ, what a mess. But if it was so confusing and uncertain, why did the other 11 jurors vote to convict him?'

'Basically because the police said he'd definitely done it and, as mad as this sounds to you and me, they couldn't imagine the police would get it so wrong, or might lie. In our deliberations people actually said, "Well, they must be sure he's done it, or they wouldn't have arrested him".'

She looked at him, mouth agape. 'What? That's ridiculous.'

'I know. I kept saying, "But there's no hard evidence", and pointed out the police screwed up.'

'Did you get any sense of what actually happened when the lad was murdered?'

'Well, that was my point, that there were very few things that we know for sure happened. Daniel Ross was stabbed seven times with a long, pointed knife. The knife found in Vokes's flat matched the wounds. Ross collapsed and died almost instantly, which meant the attack happened where he fell, in the entrance to the Zet. There was some evidence of a fight. He didn't have skin under his nails or anything, but he had a bit of his own blood on him, and a few small defence wounds.'

She drained her glass. 'Shall we get one last drink?' she asked, gesturing to the barmaid for two more. 'This picture you're painting is far worse than I would have imagined. So, who actually found the body?'

Nick leaned forward and pointed at her. 'Yeah, see, that was a weird thing, too. Someone called a taxi to the flats; nobody said who. But the cabbie was the one who found the body. Ross was already dead, but the pathologist said she thought he'd been killed at any time in the previous hour but couldn't narrow it down more than that. But the weird thing is this: the cabby gave evidence and he was a normal bloke, not some sort of human detritus. He said he got out the car and ran to the body, asked if he was OK, but then saw the blood and ran back to the cab, picked up his phone and dialled 999. The operator asked him what service he needed. He told the court that he'd just said the words, "Someone's bleeding to death" when the police turned up and he rang off.'

'That is odd,' said Julie. 'How come they were there so quickly? Was it questioned in court?'

'No. Neither the defence nor the prosecution returned to it. I raised it in discussions and other jurors said it didn't matter and that they were probably just passing, or the cabby misremembered what he'd said and how much time had passed.'

'Well, maybe it doesn't matter, but you'd want it explained all the same. Maybe they *were* just passing.'

'But you can't just pass the Zet. The road goes nowhere. It's a dead end.'

Julie scratched her head.

'So did someone call a taxi to make sure the body was officially found by someone who didn't live in the Zetland, do you think?'

'I actually suggested that to the jury. It was too perfect for it to just happen that way. It meant everyone could make out they saw and knew nothing. And that's exactly what happened. The Zet people didn't have money for taxis and in fact the cabbie, in his evidence, said he was reluctant to even go there and that a lot of cabs wouldn't bother because they thought they'd get ripped off. But it was a quiet day so he risked it.'

Julie sat and thought for a moment. 'But the jury didn't have to say who did the murder, only decide if Vokes did it and by the sound of it, there had to be doubts about that.'

'Exactly.'

He sank into his mind, scratched at his chin and bit his bottom lip in contemplation. 'It's going to bug the hell out of me, this, Jules.'

'I can see that. You've gone quiet. That's not a good sign, is it? You going quiet usually means the black dog is nearby.'

She squeezed his hand.

'Yeah, the dog is sniffing around. I've been taking my Phenibut, but it seems like it's not working as well as it has been.' He sighed. 'That man is in jail and he shouldn't be. He was distraught when the verdict was given. All it'd take is one piece of hard evidence to prove he wasn't at the flats and was somewhere else at the time of the murder, and that'd mean he'd have to be released. Just one thing. Never mind if it can't be proven who did it, at least someone who didn't do it won't be in jail. I think the police didn't want to find that evidence because then the case would still be open and their competence brought into question again. Wouldn't surprise me if they disappeared the CCTV footage that proved Vokes's innocence.'

'Could you try and find evidence? Have you got your notes from the trial?'

'No, they took them off us as we left court, but I made some notes when I got home each night, didn't I? But I wouldn't know where to start. How the hell do you find evidence that someone wasn't somewhere? Am I being crazy, Jules?'

'The CCTV is the obvious way to prove where he was. If he is innocent, it's only right and proper that someone proves it, if at all possible. Investigative journalists do that all the time, don't they?'

'Yeah, but I'm not one of those.'

'You could be. It could be a story for you to sell. God knows we need the money. I've got 50 quid on me and £98.14 in my account until I get paid next week. How much have you got?'

'I've sold a few books, but I really have no idea. You know I'm hopeless at that.'

'Right then, so look at it like this: you can sell it to a national. They love a "wrong man in jail" story. Add in some sex, drugs, a small baby and the life of the underclass and it's perfect tabloid fodder.' She flashed her blue eyes at him, encouragingly.

'OK, I'll go through the notes tonight and see if I can think of how to go about it. I could call Trevor Daley on the news desk at the *Mirror*. He's a Boro fan and I've known him for years. See if they'd be interested.'

He drained his glass and stared over Julie's shoulder and out of the large plate-glass window. A man walked into his view and, standing on the pavement, pointed at him and with an angry glare, made a throat-cutting sign, then pointed again and mouthed the words, 'You're dead'.

Julie, seeing him being distracted, spun around. 'Who the hell is that?'

The man turned and marched away at speed.

'That? That was Kev Berryman.'

'From the trial?'

'Yeah.'

'What's his problem?'

'I don't know. How did he even know I was here? What's he got against me?'

'Well, you think he's the real killer, but he can't know that, can he? Have you told anyone else that you think it was him?'

'No...oh, err...yes, actually, I have. I said it in the jury room. I said I thought he'd done it. So 11 other people know I think it was him.'

She looked at him. 'Well, that means there was a mole on the jury, then. Someone reported back to him.'

He put his hand across his eyes and shook his head. 'Oh, bloody hell. This isn't good, Jules. Berryman is a really snide, nasty, ratty bastard and, like I said, he runs the Zet from his ground-floor flat by the communal entrance. He knows who comes and goes. He knows exactly what happened that day and I really don't want someone like him as an enemy.'

'Looks like it's too late for that.'

CHAPTER 2

'Aye aye, it's Cagney and Lacey,' said Jeff, as Nick and Julie walked into his shop on Stockton High Street.

'I'd bloody love to be Sharon Gless, me. I had a crush on her when I was about 14. She wore such nice jumpers,' said Julie, walking into the cafe at the back to get some tea. 'Hi, Alisha. How are you? That's a lovely silk top you've got on. Quite psychedelic.'

'That's because there's LSD in the beans today,' said Jeff, moving his eyebrows up and down conspiratorially. 'That's right, isn't it, Argie?' He picked the little lad up and messed with his mop of shaggy fair hair. 'Just say yes, Arg. I'm your dad, you're contractually obliged to agree with me even when I'm talking absolute nonsense.'

Argie began making expressive noises which were not quite yet words.

'Groppy gaga goo?' said Jeff. 'They were a Greek prog rock band, weren't they?"

Nick perched on one of the stools beside the counter and began pulling silly faces at Argie, which always seemed to fascinate the boy. He stared at Nick intently as he pulled first a toothy, rabbity face, then a cross-eyed one with his tongue out, making him giggle and gurgle again.

'Where's Guru?'

'He's on 2 'til 10 shift. He'll be in soon. I've got to go to the JRC,' said Jeff.

'Who's on tonight, then?'

'It's acoustic night, featuring drippy lasses with long straight hair and quivering voices and their doe-eyed male equivalents.'

Nick pulled a disapproving face.

'I know. Me, too. But the students like all of that sort of stuff, so I have to cater to them once in awhile. I'm going to put every half-decent singer-songwriter onto the jukebox to try and educate the youngsters about Nick Drake, Laura Nyro, Joni, early Elton and John Martyn.' He pointed at a pile of singles in a box. 'So, what was the verdict, then?'

'Guilty by 11 to one.'

'Don't tell me, you were the one, right?' Jeff cocked a finger at him, like it was a loaded gun.

Nick nodded.

He fired his imaginary gun. 'Bang! Why does that not surprise me? Owee then, spill the beans. You took the vow of confidentiality so seriously, all I know is that it was a murder case.'

But before Nick could say anything, Guru walked in. Better known to his mother as George Urwin, he was an impressive figure at a lean six feet tall, with tanned skin and a shiny bald head. Having taken early retirement as a computer programmer at age 60, he'd turned up on the first day Jeff had advertised Emily's job, had recited the 40-year UK discography of Uriah Heep off the top of his head in chronological order, with chart placings for each album. Jeff had been so impressed he'd employed him on the spot, figuring he wasn't likely to get too many classic rock-loving applicants with top-rank computer skills and what appeared to be a photographic memory. Clearly, he was an unusually constructed chap. He put Nick in mind of his friend Josh, who had Asperger's, except Guru had social skills, albeit slightly odd ones, whereas Josh didn't, even though he'd learned what not to say and do. But they certainly shared an ability to focus and absorb information.

'Hey G-man,' said Jeff, hi-fiving him.

'Greetings to all lifeforms,' said Guru, with a smile revealing even white teeth. He wasn't at all religious but he did look like he should have been a guru or yoga master. He had that slightly rarefied air about him. The fact he was prone to dispense information via aphorisms or quotes from songs, sometimes putting his hands together as though praying and nodding his head a little, only added to the feeling that you were in the presence of a higher being.

He spoke with a basso profundo, dark-brown voice that was more Yorkshire than Teesside. Having been born and brought up in Northallerton, he retained some of that town's strange mix of Teesside vowels and Yorkshire drone. But working in London for years had diluted it significantly.

Julie called out a greeting and wiggled her fingers at him, as she talked to Alisha.

'Here, hold the Boy Wonder while I check the singles box for the club,' said Jeff, handing Argie to Nick.

Nick took him and rubbed his nose against Argie's, as he often did as a greeting. 'And how are you, young fella m'lad?' The boy looked at him with big, bright, greyish blue almond-shaped eyes.

'Neenit druff baaah.'

'No, I'm Nick, remember?' he said, balancing him on the crook of his arm.

'Nick Nick Nick Nick...neeeekekeke,' said Argie, laughing and kicking his legs around.

They all stopped and looked at each other.

'Did he just say your name?' said Jeff, eyebrows raised.

'He correctly identified Mr Guymer by his forename,' said Guru, nodding sagely.

'Say it again, Arge,' said Jeff. 'Say "Nick".'

Argie lolled his head and looked at his dad. 'Nick nic nic nic nic,' he said, looking surprised at the noises coming from his mouth.

A surge of pride flushed Nick's body. 'C'mon Jeff, that's proof. I'm his first word. Jules! Jules! Argie's first word was "Nick"!'

She came through a big grin on her face. 'What a clever Argie, you are. Now say "Jules".' She formed the word slowly and deliberately: 'Joooo-ulls.'

Argie made some random noises and then sneezed twice, but didn't seem in the mood to say any more words.

'My god, I've been trying for months to get him to say "Uriah Heep",' said Jeff, stroking his son on the head.

'Well, I'm proud to be your lad's first word.'

'So you should be. It's a great honour. Let's hope he learns a few more before he goes to university, especially "here's", "some", "money", and "dad".'

A woman in a red polo shirt and blue trousers came into the shop. Jeff turned around.

'Hi, Maggie,' he said to the nursery worker, who took Argie out along with another two kids. 'He's just said his first word.'

'Aw, that's mint that, like. Oweee, Argie, it's walkie time.'

The boy waved at them all as she carried him outside.

Julie gave a secret quick squeeze of Nick's hand as she went back to finish her conversation with Alisha.

'So, what has this Ruby Tuesday brought through the door?' said Guru, picking up a pile of newly purchased records that were on the counter. 'Ah, the mighty fine Wishbone Ash's *Pilgrimage*.'

'And it's an orange dog bone,' said Jeff, referring to the shape of the first-pressing MCA label.

Guru fixed him with a green-eyed stare, one eye half closed. 'Catalogue number MDKS 8004. If I'm not mistaken.'

Jeff checked it. '100 per cent correct. How do you do that, Guru?'

'Some things just stick in my brain. I was a big Ash fan back in the day. Saw them many times. Twin lead guitars smoking.'

He skimmed through the pile. 'I'll get these into the database and the better ones onto eBay.' As he spoke he pulled out a huge laptop, went to the other side of the counter and sat down.

'Right, I'm going to the club,' said Jeff. 'Do you want to give us a hand loading the jukey with these records, Nick?' He pointed the big box of records.

'Aye, alright.' He called out to Julie. 'We're going to the JRC.'

She put a thumb up. 'I'll catch you up in a bit.' She turned back to Alisha, leaning on the counter as she did so.

It was only a short walk to the club on Church Road.

'Must feel good that the whole trial is over,' said Jeff, as they walked. 'It took up two weeks of your time, right when you were busy selling your book. And you had that bad cold for the first week, which by the way, I think you've given to Argie. He had a sneezing fit this morning. Though he seems amazed at snot when it runs out of his nose. Keeps licking it off his hand, so he's happy enough.'

'Yeah, but it was an unsatisfactory result. I'm sure he was innocent.'

Nick gave him a quick outline of the court case.

'Do you know any of those people, by any chance? Berryman in particular.'

'Nah. I know where the Zetland flats are but that sort don't mix outside of their own weirdo druggie groups. I mean, you see that type around all the time, but they've always got that ratty-eyed, shifty look as they scuttle past you on their way to buy some...what was it...dog valium? Bloody hell. I sodding hate them, me. Just a pain in the arse and a drain on all the decent folks' money.'

'Julie and I talked about this earlier, actually. I sympathise with what you're saying, but they've sod all else to do, other than to get wasted.'

Jeff unlocked the club door and flicked all the lights on. 'That's total bollocks, that is. They don't have to get off their faces. They could get a job and stop taking drugs and stop drinking Special Brew. There's plenty of help these days.'

Jeff was being unusually harsh. His inclination was normally to take the piss, rather than be overly acerbic.

'Look, I'm not enamoured with them either, but there's reasons why people end up at the bottom of the pile. This lot were, by and large, a pitiful bunch of people with sod all in their life.'

'Aye, pitiful people scrounging off the dole and thieving from the rest of us. They wander in the shop sometimes, eyes black as coal and seeing nothing. They're bloody awful, man. Don't go having sympathy for them. They'd spit it back in your face.'

'Jeff man, you're not usually this hard-assed. You're normally sympathetic to waifs and strays.'

The big man put the box of singles down beside the jukebox, turned to look at Nick and flicked his long, greying curtain of hair over his shoulders.

'I am to people who deserve a bit of help. But running a club means you get to see a lot of the low life that only comes out at night. The only way to deal with them isn't to pat them on the head and say, "Aw diddums, there there". The way to deal with them is to give it to them hard, preferably with a baseball bat. I mean, I don't need bouncers to keep punters like you and Jules in check, do I? I have to pay hundreds of pounds out every week to employ big blokes to slap these twatty Townies down. Ratty, cheating little fuckers. You know what they do? They steal the bog rolls from our toilets and they nick the soap dispensers. They've also had a ball cock, a bog seat, and a load of spare wire from backstage. And that's before we get to their repeated attempts to break in to steal drink and rob the till, as though we'd be so stupid as to leave money here overnight. Nice people come here for a night out, but the low life come here on a shopping expedition.' His tone was fierce and angry.

He went on, warming to his theme. 'I tell you, man, they'll thieve anything that's not nailed down. They'd steal your face right off your head, if they could. And then they'll go back to their sordid pits of despair and sell it for pennies to buy a bottle of vodka or anything that will stop them from feeling anything. And the only thing they can do in life is sprog out kids. Weirdly, none of them seem infertile. Seems a life of drink and drugs makes you more fertile, if anything. Must be the grey trackie bottoms they all wear.'

'You're overgeneralising. They're not all bad. And some of those who steal from you aren't Zet druggies, they are just selfish idiots who want to ponce off society. They're not necessarily the same people. And don't think I didn't spot the Grateful Dead quote in that rant.'

Jeff raised an eyebrow. 'Thought you'd like it. Look, as far as I'm concerned, if there's one less of them around, whether dead or in jail, that's probably a win for everyone else. You know as well as I do that a lot of the decent people in Stockton don't come into town any more because of people like this Zetland crowd and all the others like them. They go to Yarm instead or somewhere nice where there aren't blokes on the corner who look like they'd steal your kidney and sell it to a sick orphan for drug money. And that means the town doesn't get money spent in it, so it's got into a downward spiral of economic despair.'

'It's not that bad, Jeff.'

Jeff looked at him like he was stupid. 'Isn't it? You remember what the High Street was like in the 70s. It was packed out with regular people going about their regular business. It's not the same now. I'm only surprised you don't see tumbleweed blowing through after 5pm. I would never talk the area down to a stranger but, owee, man, even compared to Newcastle, it's bloody bleak. You know it, I know it. No-one's got any money here and them that has spend it in nicer places. That's the truth.'

Nick blew out air and shook his head. 'That's too harsh, man. Alright, I know you're at the sharp end here, but Glenn Vokes has been sent down for a crime he didn't commit. And any way you want to look at it, that's just wrong.'

Jeff lifted the glass top of the jukebox and began taking out the singles that were stacked in there. 'Here. Take these and put them in the singles boxes behind the bar.'

Nick got the black, padded plastic boxes and began to drop the singles into paper sleeves as Jeff passed records to him.

'This Vokes bloke. OK, maybe he didn't do the knifey knifey, but he'll have already done something, or he'd have gone on to do something very illegal. When you say he's innocent, he's not really, is he? He's more correctly called a total scumbag.'

'There's a difference between stealing toilet roll and murder, Jeff. He was a petty criminal who shoplifted for drug money. And you don't know, he might have become a reformed character.'

'Might, but wouldn't. That sort never do.'

'Well, you did.'

'Eh?'

'You became a reformed character.'

'I was never a criminal, unless you've found out my secret identity as a Raffles type of cat burglar.'

'Well, you were. You used to buy dope all the time. That's illegal. You only stopped a few years back.'

'That's not the same thing. I liked a spliff, but I had the Harrogate shop and it's not like I was a waster.'

'True, but you were a major pisshead.'

'Even so. I never did anyone any harm, except myself. I mostly just sat at the bar in Jack & Danny's for hours.'

'Alright, but my point is, you were on a one-way street to an early grave. When you had your heart attack you turned your life around and cleaned up and lost weight. Who's to say Vokes wouldn't do likewise? He's only in his 20s. He isn't dumb. He went to college to do media studies, but got chucked off for smoking dope and not doing enough course work. Sound familiar?'

Jeff stopped passing him the records and raised his index finger aloft. 'Ah, but I didn't actually get chucked off my course at Newcastle Poly, did I?'

'No, but only because we had exactly seven hours of lectures a week, so there was almost nothing to miss. But they hauled you over the coals twice in three years for poor attendance and being late submitting work, and you were on your last warning for the whole of the third year.'

'Alright, alright. I see what you're getting at. But I maintain I was not a scumbag like that Zetland crowd.'

After taking out the records, he began to load the new ones as Nick passed them to him.

'Anyway, what's it to you what happens to Vokes? You voted not guilty, you did your duty, did what you thought was best. You can't do any more than that.'

'That's what Jules said, but, it means the real murderer got away with it and the police got away with being rubbish. In fact, the cops were corrupt, really. They cocked it up and needed a quick conviction to put it all to bed and draw a veil over it. Vokes was a good fit. Has Mandy talked about this case at all?'

'Nah. Lowlife stabbings are too commonplace to stand out, I think. And if Cleveland Police made a bollocks of it, she just wouldn't tell me, man.'

'But I thought you were really close now. It's been over a year since you hooked up.'

'We are, but she doesn't talk much about work, except in general terms, and the police have this informal vow of silence to civilians, don't they? Even with loved ones. I totally assume she skirts around the law when she needs to, but she'd never tell me that. I just know she deals with wasters and scumbags every day of the week. This happened last October so it's probably not even on her radar any more. In fact, there's probably been half a dozen similar cases since.'

'Is she why you've got harsher about them?'

Jeff shrugged. 'Well to be honest, when you hear even just occasional details about the shit that goes on, it's hard to feel any other way. You know what they nicked a woman for last week?'

'What?'

Jeff continued to put singles into the jukebox's rack. 'She arrested a middle-aged woman, not far from where I grew up, for sexually abusing her own daughter. No bloke involved, for once. She just...well I won't clutter your brain with the sick details. See? Absolute scumbags, man. No sympathy from me, I'm afraid. Right's right and wrong's wrong and that's all there is to it. When you've got a bairn to bring up, it focuses your mind, trust me.'

Nick rubbed his eyes and groaned. 'Christ almighty. There are some absolute evil shits out there, I know. Mandy is much more hardline than Colin Harcombe was, though, isn't she?'

'I don't know, really. They're two very different people. He was strict but Mandy is under big pressure to get results and she thinks a zero-tolerance regime is the way to get on top of the evils. So at the moment she is coming down hard on anyone who drops so much as a piece of litter. I think it's right. Summat needs doing, that's for sure.'

'But she doesn't want a murderer on the loose.'

'Nah, of course not. I'll ask her about this case, if you like, but she won't discuss it much, I know that already. It's too risky, 'cos as much as I'll tell her I won't blab, at some point, doubtless after a few drinks, I will say something accidentally to someone, or I'll be overheard in the Royal Oak and there could be consequences. So it's safer not to tell me much, and to be honest, I prefer it that way.'

They had just filled the jukebox with the 200 singles when Julie called out as she came into the club.

'Hello!'

'In here, Jules,' yelled Nick.

She strode in and looked around. 'Oooh, it smells of joss sticks in here. I've not smelt joss sticks for yonks.'

'It's not joss sticks, man, it's some sort of pot pourri,' said Jeff.

'Pot pourri? Since when did you know anything about pot pourri?' she laughed.

'I don't need to know anything about it to buy it wholesale and put it in big bowls. I think it's classy and it masks the smell of stale beer and bleach.'

'We saw Emily earlier, you know. We were in Beef and Vodka after being in court.'

'Oh, aye, how is she?'

'Great. Happy.'

Jeff smiled. 'Oh, that's good. I really miss her, you know,' he said, tapping at his phone, sending a text to Joel, his sound guy.

'Do you?' said Nick.

'Yeah, the G-man is cool, but he doesn't light the place up the way Emily did, with all her energy and her sexy little dances and stuff. She'd do these little waltzes around the shop with Tommo or any of the regulars. They all loved her. But things change, I guess. I'm glad she's happy over there and there's no arguing with love, is there?'

'Not at all. She's like a different person, in some ways. Still very rude, though,' said Julie.

'Yeah, she manages to be rude but not vulgar. Clever that.' He sighed. 'But G is great for business because he's brilliant on the computer and seems to be able to remember anything he sees. And he scares some of the shitehawks off because he looks so weird.' He looked around. 'Right, I've got to get chairs and tables put out for tonight's soiree.'

'Ah, you're making it a sit-down affair?' said Nick.

'Yeah, and table service, too. Just thought I'd try it for a quiet acoustic night. It works well for the comedy nights.'

'Come on then, you, let's get home and get out of these suits,' said Julie, linking Nick's arm in hers and tugging him to the door. 'See you soon, Jeff.'

'Aye. By the way, you look great in that suit, Jules. Like someone out of *LA Law*.'

She laughed and threw a pose.

'And if you're serious about this Vokes business, Nick, you know the place you should start to ask questions?'

'Where's that?'

'Hair Bear. He's info central for anything to do with the drug community in Stockton. Mind, you might be shocked when you go over there.'

'Why? Is the place still in a terrible mess?'

'No. The opposite. He's cleaned up. He's stopped smoking weed.'

Nick pointed at Jeff. 'See, people *can* change.'

'It's lovely out, shall we go across the road for a drink? We can sit outside,' said Julie, pulling on a loose, old threadbare pair of Levi's and a pale blue cap-sleeve top.

'You've got your Bananarama jeans on,' said Nick, because they had such a loose mid 80s look, with the bottoms turned up so they were at her ankle.

'Bananarama my arse,' she said with a snort.

'Well, if you insist, madam.' He took off the towel that was wrapped around his waist and thrust his hips at her.

She laughed 'Eee, dear me, you and your banana.' She flicked out at him with her foot as she sat in the bedroom wicker basket chair and watched him get dry after his shower.

'Yeah, OK, let's go to the pub, I could do with a whisky or two, I've still got a sore throat after that cold that Jeff says Argie's now got. Do you mind if we go over the details of the trial? I need to work out what to do now that Trevor at the *Mirror* is interested.'

'Is he a Teessider?'

'Yeah, he's from Dalton Piercy originally. I knew him on the *Northern Echo* in the 80s when he was a sports reporter. He's quite high up in the long line of editors at the *Mirror*, now.'

'If he could've done that, so could you. You've always been a well-respected writer. I remember seeing your byline on Boro match reports in the late 80s and 90s. How come you didn't make a career in newspapers?'

'Oh, that's easy, I wasn't ambitious. You've really got to push hard to climb that particular greasy pole and I just wasn't interested. I was always all about the art, not the commerce. That's why I went freelance when I moved to Harrogate in 1991. I was sick of being told what to do by men who I thought were arseholes.'

She snorted a laugh. 'Hmm, that sounds very typical of you. The rest of us accepted that there would be some people at work we wouldn't like. But not you. Ha. So what sort of money was he talking about, then?'

'Depends on what the story uncovers. He reckoned if it's a basic miscarriage of justice through bad policing, there's not too much money in that. Maybe a couple of grand. However, if there's police corruption and some human interest, preferably involving children, then it could be five figures. Terrible that it's graded in such a way, but there you go.'

'Well if you think about it, you're the only one who suspects this is all wrong. There's no competition from other investigative journalists, so it'd be a proper exclusive. Not sure how Mandy Beale will feel about you writing about her force's incompetence, though.'

'Not happy, I'd think. But the truth is the truth. If they don't want to look bad, they shouldn't mess things up so badly and then try to cover up their errors.'

'That's true. Very true. I'm on your side, luv.' She gave him her warm smile.

'Ten grand would be very useful.'

'It would, not least because I'll need five of it,' she said.

'Five grand? What do you need that much money for?'

'I want to study for a degree in Social Services. Not full time, just on day release over the next couple of years. A lot of support workers do it. More qualifications mean I'll be able to go for bigger, higher-up jobs, if I want to anyway. Sorry, but it's expensive.'

Nick waved away her apology. 'No, that's fine, man. Well, that settles it, I'm going to get a story out of this, one way or another.'

She licked her lips, rubbed her forehead and nodded. 'OK, luv. But you do realise that no-one else cares that Glenn Vokes has been jailed for 25 years, so there'll be no-one else who is sympathetic to his cause, or will want to help you prove his innocence.'

'I know that, and I also know he's untrustworthy. Jeff was really...I don't know what the word is...he was totally against people like Vokes. He was saying how much trouble he gets at the club from robbing twats like him. He said they don't deserve sympathy.'

She drew her legs up under her. 'You can understand that, though. I sort of agree with him, to a point. There's a big difference between your ideals and reality. Everyone who wants to help the dispossessed and downtrodden has this issue to deal with, because it can be so infuriating that people won't help themselves. If you're a soft touch, they'll bloody well monster you. They might seem doped up and dumb, but they'll be quick enough to mercilessly exploit anyone who gives them a sympathetic ear.'

He pulled on black underwear, a black t-shirt and lightweight jeans.

She went on, looking out of the bedroom window into the middle distance, chewing on her bottom lip. 'Sometimes, it's like this for me at work. You meet people who you really don't like, or who really annoy you. They have very different views on life to your own, and they're stupid, crude and unpleasant. Sometimes, they're racist, sometimes they call you names, but I've still got to help them. The fact I don't like them doesn't matter. My role is to make their lives safer or better. But I also understand why they're like this. Even so, there still has to be a point where you draw the line. Vokes lived a shit life and was a bit of an arsehole, but if he's not guilty, you're really the only hope he's got.'

'True.' He thought about it some more. 'Do you know if Ricky and Kev are back from living la vida loca in Benidorm yet?'

'Kev's due back tomorrow. Mam says he's got a new flat by the river. Ricky is staying out in Spain. I've not heard anything from them for yonks. Probably blown all their money. Why?'

'I think I'll go to the Zet. But I need some muscle as back up, just in case things get hairy. I'm thinking of Kev for that role.'

'Nothing he'd like better. Actually, he might even know some of the residents. It's not like those two have ever spent much time with people from the respectable end of society.'

'OK, but before that I'm going to get a bit of help from God.'

She raised her eyebrows. 'Are you now? I didn't realise you were that well connected.'

Nick walked through the gates of Ropner Park right on 9.30am the next morning. Don Preston was already waiting for him by the bandstand, dressed in black and wearing his dog collar. He'd put weight on since Nick had last seen him and was now really rather fat, with a substantial belly, a soft, jowelly pink face and receding greying hair cut short. He smiled on seeing Nick, giving him a little wave.

'Hey, Don,' said Nick, arm outstretched to the vicar.

'Nick. Nice to see you. How are you keeping?'

'Well I had a rotten cold for a couple of weeks, but apart from that, I've been in good health. Well, the usual issues crop up from time to time, obviously.'

'Your depressions, you mean?'

'Yeah, but nothing really bad or bleak, more like short but intensely low moods, really. But I've accepted now that it's who I am. I just get through them.'

'And how's Julie? Has she got over last summer's...events? She was having therapy when I last saw you.'

'Yeah, by and large she's over it, or as much as you ever get over traumatic events. The therapy did help her to emotionally file it away. And she's also got her councillor as part of her work to help her, but she's the usual bright-eyed and bushy-tailed Jules. You know what she's like, she's incredibly tough and resilient and...well...wonderful. I think so anyway. She's my hero, and I love her with every atom of my being.' He paused. 'You're the only person I can say that to, Don.'

Don grinned. 'That's not uncommon, the dog collar brings confessions out of people, sometimes ones you'd rather not hear. Julie is a superhero, though. Have you thought of dressing her up as Wonder Woman?'

'Ha ha, I don't think she'd like that. But if I could get her to be Julie Newmar dressed as Catwoman, believe me, I would.'

Don put his hands together in supplication. 'And Lord, please deliver unto your randy brethren this possibility in order to satisfy this man's holy urge to perv.'

They both laughed loudly.

'Anyway, how are you, Don? If you don't mind me saying so, you've porked up a bit. This is not a criticism, merely an observation.'

'I have. You're right. I'd like to say I'm just full of God's love, but the truth is, I'm full of parishioner cake. For some reason, a certain sort of elderly lady seems to think the vicar needs feeding with cake, cream, scones and jam. And I'm not good at saying no. It seems churlish to decline. But I must do something about it as I am getting towards the fat side of bastard.'

They sauntered around the park, a park Nick had spent almost all his summer holidays since aged nine playing in. It had seemed huge back then, but now seemed relatively modest, though still lovely.

'It's nice to see you, Nick. As ever, you look in fine fettle. And you said you've been doing your duty as decent citizen on a jury.'

'Yeah, on a murder trial.'

'Goodness. That doesn't sound much fun.'

Nick went over the case, telling Don what had happened and his conclusion that Vokes was innocent.

'Y'see, Jeff thinks that these people are all conniving wasters and if not guilty of one thing, will be guilty of something else. And he's probably right. But I can't face the idea that I was part of a jury which sent an innocent man to jail. As my unofficial moral advisor, what do you reckon, Don? Should I try and prove Vokes is innocent?'

'Well, it's not your legal responsibility to do so.' He rubbed his head.

'No, but morally, I think it might be.'

Don nodded, as he often did, as part of his consideration. 'Interesting. Well the Bible tells us that Jesus was the friend of the poor and the lowest of the low. Nobody is excluded from God's love.'

They walked around the park's small lake. Nick spoke. 'Yeah, but I'm not Jesus. I can see Jeff's point. I'm not naïve about this. I mean, I saw these people in court for nearly two weeks and they're mostly in a really sorry state. Some are on methadone because they're heroin addicts, all of them are high almost all the time. They don't seem to even live by any obvious moral code. They are, to all intents and purposes, feral. They live to get drunk and stoned. So I'm not sure I can even communicate with them, y'know? Do you meet people like that?'

'Oh, yes. As you know, I'm a big believer in reaching out to people who are in the most deprived and desperate situations. To me, that's an important part of the church's work. OK, we're never going to get much in the collection box from them, but that's not the point. If we can't try to follow Christ's example of giving succour to the most desperate, then we're letting him down.'

'These people seemed beyond help, Don.'

He shook his head a little. 'Nobody is beyond help. We can't give up on people. We're all God's children, after all. And people can turn their lives around, even when it looks impossible. I've seen it time and again and in the most difficult and challenging circumstances.'

Don's Christianity was the best sort; practical, giving and entirely without pomposity or self-regard. In fact, he totally understood why many people found religion somewhere between ridiculous and mendacious. He wasn't bothered if you had faith or you didn't. He just felt his role in the world was to help people, feeling motivated by a higher force, but he didn't expect or require anyone to believe in God in return. He just tried to do the right thing, according to his faith and was happy to be called that most old-fashioned of things, a Christian Socialist.

'Do you know that block of flats called the Zetland, just at the back of Bishopton Lane?'

Don frowned. 'I think so. Not my parish, of course. If you like, I can have a word with Tina Wallace, that's her patch.'

'Err, well, I'll tell you what I was thinking, and tell me if you think this is crazy. I was thinking me and you might go over there, along with Kev Wells. All I want to do is get some evidence to prove Vokes couldn't have killed Daniel Ross. Proving who did do it sounds like a much harder and even dangerous thing to do, but all we need is an independent witness who saw Vokes at the time of the murder and that'll do it. Now, your dog collar might help them open up. People respect a vicar.'

Don raised his dark eyebrows. 'Do they, now? Someone should have told me.'

'Don't they?'

He made a wobbling gesture with his hand. 'Can go either way. But I'm happy to help you, if you think I can. Kev is a large man of some repute, so he'll be useful in case there is negativity. It might be a nice combination, a little bit of God and a little bit of the devil!'

They laughed. 'Yeah, Kev has got a lot of devil in him. Though I've not seen him for best part of a year. He's been living in Spain with Ricky. They got a lot of money as reward for foiling those terrorists. They've probably blown it all now on beer and women.'

They sat down on a park bench and looked out over the water as house martins swooped around, hoovering up the insects that danced over the water.

'You've got a very strong sense of right and wrong, haven't you?' said Don. 'I've always thought that.'

'Yeah, my mother reminded me last year about how I hit a man on the leg who kicked his dog, when I was only a little boy. So it seems to have been in me since an early age.'

'Your mother said that, last year? But she's no longer with us.'

'Oh, she comes to see me in my dreams. Well, she did last year, but I've not seen her for a while now. I hope she comes back. I miss our little chats. Don't look at me like that, Don. It's true.'

'I didn't say it wasn't. But it is a bit odd.'

'I know. She always said I was special.'

Don folded his arms and nodded. 'Well, far be it from me to contradict your experiences, however unusual.'

'So do you think this court case is something I should pursue?'

'Knowing you, I don't think there's anything that's going to stop you. You get a bee in your bonnet about things and won't rest until you've sorted them out, or have at least tried to. And I'm happy to help you if I can, in whatever way that might be.'

'I'd feel guilty if I didn't at least try. But the trouble is, there's a man called Kevin Berryman who lives there and who seems to have taken against me.' He explained about what had happened in Beef and Vodka.

'Hmm. Well, surely, if we go around there and say we're trying to prove that Daniel Ross is innocent, he won't be too pleased about that, if he really is the guilty party.'

'Yeah, so I really need to go there when he's out. But I'm not sure how I can know in advance.'

'How's this? I'll ring his doorbell. If he answers, I'm just a fat vicar looking for new friends of Jesus God bless you my child and all who sail in you, et cetera et cetera. If he doesn't, then we're in the clear.'

'Don! This is good work. You could become Teesside's first crime-fighting priestly superhero.'

'Hopefully the role comes with an XXL superhero pair of underpants.'

'Are you confident being out in public in tight underwear then, Don?'

'I'm happy to celebrate the generous physical endowment God has bestowed upon me. Amen.' He put his hands together and closed his eyes as though in prayer.

Nick laughed. 'OK, look, I'll be in touch later when I've set up this trip to the flats with Kev.'

'OK, this is quite exciting.'

'You might not think that when you see these people.'

Don put a hand on his thigh and patted him.

'Nick, it might surprise you, but priests like me, who have spent their lives gripping the shitty end of the Christian stick, are not unused to being around the less savoury elements of society. I've been threatened with knives and I've seen terrible things both here and in Africa. So it holds no fears for me. God's love gives me strength. In my view, being a priest shouldn't be easy. It shouldn't be about tea and cakes at the vicarage, jumble sales and blarting canon at the converted every Sunday. Is that what Jesus did? No. He got down and dirty with the low life. If, as priests, we're not following in Christ's footsteps, then, to me, we're just poseurs - imposters, if you like - and we'd not be worthy to serve him.'

Emotion rose in Nick's throat. He didn't have many friends, really. He knew quite a few people, but actual friends he could count on one hand. Don was one of them. And he really admired him. He talked the talk and he walked the walk. And that was as much as you can expect of anyone in life.

'Thanks, Don.'

Don said nothing, but just smiled.

'Would you like to say a prayer for us?' said Nick, out of nowhere. He made little prayers all the time. Just put his hands together and closed his eyes and tried to become one with...with...with whatever it was. And it always helped. Or, at least, it always felt like a positive thing to do, even though he was a long way from being any organised religion's biggest fan. It all felt too tribal and divisive. But Don was cut from different cloth.

'That's a good idea.' He bowed his head and put his hands together, between his knees. Nick did likewise.

'Lord, in this endeavour, gives us strength of mind, and purity of purpose. Gives us the power of your love and the compassion and understanding of your only son. Bless Nick, for his pursuit of justice and fairness. Amen.'

Nick opened his eyes, turned to Don and smiled. 'That felt nice. Can you come up with a prayer on demand at any moment in time?'

He gave him a sparkling smile. 'Of course. You get installed with special C of E software when you become a vicar. Press F4 and it knocks out a prayer.'

'Alright, Kev. Bloody hell, you're a deep shade of orange. Helluva tan, lad.'

Kev Wells laughed and ushered Nick into his new flat overlooking the River Tees.

'You look good, son. Absolutely ripped, as per usual,' said Kev.

'I'm nowt compared to the state of you. I assumed you'd come back from Spain full of beer and chips. But you've lost a lot of weight and look like you've got down to about 10 per cent body fat. You look like you could punch a horse unconscious.'

Kev laughed again and walked into the kitchen. 'Tea? I've got green.'

That was a shock as well. 'Nice one. Yeah. How come? You're not one for the green tea, normally.'

'I'm a reformed man, aren't I?'

Nick looked around. 'How come you've come back here and not the old place? You've not bought this, have you?'

'This place? Nah. I'm renting it, aren't I? I sorted it all out online while in Spain. Nice, I reckon. I just picked the keys up for it yesterday. All fully furnished. Could never have afforded anywhere this smart before.'

Nick looked at Kev as he filled the kettle. He looked so different. All the beery fat had gone and he'd grown his hair out, so it was past his ears. Julie's natural hair colour was a light, fair brown which she coloured to be more blonde, but Kev's was much nearer being real blonde and, along with his new shape and tan, meant he looked like a Californian surfer dude.

'If you don't mind me saying so, Kev, this looks suspiciously like you've had some sort of mid-life crisis.'

Kev poured the hot water on two green tea bags.

'Aye, well. Mebees I have. Whatever one of them is, like.'

As he handed Nick the mug, he cast him an almost nervous, or maybe embarrassed look. It wasn't a look he'd ever seen Kev Wells make before. Normally he was cold-eyed and largely insensitive. Nick had always got on with him, to a point, and had found him much more approachable than Ricky, who was just an annoying twat that you'd never tire of punching. But even so, he'd led a life that, to date, had been very firmly on the wrong side of the tracks.

'So tell us all about it, then,' said Nick.

'Well, we was out in Spain, money in the bank and no-one giving us shit for literally the first time in my life. So I started to properly relax. And you know what? I realised I'd never been properly relaxed in my whole life, or not since I was a little kid. It felt great. There was nothing to worry about, nothing and no-one to fight. And like, I know this sounds soft, but it was like I felt all the shit drain out of us. I was just sitting in the sun, cup of coffee, reading a book and I stopped and looked around and thought, actually, like, this is brill. It was a proper buzz, and all I wanted to do was to not ruin that buzz. It was like all the fighting was a block to doing something better.'

'As Eric Burdon once said in a song, "When I was fighting, I could've done the right thing".'

'Summat like that, aye. Terrible rhyme that, though.'

'Yeah, it is.' Nick sat down on a black leather sofa and looked out at the slow-moving river below. Kev sat to one side.

'Jules is really brainy and everyone used to say to us, "How come you're not the same?", but I always knew I was underneath, like. Well, not quite as brainy, 'cos Jules is brilliant, but you know what I mean. Ricky is proper thick. I'm not. Never have been. And I've had a year out of my normal shit life and it's been brilliant. So I decided that I can't waste my life just pissing it up the wall and playing the hard man. I've got to do something more constructive.'

'Like what?'

'Might get some education. I was talking to my dad about it. He came out for a couple of weeks. First chance I've had to have a long talk with him. That was his advice. Education opens doors and these days, it's not just for kids.'

'He seems like a decent fella, your dad, the little bit I've seen of him. Seems a bright man.'

'He is. I mean, Julie didn't get her brains from mam, did she? He's sound. He's looking for a place in North Yorkshire, y'know?'

'Yeah, Jules said something about that. So, Kev, to reduce this down, it sounds like you're saying that not having to graft out a living by scamming a few quid here and there, has made you realise that life doesn't have to be about drinking and fighting. That's amazing, man.'

'Aye, and while I was thinking this over, I stopped drinking, went low carb, 'cos I remembered you said that's how you'd got fit and lost weight that way. Started running on the beach. Five miles a day. Just ate steak and fish and cut out chips and bread. The fat just fell off us and, don't skit us, right, but it seemed to clear my head, like. It made me think, like, err, think sort of different.' He was obviously embarrassed to even say this.

'Being sober and fit changed your thought processes?'

He nodded, still not making eye contact. 'Yeah, I think so. Yeah...I'm not that good with words but it was like I could think straight and think more than a few hours ahead. It was like I had space in me life for ideas, like. See, I was thinking about this. I'd been pissed almost every day of my life for the last 30 or more years. The only time I wasn't was when I've been inside, but then I was off me head on pills, just to relieve the boredom. In Spain, right, it was just really nice, bit of sun, comfort, no worries and after a bit, getting fucked up seemed stupid because it actually made you feel worse. I'd have a bottle of gin and then wish I hadn't. So I binned it.'

'Normally it made you feel better but when you already feel good, you don't need that boost?'

'Aye, that's it. Sounds soft, like, I know. So I just sort of stopped. Ricky thinks I've got fucking crazy. He's still out there and massively on the piss, but I don't want to any more. I might change me mind, like, but I decided I'd come back, and get me head down, do some graft and try and live like a decent bloke. Stop cracking heads, like. Maybe see if I can find a nice lass, the way our Terry has with Jas.'

'Amazing. Have you told Jules any of this? She'll be dead pleased to hear it, man.'

Kev shook his head. 'No, I thought there'd be no point until I got in here and could show her that I was serious about it all, 'cos she'd think it was all just pie in the sky. You can tell her if you want. Like I say, I'm no good with words. That's your thing. The shit we've put her through over the years...dear me...hopefully I can make it up to her, from now on. Anyway, let's stop talkin' 'bout me, it's a fuckin' boring subject. What's going on with you?'

'Not much. I published my first novel earlier this year. It's called

Kidda and it's about a Stockton lad who's a great footballer but can't handle the pressure. So the house is full of boxes of paperbacks. It's doing OK, though. The past two weeks I've been on a jury in a murder trial.'

Kev raised his eyebrows. 'At Teesside Crown Court?'

'Yeah.'

'Who was it?'

'A bloke called Glenn Vokes. Do you know him?'

He nodded in recognition. 'I knew his dad. Vodka Vokes, we called 'im. Major alkie. Died about 15 years ago. Glenn must've been about 10 at the time. Who did he kill?'

'A lad called Daniel Ross.'

'Don't know him.'

'He was only 25. He was stabbed seven times in the entrance to the Zetland flats off Bishopton Lane.'

Kev nodded and sneered. 'Bloody horrible flats, them. It's always been a drug den, that place, going way back to the 70s. The hippy druggies all hung out there. So what was the fight over?'

'The prosecution said it was a fight over Glenn's girlfriend, who was supposed to have been unfaithful to him with Daniel Ross. Glenn had it out with him, pulled a knife and that was that. That's the story, anyway. I don't believe it.'

'Sounds quite typical. Someone coked up, or whatever, gets a rage on. Wham. All over.'

'Yeah, but the problem is, Glenn said in court that he wasn't even there and that he's been stitched up.'

Kev snorted with contempt. 'Trust me, everyone in jail will tell you they were stitched up.'

'Yeah, but I think he was telling the truth, even though the rest of the jury disagreed. I think a bloke called Kevin Berryman did it and I said so in the jury room, and somehow he's got hold of that info and threatened me.'

Kev gave him a weary look. 'Oh, Kev Berryman? He's a snidey shite, that one. Fancied himself as a moneylender a year or two ago. Had a bent copper on his payroll to scare the punters into paying up. I once had to sort Berry out on behalf of someone who he was giving a hard time. Full of shit.'

'Sort him out? Physically, like?'

'Sort of. I threatened to rip his lungs out if he didn't waive this debt on a pal of mine. He did. So I didn't have to hurt him.'

'Right, so you know him quite well?'

'Yeah. And he knows me. And I know how he knows what you said in the jury room. He'll have paid off one of the security blokes to eavesdrop.'

'Does that happen much?'

'Not often, but I've known it more than once. Typical snidey move of Berryman. He's a nasty, oily little shitehawk.'

Nick explained more about the court case.

'Y'see, Kev, all it'd take to get Vokes off is hard evidence that he wasn't there. He says he was wandering around all over the town because he was speeding. I don't want to be part of sending an innocent man down and I want to speak to some of the others in the Zet to see if I can get any evidence of Vokes's innocence. But, it might be a bit dangerous - druggies are unpredictable, so I need a bit of back-up and I thought of you. But now you've turned over a new leaf, you might not want to play at being a henchman.'

He shrugged. 'Aye, that's no bother. I'll have a wander down there with you, but they'll be stoned, so you won't get any sense out of them, I'll tell you that for nowt. There'll be no bother unless someone is raging on crack.'

'Yeah...you're right...maybe it's a daft idea. I just wanted to be able to see where it had all happened and I just don't trust the police's account.'

'They let a bloke into a flat which could have been a crime scene, that's useless, but the cops *are* useless, Nick. I know a lot of people slag them off as corrupt, but I don't think hardly any really are - not proper corrupt - most are just a bit shit at the job and it makes them seem bent when their stories don't match up or they let someone go somewhere that they shouldn't. Most of the time they just want a conviction. Whether it's right or wrong isn't as important as just getting one. Then they can tick a box and make out they're on top of things. A lot of it is just PR.'

'Did you know that Jeff is going out with Mandy Beale?'

'Big Mandy? I did hear something about that, aye. Mam told me about all the shit at his club and those rapists and Jules and that little Emily lass. Fucking disgusting.'

'Yeah, appalling.'

'In case you've not heard, they've been sorted inside, them four.'

'Really? I didn't know. So...err...you put the word out?'

'Yeah. Sorted. They'll fucking wish they were dead. They're going to have to look over their shoulder for the rest of their lives.'

He made a cutting sign across his throat and made a face as cold and scary as any Nick had seen. That side to Kev Wells, forged in a life of violence and crime, he didn't really want to explore. It sounded ominous for the four of them. Sex offenders were not exactly everyone's favourite criminals, even amongst criminals. Yeah, well, fuck 'em. Evil bastards.

'Aye, well, Jeff must have started going out with Mandy after you went abroad. They're quite close now.'

'She's a tough old bitch, that one. Had a few run-ins with her, over the years. Hope I don't have any more. She's alright though, y'know. Massive tits on her, mind. Seems weird that Jeff is banging her. She's a good shag, though, like. I knew Sid, her first husband, and that's what he always reckoned. He only stayed with her as long as he did because of the sex.'

'Like having it off with a huge blancmange, apparently!'

Kev laughed. His laugh weirdly sounded very like Julie's low, woody chuckle, like she was living inside him, and suddenly it was easy to see that they were brother and sister.

'So, when do you want to go down to the Zet?'

'I'll give Don a call and see if he's available.'

'Who's Don?'

'Don Preston. He's a vicar, a mate of mine. He married us, remember?'

'I remember someone married you, don't recall him much. A vicar? You're not religious, though.'

'I know. It's probably a daft idea. But he can scout out whether Berryman is there. There's no point in us being there if he is.'

'Aye, he's the boss of there, I should think. Alright, well, whatever. I don't see what you're going to get out of this visit, though.'

'No, I don't either, but I've gotta start somewhere.'

He called Don, and arranged to meet on Bishopton Lane, outside the station, in 20 minutes.

It was only a 15-minute walk across town. As they set off, it felt weird to be with Kev Wells on his own, which almost never happened, weird that Kev looked like a buff surfer, and weird that he'd turned over a new leaf. Would he be really be able to do that? He was in his late 40s and had led a dodgy life all his adult years. He and Ricky had a well-earned reputation as hard men, and had made a lot of enemies over the years. Even if he didn't want trouble, there was a good chance it would find him, regardless. If he was serious and really did want a quiet life, he'd be better off going somewhere a long way from Teesside, somewhere such as Spain, in fact.

'Wouldn't you fancy staying out in Spain, Kev? I mean, surely it's nicer than here.'

'It is, like. But I don't know anyone out there, do I? It gets boring just being with Ricky. I've seen far too bloody much of him, as it is. It's time I grew up and stopped hanging around losers like him.'

'Yeah, but you could make friends out there. It's just that a lot of people round here have got a beef with you one way or another. Staying out of trouble might be impossible.'

'I'll be alright, man. Anyway, I sort of want to prove I can do it, not just run away from the past.'

Nick wasn't so sure, but he silently wished Kev luck.

Bishopton Lane ran off either side of Bishopton Road. On the north side it led down to the railway station and around to the Zet. Don was waiting for them outside of the station.

'Hello, Kevin. Hello, Nick.' They shook hands.

'So what shall we do?' said Kev. 'Knock on a few doors?'

'Let's just have a look of the lie of the land first,' said Nick.

They walked around the bend in the road and stopped. The flats were 10 yards ahead on the right and were totally decrepit. All the windows looked filthy, with rotting frames. A huge pile of bin bags and carrier bags and assorted rubbish was piled up to the side and back. Graffiti was daubed all over the walls in black and blue and red. With litter blowing around in the breeze, everything seemed completely run down. At the end of the road was a tall metal fence, beyond which were a few trees, some sort of industrial building and Nolan House, a 17-storey block of flats which overlooked the whole area.

Kev asked, 'You said the kid was stabbed in the entrance of the flats?'

'Yeah. Right in that doorway,' said Nick, pointing to the entrance. 'He died almost instantly. I saw the photos of the bloodstains and the outline of where he had been lying.'

'Was he on his front or back?' said Kev.

Nick thought for a moment. 'I don't know. They didn't say.'

Kev shrugged and pointed at Nolan House. 'Did anyone from those flats give evidence?'

'No.'

Kev frowned. 'You're not telling me that no-one in there saw anything? That's crap. There's a lot of flats in there. Dozens of people live there. Someone would have seen something.'

55

'Ah, but surely, it doesn't take long to be stabbed. It'd be all over in an instant,' said Don. 'What time of day was it?'

'Middle of the afternoon,' said Nick.

'Well, a lot of people would be at work then,' said Don.

Kev snorted derisively. 'This is Stockton, Rev, remember,' he said, his thick forearms folded across his chest.

'The communal entrance is right in the centre of the block. You go in through that door into an internal corridor and stairwell. There's a flat on each side of the stairs. Six in total,' said Nick. 'The two downstairs flats can therefore see anyone, any visitor who is at the communal door.'

'One of those would be the ideal flat for a block boss to have,' said Kev. 'He can keep track of everyone who comes and goes. If any dealers, hookers, loan sharks, bailiffs or coppers are coming round for others in the block, he'd know. Anyone shagging someone's missus, he'll know. Pound to a penny, he's got a chair out of view where he sits and mirror set by the window to watch it all happen without being seen. And he'll use that info to boss everyone.'

'Is that really how it works, Kevin? That's quite clever,' said Don.

'Yeah. You see it all over the place. Ragworth estate was terrible for it, back in the day. A couple of families ruled the place, or reckoned they did. Caused a lot of rucks. Used to be good money in that.'

'How come, like?' said Nick.

'One side or another would give you a wedge to fist the other lot, when push came to shove. Me and Ricky were like paid vigilantes for a while.'

Nick must have looked both shocked and appalled because Kev added, 'I know. Not exactly what you might call civilised, like, but it's how it worked back then.'

'OK, well, I'll go and see if Berryman is in,' said Don, striding towards the flats purposefully.

'How come you've got a vicar as a mate, then?' said Kev, turning to Nick.

'I told you, he married us, didn't he?'

'He looks loads fatter than I recall. I didn't know you were mates.'

'Yeah, he's a brilliant bloke, is Don.'

'Yeah?'

'All he does, right, is try to make people's lives better. Went all over Africa, came back and got Dormanstown as a parish at one point."

Kev puffed out his cheeks. 'Fuckin' hell. Good luck, with that, son,' he said, rhetorically, laughing a little.

'Exactly. I know he's just a chubby bloke. But honest, man, he's made out of steel. Tough comes in different forms. Don is seriously tough.'

'Aye, well, fair play, like. As long as he's not a kiddie fiddler. Bloody church is sick for that shit.'

They stood and watched as Don walked up to the communal entrance, looked at the row of bells and pressed the top one, even though it was probably broken. He took a step or two backwards, and rocked on his heels a little as he waited for someone to answer.

Suddenly, a man sprinted out of the building at speed, his right arm outstretched. In that instant, Nick realised he was wielding a knife, like a short vegetable knife. The man ran at Don and, without slowing his pace, slashed out at him in a big swipe, from right to left, right across his throat.

Nick and Kev stood and looked in shock for one, two seconds.

Don had sunk to his knees and was already holding his throat, dark red blood leaking through his fingers. He made an unearthly noise that was somewhere between a scream and groan.

Suddenly, all the information flooded into Nick's brain and into Kev's, too. Nick sprinted towards Don.

The man with the knife ran in a wide arc, but had to get past Kev. There was no other escape route. He still held the knife in his right hand, ready to use it. Kev's new leaf notwithstanding, some instincts run too deep to resist.

Nick glanced back to see Kev volley the knife out of the man's hand with a big swinging kick of his right foot, then grab the man by his hoodie, yanking him up into the air, like a grizzly bear catching a leaping salmon. He dispensed one punch into the man's face; one utterly incredible punch, that looked more like someone throwing a javelin. The energy seemed to drain out of the man as consciousness left him via Kev's right-hander. The big man threw him to the ground like a bin bag of rubbish.

Don was in a bad way already, pale and woozy, half making words but not saying anything. The knife had clearly nicked his jugular and blood was spurting from between his fingers with every pulse of his heart.

Nick ripped off his t-shirt, bit into the side seam and tore it apart and rolled it into an improvised bandage. 'Let go, Don. I'll tie it off.'

But Don was spaced out and going down quickly. Nick pulled the vicar's hands from his wound, sending a pulse of blood into the air. Squatting behind him, he wrapped the cotton and elastane stretchy fabric around Don's neck, pulled it as tight as he dared and tied it off. The blood oozed into the fabric immediately but at least it was putting pressure on the wound.

Kev came running towards him. 'I called 999. Shit, he's bleeding like slaughtered pig. Who is that?' He pointed at the prone body of the man he'd hit.

'I don't know. I didn't really see him. Is it Berryman?' said Nick, fixing the fabric so it was tight and evenly distributed.

'No. He's only about 18.'

'Well go and fucking ask, Kev. Find out why the fuck he just did this.'

Nick's heart was pounding painfully in his chest, scared to death that this was going to be a fatal wound.

Kev did as he was told, went over to the kid and picked him up by his hoodie.

'What's your name son, eh?' he shouted into the man's face.

He shook him and shouted back to Nick.

'He's stoned on something! He stinks of shit as well. Urgh. Fucking hell. You dirty bastard!!' He cast him to the ground again in disgust. A police car came up Bishopton Road and screeched to a halt at the end of the lane.

'What's happened here?' said a tall, rangy copper, getting out the passenger side. 'What have you done, Kev?'

'I've done fuck all. Bloody hell. This little fuck knifed Don there, I twatted the kid to stop him getting away. You should be bloody thanking me! Cheeky bloody sod!'

'Where's the ambulance?' yelled Nick, fearful that it was too slow to save Don, who was breathing very shallowly now and still mumbling something that sounded like prayer.

It only took about four minutes for the ambulance to come roaring up the road.

'It's not a big cut,' he yelled as the two paramedics ran up. 'It looked like a deep nick in his jugular. I've bound it as tightly as I could.'

The paramedic took a look and nodded her approval. 'Good work. We'll get him to hospital.'

'Will he be OK? He's not breathing well.'

'We'll get him hooked up to some oxygen.'

They fussed around Don, chatting to him as they did so, and then loaded him into the ambulance.

There were now four police cars and seven officers present, taping off Bishopton Lane. A big fat man, who Nick recognized from court as the man they called Blobby, was talking to an officer, as was a skinny, small woman that he realised was Tracy Berryman. Nick was running on some sort of autopilot, unable to really grasp what had happened to Don, how everything can change within one second, and with one small movement.

A policeman came up to him.

'Who's the kid?' said Nick.

The lad had made a partial recovery, and was now locked in the back of one of the patrol cars, the large red swelling on one side of his face suggesting Kev had broken his cheekbone, or perhaps more accurately, smashed it into several pieces.

'We don't know, yet,' said the officer.

'I've never seen him before,' said Kev, as though his mental database of Teessiders was infallible.

'Yeah, but you've been away for a year,' said Nick, feeling really awkward now, standing there half-naked, even though it was quite warm. 'Can I go and talk to the people from the Zet?'

'No. This is a crime scene. I'll need you to make a statement.'

'Alright, but can I go down to the station to do it later? In case you've not noticed, I've no shirt on.'

'Oh, right. I assumed you'd come out like that,' said the copper, a thick set man in his mid-30s.

Nick looked at him with incredulity. In which world does a 50-year-old man walk around a town like Stockton without a shirt on? Only crazy people and drunks do that. Then it occurred to him, that's what the copper thought he was; one of the wasters and crazies from the Zet.

Thankfully, he was soon disavowed of this notion by a younger, female colleague, blonde hair scraped back into a short ponytail, who had just arrived in a fifth patrol car.

She gave him a quick smile then turned to the other copper. 'It's OK, he's Nick Guymer.' This clearly meant nothing to the officer, who looked at her with a loose jaw and a fat, dumb bottom lip.

'I'm PC Shirley Mason. Just give me a brief account of what happened and we can come round your house later to take a full statement, if we need to. We've got SOCO coming down.'

She took out a pen and notepad. Why didn't they just have a recording device? It's not like they cost much more than a pen and notepad. Nick said what little had happened. There was nothing to tell. Kev nodded, confirming it. And that was it.

They walked away. Nick felt really emotional, to the point of being on the verge of tears. Poor Don. He'd have to go to the hospital and see how he was doing. He rubbed at his forehead, as though to massage away the psychic distress.

'You walk on, Kev. I've got to have a minute to myself,' he said, stopping by a low wall.

'Why, like?'

'I just...I just need some time on my own, man.' A surge of upset and anger swept up into his throat. 'Just fucking leave us alone, right?!' He yelled it into Kev's face, nose to nose. Fuck it. The bloke had to learn some sensitivity, sometime. Two old women walked past them, giving them funny looks.

Kev raised his eyebrows, and for a moment, Nick thought he was going to say something disparaging, or even hit him. He might have in the past. Nick sat down on the wall and ran his hands through his hair, then pushed at the tears in the corner of his eyes, craving to be alone and not have to think about human interaction. He wasn't having a depressive episode, he knew that. He just felt crushingly guilty for what had happened.

'Are youse alright?' said Kev, looking down at him.

'Not fucking really, no. Don's a close friend. He helps me, he gives me good advice, and I put him in danger. It's my fault.'

'Yeah, it's pretty shite, like,' said Kev, sitting down beside him but not saying anything else for a minute before clearing his throat.

'First night I ever spent in Durham jail, I was 19 and scared shitless. It's a fucking terrible place; like being told you've got to live in hell. They put me in a cell with Tom Yarrow. He was great. Told us how to survive the six months I'd been given. Told us how to avoid getting my head kicked in. I was full of it, but shit scared underneath. You know that episode of *Porridge*, "A Night In"? That was me and him. I was a kid, he was an old lag. Had done a lot of time. Next day, there was a ruck in the dining hall and a bloke smashed his plate and slashed Tom's throat with it. Reckoned he'd grassed him up on the outside. They took Tom out and put him in hospital for months. He survived, somehow, but I never saw him again. So I only had the first night with him. I was devastated, even now, it brings a lump to me throat. Everyone needs someone to help them. That's how I look at it now.'

That didn't help at all, it just made Nick's emotions rise further. He bowed his head and let silent tears drip onto the dry pavement, unable to look up, and especially unable to look at Julie's brother. Emotions were embarrassing in front of most men, and especially men like Kev, and especially when you were half sodding naked and milk-bottle white.

He just couldn't say anything.

Kev went quiet as Nick tried to compose his thoughts.

'Kev, man, how do we deal with this sort of shit? The three of us were just there, Don walked up to the door and then that happens to him. How are we supposed to compute that? God willing, he'll be OK, but his life is forever changed by that one-or two-second moment.'

'Yeah, see, I've never thought much about that before, like. It is a pisser. You've just got to deal with it. Nowt else to be done, is there?'

'Why did that kid do that? Did he say anything?'

'Nah. Nothing. He was trippin' on something. Lost in his own world. I broke his face, but he wasn't over bothered, I don't think he even really felt it. If you ask me, he was fucked up on something heavy. Some extra strong skunk is my bet. It numbs you up good, it's like a sodding painkiller. He was obviously paranoid and scared and just lashed out at Don. He must have thought Don was someone who was after him. When you get into that state of mind it seems like everyone is coming for you.'

In an out-of-character move, Kev patted him on his bare back, almost gently.

'Don will be OK. You got him sorted right away. I'd have stood there just looking at the blood.'

But Nick couldn't respond. Wrapped up in his own upset, he still really wanted be alone.

They sat without speaking for a few more minutes. Normally, Kev would have lit up a fag, but he must have stopped smoking, as well as drinking. Nick recomposed himself and let out a deep sigh. Just as he did so, Kev tapped him on the leg.

'See that bloke crossing the road at 2 o'clock.'

Nick looked out the top of his eyes at the man. He was middle-aged, stocky and wearing a black hoodie, black t-shirt and black jeans. He didn't recognise him at first.

'Yeah? Do you know him?'

'Oh, aye. That's Kev Berryman.'

CHAPTER 3

'Oh, yeah, of course it is. I remember him from court.'

'He's going home, look. Walking down Bishy Lane.'

Nick watched as the man crossed the road and walked down towards the station. As soon as he saw all the police cars and officers, he stopped in his tracks, reversed up and ran down a side alley, out of view. The alley led to the back of the Zetland flats.

Kev looked at Nick. 'I know I'm a cynical old sod, but I reckon if we sit here for five minutes, Berryman will come back up that rat run and leg it.'

He was almost 100 per cent right. It actually took him less than three minutes to emerge holding a carrier bag. Not even enough time to get into his flat. The police probably wouldn't have let him, anyway.

'How come he's got a bag now? There's not been enough time to go in the Zet,' said Nick.

'He'll have had a stash bag out the back, probably in a bin or summat. He's just picked it up and is offski. We won't see him again.'

'A stash bag? What's that?'

'Essentials that you'd need to survive away from home for a few days.'

'Really? Is that a thing?'

Kev looked at him like he was a small boy, and shook his head. 'Yeah, of course. Classic. Means he's been up to no good, and was expecting something to kick off. I'll just have a word, eh,' said Kev, getting to his feet and sprinting with power and speed to intercept Berryman. Nick followed in his wake.

Knowing Kev was experienced at this sort of streetlife, Nick watched him step in front of Berryman, the way a defender does to an onrushing striker, sending him crashing to the pavement on the downward slope of Bishopton Road.

'What the fuck do you think you're doing?' said Berryman, sprawling on the ground.

'I'm 'avin a word with you,' said Kev, standing over the man, who clearly hadn't recognised him initially, but now did.

'Fucking hell, it's you, Kev. I've not seen you for yonks. What's this about, eh? I'm a busy man. You didn't have to deck us.'

Straight away, it was obvious that Berryman was deferring to Kev. Maybe Teesside thugs, like wild dogs, had an innate hierarchy that they all knew, and he certainly knew his place in that hierarchy and it was well below Kev, even though Kev had been away for a year and now looked like a Californian surfer.

Kev pulled the man up to his feet. 'A fella was cut earlier, outside the Zet. A vicar...'

'...a vicar?!' Berryman screwed up his ugly, frog-like face.

'Aye. Dressed in black, fat gut, balding. You know what I reckon? I reckon the kid that did it thought he was you.'

Kev leaned on the wall that ran down to the bridge, blocking Berryman's escape route.

'Eh? How's that, like? I've done nowt, me, Kev.'

Kev barked at him, impatiently. 'Fuck off, Berry. Don't give me that shit. You've just pulled your stash bag.' He nodded at the Tesco bag in Berryman's left hand. 'This is something to do with that court case, isn't it?'

'Eh? What court case?'

The scumbag instinct to lie about everything was innate to a man like Berryman, and it put Nick in mind of his appearance in court, where he'd lied about everything, including his date and place of birth, and the fact he'd once been married. That was before they even addressed any of the facts of the murder. Kev wasn't having any of it. He tapped Berryman on the cheek with the flat of his hand in a way which was extremely menacing.

'Don't piss me around, son. You know fine well what court case. Who really killed Danny Ross, eh?' said Kev, who, in a situation like this seemed more like some street barrister, questioning a witness.

Nick kept his distance as the underclass went about their business, arms folded across his hairy chest, still inhibited to be in public without a shirt on and still getting the occasional funny look from passers-by.

'I don't fuckin' know, Kev. They busted Glenn Vokes for it.'

'Did he do it?' Kev pushed the man hard in the chest. 'Well? Did he?'

Berryman threw his arms up in protest. 'I don't know, do I? I didn't even know the lad that was killed.'

'Stop lying, man. Yes, you did. I know all about it. Your daughter hung around with him. She's probably had a bairn with him.'

'Our Tracy is no better than she ought to be. Look, I didn't tell the cops anything. I'd never tell the cops anything, would I?' said Berryman, seemingly noticing Nick for the first time, and doing a double take at his half-naked muscular torso.

'Yes, you bloody did,' said Nick. 'The police said that you told them that the body was Danny's.'

'Is that right?' said Kev.

'No. Who told you that? Nah, you've got it all wrong, mate. I never said nowt to the police. I wouldn't do it on principle. Fuck 'em,' he said, to Nick. 'Where's your fuckin' shirt, anyway, mate? It's not that bloody hot.'

'Don't you ever tell the truth?' said Nick. 'The police went to Vokes's flat, found the knife and that blood-soaked sweatshirt and when he turned up at the Zet a bit later, he was nicked.'

'The police are liars,' said Berryman. 'You don't believe what they say, do you? You're a mug if you do. They're all bent. Trust me. Half their evidence was made up.'

'But you agreed in court that you told the police that it was Danny,' said Nick, almost incredulous.

Berryman shrugged. 'Did I? Well maybe I did, or maybe I didn't, and maybe the pigs lied. Does it matter?'

'But you just said you didn't tell the cops anything, and that you didn't even know him,' said Kev. 'Try and keep up with your own lies, Berry, you prick.'

Berryman was getting frustrated. It was just like this in court. None of the witnesses could remember what lie they'd told to which person or when, so they ended up contradicting themselves so often, that at times, it seemed like they didn't know the truth themselves anymore.

'Stop asking us questions. I don't fucking know, right? Vokes is just some doped-up loser who was around the Zet all the time. The sort of fucked-up loser no-one would be bothered to see go inside.' He seemed to suddenly focus his mind. 'The police fitted him up for it because they made a bollocks of the crime scene and they knew it. They let Davey Foster into the building to go and get a tracksuit from Ross's flat. They never should have done that. Foster could have done anything with any evidence in Danny's flat - but they're fuckin' idiots, the coppers. You know that as well as I do, Kev.'

It was a sudden outburst of articulation. Suddenly, it sounded like he knew exactly what had happened.

'And you gave Foster the knife you used to kill Vokes, and the bloody sweatshirt that you were wearing when you did it, didn't you?' said Nick. 'He took them right past the police, planted them in Vokes's flat. You told him to do that, didn't you?' said Nick.

Berryman pulled an ugly, disgusted face. 'Fuck off. You're talking shite, son. All of that is pure shite. I never killed no-one and I don't know who did, so there's no point in asking me any more.'

'I'll ask you again, 'cos I know you know, who really did kill him?' said Kev, leaning right into the man's face. 'Don't lie to us, I know you know, I can see it in your eyes.'

Berryman looked right at him. 'No-one knows, Kev. Honest. I don't reckon it was anyone in the Zet. It probably was Vokes.'

Kev gripped him at the base of the neck with his big, tanned, strong hand, blue veins dilated. Now he growled in a much more exaggerated, hard, Teesside accent, as though he had slipped into a different persona.

'You're fuckin' lyin', son. I'll fuckin' beat it out of youse, if I 'ave to. Was it you, eh? Did you knife 'im, eh?'

Berryman was clearly scared now, as anyone would be with Kev Wells gripping them by the throat. 'No. No, I didn't. I did say in court I thought it was all about our Tracy. Vokes fancied her and so did Ross, they were both knobbing her, but I don't even know if that's right. I don't reckon anyone knows who did it except whoever did it, like. A taxi driver found him lying there. As far as I know Kev, no-one saw it happen. That's the god's honest truth. I swear. Vokes was always hyped up on something. He was mad for it, any drug you like. And he could get a proper rage on, like. So if he did it, it wouldn't surprise me.'

Berryman was obviously scared shitless of Kev Wells. He thought he was in for a proper beating here. He was wincing and trying to turn his head away as far as he could, almost feeling the pain before it was administered. It was quite something to see from a man who had been so cocky, and who had played the hard man in court, and again towards him outside of Beef and Vodka.

Nick took a few steps to one side, so he was now face to face with him. He raised his eyebrows and waved. 'Remember me in Beef and Vodka, after the trial?'

'Yeah, why did you have a pop at him, eh? Telling him he's a dead man. That's just rude,' said Kev, pushing at Berryman's neck again.

Berryman was not quick-witted enough, and was now too scared to make up a lie this time.

'Fuck. Was that you? Look mate...err...look I just heard that you thought that I was the killer. I was pissed off about that like, 'cos I'm not and I don't want people thinking I am.'

'So you paid a court official to snoop, didn't you?'

'Yeah, yeah. And I was just walking past that place and I saw you in there in your black suit and I thought I'd 'ave a pop at you. Gotta protect your reputation, Kev. You know that.'

'Christ man, it's a bit late to worry about your reputation. Everyone in this town knows you lot in the Zet are bunch of lying, cheating, thieving, druggie scumbags. You were playing the hard man, trying to scare me. Well, I'm not impressed and neither is Kev. Are you, Kev?'

'No, I'm fuckin' not. And it's all I can do to resist breaking every bone in your snidey fuckin' body, Berry. You evil little shite.'

Berryman began stuttering a bit. 'I'm s-s-sorry Kev, I didn't know he was your mate, did I? You've got to stand up for yourself 'round 'ere, you know that. I thought you'd fucked off for good, anyway.'

'Nick's my brother-in-law, you fuck face.'

'Is he? Shit. Sorry, mate.' He turned to Nick. 'I was bullshitting you. I wasn't going to do nowt. I was just bluffin' it, like.'

'So why did that kid knife someone? He thought Don was you,' said Nick.

'How do you know that's what he thought? I dunno. I don't even know who it was. He better not have robbed my gaff.'

Kev released his grip. 'I know you're lying, or you're not telling me everything you know. You're the boss of the Zet. You know everything and everyone that goes in or out of that fucking rat's nest. Nowt gets past you. So where are you going now?'

'Me cousin's.'

'Where's he live?'

'Just up Durham Road, like. I'll just bunk down there until the cops have cleared off.'

Kev released his grip. 'Alright. But if I find out you've lied to us about any of this, you know what'll happen, don't you, you ratty little twat? I'll find you and I'll snap you so hard that they'll never mend you.' He shook him hard to enforce the point.

Berryman nodded vigorously and sprinted off as soon as Kev pushed him, away down the road.

Kev turned to Nick and grinned. 'I thought I showed a bit of class there not to break so much as his little finger. See, I am turning over a new leaf.'

'He was bricking himself. That shows me that he's not the hard man he likes to pretend to be.'

They watched him disappear into the distance, then began walking back to Kev's flat. 'Nah, he's not hard in one way, but he's hard in others. He is a nasty, devious sod - most of what he said there was lies.'

'How do you know?'

'Years of experience. Too many years. He knows something, or he saw something.' Kev scratched at his greying blonde hair and winced. 'But it's something, or someone he's so scared of that he'd still rather take a kicking off me then tell us.'

'So you think he knows who killed Ross?'

'Yeah. Yeah, deffo.' He nodded his head. 'I'm sure of it. Y'see, alright, he was a shit liar, and we caught him out, or we think we did. But did we really? Pretending to be confused or messed up is a great cover. Everyone is so busy trying to work out what, if anything, you've said is right or wrong, that they stop looking for the real truth. That way, you use being thought to be fucked up to your advantage.'

Nick looked at his brother-in-law. This was a different Kev. Sharp and thoughtful.

'That's fascinating. It's an intellectual equivalent of playing dead.'

'Yeah. Like I say, he's a schemer. Always has been. He's left us confused just by contradicting himself several times, and while we try to pick the bones out of it, it stops us thinking about whatever it is he doesn't want us to even think about.'

'He was crapping himself that you were going to whack him around.'

'Yeah, I know. But he still wasn't even near to giving up what he knows. Hmmm...' he ground his teeth together in contemplation '...some blokes like him have literally nothing to lose. Half of them expect to snuff it soon enough. That's why they're so hard to scare. Once you've lost self-respect and have no-one to care about, and don't care much if you live or die, just threatening you makes no odds. So the fact he was shitting it, means Berryman has got something invested in not telling us what he knows about the murder. Something it'd be well worth taking a beating to keep secret.'

Nick rubbed a bicep, as they walked. 'This is a good stuff, Kev. You're like a criminal psychologist. Come on, I've got to go home and get a shirt on and then go and see how Don is.' They walked towards town. 'So what could that investment be?'

'My guess is simple, good old money and a route out of the Zet. Keep quiet and we'll wedge you up and get you out of that shit hole. He'd go for that and, for what it's worth, like, I don't think he's anywhere near being as big a stoner as the rest of them in there. He looks too healthy.'

'Yeah, I thought that in court, as well.'

'But I still can't see how you're going to get hard evidence that Vokes didn't do it. Vokes's lawyer would have found evidence, if it was easy to get. They'd have tried and just came up with nowt. So maybe he really did it. Don't rule that out.'

'I'm pretty sure he didn't.'

'Alright, but don't be naïve about these people, Nick.'

'I saw Tracy Berryman outside the Zet and she was in court, too. Do you know what she's like?'

'They used to reckon she banged like a shed door in a storm. For a druggie she was a little cracker. Probably won't be now if she's kept on the dope an' that.'

'I meant what's she like as a person. Women aren't just eye-candy Kev. They're, like, people, y'know.'

Kev turned to look at him with a squint and a withering curl of his top lip. 'Bloody hell, Jules has got you well trained. That's the sort of thing she'd say. What's the word, err...objectifying women. Always went on at us about that, saying that they weren't just sex objects, even though I never said they were, like.'

This didn't seem like a good moment for a gender politics discussion, especially when you didn't have a shirt on.

'Apart from being a quality piece of fanny...' he raised an eyebrow at Nick, to let him know he was saying this deliberately, to take the piss '...as far as I know, she was a drifter. Truanted from school, started on the grass early...was probably getting poked by some dodgy uncle from an early age. She's got them hard, seen-it-all eyes that abused kids always have. Pretty, but you know it's all dark in there.'

'She wasn't much use to the defence or the prosecution in the trial. She seemed so vague about everything, like her mind was a glacier that memories just slid off of. So she was an unreliable witness to whatever she *had* witnessed. She couldn't even get her story right. She'd told four different versions since being questioned initially. In two she was on her own all day, in another one she met with Vokes, but the one she settled on was that she was with Ross, in his flat. He went downstairs for some reason and was killed in the doorway. She was smoking heroin at the time. While he was gone, she passed out and was only woken up by the police an hour or more later. None of those stories might have been true, but I could easily imagine the scene.'

He stopped beside his old BMW and unlocked the door.

'Jules will be in soon. I want to get to North Tees. Thanks for riding shotgun, Kev. Is your hand alright? You proper caned that kid.'

Kev looked at his knuckles. They were red and a little swollen. 'I've had worse. If I hear anything about Vokes, I'll let you know. I'm going home to stay out of trouble. I'll think on about Berryman and see if I can dig up anything else on him. That toe-rag isn't getting the better of me. I'll dig him out, one way or another.'

'Nice one, Kev. Thanks for your help.'

Nick cursed under his breath as he put money into the parking meter at North Tees hospital car park. Why did you have to pay to visit the sick? It was a charge on compassion, that's what it was, and it was wrong.

He handed the ticket to Julie, who stuck it on her mid-blue 1975 Porsche's window.

They walked hand in hand into the reception area of the hospital and said who they were there to visit, then made their way to intensive care.

'We've all spent far too much bloody time in this place,' said Nick, hating even the smell of its corridors, which still evoked having to visit his mother.

'Huh. They'd go out of business without us, one way or another,' said Julie.

He approached a reception counter. A tired woman in her late 50s looked up at him.

'Our friend Don Preston was brought in earlier today. He'd been stabbed. We've just come to visit him. Is he OK?'

She said nothing, but looked at her screen and then at something on her desk, then back to her screen.

'Sorry, what's your name?'

'Nick Guymer.'

'I'm sorry to have to tell you, Mr Guymer, Mr Preston died shortly after he was brought in.'

CHAPTER 4

A cold horror swept through Nick's body, and he felt like he was going to puke. He put his hand over his mouth and let out a groan of pure shock. He just hadn't expected to hear this. Julie grabbed his hand.

'But...but I tied off his wound just like you're supposed to, like I did for Julie once. It saved her.' He began panting, short of breath as the shock reverberated around his central nervous system. 'He can't be dead. He's Don. He's...he's my mate...he's a man of God. God wouldn't let this happen to him.'

Julie put her arm around him. 'Ssshh, there, there.'

'I'm sorry, Mr Guymer, it's obviously a shock, please take a seat. I'll get you some water.'

She filled a paper cup from a water cooler and handed it to him. He knocked it back and crumpled the cup in his hand.

'It's terrible what goes on today, son,' said an old woman, sitting with a bandaged arm and a purple bruise on her face. 'There's thems what'll do owt to anybody these days.'

'Poor Helen,' said Julie. 'I wonder if she's here?'

Nick was disconsolate. Don was a relatively new friend but perhaps one of the closest he'd had. Why do bad things happen to good people? No-one had a satisfactory answer and those that thought they did were just fooling themselves. It made no sense for a loving God to let someone as good as Don to die like that. What the fuck was the point in being omnipresent if you couldn't stop shit like this happening? Useless fucking deity.

It hurt inside his heart and inside his gut. No. No. No. He couldn't deal with this. It was too much. He wanted to hide from it, to curl up into a ball, close his eyes and wish it all away.

Julie squeezed his arm again. She knew Don, but Nick's friendship with him was conducted with only the two of them present. He was his confidante, his spiritual helper, his funny holy man.

'Let's go home, luv. There's nothing we can do here.'

They stood up and began to walk out of the waiting area when there was the sound of a door opening and closing behind them. Almost instinctively, Nick turned to see who it was.

It was Helen Preston, Don's wife.

'Helen! Oh, Helen. I just heard...' he ran up to her and put his arms around the rather slight woman, giving her a quick tight hug. 'Are you alright? It's so awful, so terrible what's happened.'

'I know. It was such a shock,' she said, her face pale and drawn. 'Do you know what happened?'

'Yeah. I was there with Julie's brother, Kev. This lad ran out of the Zetland flats and just did this short slash of the knife, towards Don, it nicked his jugular...it wasn't a big cut, but it was in just the wrong place,' said Nick.

'They told me he lost a lot of blood. Did the lad get away?'

'Kev caught him. The police arrested him. He hasn't got away with it, Helen. I did my best for Don, honestly. I tore off my t-shirt and used it to try and bind the wound to stanch the blood. I thought I'd done enough to save him.'

'I'm sure you did everything you could, Nick.' She smiled a thin smile.

'Is there anything we can do for you, Helen?' said Julie.

'No thanks, Julie. I'm fine. It was a shock. But I'm over the worst of it now.'

Nick looked at her in desperate silence. How could she be so composed?

'Is it your faith that makes you so strong at a time like this?' said Nick.

'Perhaps. We're all in the Lord's hands. What will be, will be.' She smiled once more at them in turn. 'Well, I'll get off. Thanks for coming. That was very kind.'

'We just came to see how he was. I can't believe he's gone,' said Nick, feeling beyond desperate.

Helen paused and frowned at him. 'Gone? He's not gone anywhere. What do you mean?'

'What?' said Nick.

'He's not gone. He's still here,' said Helen, pointing to the door she'd come out of.

Julie picked up on it first, letting out a yelp and then covering her mouth with her hand. 'You mean, he's not dead, don't you?' said Julie. 'Eee, my god...oh, bloody hell.'

Nick couldn't grasp her words.

Helen spoke again. 'No no no. He's not dead...no no no. He's sedated while he recovers from the blood loss, but he's alive and will make a full recovery. Thank the Lord.'

Nick couldn't deal with this. A surge of intense relief and happiness flooded his synapses along with a fury that the woman on reception had made such a profound mistake.

With a righteous indignation he strode back to the desk, intent on shouting the odds. But as he got there and saw the tired woman, his mother's words, *"Just be a good lad and have nice manners, our Nick,"* echoed in his head, as they often did in moments of stress these days. So he cleared his throat and leaned on the counter.

'I think you've got confused. Don Preston is alive. Not dead.'

She frowned and tapped at her keyboard. 'No, Don Preston died today. It's quite clear.'

'Well, would you like to tell his wife, who has just come from his room?'

'How are you spelling his name?'

'Don, short for Donald. Preston.' He spelt the surname out.

She began rubbing her forehead hard with two fingers on her left hand. 'I'm so sorry, Mr Guymer. My system says he's de...err...not alive.'

Nick gestured to Helen to come over.

'Helen...tell this woman, is Don, your husband, alive?'

'Yes. He's in there.' She spoke with a calm assurance and pointed to the door again.

'This woman thinks he's dead.'

'I'm sorry, I don't understand, why do you think that?'

The woman looked both guilty and confused.

'I'm sorry, clearly there's a discrepancy between the information in the system and...err...reality. I'll get it cleared up for you. I am so sorry, Mrs Preston - and you, too, Mr Guymer. I'm very sorry for the upset and confusion.'

And she really was sorry. She was clearly overworked and under-resourced.

Without hesitation, Helen said, 'That's OK. Everyone makes mistakes. God bless you.' She was as good an example of her faith as you could ever wish to meet. Nick wished he had even half of her magnanimity because he was feeling a lot less charitable, having been put through the emotional wringer.

Nick and Julie looked in on Don, but he was, as his wife had said, sedated, his neck heavily bandaged, a drip in his arm, topping up his blood. Even so, the fact he was alive was a brilliant and wonderful thing. Nick squeezed the vicar's hand and said a short silent prayer before they left him.

The next morning Nick was up at 6.30am. He made a pot of strong coffee and sat down at the kitchen table to look at the notes he'd written up after every day of the trial. The court had allowed the jurors to take notes, but had required them to be left with the court at the end of each day, and when the trial was over, they'd had to hand them in. He'd forgotten some details by the time he'd made his own notes, but even so, it was quite well recalled. He'd wanted to preserve the experience because, when you're a writer, life is the only capital you've got from which to draw your inspiration. And this was a story of life at the very bottom of society.

Life in the Zet was simple. You had a roof over your head, albeit in a squalid environment, and you had a drug habit and a drink problem. Most of your bills were paid by the state, after which you had a few quid left over to buy just enough food to keep you alive, but not enough to enjoy life. Only being drunk or high made it bearable, consequently it was a life of almost total dissolution. Everyone had given up on you and officials were happy enough to tick whatever box meant that they didn't have to see or deal with you again. You could apparently get away with regularly breaking laws, such as possessing narcotics or lying to the police, because you were much less trouble shut away in the Zet than if you had to be processed through the justice system.

The best-kept secret of modern life was that the state was very happy for a certain sort of waster to shut up, take the money and go away. They were too much trouble, too much hard work, and too non-productive to expend effort on, or invest money in. So they were written off and put in society's bins, bins like the Zet. Just close the lid and forget about them for as long as possible. And weirdly, those people knew it and, in a perverse twist, had grown to quite like it that way. Anything for a quiet, if stoned, life. Even when one of them died, things didn't change. In fact, when someone did die, it was largely viewed as a blessing for all concerned.

Throughout the whole trial there hadn't been anyone who shed any tears at Daniel Ross's death, or even, apart from Tracy, had a sorry word for his passing, even though, as far as it was possible to ascertain, he wasn't guilty of any great crimes against humanity and there was no evidence that anyone hated him or wanted him dead. No-one had anything against him, or if they did, it hadn't come out in court. In fact, he seemed to have lived a relatively quiet life, sitting in the flat drinking vodka, smoking heroin and eating crisps. The only food in the flat had been crisps. It was all just really sad.

After highlighting a few details, he went into the kitchen, took a smoked-salmon fillet out of the fridge, splashed some olive oil into their big wok and let it heat up. As soon as it was hot, he put in the thick piece of fish, waited 30 seconds, flipped it over, put a glass lid over it and turned off the gas to let it finish in the residue heat.

As he was buttering a couple of oatcakes, and placing a handful of baby spinach onto a plate, Julie came into the kitchen and grinned as she clipped up her hair on the back of her head.

'That smells good. Is that for me?'

'Of course, sit down, it's ready.'

She poured herself the last of the coffee.

'Found anything in your notes that might be useful?'

He arranged the fish on the leaves and squeezed some lemon juice over it.

'Yeah, a couple of things that I'd forgotten about. There you go.'

'Aw luv, it's like living in a restaurant here.' She cut a soft, smooth flake of fish off the fillet and held it up to the light. 'And it's perfectly cooked, as per usual. What a clever boy you are. You know I work with women who leave the house in a morning having only had a slice of toast, or a bowl of cereal. Then they eat chocolate and biscuits all morning. They can hardly believe what you serve up for me every day. It's become a running joke, in fact.'

'That's daft. It's not that amazing. It takes literally two minutes to cook the fish, that's probably quicker than the time it takes to make toast. If you ask me, people need to just learn a few basic skills, have some ambition and feed themselves properly. It's not that hard. If I can do it, literally anyone can.'

'You're a great cook, most people aren't as good as you. You've got a real talent for it. This is perfectly seasoned and it's as good as anything you could buy if you ate out at a nice place.'

Nick shrugged and picked up his notes. 'It's just basic food. Nothing fancy, but you know I love cooking for you. Feels like I'm looking after you properly.'

She hunched up a little and grinned as she finished her plate. 'So what did you get out of your notes?'

'Vokes detailed where he walked. I forgot about that. He knew exactly where he went. Or he said he did.'

'Why does that matter?'

'He said he left his flat in Roseworth and walked past the shops. Now, there was CCTV there but the police said in court that he wasn't on it. This was used to discount his story, but he claimed the police must made the relevant recordings disappear.'

She raised her eyebrows. 'Really? How did that go down?'

'Well, lying drug scum like Vokes can't go up against the police in court and win, can he? He had no proof, so everyone assumed he was just casting aspersions.'

'Doesn't mean he was wrong, though.' She finished the coffee, patted her tummy, stood up and brushed her loose black pants down and slipped on her jacket over her white shirt. 'Lovely scran, that. Right, I'm off. Are we doing anything tonight?'

'Yeah, we'll be having vigorous, noisy sex,' said Nick, immediately, not missing a beat.

She wasn't fazed. 'Well, that goes without saying, but before we do that, are we going out?'

'Do you want to?'

'I'd like a drink-up. How's your throat?'

'A lot better today.'

She opened her arms for a hug. He pulled her into him, breathed in her air; a mix of shampoo, soap and Calvin Klein's Escape, and ran his hands over her backside, giving her a firm squeeze.

'OK, but let's have a drinking session here. I'll make us tapas, as well. Is that OK?'

'Of course. Brill.'

They kissed, maybe much more passionately than most couples would at 8.30 in the morning, but their lust for each other was never far below the surface. She gave him a squeeze between the legs and made a faux shocked face at him, as though she was amazed at what she'd got hold of, then laughed.

'It's never too early in the day for you is it? Dear me. Rock hard. You'll have to sort that business out for yourself, I've got to go to work.' She kissed him again, quickly. 'Save a few inches for me for later, though.'

'There's always plenty for you, Jules, you know that.'

She laughed her deep, woody chuckle as she grabbed her bag. 'Well, I'll be getting my ruler out, just to make sure I get the full amount. I don't want to be slipped a short length.'

75

'You always get every inch of my love,' he said, laughing.

She planted a kiss on his lips. 'Mmm, I know and I can't wait. See ya later, randy boy.'

After she'd left in her old Porsche, Nick made himself some bacon and eggs and tea and looked through his notes some more. Assuming for a moment that Glenn Vokes had been telling the truth about where he was walking when Daniel Ross was murdered, he'd have to have been caught on CCTV at some point. He'd said he'd walked for miles all over the area from his Roseworth flat, going to Norton and then on to Billingham, walking all around the town centre, then somehow he'd gone to Billingham golf course and said he'd walked across there to Wolviston Road and eventually finding his way to Junction Road and from there, heading into town on Durham Road, ending up at the Zet where the police had pounced on him and nicked him.

Even if one or two cameras were turned off, or not working, on a walk of that length, at some point he'd have been filmed. It was the fact that he hadn't been that made everyone assume it was a lie. And it could easily all have been a lie. Vokes was a stone cold, 100 per cent lying machine. He lied as a matter of course, often when he had no need to, or there was nothing to be gained by lying. But even so, the look on his face as he was found guilty, that wasn't a lie. His protestations of innocence didn't feel like lies, either. So why wasn't he on any CCTV? That was odd for a start.

Loading Google Maps on his phone, he traced out the route that Vokes said he'd taken, starting from his flat above a bookie's on Redhill Road in Roseworth, and ending at the Zet, where he said he'd gone to see Tracy and had instead been arrested for the murder of Daniel Ross at 5pm.

They say criminals often return to the scene of their crimes, but even so, it had struck Nick as odd that he'd done so. The defence in court had pointed this out, too. But it didn't sway the jury at all. They found it easy to believe he'd do something that stupid. There was nothing too dumb, nothing too odd, irrational or horrible, that the jury wouldn't have believed of him.

But the knife had been bleached to remove evidence, and there was no proof the bloody sweatshirt was actually Vokes's. Nick had tried to point out to the jury that all they knew about the knife was it fit Danny Ross's stab wounds. The fact that it was in Vokes's flat didn't prove he'd done it. It had been almost professionally cleaned. Nick had doubted

Vokes was in any fit state to do that so efficiently, simply because he was always stoned.

Nick drove his old BMW to the row of shops on the Roseworth estate and parked up outside them on Redhill Road. Built as one of the biggest council housing projects in the area back in the late 1950s or early 1960s, it was a huge, open, sprawling estate of perfectly decent semi-detached houses, exactly the same as the one that Julie had grown up in, in Hardwick.

Walking along to the bookie's, he looked up at Vokes's flat. It was accessed via a grubby white door beside the shop. The row of retail units had been built back before there were supermarkets. This would have been where you got most of your food from a green grocer, butcher and baker, in the same way his own mother had at the shops at the top of Palm Grove in Fairfield.

The first thing he noticed was a CCTV camera mounted on the wall above the entrance to an off licence, one door down from the bookmaker. If Vokes had come out of his flat, that would definitely have filmed him. Definitely. He stood back and took a photo of the shop so he could remember exactly where the camera was. Was it even working? How did you tell? There was no light on it and it didn't move. In the trial it had been said that at any one time at least 20 per cent of these sorts of older cameras are not working properly. He took a close-up photo of it and then walked to the end of the row of shops. That was the only CCTV camera on the block or in the area. The last shop was a local convenience Co-Op store. Walking in, he turned and looked at the ceiling. These sorts of places always filmed people as they entered or left the store. They had to for evidence against shoplifters. Sure enough, there was what looked like a black plastic egg in the roof, which had to be a camera. Could that film anyone passing on the pavement? It was hard to tell. He stood for a moment staring up at it.

'Eee, it's you, isn't it?' said a woman's voice, in a very Roseworth accent.

Nick turned to see a woman about his own age with a bob of blonde hair and a large heart-shaped face. She was dressed in a navy blue suit and pale blue blouse.

'You don't recognise me, do you? Have I changed that much?' she said.

It took a few seconds before it dawned on Nick who it was. Bloody hell. Sue Thomas.

'Hello, Sue. Wow. Amazing to see you, after all these years. No, you've not changed at all.'

'Neither have you, except you didn't have greying hair when you were 16, and you've thickened out. You used to be a right skinny lad, you.'

She smiled at him with nice grey-blue eyes. She was good-looking in a robust sort of way, what Jeff would have called 'all tits 'n' hips'.

'How have we not met since 5th year at Ian Ramsey?'

'I moved away that summer, didn't I? To Newcastle.'

That sounded familiar now that she said it. He and Sue had gone out for three or four months when they were 16. She'd been the first girl he'd had any sort of intimate sexual contact with. Not actual sex, but pretty much everything just short of that. She'd been a forward girl, which he'd always loved, both then and now. She'd shown him where to put his hands and what to do with them, and had even given him his first up-close anatomy class on the fascinating, if complicated, subject of female genitalia, sitting on his bed, legs apart, pointing to all the relevant parts. On reflection, she'd been a very liberated 16 year old. Very uninhibited, at an age where inhibition seems built into your DNA.

'So, do you live here now? Your family were from Roseworth, weren't they?' he said.

She nodded. 'I've been back in Stockton for about five years.' She laughed, bent her knees slightly as though in surprise at meeting him again. 'Eee, well I never. So what do you do?'

'I'm a writer. Mostly about football. I've just published my first novel.'

'That figures. You always did have a vivid imagination.'

'What about you?'

'I've worked for the Co-Op in management roles for decades. I'm now a regional manager, so I tour all these local convenience places and iron out problems, or whatever.'

'Amazing.'

She scrunched her face. 'Not that amazing.'

Nick glanced up at the CCTV camera.

'So, are you married?' she said.

'Yeah, to Jules. Julie Wells, that is. You remember Kev and Ricky Wells, don't you?'

'Oh, god, yeah. They were real thugs. You married their sister? Blonde lass?'

'I did. Only about 18 months ago, but we've been together, off and on, for years.'

'OK. I see. Kids?'

'No. We left it too late, sadly.'

She cocked her head to one side and turned her mouth down. 'Aw...I didn't want them. Married the wrong bloke in my 20s, luckily didn't have any kids with him and since then...well...I never fancied it. I realised marriage wasn't for me and I just like to have a good time.'

'Funny how time passes so quickly. You always think you'll have more time, but it just goes like that.' He clicked his fingers together.

She rested her weight on one hip. 'No, it doesn't seem long since I was snuggled up to you on that single bed in your bedroom in Palm Grove. My my my, we enjoyed ourselves back then, didn't we?' She laughed in a familiar way, a way he'd forgotten all about; a sort of dry cackle.

'We certainly did. You educated me, Sue. I was an innocent lad before you quite literally got hold of me.'

She laughed and touched him on the arm, affectionately, briefly stroking him a little. 'Yeah, you were quite naïve, if I remember. Well we both were, really, even though I thought I knew it all. It makes me feel funny to think about those times. I can recall them like it was just the other day. It was fun. You were such a nice lad.'

He shook his head. 'It's funny that you've changed so little. Sometimes you meet people who are transformed from their teenage selves, but you're not at all.'

'I wish I was still that eight-and-a-half stone girl, I can tell you that. I've not been that weight since the 80s.'

'Still looks like there's nowt on you, Sue. You look great.'

'Aw, thanks. And you've got some muscle on you, mind. You must work out.'

He shrugged, hating compliments. 'I do weights, it helps with my depressions to exercise a lot.'

She paused. 'Oh, I see. Yeah, I've heard that. Mind, you always did have at least one well-developed muscle on you. I do remember that much.' She cast him a wry, sly smile. 'I often thought of it later on.'

Nick looked at his boots and felt like this would be a good time for a hole to open up and swallow him. What could you say to that? She wasn't going to try and flirt with him, was she? He couldn't tell. Best just ignore it.

'This might sound weird, Sue. But do you have access to the CCTV footage taken on that camera up there?'

'CCTV? Eh? I don't understand.'

'I'm trying to prove someone isn't a murderer. It's a long story and I'll tell you about it sometime.'

'Is this for a book?'

'For an article, probably. Like I say, it's a long story. I was a juror in a murder trial and the man that was convicted for it, I think, is innocent. That camera might help prove his innocence.' He pointed at it.

'Come on.' She turned away from him and gestured for him to follow her. As he did so, he couldn't help but notice that she had a nice arse, and was clearly wearing some sort of small thong. He then immediately felt guilty for even noticing her arse. It seemed to be such an ingrained thing in his psyche that his subconscious had already assessed and judged it before his conscious mind had caught up. For all his intellectual desire not to objectify women, his libido hadn't got the memo.

In fact, in some ways she was physically very similar to Julie, only about two inches shorter and a little broader in the hips, smaller in the shoulders. Maybe you got a physical shape or type you liked and just, albeit subconsciously, stuck with it. It was a really odd feeling to meet someone with whom you'd learned about sex with, that you had an intimate history with, and yet hadn't seen pretty much ever since.

It felt like being intimately acquainted with a stranger. As they walked, he had a strong memory of them doing was weirdly called 'heavy petting' at the time, even though petting was entirely the wrong word for it. It had been effortlessly the most exciting thing that had happened to him in his first 16 years, perhaps with the exception of buying a copy of *The Allman Brothers Band at Fillmore East* earlier in the year.

She led him out the back of the store and up some stairs. Flicking a strip light, a windowless room was illuminated. She shook a mouse on the desk to wake up a wide computer monitor on which was four camera views from the shop downstairs.

'These are the shop's CCTV views. The top right is the one by the door. When did this murder happen?'

'Last October. Did the police requisition the footage, do you know?'

'I wouldn't know, but Dave, the manager, will.'

Nick pulled a chair up to the screen and sat down to study the four images. Only the entrance camera could film anything happening outside, and then all you could see was a little section of the pavement. A shadow passed by, cast by someone out of view, followed quickly by a pair of legs in black trousers, only visible from just below the knee, then a pair of legs and part of a skirt were visible. As he leaned into the screen, Sue stood behind him.

'Is this of any use?' she said, putting her hands on his shoulders. Nick tensed a little. Why was she doing that?

'Yeah. At least in theory, the man that I think is innocent could have been caught on this camera.'

'If he came into the shop, obviously.'

'Yeah, but also if he walked by close enough to the doors. It'd only film the lower half of his legs but that might be enough.'

'Surely only enough if he was wearing something uniquely distinctive, though.' She squeezed the muscles at the base of his neck, massaging them a little with her warm fingertips. Shit. What did she think she was doing? He had to stop this, but he needed to see the CCTV footage from the murder day.

'True. But I know when he says he was walking around here, and I know what he was wearing. How could I get to see that footage from that time of that day?'

Thankfully, she removed her hands from his bare flesh and he stood up. She pointed to a large cupboard set into a wall. It held DVDs of footage.

'Looks to me like that's where they're stored. Help yourself. I'll go and ask Dave if he remembers the police looking at them back in October.'

They were all filed chronologically, so he went straight to October, and flicked through until he reached the week of the 18th and pulled it out. Turning off the light he went down the stairs, just as Sue was coming back up.

'Oh, did you find it?' she said.

He held up the disc. 'I'll take a look at this at home, if that's OK. Did Dave remember the police coming for it?'

'No. They've only come for proof of people nicking bottles of booze and that sort of thing.'

'Oh, that's interesting. OK, err...I'll bring this back once I've looked at it. Thanks for your help, Sue. And it's great to see you again.'

'Great to see you too.' She looked him up and down. 'You could thank me properly, if you like.'

'Thanks, Sue.'

'I don't mean with words. I mean with your body. Now we're all grown up, we can have proper grown-up sex, can't we?' Her words shocked him. Women didn't say this sort of thing to him. Ever.

Nick felt panicked. She licked her lips. There didn't seem much doubt she was feeling horny. Weird. This was a Co-Op. You can't be horny in a Co-Op. It seemed wrong. And it was a bit scary.

'I'm a married bloke, aren't I? I'm not interested in having affairs.'

She pulled a face. 'I'm not going to say anything to anyone. Just come over to my flat one night. We can do anything you want. I'm very broadminded. Any fantasy you've ever had, I can make come to true.' She looked south again.

'This is too weird for me, Sue. I'm not that kind of guy, and I'm madly in love with Julie. There's no way I'd ever be unfaithful to her. Sorry. But thanks for the invitation.'

She put her hands on his belly and let out a sigh. 'What hard stomach muscles you've got. Are you sure? You don't know what you're missing. I could just be an intimate friend for you. Doesn't that sound good?'

If Julie had stroked his belly, he'd have had an immediate redistribution of blood below the waist. But not here with Sue. The opposite, if anything. It wasn't sexy, it was oppressive and unpleasant and he really didn't like it. It felt like some form of bullying. Maybe Sue thought all men were flattered by the sexual attentions of women, but it really wasn't true, at least not for him. It was so embarrassing and he had so few social skills that getting out of it was some shade of impossible, so he took her card to make all of this end.

He'd never been so pleased to get into his car and drive away. Christ, you heard about women like Sue, but you never expected to meet one. It was awful. God knows what having sex with her would have been like. He didn't even want to imagine it. Even if he'd wanted to, he probably couldn't have managed it. She would have provoked sexual dysfunction in him, almost certainly.

As he drove away, he shuddered and let out a nervous laugh. To some men, that would have been their dream situation, a woman offering him an unaccountable, no-holds-barred sexual adventure, but to him, it was most definitely a nightmare. Wildest fantasy, she had said. How did you even have wild fantasies? He'd never had them, not at any age. Regular sex was easily wild enough for him and for Julie, and no amount of additional weirdness would make it better. They had three positions they liked doing it in, add in oral sex, and that was it. That was plenty. In fact, any one of them was enough. Maybe they were just conservative, but who even has the time, energy and inclination to do anything more elaborate?

Once home, he made some Sencha green tea and put the DVD into his laptop, then went back to his notes. Glenn Vokes said he'd left the flat and gone walking at around 3pm in the afternoon, but Vokes's 'around' could be half an hour either side of that. The pathologist said that Ross had likely died roughly between 2.15pm and 3.15pm. There'd been no description of what he'd been wearing, but people like Vokes had few changes of clothes. All the way through the trial he'd worn a grubby pair of white Adidas trainers with three stripes on the side. Nick knew that because Vokes, in an act of contempt, had, at one point, put his feet up on the rail that surrounded the dock. It didn't seem likely that he'd had any more shoes. Why would he? A pair of trainers might cost £30. You could buy a lot of dog valium for that. Admittedly, he might have stolen a pair of trainers, but from everything he knew of Vokes, that wasn't likely, if only because he was so messed up on drugs, so much of the time, that stealing anything successfully was beyond him.

The footage was time stamped. He rolled it forward to just before 3pm and watched. It was all dull footage. Regular life going on. People coming in and out of the shop. No sign of Glenn Vokes. But at 3.16 the camera captured a pair of dirty white trainers walking up to the front window of the Co-Op, just to the left of the sliding front doors. Nick hit 'pause' and stared at them. Was that Vokes? The trainers were very similar to what he'd worn in court. Dirty white. Three blue stripes. Not just similar. They were the same. Grey trackie bottoms; the loser's uniform. Whoever it was stopped to do something. Nick watched. The feet shuffled from side to side for a few seconds, then a match was dropped. He must have been lighting a cigarette. If that was Vokes, he'd come from the direction his flat was in, and left to walk in the direction of Norton, or possibly to Ragpath Lane which led into town.

He rewound it and watched again. Yeah, that could easily have been Vokes. The pathologist's best guess as to when Danny had died was around 3.10pm, but she was keen to point out it could have been any time in the previous hour and didn't want to be categorical. But if it was 3.10pm, this was less than six minutes after that. He couldn't have stabbed Ross at that time and been there five minutes later. It was way too far, unless he had a car. But he didn't. The police hadn't even bothered to look at this footage. That was so sloppy, to say the least. Checking his notes again, he found a short comment that he'd made about the senior investigating officer in charge of the case: 'George Dunne said they'd pulled in all CCTV for 18th but no image of Vokes on any of them'.

The thing was, now he thought about it, Dunne's statement wasn't reliable evidence, really. It was just an assertion that the court hadn't even challenged. No-one questioned the detail of this routine police act. It seemed to have been taken for granted that they'd done it efficiently. If Vokes had had a top lawyer, they'd probably have been more forensic about the police's work, but he didn't and Vokes was a doper, so no-one would side with him over the police. That just wasn't going to happen. The prosecution had known all along that they could assert the probability of criminal behaviour at every turn and everyone would believe it because of who and what Glenn Vokes was. But there were only two reasons for him not to have been filmed. One was corruption, the other was incompetence.

The other CCTV camera on that block of shops was outside the off licence.

Nick loaded the photo he'd taken of it onto his laptop. It just looked like every other one you saw; a black rectangular box mounted on a bracket, screwed to the wall at a height of nine or so feet. Off licences were always hot spots for kids and low life to hang around outside. That was even the case back in the 1970s, so that had to be why it had been placed there.

He stared at the black box mounted on the wall. There was nothing distinguishing about it. A small blue chalk cross was underneath it. He knew there were local monitoring suites where some poor sod, on behalf of Cleveland Police, sat and kept an eye on them at certain times of the day, but the cameras themselves had to be maintained by a separate company. The police didn't fix their own CCTV cameras. Like so many things in public life, it'd be a contract each force would put out to tender and given to the cheapest bidder, regardless of whether they were any good. That's how it seemed to work. If he could find out which company it was, maybe he could find out if it was actually in operation. But there was no way to know which company it was and even if he did, the security of info about cameras had to be paramount, or else every other criminal would be up their backside.

Looking again at the six-mile route Vokes said he'd taken, he'd surely have to have gone past several cameras. The fact Vokes wasn't caught on camera doing what he said he'd been doing had swayed a lot of the jury on the first day. It had established Vokes as a liar, a liar who had taken a route into town where he wouldn't get filmed, or got lucky and the cameras that could have captured him were out of action. There was no way back for him after that. But guilty or innocent, why hadn't Vokes appeared on *any* CCTV? He would have, no matter where he was going and whatever he'd done. It wasn't credible that he didn't. To get from his flat to the Zet you had to go through some major junctions. He couldn't have avoided it. But the police simply asserted that he wasn't filmed and that was that. It was used only as proof of Vokes being a liar. But the police had access to the recordings before anyone else, so they could assert anything at all as a fact, in the hope the defence wouldn't rigorously analyse them. Or they could doctor the evidence, or just make recordings disappear. There'd been no issue made by the defence over the CCTV non-evidence. Again, if it had been a posh trial, they'd probably have requisitioned it all, and looked through it themselves, but no public defender lawyer was going to do that scrupulously. There wasn't time. And anyway, everyone already thought he was guilty.

He called up Kev Wells.

'Now then, Nick.'

'Just a quick one, Kev. If you wanted to walk around Stockton and avoid being on CCTV cameras, could you actually do it, or are there too many?'

'Pffft. Good luck with that. You'd have to avoid shops, schools, public buildings and major junctions. But I don't think you could do that in Stockton. It's too small. You could trying going on minor roads and across fields, but all sorts of places have got cameras now. Why do you want to do that, anyway?'

'I don't. I just wondered if Vokes could have gone from his flat in Roseworth to the Zet and not have been picked up, if he'd known the right route to take?'

'Nah, too tricky. At some point you've got to hit Bishopton Road and there'll be cameras on the lights because it's a major road. Nope, I don't think he could. And there's only one way in and out of the Zet. There are no alternative routes. It's a dead-end street.'

'Yeah, of course. OK, thanks, Kev.'

'Have you heard if Don is OK?'

'Yeah, he'll recover, Kev. Thanks for asking.'

'No worries. Nasty cut, lost a lot of blood. God must've saved him, eh.'

'Yeah, well, maybe he did.' It was nice that Kev had asked. Maybe he really was turning over a new leaf.

A text made his phone buzz. It was from Jeff.

'Are you around? If yes, want to get fish and chips?'

Nick replied. *'Am at home. Yes to food.'*

Fifteen minutes later, they were on their way to Seaton Carew in Jeff's white van, to their favourite fish and chip restaurant.

'I've had such a weird morning,' said Nick as Jeff drove on the B1275, then the A1046 to Seaton Carew Road, the still-impressive remains of the chemical industry to their left.

'Oh, have aliens been abusing you again?' asked Jeff. 'Little grey feckers fiddling with your nadger?'

'Not aliens as such. It was Sue Thomas.'

Jeff yelped and hooted.

'Sue Thomas from school? Sexy Sue? Totty Thomas? What other names did we have for her? Spunky Sue!' He laughed loudly. 'Oh, she was proper sexy, her. God, I loved her. I did. I loved her. No, OK, I lusted her. But she was something. Man, I hated you for going out with her.'

'I don't think we actually went out. We just got naked and administered orgasms to each other.'

Jeff laughed as he looked in his wing mirror. 'So what's she like these days, then? She was a cute as cute thing with an extra frosting of cute back in the day. All sort of rounded off on the corners.'

'She's not changed much at all. Still got a really nice arse.'

'It's always the arse with you, isn't it? Didn't you say she had outsized nipples?'

'She did. As big as coasters. Never seen any bigger. And I'm sure she still has. Your nipples don't shrink with age, do they?'

'I've not measured mine, but it seems unlikely, unlike the male appendage, apparently. Gravity takes its toll on a chap's plums.'

'Oh, mine will be at my knees by the time I'm 70.'

'What a terrible thought. So, is Sue married with kids?'

'No, but she is still absolutely sex mad.'

Jeff looked at him and gave him one of his mad-wizard looks. 'How do you know that, like?'

'Even though we'd only met 10 minutes earlier, she wanted to have it off with me and offered to satisfy my wildest fantasies.'

'Get out of here! She didn't.' He whooped. 'How does this sort of shit happen to you, Guymer? I think it's the fact you're so naïve to it. Everyone else would have their tongue hanging out. Not you. You're straight away overthinking it. So she offered to make all your sexual fantasies come true?'

'She did, yeah.'

Jeff laughed again. 'But you famously don't have any wild fantasies, or none you've ever trusted me with, at least.'

'I don't, no. Never have had. All my fantasies just involved an intelligent, attractive lass being nice to me, then taking her pants off. That's pretty much it. These days, all my fantasies just involve having it off with Jules in one of a maximum of three different positions.'

Jeff cocked his head and raised his eyebrows. 'Three Positions Guymer has always been your nickname.'

'Has it?'

'Has it bollocks. I just made it up. So what did you say? I bet you almost shat your nest, didn't you?'

'I did. Just said thanks but no thanks and got the hell out of Dodge.'

'Well, she was always a precocious kid. Not backward at coming forwards when it came to matters trouser-based.'

'That seems to have remained her modus operandi.'

'Didn't she just walk up to you in the school yard and say something like do you want to see my fanny?'

'Not quite. She waited until I was on my own, walked up and said, bold as brass...err...let me think..."I need see your erect penis, please; if you show me it, I'll show you my fanny"...or words to that effect. I shat me nest that day, as well. Wasn't the sort of thing that ever happened back then, or since, in fact. Not that it stopped me from saying, "Alright then, come round our house later". I was in shock that this was even going to happen. But happen it did. Believe me, a girl undressing in your virginal bedroom is something you don't forget. I literally couldn't believe it when she was standing at the end of my bed, totally starkers.'

'Ha ha...I love the word *starkers*, very 1970s. Funny then that you didn't actually have it off with her.'

'I know. Given she was so upfront and uninhibited, you'd have thought she'd virtually demand I did it with her. But she was still sort of sensible under all the lust, and was scared of getting pregnant, I suppose. And I was happy with things as they were. I thought it was ace just being naked and getting a hand job and being able to rub her naked body. I'd still be happy with that now, actually. I've never had much sexual ambition.'

'Then she moved away, didn't she?'

'To Newcastle. I wasn't bothered at the time. I think we only wrote once. Odd, really.'

'Especially for you - someone who famously kept falling deeply in love with every girl who gave you the eye, and plenty that didn't.'

'I didn't understand it at the time, but it was all physical with Sue. Very little affection. We didn't even like the same things, or have much in common. I think I'd had my fill of it by the time she moved away, so I never got the blues over her the way I did over every other girlfriend.'

'You're a weirdo, you are, Guymer.'

'It's not that weird. Sex with someone you love - even teenage love - is way better than sex with someone you don't love at all, and I never loved Sue Thomas, no matter how good she was at hand jobs.'

'Oh, god, you're not going all Clinton Cards on me, are you? I think lasses like Sue have always done us all a favour by putting it out there in an uncomplicated way. No messing around. "Fancy a fuck, luv?", and that's it. All so much easier than the wining and dining, which by the way, is not why I'm treating you to chish and fips, so don't go getting ideas, you saucy goose.'

'Oh, I thought I was on a promise.'

'You are. A fishy promise. Hang on, that sounds a bit dodgy.'

'Wouldn't surprise me if that's what Sue was as well.'

'Well, by the sounds of it she likes a bit of batter.'

'Are we going to keep making sexual innuendos for long?'

'I think I'm done now except for once last reference to a saveloy.'

'Do saveloys still exist? You never see them any more. I used to like one from Oxbridge chippy,' said Nick.

'I suspect they've been relocated to planet hot dog. It's all the same extruded meat product type thing, isn't it?' He raised his index finger to 45 degrees. 'Here's a foodie question for you: whatever happened to rock salmon? That's what I want to know. You used to see it all the time in chip shops and in tins.'

'Good question. Was rock salmon an actual salmon?'

'Of course not, it'd have just been called salmon if it was. If I recall rightly, it was some sort of tasty dogfish, which was renamed to make it sound more palatable,' said Jeff.

'Oh, yeah, you're right. Confusingly, a dogfish is actually a shark. So not only is it not a salmon, it's not even a fish.'

'Aren't sharks fish?' said Jeff.

'They're sharks, aren't they? Sharks are mammals.'

'Are they bollocks. That's whales, man. They're the sea mammals.'

'Are you sure? Don't you have to have breasts to be a mammal?' said Nick.

'I think it helps, like. Do whales have tits?'

'I've never seen a whale tit.'

'You'd need a huge bra for a blue whale,' said Jeff, then frowned and looked at him, puzzled. 'What the hell are we waffling on about?'

Nick shrugged. 'I have no idea, but I was enjoying it.'

They hi-fived.

'Rock salmon is typical of the food industry. Pretending something is something it isn't. It's like when they use the word "flavour" on a product. Strawberry flavour just means, no actual strawberries are in this,' said Nick.

'True. Do you remember back in Harrogate, in about '95, when we tried to eat every single one of the 182 colouring E numbers in a week?'

They both laughed.

'Yeah, we did well. We had all of them except two. I bet you can remember which two we couldn't find as well, can't you?'

Jeff raised his index finger to 45 degrees again. 'Of course. E153, vegetable carbon. That was black. We thought it'd be in black jacks or Pontefract cakes, which by the way, are annoyingly not actual cakes, so don't get me started on them, but anyway, it wasn't. And the always elusive, white E171, titanium dioxide, we just drew a blank on. I thought it'd be in olde English mints.'

'I love a Pontefract cake. It is annoying that they're called cakes, though. Here's a bit of learning for thee. *Cake* is originally a Viking word, it's derived from their word "kaka". True story.'

'Well, I never. Pontefract kaka might be a hard sell, I suppose. Can't think why. Here we are. The Costa del Carew.'

They parked up in Seaton Carew town centre and took a walk along the front to Georgio's. It was one half chip shop; the other half rather ambitiously called itself a restaurant, when all it essentially was, was a collection of over-worn red melamine topped tables, where you could sit and eat your food and get a cup of tea.

'I love it here,' said Nick. 'I always feel more comfortable being downmarket.'

'Having high standards is overrated. Too much pressure, if you ask me.'

They ordered haddock and chips and two mugs of strong tea.

'I bet if you asked for green tea in here they'd think you were taking the piss. "Tea's brown, not green, luv",' said Jeff, looking at the dark orange brew in a chipped white-and-blue enamel mug.

'At least they cook in beef dripping, though, and not that heinous long-life vegetable oil stuff that almost everyone uses these days.'

'Aye, no concessions to vegetarians or food ponces in here. Proper,' said Jeff, tying his hair back.

The waitress, wearing a floral pinny, put down two plates groaning with food. If she could have had a fag balancing on her bottom lip, she would have. She was straight out of a post-war cafe, though only in her mid 40s.

Jeff put a fork full of chips into his mouth. 'Hmm, sweet, sweet animal fat is the order of the day. Makes everything taste like it's still 1965.'

'You can have most of my chips if you want. I don't potato, really.'

Jeff pointed at him with his fork. 'Using *potato* as a verb. I like it. I treat them like an exotic vegetable these days, myself. Potatoes that is, not verbs.'

'This fish is brilliant.'

They scoffed the food down, hungrily. The smell of hot beef dripping and steam from the fish, mixed with vinegar and sea air, was a timeless smell that evoked more simple days.

'I like how the fat coats your lips like a primitive lip balm,' said Jeff. 'You'd pay a fiver in the Body Shop for that, here it's a side effect of eating your dinner. So have you made any progress in proving Glenn Vokes is innocent?'

'Nah. Not really. That's how I met Spunky Sue. But I got distracted and then scared by her sex drive.'

Nick explained about the CCTV cameras in the store and outside the off licence, as they finished their food. Jeff took a drink of tea, then raised his right index finger to a 45 degree angle for the third time that afternoon.

'Did you know that you have the legal right to request CCTV footage of yourself from whoever it is that filmed you, even if it's a store or the police? They're legally obliged to provide it within 40 days. That's straight from the horse's mouth, not that I'm saying Mandy is a horse because...that would make me a jockey.'

'And you're too big to be a jockey.'

'I sense we're creeping into off-colour territory, here so I am backing away politely before I make a joke about riding and whips.'

'More seriously, that means Vokes could do that - demand to see the footage he's on in order to prove he was somewhere else when the stabbing happened,' said Nick.

'Well, he could if he was on any, but he doesn't know for a fact that he is, does he? And the cops say he isn't. When did the murder happen? What time?'

'The pathologist said Ross'd been killed roughly between 2.15 and 3.15pm. So if those trainers were him outside the Co-Op, that was at 3.16 and it couldn't have been him at the Zet doing the butchering, depending on exactly when the knife went in,' said Nick.

'Seems to me that you need to get a proper rage on to stab someone seven times. It's not exactly accidental. Did Vokes have any history of violence?'

'That's a good point; no, he didn't. All of his many offences were for theft, drugs, criminal damage and other minor stuff. Kev Berryman said he could get a rage on, but I don't trust anything he says.'

'What criminal damage did Vokes do?' asked Jeff.

Nick laughed a little. 'A year ago he managed to set fire to a cash point machine in Thornaby...'

'...as you do. It's happened to the best of us. One minute you're minding your own business, the next you've thrown petrol over a cashpoint and set it alight.'

Nick laughed again, as he finished his tea. 'Maybe he spontaneously combusted.'

'He probably drinks kerosene, so that might not be far from the truth.'

Nick couldn't stop laughing. 'You're on good form this afternoon, man. Well, he said he didn't do it, obviously.'

Jeff adopted a posh voice. 'And I for one believe the chap. Many's the time I've taken some money out of a cashpoint and the damn thing catches fire and the police turn up and arrest me for criminal damage,' said Jeff, wiping his mouth on a paper napkin. 'Bloody unfair, I tell you.'

Nick finally calmed down, and explained his doubts about the CCTV evidence.

'The cop's version of the crime is that Vokes left his flat, walked to the Zet down Durham Road to meet Tracy. He gets there and Danny Ross is standing in the doorway. For some reason, there was a fight. Vokes carries his knife for general drug chopping up, et cetera. For reasons unknown, Vokes pulls out the knife and stabs him seven times in his back and round to his side. And he does it so hard that he breaks one of Ross's ribs in the process as he slams the knife in.'

Jeff winced. 'Bloody hell, that's awful.'

'But the thing is, Vokes not only has no history of violence, he's not a big bloke. He's 5'7" and skinny. My point was that breaking someone's rib with a knife is the work of a powerfully built person. But the jurors just thought he was off his head and you could do anything when you were off your head.'

'Well, it depends on what you're off your head on. They'd clearly never been off their heads on anything,' said Jeff.

'Never. All as straight as a ruler. Scared to take more than two Ibuprofen.'

Jeff pushed his plate away and belched. 'Yeah, I'm beginning to see why you voted the way you did.' He paused again. 'When you hear the details of someone's death, even if they are a scumbag...I dunno man...it does bring home what you said in the club - there's a difference between being a thieving toe-rag nicking my bog roll, and murder. What was Danny Ross like, any idea?'

'They didn't tell us much in court, except that he was 25. Like Vokes, he'd got decent grades and had gone to college but dropped out before they could chuck him out. Tracy said in court he'd got into heroin about a year previously. She said he always had a lot of it in his room.'

Jeff shook his head. 'Man, that's sad. You can't dress that up any other way. What a waste. Was he going out with this Tracy lass?'

'Not going out like we normally think of it. She was a junkie as well and she probably did some prostitution. She'd got to know him when she'd visited and stayed with her dad, Kev Berryman. She said in court she thought he was nice, but frankly, I was surprised the defence even put her on the stand, because she was not in a fit state. She didn't have access to her memory, really. I think she just guessed and made up stuff. You could tell she wanted to do the right thing. But she was high, y'know, and just dead inside. All that it did was confirm the jurors' notion that these people were worthless scum and capable of anything. Honest, Jeff. It's genuinely upsetting to see these people. I totally understand what you said about them being scum. They are. Totally. And I couldn't stand to spend time with any of them. Horrible. But...'

'...but they're still human.'

'Exactly. The worst thing is when you can see the perfectly decent people that they could have been peeping out from behind the veil of drugged-up dissolution.'

Jeff smoothed out his long beard in contemplation.

'I do totally get what you say. I think you're just a nicer bloke than me, because I still can't stand them. Who they might have been is one thing, but who they are is another and who they are is who we have to deal with.'

'I know. I'm confused about how I feel, but I take inspiration from Don. He's spent his life around low life trying to get them to a better place.'

'Yeah but in fairness, via the extremely dodgy route of religion. I mean, religions - it doesn't matter which flavour - have all got a bad reputation due to being a mixture of bullies, pervs, terrorists, paedos, misogynists and peddlers of superstitious nonsense. More people have been messed up by religion than saved by it, if you ask me.'

'And ironically, Don would agree with you. He'd say that's the fault of people, not the religion.'

Jeff twitched an eye and shrugged. He didn't know Don at all and had only met him once.

Nick went on. 'All I'm saying is...actually, I don't know what I am saying...' he rubbed his forehead and thought for a minute '...there's something not right about Vokes's guilty verdict. I'm the only one who cares if this innocent man goes down for 25 years. So I have to find out what really happened. I feel like I have a duty. Kev Wells reckons Berryman knows who did it and he reckons he's been bought off and told to confuse the picture by lying a lot. All I need is one piece of hard evidence that Vokes couldn't have been there and that would get him out.'

They got up and went outside into a brisk breeze coming off the sea. Jeff jammed his hands into his pockets.

'No, you don't have any duty - you've just made that up in your own head. But if you feel you have to, fair enough, and I'll support you in that, but I'll tell you this now - these people will let you down. You don't meet them like I do. If you want to believe they're not as bad as they appear, believe me, Nick, they bloody well are - and worse - much, much worse. You're a nice lad, these people are not, and once you pull back the curtain on them, you'll be shocked at just how bad they really are. I'll tell you this only once, you'll regret the day you got caught up in their shitty world. You really will.'

CHAPTER 5

By the time Julie got home from work, Nick had prepared a range of bite-sized snacks - not exactly authentic tapas, maybe, but a fair Teesside equivalent.

'Hiya!' she called out as she came in.

'Hello, wife,' he said, kissing her on the lips. 'Good day at the coalface of misogynist abuse?'

'An easy day, for a change. No new punters, just paperwork to do.'

She looked at the plates of food lined up on the kitchen bench with wide eyes. 'Have you made all this? You've not, have you? You've bought it from Marksies.'

'All my own work. Here, taste this.'

He gave her a fork with a curl of smoked salmon, a bit of avocado, a single coriander leaf and chili oil on.

'Oh, god. That's lush, that is,' she said, closing her eyes to concentrate on the flavour.

'There's plenty more where that came from. Drink?'

'Have we got any Red Bull?'

Nick opened the fridge. 'No. We've got four cans of Bulldog, whatever Bulldog is.'

'Oh, aye, I bought them from the pound shop. Four for a quid. They're obviously a cheapo imitation of Red Bull. Give us one of those with a big slosh of vod in.'

'Your wish is my command, my Queen of Sex Bottoms.'

She let out a loud, woody laugh, shook her backside at him, and went to get a shower.

Neither of them normally drank pop, but they'd recently developed a taste for energy drinks - basically any sugary drink with caffeine in - with a large glug of vodka or gin added. It was a very good perk-up at the end of a long day

He fixed them both the same drink, added some ice and lime and put them to one side on the kitchen counter while he finished making the food, skewering a stuffed olive and a small sliver of dressed raw beef, adding a few chili flakes. Then he roasted some macadamia nuts and crushed them on top of small ramekins of Greek yoghurt with cucumber and mint stirred through. Finally, he tossed some chunks of roast chicken in pesto and skewered them to half a cherry tomato and a basil leaf.

Taking the plates of snacky food into the lounge, along with a bowl of spicy peanuts and their drinks, he flopped onto the sofa feeling like this was a simple but wonderful thing: feeding Julie, having a big drink and looking forward to some bedroom gymnastics later. Being on a promise was one of the little things in their life that both amused and excited them. Somehow, looking forward to the sex made it more exciting, as though the waiting throughout the day was part of the foreplay.

She came in, having changed into pale blue pyjamas bottoms and a long white t-shirt. He held out his arms and she fell onto him.

'Hello, you,' she said nuzzling and kissing him.

'Hello, gorgeous,' he said, once again feeling like he had to hang on to these moments while they lasted because, when you weren't happy, when you were low or depressed, the times you'd felt happy were like a distress flare on the stormy seas of life. 'Ooh, hello, you feel all underwear-free and funky,' he said rubbing at her backside.

'Well, you're only going to take them off me, so I thought I'd save you some time. I like to reward you for your culinary skills and all I have to give you is my sagging 47-year-old body.'

'That's plenty enough for me.' She kissed him passionately, grinding slowly on his leg, then sat up, panting a little.

'Whoo, I've got the proper horn. I've been thinking about this all day. Give us a spoon and I'll eat you.'

'Aye, my heart's pounding in my chest, like a teenage boy waiting outside the Odeon for his first date.'

She patted him on the leg. 'Plenty of time for all that, later. I'm starving. God, this all looks brill.' She got a plate and put two of everything onto it. 'So, what sort of day have you had?'

'Interesting and varied. I think I found Vokes on a CCTV at the Co-Op along from his flat, at 3.16.' He explained what the DVD showed.

'That's interesting. So he couldn't have done the murder and got back there in time.'

She sat, legs crossed underneath her, eating.

'Not if it happened around or just after 3pm. Not on foot, anyway. Trouble is there's no way to prove those trainers are actually him.'

She nodded. 'Oooh, I love the raw beef and olives. And these little lightly pickled quail's eggs are delish, but they're going to give me the farts, I can tell.'

'They are nicer than the old-school pickled egg, though. There was always a massive jar of pickled eggs in most pubs when we were kids, remember?'

'It was dying out by the time I started going out. There was that hairy pub in Durham city centre. It used to have a massive jar of them. I used to drink in there sometimes when I was at Newcastle Uni.'

'Oh, yeah, I remember that. The Angel. I'd like to go back there sometime.'

'That's it. Hey, something very interesting cropped up at work today. I was finishing and sorting out and filing away the paperwork on Ruth Small. I'd written a profile of her husband's behaviour towards her. I re-read it and one thing jumped out.'

'Oh, yeah, what was that?'

'She mentioned that he had a friend called, wait for it, Kevin Berryman, who lives in the Zetland flats!'

'Really?!' Nick dropped a pickled egg in shock and it rolled across the room.

'Yup, and it doesn't stop there. If you remember, husband Harry was a policeman, at least until last November when he was pensioned off at 55.'

Nick looked at her. 'Wow! Kev told me that when Berryman was into being a loan shark, he had a bent copper who went around bullying people who fell behind with payments. I took that to mean physically bullying people, but you said he psychologically tortured Ruth.'

'Yep. Never laid a hand on her, but had a real talent at getting inside her head and undermining her ego. So maybe he was doing that for Berryman. Menacing people to cough up money. A pension at 55. That's not normal is it?'

'No it's not.'

'She said he was given early retirement for some reason, which he'd never talked about.'

'Early retirement? From the police? Well...there's only one reason they do that, isn't there? They pension off someone who they know has badly screwed up, so they're no longer on the force if and when the story comes out in the media.'

'Of course, yeah. It's like with Hillsborough, isn't it? Disgraceful. Loads of them jumped ship before they could get nailed to the wall,' she said, chewing smoked salmon.

'It's standard policy in a lot of public life, from the NHS to local government.'

'I wish someone would pension me off for being shite. Bloody hell.'

Nick tugged at his stubble in silent contemplation.

'That was some seriously tasty scran, luv,' said Julie, putting her clean plate onto their big coffee table. 'I'm going to save room for some spicy peanuts with the booze.'

'Hmm,' said Nick, hearing her voice, but lost in his own thoughts, as something began to stir in his brain; thoughts that were not quite ready yet to coalesce into a definite idea. But he knew himself well enough to know that his subconscious was hard at work and would, sooner or later, deliver a truth to his conscious mind.

He cleared his throat and took a sip of the sugary energy drink, fortified by a triple vodka.

'That place is a vortex of evil, if you ask me,' he said.

'The Zetland flats?'

'Yeah. Tomorrow, I'm going to have a word with Hair Bear and see if he knows any of the people who live there. In my notes I made the point that it wasn't definitively stated in court who are actually the tenants in the six flats in that block. Danny Ross lived in Flat 6, Kev Berryman in 1. Sid Smith was in 5, Blobby in 3. Apart from that, we never heard from the others, though it was said that at least 11 people lived or stayed there at any one time, and that there was an endless tide of itinerant people coming and going all the time, people like Tracy Berryman. There's a chance someone saw something that day and then left, so the police never even had a chance to interview them and don't know about them.'

She sat cross-legged on the sofa, leaning against the arm, her drink on her lap.

'I meant to ask. How the hell did you get hold on the DVD from the Co-Op?'

He let out a laugh and rubbed at his hair. 'Quite a story there. Remember Sue Thomas, from Ian Ramsey?'

She grinned and nodded. 'I remember you telling me about her and what you used to do to each other. You dirty boy, I never heard the like, letting a girl play with your naughty bits. Shocking.' She chuckled a laugh. 'As an aside, were you fully...err...developed, like? As a 16 year old?'

'Yup. I was a late starter. Puberty didn't kick in until I was nearly 14 and then it came on super fast and by 16 I was, what Muddy Waters once called, "a full-grown man". Chest hair and ear hair aside, how I am now, was how I was then. It was an amazing time. You look at your body changing with a delicious sort of fascination, and your body becomes this amazing playground of pleasure.'

She pursed her lips. 'Phwoarr. If I'd been your age, I'd have been all over you like white on rice. Sue Thomas would have had nowt on me. And I'd have let you have it off with us. In fact, I might have insisted you did! I don't think I could've just been naked with you on a bed and not done it. My will power isn't that strong!'

He laughed. 'I'm not sure I was quite ready for that and I was happy to get any action at all. It seemed very daring at the time.'

'Aw, don't worry, I'd have shown you what to do and would have happily popped your cherry for you.' She said it in her original Hardwick accent and somehow, that made it all the more sexy.

She kept chuckling. 'What about Sue Thomas, anyway?'

'She was at the Co-Op in Roseworth.'

'Get out of here. Really?'

'Yup, she's a senior Co-Op manager. So we got talking and I said what I was trying to do, so she showed me up to the room where all the recordings were stored. It was then that she tried to seduce me.'

Julie gave him a wide-eyed, shocked look. 'Eee, she did not. Just like that?'

'Oh, yeah, she did, just like that. I think she'd have done it there and then, actually. She said I could go round her flat and make my wildest fantasies come true.'

Julie folded her arms across her chest and jutted out her jaw. 'Bloody hell, the cheeky cow. What did you say?'

'I said I was married, said I loved you and would never cheat on you, and that I wasn't that sort of bloke.'

'Did you now? Are you sure you're not just trying to make yourself look good?'

'That is what I said, Jules. You know I would never...'

She interrupted him. '...I know you wouldn't, man, and you don't have any wild fantasies, anyway, do you?'

'No. I don't know how anyone does. Where do you get them from?'

She shrugged. 'I once knew a man who said he'd pay me £100 to watch me have a poo. I told him to sod right off.' She rolled her eyes.

'That's gross and he's probably mentally ill.'

'Exactly. But I have to say that at work I see women who have been subjected to all sorts of pervy behaviour as part of abusive relationships.'

'I suppose you must do. What sort of behaviour?'

She shrugged. 'Oh, it can be anything. There's nothing that could shock me anymore. A threesome with his mate, or his mate's wife. S & M. Dressing up. Nipple clamps. Getting an aubergine up your arse.

Anything. I even had one woman whose husband liked to piss on her. She had to lie in the bath while he did it.'

Nick winced. 'Bloody hell, Jules. What the hell is that about? I'm sorry...that's just gross.'

'It was all part of his way of humiliating her. With our help, she eventually left him.' She said it very matter of factly.

'Good.' He shook his head in disbelief. 'Where do people get these ideas from? Why does it turn them on?'

'In my experience, much of it is to do with power and domination. It's more common than you might think. Women sometimes go along with it to please their man, or because they're scared to say no, in case he turns nasty. And, occasionally, the woman is into it, of course, though quite often, extreme sexual behaviour is the product of abuse when younger.'

Nick finished his drink, got up to fix them two more. When he got back into the lounge, Julie had gone to the music room and selected a few records and was dropping the needle on Mike Oldfield's *Tubular Bells*. 'Thanks, luv. I love this record. It's so melodic. Reminds me of being little.'

He put the glasses down. 'That's a first pressing. You know how you tell?'

She made a comedy slack-jawed look at him. 'How, like?'

'The Virgin label is black and white, not colour.'

She made a mocking yawning gesture.

He put an arm around her waist and kissed her on the lips, enjoying their funny, easy love for each other.

'Do you have any wild sexual fantasies?' he said, sitting down on the sofa. 'You can say, I won't mind.'

She took a big drink and resumed her cross-legged position on the sofa.

'I'd have told you before now if I did, wouldn't I? It's not my thing. I don't think it's most people's thing. Though I do quite like the idea of a naked 16-year-old you. Ha ha. Actually, you know what I do love?'

'Being spanked with a table tennis bat and then covered in goose fat?'

'Well, obviously, there's that...but my fantasy is just making love with you. It's what I was thinking about at work. Y'know, everything we get up to. It's brill. We're lucky we're so sexually compatible, it's not always the case. I suppose we both have our little preferences, which we accommodate for each other, like you with the dirty talk, that's all part of being a nice couple, I think.'

'Yeah, one thing Sue Thomas made me realise all those years ago was that there was as much pleasure in giving pleasure as there is in being pleasured yourself, and I never forgot that.'

'How did she make you realise that?'

'Well, she'd take my hand and put it between her legs and basically explain which bits felt nice when I touched them, and how I should go about the whole thing. I think she got turned on by telling me, as well. I mean, she was very gynecologically focused and she was also very keen on expanding her phallic education.'

She leaned against the arm of the sofa, hands behind her head, grinning. 'I think that's brilliant, that is. That's proper feminism, in my book. I'm a great believer in being educated about and in control of your own body. I should shake her hand for educating you so well.'

'I was saying to Jeff, though. I never really had any massive affection for her. I mean, I liked her, but the attraction was all physical, really.'

'Well, you were young and immature, weren't you? So what did she say to you today?'

'Just that she remembered what I was like and now we were grown up we could have grown-up sex.'

Julie cleared her throat and took a drink. 'In a way, if you think about it, all she's doing there is taking the role blokes normally take in trying to get some sex. It only seems more shocking because it's a woman. But she's really just not being passive. She's asking for what she wants.'

'I suppose so. But I really didn't like it. It was oppressive and, I know this will sound prudish, but it was rude and presumptive. And it made me really uncomfortable.'

She nodded. 'Yeah, well, now you know how women feel from about the age of 13 onwards.'

'Yeah, that did occur to me. It's funny really, men traditionally think that women should be flattered by their attentions, like it's a compliment. But actually, it doesn't feel like that at all. It feels closer to bullying when it's unwanted.'

Putting her drink down, she stood up, took off her clothes and stood hands on hips in front of him.

'Well, I hope you don't think what I'm about to do to you is bullying, darlin'. C'mon, get your kit off and let's pretend we're still 16.'

Hair Bear's house on Hartington Road was one of the few in the street which hadn't been done up. But then, when you spent your days smoking dope and listening to Hawkwind, DIY was a long way down your 'to do' list.

Nick rang his bell the next morning. It was a long time since he'd been there. Previously, it was a bit of a trial to get in, but this time, Hair Bear opened the door within a few seconds.

His appearance was radically changed. His big mop of curly greying hair was now cropped short and there was a colour to his skin that Nick had never seen before.

'Hey, man. Nick Guymer. Remember me?' said Nick, pointing to himself.

'Of course. Nice to see to you, man. What brings your sun into orbit around my planet?' He held out his hand. Nick shook it.

'It's quite complicated.'

'Life is complicated, man, but also very simple and maybe that's the most complicated thing to get your head around.'

Hair Bear smiled almost beatifically. Talking to him was like having a conversation with a book of hippy aphorisms.

'Can I come in?'

'Yeah, man. Be my guest.'

The last time Nick had been in there, the place was ruined. Crunchy carpets, fag-burnt sofas and chairs, and a big magic eye poster on one wall. But those days were gone. Now, the living room was clean and though hardly something out of *Homes and Interior*, was tidy and fresh. The walls had been painted cream and the matching carpet still had that new-carpet smell.

'Things have changed here, HB,' said Nick, with a smile. 'Don't tell me you've become a respectable Teesside citizen.'

'Not exactly, but times change...I met a nice chick. She changed my life. Stopped smoking so much and started livin' right.'

'Ah, women. Men are so much better for loving them. They make us into better humans. I genuinely believe that.'

A big grin broke over Hair Bear's lantern-jawed face.

'Too right, brother. It's all about their yin to our yang. Hey, but you're looking cool, man. Can I make you some green tea?'

'No, it's OK, I won't keep you for long, but thanks anyway. I just wanted to pick your brains about a block of flats called the Zetland, or the Zet as it's more usually known.'

Hair Bear sat down on a big, padded, brown leather chair and invited him to do likewise on the matching sofa. It was odd talking to him when he wasn't stoned. A first, in fact.

'The Zet, huh? Hmm, that's one bad place. Didn't some dude get killed there last year?'

Nick explained briefly about the court case. Hair Bear listened, fingers together at the tips, forming a pyramid. Here was another man, like Kev Wells, who had changed. Maybe there was something in the air.

'I think Glenn Vokes is innocent and I can't be part of sending an innocent man to jail.'

'Well man, you know, innocence is fluid concept.'

'I know he's not innocent. I know he's a scummer, but I don't think he killed Danny Ross. Do you know anyone who lives there?'

'There's a bad dude called Berryman that used to live there, I don't know if he still does.'

'He does. He's the boss of the block, apparently. Why is he a bad dude?'

'He was into money lending for a while, in a money with menaces, kinda style. Man, those people are the worst.'

'Yeah, I heard about that. But he's quite pudgy. He's not a big thug, so did he have hired muscle?'

'He had the best muscle there is, man.'

'What? A boxer or something?'

'No man, he had the Law. I always thought "the fuzz" was a too-nice name for them. All kind of soft and fluffy. Not like the police at all, in that respect.'

'Ah, yeah, I know about this, do you mean Harry Small?'

Hair Bear made a circle with thumb and forefinger. 'That's the man. Small made your life hell if you owed Berryman money. I was always self-sufficient so it never affected me, but plenty had fingers broken and worse. Not that Small did the breaking. He'd hire some low life to do that for him but only as a last resort. Small's gig was to menace people, y'know? Get them full of The Fear. Get them scared, so scared they'd find the bread one way or another. One dude told me it was a kind of mental warfare. Sounds over the top, man, but I believe it. Then he was pensioned off, so the top brass must've got a whiff of scandal.'

'I know a bit about Harry Small. His wife committed suicide, y'know.'

Hair Bear winced. 'I prefer the term, "altered her consciousness". When was that?'

'Not long ago. She jumped in the river. There was no evidence of foul play.'

'Sometimes there isn't,' said Hair Bear, cryptically narrowing his eyes.

'So did anyone from the Zet buy dope from you?'

'The word "from" suggests that anyone actually lives there on anything like a permanent basis, man. Blobby and Berry apart, everyone just drifts through for a while and then moves on. And it's not like I asked for proof of address, man. So, y'know, I might have done.'

'No, I realise that. Does a dealer have that area as their territory?'

Hair Bear had a surprisingly high-pitched laugh. 'It's not like they're postmen, Nick. They don't have a round.'

'Sorry, I don't have much idea about the way drugs get bought and sold.'

'Mostly, hardcore Class A users go and score, especially as that place is notorious. No dealer would want to get caught around there by a passing policeman 'cos they'd know you were there for only one reason.'

'Yeah, but as far as I can tell, it was never busted. It was as though the police just allow them to stay in there taking drugs. They know they could bust them for possession at any time, but choose not to.'

'Yeah, man, but that's the same deal I had with them. They all knew what I was doing here, but they turned a blind eye because they knew I was no trouble and didn't deal anything besides pot. I'd have just choked up the system and soaked up resources. It's all unofficial policy, of course, but it's policy nonetheless. They'd rather have a cool dude like me selling, than a gangster.'

'So have you stopped dealing altogether?'

'Totally, man. I'm getting out of town soon, too. Karen has got a job in Darlington, so I'm going with her.'

'Oh, wow. Well, that's good. What will you do for work?'

'Haven't quite worked that out yet. I might get into painting.'

'I didn't know you were a painter.'

'Yeah, man. I went to art college back in the day.'

Nick nodded. 'I'm pleased you're moving up and on, HB. It's all good, I reckon.'

'Thanks, man. It was time for change. I've been living a hermit life in this place for too many years.'

'Any good ideas as to how I can get evidence to prove Vokes's innocence?'

Hair Bear sat and thought for a full minute without saying anything.

'The Zetland flats are overlooked by Nolan House, that big tower block...'

'...so someone must have seen something?' interrupted Nick.

'More likely no-one actually saw it. It was a only few seconds in time. What I was going to say was that each of the floors of those flats has a security camera on the landing where the lift doors open. The side of each of those is glass. Depending on which side the camera is on, it would film the Zet behind, or it would from some of the lower floors.'

He stood up to illustrate. 'You've got the lift door here in front of you. The Zet is visible on your right through the ceiling-to-floor window. If the camera is on the top left, it'll have a clear view of the Zet. If on the right, it's facing in the wrong direction. Now, all you're gonna need is one on the left that's not too high up.'

'How do you know those flats so well?'

'My buddy, Hal, he lived in there for a while. Of course, if anything was filmed, where do you get the footage? Does it still exist? Have the police taken it? It's relayed to a surveillance and security centre in Thornaby. That's what Hal used to say. He was paranoid of getting filmed bringing drugs into the place, though it was mostly the drugs that were making him paranoid, ironically enough. Ha ha. That's as good as I've got, man.'

'It's a great idea. Thanks, man.'

'But y'know, be careful with those Zet people. People think they're all messed up and wasters, and like, man, they are. But they're not stupid. In fact, major dopers are often very good at scheming and conniving, and like, totally without morals and when you've no morals, you'll pretty much do anything to anyone at any time. So watch your back, man. Don't underestimate any of them. Nice people tend to give them the benefit of the doubt, but nice people are stupid to do that.'

'You're the second person to tell me that. Thanks, HB.'

Nick left the house and walked the short distance to the Nolan House flats. He stood on the pavement looking up at the 17-storey block which had probably been built in 1970s and refurbished in the early 90s. Back in the day they'd have been called council flats, but now probably had a fancier name which amounted to the same thing. It was mostly public housing and none the worse for that. This was a decent place, where decent people lived. It'd have 24-hour security and maybe some sort of concierge. It'd certainly be locked, so how was he going to get in there? Walking up, he noticed an illuminated strip of buttons with names on the right-hand side.

Fearlessly he pressed six buttons, one after the other and then put his ear to the door. It was late morning, most people would be at work. A voice came out of the speaker.

'Hello?'

Nick ignored it and pressed more buttons. Four seconds later he heard the door-release buzz, pushed at it and went in. It was a lucky guess, but there's always someone waiting for a delivery or a visit who just lets someone in, without asking who it is.

No-one was around, though there was a small admin office that was locked up with a sign on it saying, 'Gone to Lunch, back at 1pm'. He'd got lucky. The lobby had postal boxes on one wall, stairs to one side and the elevator in the middle. Taking the stairs up to the first floor, he emerged onto a small landing, laid out exactly as Hair Bear had said. A small egg-shaped CCTV camera mounted on the wall the lift doors were on, so it could film people coming out of the lift, going through the fire doors and to the corridor beyond, off which were the flats.

Bugger, the camera was on the right and couldn't film anything out of the right side window. Taking the stairs up a flight he checked it again. Same situation. Third floor, the same. The fourth floor didn't have a camera. The holes in the walls suggested one had been there at some point. Maybe it had been broken. He took the lift to the next floor, as the doors parted, his heart sank when he saw no camera there, either. He got back in the lift and went to the top floor. The camera was on the right again, too. They'd obviously made a policy of where to put them for the whole block, and it was in exactly the wrong place for what he needed. So he went to the window and took a look out. The Zet stood below, dirty and forlorn, its flat roof green with mold. Christ, it must be damp in there. As he looked back to the camera and tried to follow its line if it had been on the opposite side, he suddenly realised that there was no way that it could have filmed the flats at this height. It was at an impossible angle on the top floor, so he took the lift back down to the fifth floor and tried to judge the line. Still a bit too high.

As he got to the fourth floor, it was obvious that was just the right angle to film the landing and in doing so, get a full view of the Zet below, if only it had been on the left of the lift doors. But the fourth and fifth were the floors without cameras. Was that a coincidence? Surely, it had to be because they would still be on the wrong side. Oh, well, it was a nice idea.

He trotted down the stairs to the lobby, noting as he went that the view from the lower floors was blocked by trees and another building. A middle-aged man in navy blue overalls had just come in carrying a stepladder under one arm and two boxes under the other, along with a carrier bag which looked to have metal brackets in it. He was obviously a builder or workman of similar description. He pressed the lift button and gave Nick a perfunctory nod. As he did so, Nick noticed the printing on the boxes: 'See-all Security Camera'.

'Hiya, mate. Are you putting one of those in on the fourth floor, by any chance?' said Nick, stopping alongside him.

'Aye, I am like. Fourth and fifth both.'

'Are they any good? When you see CCTV on *Crimewatch* it's always really ropey footage.'

'That's from them old black-box cameras the police use, or newsagents who get secondhand rubbish. This is state of the art, this is. Best part of a hundred quid a go.'

Nick had no idea if £100 was a lot of money for a security camera.

'What's so good about it, like?'

The lift pinged as it got to the ground floor.

'This? They're 180-degree cameras. They go around from side to side.' He made a circular gesture with his middle finger, then made a short laugh. 'Less hiding place for scumbag villains!'

The man got into the lift, the doors closed and took him up to the fourth floor.

Nick stood still as this info dropped into his brain. So it could have filmed the Zet from the right-hand side; it didn't need to be on the left because it wasn't fixed. Shit. And that fourth-floor camera was the only one on the block that was in just the right position to catch the action in the doorway of the Zet, and was missing. But it was eight months since the murder, surely it couldn't have been missing that long, if it had been taken off to prevent recording the murder. That was a conspiracy theory too far, surely.

Sprinting up the stairs to the fourth floor, he found the man fitting the camera onto a bracket in the same location as before.

'Alright, again,' said Nick, trying to be pretend to be a resident who lived on that floor. 'It's about time that got fixed.'

'Aye, well, you know what the companies who run these places are like. They save all the jobs up and give them to us in one lump so they get a cheaper deal. Always happens in April and May.'

'Huh. I wonder why.'

'Ah, it's all to do with the tax year, or whatever. These cameras were first reported as broken in mid-October. Probably some punk kids having a bit of fun. Eight months to get new ones is just stupid. These should be council run, if you ask me. Not some private company making profits from renting them out. Mind, I'm an old-fashioned socialist, so don't listen to me.'

'I agree with you. You know what, I've lived here for a couple of years and I still don't know where the CCTV film goes. Is it in this building?'

'Nah. It's fired over to a place in Thornaby. The company that owns this block owns others in the area. They all feed the CCTV into the security centre.'

'Getaway. I never knew that. So some poor sod just sits there looking at people getting in and out of lifts?'

'Nah, man. It's all automated and stored on servers. It'd be against human rights to have someone just sitting there, looking at people coming in and out of a lift on the off chance something was going to happen.' He laughed. 'It'd be torture. The cameras are just so the police can get footage of a robber or of criminal damage, or whatever.'

Nick feigned disbelief. 'I'm such a Luddite for technology. I think I reckoned it was all on VHS tape.'

The man laughed again as he finished setting up the camera. 'Aye, I know what you mean. It's hard to keep up, like.'

Nick said his goodbyes and went down the corridor to wait for him to go. There was a flat doorway every 20 feet or so. Walking down to the end of it, he realised there was another set of stairs at that side. So he took those down a floor and made his exit.

The camera was broken before the murder happened, so there was no filmed evidence to find. OK, it could have been a coincidence, but it was a hell of a big one, if it was. The floors below had their view of the flats obscured. The ones above were at too steep an angle for anything but the roof to be caught by the camera's eye. That fourth-floor camera was crucial. This was surely proof that it was a preplanned murder, which in itself was proof Vokes hadn't done it because he was constitutionally unable to plan anything. He lived in the now, and even that seemed to be something of a struggle for him. Planning how to make sure there was no film of the murder you were about to commit was, if nothing else, well beyond his organisational skills.

He walked around the block to the Zetland flats. Don's bloodstains were still on the pavement. He shuddered as he stepped over them. He must go and see how Don was.

Kev Berryman's flat was on the ground floor, on the right of the entrance. Nick looked into his living room window. No-one there. He'd probably not returned yet. It was a normal enough room, not much to it, but not a filthy drug den, either. But Kev Wells had been right. There was an armchair to left side of the room, and a long free-standing mirror against the right wall which he could see his own reflection in. It had been set up to monitor who came and went, but without it being too obvious.

As he walked to the communal entrance, the door opened and a slight figure came out, a baby on her arm, a cigarette and lighter in one hand. It was Tracy Berryman. Would she remember him from court? It was doubtful. None of the witnesses seemed to pay much attention to the jury, oddly enough.

She lit the fag, and looked at him as she did so.

'Alright, Tracy,' said Nick, putting his hands in his pockets to make his body language seem unthreatening.

'Who are you, like?' She scowled at him. It was the innate defensiveness that he recognised from the court.

'Jack Casady. Remember? Everyone calls me Cass. Is Danny in?'

'Cass? Don't remember you, mate. You want Danny?' she said, blowing smoke away from the baby as it slept in her arms. 'Are you takin' the piss, like?' She spoke with a classic Stockton accent where 'taking' is transformed into 'taaakn'.

Nick affected a dumb look and broadened his accent. 'Eh? What d'ya mean, like?'

'Don't yer know?'

'Know what?'

She sucked on the fag again. 'Danny's dead. He died last October. He were murdered, they said, like.'

'Eh? Murdered?!'

'Aye, right where I'm standing an' all.'

'Bloody 'ell. Eee, my god. Poor Danny. I wondered why I'd not 'eard from him. I've been in jail for a year. No-one said nowt. So who murdered 'im?'

She carefully, Nick thought, didn't answer that. 'They've sent Glenn Vokes down for it. Do you know 'im?'

'Oh, aye. A bit. But not much.' Nick was rather enjoying playing this role as an ex-con with Jefferson Airplane's bass player's name. 'Why did he do it?'

She shrugged, but didn't say anything.

Tracy was only in her mid-twenties but looked older. She was a small woman, but a hard woman. With hollow eyes, gaunt and without an ounce of fat on her, there was no doubt that her lifestyle had taken its toll on her, but even so, it was possible to see the attractive young woman she would have been, if healthy. She had long eyelashes, green almond-shaped eyes and full lips. But those eyes had a disturbing, strange look. A look that no-one who has lived in the nice, respectable world ever has; expressionless, unemotional, almost dead. It was upsetting to see in court and worse up close, here and now. Those eyes showed a soul that had been locked away to protect it from any more pain.

The baby woke up and looked around. It was about a year old or maybe a bit less. It looked at Nick and reached out a hand to him, the way inquisitive kids do.

He took hold of the little paw, squeezed and tickled it. You poor kid.

'So how did he die, then?' said Nick, still holding the baby's hand.

'He were stabbed.' She said it with no emotion.

'That's terrible that is, poor old Danny,' said Nick. 'Why did Vokes stab him?'

She just kept smoking, but said nothing more.

As Nick waited for her to say something, an idea occurred to him. Danny Ross had supposedly gone outside before he was killed, maybe because he wanted a smoke. Tracy had the baby with her, so he'd stepped out to not smoke in the room with the baby. Not the act of a totally irresponsible, couldn't-care-less person.

'Shit. Danny was a good lad, I can't believe he's dead.' The baby reached out to him with both arms now.

She gave half a smile at the baby. 'Can I take him, Trace?' said Nick. 'I like kids. I'm good with them.'

'Go on then. Don't drop her.'

Nick scooped the child into his arms the way he did with Argie. 'Now then, what's your name?' he said, pulling a silly face at the kid.

'She's Katie,' said Tracy, softening in her stance towards him, relaxing a little.

'Aren't you lovely, Katie, eh. You've got your mam's green eyes, haven't you?'

'She does, yeah,' said Tracy. 'She's really good. No trouble like.'

'Aw she's a proper bonnie lass,' said Nick, realising that he was being too like his real self now. 'So do you live here now, Trace?'

She ignored that. 'How do I know you? You look familiar, like. Can't place you, though.'

He had to be creative. Drawing on what he'd picked up about her in court, he bluffed it.

'We used to go drinking. Me and you and Danny and a few others. Glenn was around as well, I reckon. He lived over Roseworth way.'

'Oh. Oh, right. Yeah.' She tossed the fag end to the pavement and ground it with the tip of her training shoe.

'It was earlier last year. Like I say, I've been inside.'

'What did they nick you for?'

'Oh, not much. Drug dealing. Occupational hazard though, innit?'

Katie had now fallen asleep against his arm. Tracy smiled a wide, proper smile for the first time. It transformed her face for a brief moment, the way sun emerging from behind storm clouds casts hope of better weather.

'You're good with her, you, like.'

'Kids like me. I must give off a good vibe or something.'

'I'll have to give you a ring when she's playing up, then.' He smiled at her. She smiled at him.

'So how are you then, Trace? Still on the gear?' In court, she'd said she was on methadone.

She took out another cigarette from a packet which looked like it had begun its life in Albania or Bulgaria. Cheap, untaxed knock-off fags were a standard lifestyle accessory.

'I'll be honest with yer. I'm tryin' to stay clean, me, like.'

'Are you? How's it goin'?'

'Bloody hard, man. I miss Danny. Doesn't exactly help staying in his old flat.'

'Sounds heavy, that. So were you two living together?'

She shrugged non-committedly. 'Sort of.'

'Is Katie his lassie?'

She shrugged again. 'I don't know, Cass. Might have been. You know how it is when you're fucked up. I just want to make it nice for Katie. They'll take her off us if I don't. But I need money to make sure she's alright.'

It was impossible not to feel sorry for her.

'Look, shall we go and get some coffee? I'll pay.'

'Aye, alright, then. Nowt else to do. I'll just lock up.'

He continued to hold the kid, watched her go back into the Zet and glanced up at the Nolan House tower block. He couldn't really see the first three floors through the trees and buildings. But that fourth floor was right in his eyeline. So plenty of people had the potential to see Danny being stabbed.

As he looked back to the Zet, a big fat pink head peered out of the flat above Berryman's. It was the man everyone referred to simply as Blobby. No-one was at any of the other windows, but it was easy to see how anything that was going on outside the building would attract the attention of residents, immediately. The idea that no-one had seen who stabbed Danny in the middle of the afternoon beggared belief.

Tracy came back out with a small black leather shoulder bag. She'd also passed a comb through her shoulder-length brown hair, straightening out all the bed-hair tangles on the back.

'Are you alright carrying her? I can get the pram if you like.'

'No, she's fine. We'll just go to Costa on the High Street. It's only five minutes' walk.'

The thing was, she was being very trusting. She didn't know him, or anything about him. After her initial defensiveness had been dissolved by him being nice to her kid, she now seemed *too* trusting. This was almost certainly how you got mixed up with bad people. Despite being hard-faced, she was very vulnerable. Every human needs someone to be nice to them, and the worst people know that and exploit it for their own ends, whether that's drugs, sex or money.

'I'm still shocked at Glenn Vokes doing what he did,' said Nick as they walked slowly towards the High Street. 'I don't remember him being that sort of bloke. Was he raging on meth or something?'

She offered him a cigarette.

'No, ta, Trace. I've given up.'

'Bloody wish I could. Are you clean an' all?'

'Aye. Packed it all in. It's a dead end, all that shit. I just realised one day that it was making life shit and not better.' He found himself plugging into what Kev Wells had talked about as source material for his act. 'Just want to settle down, get a job and maybe find a nice lass.'

'That's a nice idea that, like, Cass.'

He wanted to get the conversation back to Vokes.

'So when was Glenn sent down then?'

'Just the other day. He got 25 years.'

'Shit. What made him do it? Did he say?'

'Said he never did it.'

'Is that right? I mean, did he do it?'

She didn't reply and he wasn't sure if he should push it any more. Probably not. As they reached the coffee shop, he handed the little girl to her and went to the counter.

'What do you want?' he said.

'Eee, god, the prices in here. Err...just normal coffee with milk in.'

When you're not totally skint all of the time, you forget how even the price of a coffee in Costa is unaffordable. Spending a precious fiver on two coffees was a waste when you could buy three litres of white cider instead. He put the two cups onto a tray and paid for them with a £20 note, then put the change on the tray as he carried it to the table she'd sat at, right at the back of the shop, in the same way that the rough kids always sat at the back of the bus, as though to keep an eye on everyone else.

'I'll just go the toilet,' he said.

As he looked at himself in the mirror while washing his hands, he clearly didn't look like a man who had just got out of jail. He was too healthy looking for a start. And he'd caught the early summer sun, so had a light tan. She must know he was lying, surely. Hair Bear had said not to underestimate the Zet crowd.

Returning to the table, he sat down. Katie was gurgling and making squeaky noises. She shushed her and bounced her a little on her knee.

The £14.84 change that had been on the tray was gone.

'Where's the change?' he said, pointing at where it had been.

'What change?' she said, innocently enough.

'There was a tenner, four pound coins and some change on here.'

She shrugged. 'Have you dropped it?'

But it was obvious she'd stolen it. It wasn't even as if someone could have walked past the table and picked it up. They were against the back wall. He wasn't sure what to say or do. If he really was Cass, just out of jail, how would he react? He wouldn't let her get away with it.

'You've nicked it. You cheeky cow.'

'I've not taken nowt, me.'

'Trace, man, you could've had the money. You just needed to ask.'

That obviously sounded weird to her ears. No-one gave you money without wanting something in return in her world.

'I'm not turning tricks any more, Cass. Right?'

'Fair enough. I didn't say you were.'

'But if you want to have it off and have got a spare 20 for us, that'd be alright, like. You were always good to me, Cass. We could sort something out between us. Whatever you fancy, as often as you like. Just as mates, nowt heavy. I'll come round to your place if you want. I'm still good in bed and I'm clean, honest. You must be really gaggin' for it after being banged up.'

Nick felt shocked. He'd never heard anyone say anything like that before. What did you say in response? It was pretty much still prostitution, even if you tried to dress it up as a more informal arrangement between friends, even though he wasn't her friend and even though she'd never met him before in her life. And with your little daughter on your lap, too. How many blokes did she have a little arrangement with? Not enough, presumably, or she'd not be stuck in the Zet. Bloody hell, this really was a different world and he felt out of his depth in it. Until you see it up close, it's hard to grasp the reality of what this kind of life was all about. Desperate didn't cover it. It was tragic. How could society let people fall through the net like this?

'Nah. I don't think so, Tracy. Thanks, though. I'm fine.'

Again, he could tell he wasn't saying the words that the sort of man he was pretending to be would say. She didn't say anything for a bit, then gave him a narrow-eyed look as she drank the coffee.

'Are you a copper?' she said, suddenly.

'Eh? Of course not. How could I be a copper?'

'There's summat not right about you.'

Bloody hell. There wasn't going to be any chance of getting anything more about the murder out of her.

'Don't be paranoid, man.'

She finished the coffee. 'You can't blame us for being paranoid, living in that bloody dump. You can't trust no-one and nowt.'

'What about your dad? Does he still live there?'

'Yeah, and he's the fuckin' worst of them all. The things he did to me as a kid,' she added, almost under her breath.

She put her bag on her shoulder and picked up Katie. 'And by the way, Vokes never killed Danny. That was a load of old rubbish. Thanks for the coffee, Cass. Give us a ring if you change your mind. I always need the money.'

'Yeah, I will, but I haven't got your number, Trace.'

She took out a Biro and wrote it down on the till receipt that his change had sat on before she'd pocketed it.

Nick picked it up, reached out and gave the kid's little hand a squeeze.

'See you, Katie.'

Tracy looked at him again with narrowed eyes.

'Deffo summat weird about you, son.'

'Eh? Weird? What's weird about us, like?'

She shrugged. 'Yer too nice, son. Far too nice.'

He watched her walk out. Where was she going now and what was she going to do? It didn't bear much thinking about. The funny thing was, he'd thought he was manipulating her to tell him about Vokes and Ross, but in fact, she'd seen him as an opportunity to exploit for money, one way or another, and she was already £14.84 up. Hair Bear was right. These people were not to be underestimated. Tracy had a survival instinct and that was just about keeping her alive. But only just.

It seemed unlikely that she was telling the truth about being clean of drugs, though she was clear -eyed in a way that she hadn't been in court. Maybe he'd caught her on a sober day, or just a sober morning. It was certainly unlikely that she'd be allowed to keep Katie unless she was sober. But even so, he sort of liked her and her contempt for her father seemed genuine enough, as did her statement that Vokes didn't kill Danny. But 'seemed' was the crucial word. You could never quite tell what was truth and what was lie when you listened to people from the Zet, and that was exactly how they all liked it.

After a few minutes he left the coffee shop and was about walk up the road to Jeff's shop when a large, fat, bald man stepped in front of him.

'What was she telling you, eh?' he said, putting a flat, flabby hand on Nick's breast and pushing him.

Nick was caught by surprise and took a step back. It was Blobby from the Zet and he stank of booze and sweat. 'Who? What are you on about?' said Nick.

'Never mind that, what did that bitch Tracy Berryman say?'

'Why should I tell you anything about anything?'

'Because I know who you are.'

'Sorry, that's not a good enough answer, mate.'

Nick tried to walk away but the man stepped in front of him again, and again pushed him, with both hands this time. A couple of people stopped nearby to watch, no doubt hoping to see a fight breakout.

'What did she tell you?'

Nick sighed. 'Don't try and play the hard man with me, Blobby. Why do you care what she said?'

'I'm asking the questions and how do you know who I am?'

Nick put his hands on his hips and took a chance with a big guess. 'Look son, I know you're from the Zet. I know which flat you live in. And I know that you know who really killed Daniel Ross. And I know that you know that Tracy knows as well and you're worried that she's told me.'

The man went a deep pink colour as though flushing with embarrassment. Nick knew he'd hit the nail on the head just by the shifty way the man looked.

'So, did she?'

'No, she didn't.'

'She's a liar, you know.'

'I know.'

'So if she does tell you anything, you're as well not believing it.'

'This is such a weird conversation...'

'If she does tell you anything, come and tell me.'

'...and it's getting weirder.'

'Just do it, Guymer.'

'So how do you know me?'

'I saw you with Kev Wells, having it out with Kev Berryman on Bishy Road. I thought you must know him quite well. Everyone knows Kev Wells and everyone knows his sister. I Googled her on the library computer and found pictures of her with you. Easy.'

Did this man know he'd been on the jury? Berryman certainly did via his paid-off court official.

'OK, well done, Sherlock.'

'And I know you think that Glenn Vokes wasn't guilty and you were the only one on the jury to vote not guilty.'

Nick crossed his arms and flexed his right bicep as he did so. 'OK, so you're a pal of Berryman's.'

'I never said that. I hate the man. He needed sorting out. I hope he never comes back. I wish Wells had caned him.'

'So who did murder Danny?'

'Everyone knows what happened.'

'Everyone? Who's everyone?'

'Everyone in the Zet, but no-one will tell you.'

'Why not?'

'Because then we'll all be murdered. Only we know, so if anyone else finds out, it'll be obvious one of us has told someone. And that means death.'

He spoke with quite a slur, which initially Nick thought was a strong Teesside accent, but soon realised that the man was just drunk.

'That's all a bit melodramatic, isn't it?'

'It's the bloody truth and you're already too near to the truth. So think on. If we're all found dead, it'll be your fault.'

The man walked past him and south down the High Street.

Was that the truth? Or just more Zet lies? Or, perhaps more likely still, just the deluded ramblings of an alcoholic?

CHAPTER 6

'I'm not sure there's anything more you can do,' said Julie from behind the wheel of her old Porsche, as she drove on the A177 towards Durham. 'OK, it'd make a great story to sell and we could use the money, but it's not fair on you to have to cope with the pressure of putting people's lives in danger, potentially. Like I said last night, I really think you should just drop it now.'

'Yeah, I think you're right. Something odd happened there. That's totally for sure. And I'm sure Glenn Vokes and Danny Ross were, in different ways, the victims of it. But Christ knows what it's all about and I'm still not convinced any of them has ever told the truth about anything that happened. In fact, I do wonder if they even really know the truth. Even as he was getting sent down, Vokes was lying in saying he didn't even know Danny. It's a reflex with them.'

'Oh, well, let's just forget all about it and enjoy our dirty weekend in Durham. Haven't been back since I did my Master's degree.' She rubbed his leg and grinned at him.

'Yeah, this was a good last-minute idea of yours. Two nights in a nice hotel, a record fair, hiking and hopefully some good food. Perfect.'

'We don't get away enough - or at all, in fact. We should have a dirty weekend once every couple of months at least. It doesn't have to be pricey.'

'How dirty is it going to be?'

'As dirty as you like, luv.'

'But what does *dirty* actually mean? Dirty is one of those words that hints at more than what the reality is.'

'I know, it's a bit of a cliché really; a bit *Carry On*. I like it, though. Makes it feel a bit naughty and I like that at our age. And I have packed me sex pants.'

'Oooh, which ones?'

'You'll have to wait to find out, won't you? I've packed yours as well.'

'I didn't know I had any.'

'You do now, lad.'

'Cor. This *is* starting to sound properly dirty.'

It was only a half-hour drive to the city centre. They checked into a small independent hotel which had been doing a 2-for-1 deal on weekend breaks and were given a spacious room on the top floor, overlooking the River Wear.

'This is a quirky old place, isn't it?' said Nick, looking out of the window. 'Must be early Victorian.'

'My friend Diane recommended it. She lives in town. I'm meeting her for coffee tomorrow while you're at the record fair. I love old hotels. Your Travelodges are fine if you've just got to kip down for a night, but I like something a bit different for a break.' She flopped down on the bed and bounced up and down. It made a loud creaking noise. 'Listen to those springs go! Ha ha...boing boing!! They're comedy springs.'

'We're going to have to have it off on the floor or somehow do it without moving at all.' He looked under the covers. It was an old iron frame and springs, the like of which he'd not seen since the 60s. 'My gran in Castleford had beds like this. I was told when I was very little that if I used the potty for a piss, not to put it back under the bed because the steam off it on a cold night would make the springs rusty.'

She laughed as she went to the toilet. 'We forget how cold it was before central heating, don't we? Frost on the inside of the windows and all of that.'

'Yeah, but I'm not convinced we're happier for being more pampered. Deprivation made you appreciate simple things. Having a lot more choice, more often, has reduced our quality of life in so many ways.'

She came out the bathroom, drying her hands. 'Talking of choice, I've booked us a table for 6pm at a French place, so we can get some food in us and then get a good drink-up on the go.'

'OK, cool. Let's just go for a short walk by the river until then.'

It was a grey, cloudy but mild afternoon.

Julie spoke thoughtfully. 'Funny how your life turns on the choices you make. You know the day I met you in Jack & Danny's bar in Harrogate? I nearly went back to the hotel to get changed, but couldn't be arsed. And we nearly went to another place, but I'd been in Jack & Danny's before and knew they played rock music, so I said we'd have one in there and then go on somewhere else. We could easily never have met.'

'When you think about it,' said Nick, 'life is all just random events that could so easily never happen. I mean, just ask Glenn Vokes. He turned up at the Zet after walking six miles around the town, only to get nicked for a murder he didn't do. Just like that. Life changing.' He clicked his fingers together.

'It bothers me that Ruth Small's husband was mixed up with that lot, or with Kevin Berryman, at least. Danny Ross dies, Ruth dies. Dunno, feels weird.'

'Yeah, I think that as well. I've asked Jeff to ask Mandy about Harry Small. He said he'd have to wait until they were having a good drink-up this weekend, because she didn't like to talk a lot of shop.'

'Well, we already know he's a wrong 'un - but just how wrong, exactly? Our Kev always said there was only ever a handful of proper corrupt coppers, and all the criminals knew who they were - but they always got away with it because if it got out into public knowledge, it'd make people think the whole force was bent. So the few that were, or are, have to do something pretty bad for a long time to even get pensioned off. Everyone would rather turn a blind eye.'

They walked to the French restaurant just across Elvet Bridge. The town, just like all northern towns at 6 in the evening on a Friday, was filling up with Friday-night drinkers and plenty had already had three hours of necking pints and big glasses of wine under their belt. When you've been brought up around it, you don't really notice it. You take it for granted. It's the way it's always been. The industrial north was always fuelled by alcohol, going back to the start of the industrial revolution, and it's still part of the region's identity. The health lobby can go on about how bad it is for you, how it leads to ill-health and injury and fights and all of that. It's all true. But it makes no difference. Drinking is how the North knows itself.

It was a small restaurant. They were shown to a table about big enough for two plates and nothing more. A young woman, probably a student, took their drinks order and then didn't return with the bottle of white wine and no-one came to take their food order.

'This is so typical of so many restaurants,' said Julie. 'It's poor management. It does my head in. There are only 30 covers in here and no-one is getting their food.'

They waited another five minutes, still no wine, never mind food. They got up and left.

'Owee, let's find a chippy,' said Julie. 'I'm starvin' and I'm chokin' for a drink.'

They soon found one, ordered fish and chips and took them down to the river to eat.

'It all goes to show why Big Meat and Beef and Vodka are so popular. They run such tight ships. Everything happens properly,' said Nick, dropping the last of the delicious haddock into his mouth.

'Yeah, people think success is random, but it's not. Do great food and have great service. That's it.'

119

'I remember once waiting for a coffee in a cafe in the Lake District. It never came, so I asked the idiot running the place where it was. And he said, "I've got six coffees on the go, y'know!" like this was a valid excuse. We need to learn customer service from America. OK, they might shoot you in the head, but at least you won't have had to wait for your food beforehand.'

'Ah, well. Sod it. Let's go to the Angel and get some vodka behind our eyes.'

They'd each just got a triple vodka and tonic when Nick's phone vibrated. It was a text from Jeff. He read it out.

' "Mandy says Harry Small was Durham police force, not Cleveland. Was always odd rumours about him. Pensioned off last year. Mand thinks there was more to it, but doesn't know anything specific about him".'

He put the phone down.

'Well, that's interesting.'

'Whatever he was, he was a horrible bully to Ruth.'

'Hmm. Seems like that's what he did for Berryman as well. Tracy didn't have a good word to say about her dad, either. Said something about what he'd done to her when she was a kid - it suggested abuse, really.'

'Was Tracy bothered that Vokes was in jail?'

Nick sipped at his drink and shook his head. 'Not in the slightest. She was a bit sad about Danny, I think, but she'd swallowed down so much hurt and upset in her life that this latest tragedy was just another brick in her emotional wall.'

Julie pushed a strand of hair off her eyes and chewed at her cheek a little.

'It's sad, isn't it? Your life is reduced to offering up this small hole in your body to men for a few quid.'

'Yeah, awful. In a way, the fact she was almost pretending that it was just a favour she'd do for a mate made it even worse. Like that was obviously how she was rationalising it for herself.'

'And she's hardly operating at the high-end call girl level, is she?'

'Is her situation something you might come across at Teesside Women?'

'It's not unknown. After all, the likelihood of someone being abusive towards a sex worker is quite high.'

'And is it always drugs that leads women down that road?'

'Pretty much. I did recently see a 20-year-old girl who was paying her way through college by granting fellow students intimate favours - male or female. And in the course of doing this was gang raped by three men.'

As usual, she said it so matter-of-factly.

'Christ almighty. What did you say to her?'

'I didn't say much, I just listened a lot. She felt guilty. She knew who the men who raped her were, but couldn't face pressing charges and going through the courts and y'know, who can blame her for that, given the circumstances?'

'So they got away with it.'

'Yup. Men almost always get away with rape. I've told you that often enough. That lass isn't even on any official rape statistics because she didn't report it to the police. And as I say, she had this veneer of middle-class respectability so you'd never have thought that behind it she was, in essence, a prostitute. Her public face and private life were two very different things.'

'I don't think any bloke I've known has ever told me they've paid for sex with a prostitute.'

'Probably too ashamed to tell you.'

'It's always been beyond me how men can even do it and I don't see why they even feel the need to. I mean, it's just, to put it crudely, ejaculation.'

'That's not putting it crudely. That's putting it biologically.'

'Whatever. I mean, even if you're having a one-night stand, you at least entertain the hope that the woman wants to have some fun and feel good, too. It's part of the night's fun. Sex is about the giving and getting of pleasure. But if you're with a prostitute, there is no concept of giving pleasure, there's just the sex act. Without the mutual desire, it really is just ejaculation and any man can achieve that on his own, so I don't see the point of going to a prostitute, regardless of any moral issue.'

She grinned at him and shook her head. 'You really don't get it, do you?'

'Get what?'

'What you just said isn't how some men view sex. To them it's not a sharing thing, it's a selfish thing. They want what they want and don't care about the woman at all. Just because it's second nature to you to care, don't assume it is to everyone. Though as I've said, by the way, that's why you're good at it.'

'I'm happy to take compliments for being a good shagger, but actually, in a way, it's selfish, because you enjoying it is part of my enjoyment. I mean, I didn't need any education in that even as a teenager. I felt that way from the first time me and Sue Thomas started messing around with each other's downstairs bits.'

'That's so funny. Fancy being in the nuddy with someone and not actually having proper sex.'

'I vividly remember the first orgasm I saw her have.'

'Go on then, what was it like?'

'Her whole body tensed, she seemed to hold her breath for about 10 seconds and then let out about half a dozen high-pitched squeaky groans in quick succession while wearing a look on her face that suggested she was trying to shift an especially large stool.'

He did a passable imitation of her. Julie threw her head back and laughed.

'Ha ha, very expressive.' She burst out laughing again.

'I was amazed. For at least five seconds I thought she was in agony, then it dawned on me, this was that orgasm thing I'd read about in a well-thumbed copy of *The Joy of Sex* in Fairfield library. Then after that, because she said how brilliant it was, I just wanted to make it happen for her every time. I mean, that's just natural, surely. It's nice to be able to give someone pleasure.'

Julie dabbed at her eyes, wiping away tears of laughter. 'I owe her a drink. She obviously trained you up well in the whole caressing of the lady parts thing. I've never had any complaints in that department.'

'Like you said the other day, I'm glad we still fancy each other after all these years. I mean, it's 12 since we met and I still can't wait to get back to the room and do some horizontal dancing.'

'You've forgotten, we've got a squeaky bed. The whole hotel will hear us and I'm not going down to breakfast with everyone looking at us.'

'We'll have to be creative, then.'

'The floor seems a bit insanitary, but you can bend me over the Corby trouser press if you like.'

'That's a nice idea and that'd be the first time one of those things has ever been of any use.'

'Or we could just do it standing up, like we did in that hotel before we went to see Rush, remember? I was leaning against the door.'

'Aye, and the door handle went right up your bum!'

She burst out laughing again. 'One knob in the front, one in the back, y'see. No wonder I had a good time!'

Saturday morning dawned damp and a little misty. There was a record fair at a church hall in the centre of town. It started at 9, so Nick and Julie had a quick breakfast with the intention of getting there early just in case there was anything rare and cheap, which wasn't likely, as most dealers knew what everything was worth.

Nick was cleaning his teeth as he heard his phone vibrating as a text came in. Julie passed it to him. He spat the toothpaste into the sink.

'It's from Kev.'

'My Kev?'

'Aye.' He frowned as he read it. 'This is weird Jules. Listen. It's really badly written, mind. It's like he's illiterate. Absolutely no punctuation. "I told Ricky about Berryman and your trial etc last night Ricky called us and said his mate from Roseworth what is staying with him saw a bloke what looked like Danny Ross in a bar in Benidorm I said he's dead so it can't be him you prick but he says it was tho so I told him to take a photo if he sees him again probably all shite but berryman is a skeeming twat so you never know thought youd like to know anyways".'

She put on a blue, green and white checked flannel shirt over a white t-shirt.

'Well, that's just stupid. Ricky's mate was probably high on something. And Ricky gets daft ideas stuck in his head. Always has done. Ross was murdered. He just can't suddenly be alive. Nah. Not havin' that.'

Nick stared at the text in thought. It made zero sense. In court, he'd seen photos of the stab wounds that had killed him, taken in the morgue. The pathologist had looked at the body. The taxi driver and the police found the body slumped and bleeding heavily in the doorway. None of this was hearsay, it had all happened and there was plenty of evidence to prove it. And yet...Tracy's words came back to him. She'd said that Vokes didn't kill Danny. He'd taken that to mean Vokes was innocent, but actually maybe it meant he had killed someone, but it wasn't Danny. And that triggered something his subconscious had been working on. When Vokes protested his innocence in court he'd also said, 'I didn't kill him', but the emphasis, at least one time, was on the word *him*, which could be taken as an admittance of killing someone, just not 'him'.

'I know Ricky is daft in the head and his mates are just as bad, but let's just say he's right and Danny Ross is alive. Was someone actually killed that day? Maybe it was all staged for some reason.'

She gave him a withering look. 'Oh, come on, Nick, that's all too mind-blowing. It'd mean that the police, Danny, and the taxi driver, paramedics, pathologist, Vokes and the rest of the Zet have all conspired to create a fiction.' She counted them off on her fingers as she spoke. 'All for why? That's the stuff of the movies, not of real life. And why would Vokes knowingly and willingly go to jail for a murder that he hadn't done, and hadn't even happened?'

'It's totally out there. I agree. But that doesn't mean it's not possible.'

She pulled a face. 'I think it does mean exactly that. In practical terms, it is not possible. The wider any conspiracy, the more potential compromises there are to the story, but this has survived intact for over eight months and made it through an eight-day trial.'

'True, but all through the trial I thought there was a lack of hard evidence that Vokes had done it, though I never suspected for a moment that it hadn't happened. There was too much apparent evidence that someone had died there. I mean, there was a pathologist there. It wasn't all just the police's word.'

She pulled on her baseball boots and sat on the edge of the bed, thinking about it. After a moment, she spoke.

'Maybe it wasn't Ross that was murdered, but it was someone else. Would it be possible for a dead man to be processed as Danny Ross, but not be him? Because if it is, it'd be a great way to hide who was really killed, if you didn't want it known he was dead.' Nick looked at her as she continued. 'We've been thinking about this in terms of Danny Ross - is he alive or dead, and why either might be the case. What we've not thought about is, who is the real dead person? If you wanted someone dead, but wanted it to be covered up, a great way to do it would be to have him killed and then assign the death to a different identity. That way, whoever has been killed just disappears. No body can be found. No-one knows what has happened to him and as long as the supposed dead man doesn't reappear, no-one is the wiser.'

'OK, but why hasn't anyone said it wasn't Danny? Tracy said Vokes didn't kill Danny. Maybe that's a kind of admission.'

'What about your encounter with Blobby? In effect he told you there was a conspiracy of silence by everyone in the Zet to keep quiet about who the real killer was, under pain of death.'

'Yeah, but he could easily just be full of trippy, mind-fried drunken bullshit.'

'I know. He could,' said Julie. 'But why make the effort to follow you and Tracy and then have it out with you? Think about it, how do you keep a flat full of druggies quiet about anything? Tracy is selling herself for £20 a go. I'm sure if anyone offered her £500 and a bottle of vodka she'd spill the beans, in fact she's probably spilling someone's beans right now, with her right hand.' Nick winced at the thought.

It was a short walk to the church hall. As record fairs usually are, it was largely populated by middle-aged men, most of whom looked like they could do with the love of a good woman and a lesson in personal hygiene.

'You're a weirdo, Guymer, and yet here, you look like the sexy modern fella,' said Julie, laughing as they walked in. 'Eee god, look at him.'

She nodded toward a man with lank greasy long hair which had left an oily residue on the back of a green army jacket.

'It smells funny in here,' she said, looking around the room, which had long tables around its perimeter, all covered in boxes of vinyl records.

'Yeah, it's always like that. A sort of sour waxy smell. These kind of blokes seem to exude it. It's some sort of collector's pheromone.'

'Well I'm going to leave you to hang out with the whiffy men for an hour or two. I'm going to meet Diane for a coffee.'

'OK, Jules.' She patted him on the chest with the flat of her hand and pecked him on the lips. As Nick watched her walk away, a voice spoke to him.

'Your missus is gorgeous, if you don't mind me saying so.'

It was one of the dealers, a rather sleazy man he recognised and half knew from going to fairs all across the region for so long. He was in his late 60s, but had a rather modish haircut and wore tight jeans. Jeff had told Nick the man was a bit of a perv, always leching after women.

He was just about to say something when he was surprised to see Jeff walk into the room, so made his excuses and went over to meet him.

'Hey, big man. I wasn't expecting to see you here. I thought you were too busy.'

'Ah, there you are. I farmed Argie out to Mandy for the morning. Thought I'd better come up just in case there's anything decent. Seen anything good?'

'I've just arrived. You've just missed Jules, she's gone for coffee. I'm glad you're here, actually. I need to pick your conspiracy theorist's brain.'

'Right, well give us an hour to get through everything and then I'm all yours. Well not all of me, obviously. Nothing below the waist and not me nipples either. But apart from that...' he flapped his long hair up and down like a large pair of grey ears.

When you had as big a record collection as Nick, it was harder to find items you wanted but didn't have. So he was glad to pick up a copy of the Peanut Butter Conspiracy's final album, *For Children of All Ages*, and to find a UK copy of Ten Years After's debut album, which he only had as an American release. There were a few other items he'd have liked but couldn't afford.

A man in his 50s, who'd just turned up to sell his collection of records, put the boxes onto a table. When a member of the public did this, he was descended on by the dealers who, like vinyl locusts, swarmed over the fresh meat and harvested all the best records. Jeff was at the front and soon emerged with a huge armful.

'Here, hang on to those, I've got to dive back in and pick up some cheapies.'

Twenty minutes later he returned with several carrier bags full of records.

'That was successful crate digging,' said Nick.

'Yeah, much better than usual. I spent nearly a grand but have probably got about £6,000 worth of records, so it's a decent haul. I'm parked up on a meter. Will you give us a hand to take them back to the van?'

They walked out into the Saturday morning sunshine which had burnt off the early mist.

'So what did you do last night?' said Jeff, unlocking the van's back door.

'Had fish and chips and vodka.'

'Ah, a classic triplet.'

'Then back to the hotel for some adult fun, involving a trouser press.'

Jeff put the bags into a couple of boxes then put his fingers in his ears. 'La la la. Don't want to hear, don't want to hear. You can't make me listen.'

Nick laughed.

'So what's with the conspiracy theory?' said Jeff, locking the van up while Nick texted Julie to tell her they'd be in Starbucks.

'Ah, well, there's a chance, an outside chance, admittedly, that Danny Ross isn't dead and wasn't murdered.'

Jeff stood and looked at him like he was stupid. 'That's absolutely, bloody, and a second bloody...and a third bloody, ridiculous. Even at my most wacko, I'd not have come up with that one. Err...let's think...does it involve crash test dummies and dead pigs?'

'What?'

'Crash test dummies and dead pigs - that's your conspiracy theorist's standard way to explain why some terrible terrorist incident which kills a lot of people hasn't really happened at all and it's all a false flag event staged by the government to keep the people scared and pliable. Anything which contradicts this is merely black propaganda that only a fool would believe, anything that supports it is always 100 per cent true.'

'That's the beauty of a good conspiracy theory; even the evidence proving it's wrong is proof that it's right.'

'Exactly. Some of the nuttier people don't even realise that, either. All they see is a perfect circle of logic.'

Nick pushed open the door to the Starbucks.

'So how is your dead man really alive?' said Jeff. 'And who was the corpse? That's where the crash test dummies and dead pigs come in.'

Nick explained. Jeff blew out disbelieving air as he did so.

'See, your trouble there is that Ricky and his mate have nothing to do but drink all day and think up mad stuff.'

'I know. But, Ricky said his mate recognised him from back home, after Kev texted him. Something is odd about the whole thing. Tracy said Vokes being arrested for murder was "a load of old rubbish" and that Vokes "didn't kill Danny" and the Blobby bloke had his story about not telling anyone who the real murderer was. We've got corrupt copper Harry Small mixed up with Berryman, who Kev Wells thinks knows who the killer is, but has been bought off. And there still wasn't any hard evidence that Vokes had murdered anyone. The camera that could have recorded it in Nolan House was conveniently missing at the time. All they had was the bleached knife and the bloody sweatshirt and the fact Vokes couldn't come up with an alibi, almost certainly because someone took the CCTV evidence of where he really was and binned it.'

'Just enough evidence to get a jury to convict. Enough to suggest his guilt, but not actual proof of it. Yeah, I see what you mean,' Jeff stroked his long beard. 'That's quite clever, actually.'

Nick bought them both black coffee.

'You know, setting up a scenario like this wouldn't be that hard for the police to do,' said Jeff, flicking his hair over his shoulders, so it fell down the back of his denim shirt. 'Let's ignore why they might want to, for now. Say they want Ross to appear dead. So they photograph him apparently stabbed in the doorway, blood everywhere.'

'They didn't do that. There was no photo of the body in the doorway. Only a photo showing an outline of where he'd fallen and the bloodstains he'd left. There were photos of the stab wounds, but those could have been anyone, I suppose. There was a body, though, because the cabbie found it and began to call 999 just as a police car arrived. The ambulance took it to the hospital morgue.'

Jeff narrowed his eyes and raised an index finger. 'That's the bit I don't like. That, and no photo of the body, is your proof of a conspiracy. You're not telling me that a police car just happened to be going up a dead-end street right after a murder was committed. If you ask me, they knew something had happened, somehow. And if their evidence is fake, then everything else has to be as well. One non-fake element in the chain would reveal the con.'

'So even the pathologist was fake? That's crazy. She was a real pathologist. They gave out her credentials in court. She wasn't an actress.'

'OK, she's a real pathologist but is working to an agenda, for reasons as yet unknown. Everyone in the whole thing is playing to an agreed story, up to and including the barristers. It won't work otherwise.'

Nick shrugged. 'Well, I wanted your conspiracy brain - and you gave me it - that's a doozy of a conspiracy. I guess it's not totally impossible, but it's not far short and it'd be a massive thing to have to organise and very, very illegal.' He paused. 'What about Davey Foster, the bloke who was let in to get a tracksuit?'

Jeff speculated some more. 'The cops that attended were sloppy because they knew it wasn't a real crime scene, and Foster saw a chance to get Ross's designer tracksuit. He's not implicated in any crime or cover-up. He did what he said he did. But we're still left with one big question: Why go to such lengths?'

'Exactly. Why go to such lengths to get Vokes banged up? He was living a largely illegal life, they could have banged him up for any number of things if they'd wanted to,' said Nick.

'Hmm. Maybe it's an elaborate double bluff. Maybe he's not a scumbag druggie at all.'

'Well, if that was true, he must be some sort of top-notch method actor because there was plenty of CCTV footage shown in court of Vokes and others from the Zet just sitting around town drinking, day after day, until they could hardly stand up on more than a few occasions. The prosecution used the footage to establish Vokes's character. I mean, obviously, at least in theory, everything could be brilliantly faked. The whole thing, from start to finish, for reasons we couldn't even guess at...'

'...but you're right. It seems like a herculean task to set it up and maintain, especially when it involves dopers and wasters like those who live in the Zet. Mandy said it's been notorious for years as a hub for the dissolute and degenerate.' He took a drink of coffee. 'Who actually identified the body?'

'As ever, that was a point of contention. The police who attended said they searched him for ID but found nothing. However, they found a piece of paper in his pocket with a phone number on. A mobile. They called it and it was Danny's father. He went to the morgue and identified his son.'

'Sounds straightforward enough. Seems weird Danny didn't have a phone, though. Everyone has a phone, even if you're from the Zet; you've got to arrange to buy your dog valium somehow.'

'Yeah, but another copper said Kev Berryman told him it was Danny Ross. Berryman denied this in court. But then sort of admitted it when me and Kev stopped him, but he still could've been lying.'

'See, they're not stupid, these people. By saying one thing then another, you undermine faith in anything they say. And that's very much to their advantage.'

'So Mandy didn't know much about Harry Small?'

Jeff shrugged. 'I don't think so. There's not a lot of love lost between some elements of neighbouring forces and quite a lot of competition. There's so much internal politics to the police these days, all related to funding and performance measurements. To be honest it's really boring, so she doesn't go on about it much. Small was pensioned off by Durham police before Christmas.'

'But she was aware of the Zet, thus of Kev Berryman, thus she must have known of his relationship to Harry Small. Also Ruth and Harry Small lived in Stockton all their life, only round the corner from Vokes, in fact. It beggars belief in a town like Stockton, where all the crims know each other and all the police know the crims, that she didn't know what Harry Small was doing with Berryman. She absolutely has to have known something, Jeff. She might not want to say what or why to you, but she must.'

'I know, I know...and I know how it looks, but she said she'd never even met Harry Small. I wouldn't be surprised if she was just keeping schtum, though. Like I said, the cops are like a secret society. They really are. Even family are kept on the outside.' Jeff finished his coffee. 'Look, I know you set out to try and do right by Vokes, but I don't think you can and I don't think that Vokes is even deserving of it. You should just drop it.'

For a moment Nick wondered if that was really Mandy speaking and she'd told Jeff to put him off the whole case. Then again, maybe he was just in paranoid conspiracy overload.

'Yeah, maybe. Though there's the chance of money from the *Mirror* for the story. Ah, here's Jules.'

'Right, I'm getting off home. I don't want to leave Argie too long, he's got a right cold now - your cold, like I told you - and he's not had a bad one before, so I want to keep an eye on him.'

'Hello, big boy,' said Julie, patting Jeff on the back.

'Hello and goodbye, blondie. Have a good day yomping around the Pennines.' Jeff left them.

After a four-hour walk on the moors around Allenheads in a low mist, they ended up back at the hotel, showered and got dressed for a night out.

'You know, all I really want is a big burger and then a skinful,' said Julie, pulling on her old blue jeans and a grey sweatshirt. 'We didn't get a good drink in last night, due to being severely distracted by our mutual lust.'

'Aye, normally it's the drink that makes us randy, so we got it arse over tit.'

'Or arse against door, or indeed, tits over trouser press, as the case may be.' She pulled a faux shocked face and fanned herself with the flat of her right hand.

Nick laughed and shook the machine. It rattled. 'I think you've knackered it, y'know. It's falling apart and the plastic hanger thing is cracked and coming off.'

'Well a girl has to hang onto something tightly while she's getting vigorously serviced from behind, doesn't she?' She said it like it was obvious.

'Pity the door knob wasn't at the right height for you this time.'

She went to the room door and flicked at the old wooden handle.

'And it's a small handle, not a big knob.'

She gave him a shrug and a look which said, 'What's a girl to do with that?'

After eating, they went to a pub. In the middle of evening, Kev Wells emailed Nick a photo that Ricky had sent him from Spain. It purported to be Danny Ross.

It was a man of about the right age. Mid-twenties, wearing a red t-shirt and jeans, drinking a pint of lager in a typical downmarket Spanish bar. He was with two other men and a woman, all the same sort of age.

'Do you recognise any of them?' said Nick. 'Kev says he's not sure who it is. He didn't know Ross, but Ricky's mate was so certain that he went up to him and asked. The bloke denied it but Ricky said he was Northern.'

Julie squinted at the screen. 'He just looks like every other lad of that age. Healthier than you'd imagine a druggie from the Zet might look. A bit thin, maybe.'

'You know, I should show this to Tracy Berryman. See how she reacts. Might do that tomorrow as long you'll come with me. I don't want her thinking I've turned up for sex.'

'OK. If you're sure. I thought you were giving up on this whole Zet thing.'

'I am. This is the last thing, I promise. I'm fed up with thinking about it, to be honest and I've got to put my shoulder into marketing *Kidda* instead of messing around with doped-up losers.'

They got back into Stockton by noon on Sunday. Julie parked the Porsche outside the Zet, got out and looked up at the windows of the flats. Blobby came straight to the glass and stared down at them. Kev Berryman still didn't seem to be back home.

'Danny's old flat is number 6. Top left,' said Nick. 'The bells don't work.'

The communal entrance door once had a Yale lock on it, but it had long since been kicked in, the door frame splintered and never replaced. Inside it smelled of stale smoke and rancid dustbins. The concrete stairs were thick with dust, filth and fag ends. There was graffiti painted on the walls and something plastic had been burnt in one corner and left a big black burn mark half way up a wall. How did people live like this?

On the first floor was a pile of what looked like dog shit, but could have been of human origin.

'This is disgusting,' said Julie, her hand over her nose and mouth. 'It shouldn't be allowed. How can you bring up a child here? This is so wrong.'

They got to the second floor. Flat 6 was on their left. The dirty, cheap, plywood door was covered in black marker pen tags and scrawls, along with the obligatory cock and balls. The bell didn't work, so he knocked on the door.

'It's already open,' said Julie, as it swung ajar a little with the force of his knock.

'Tracy! It's Nick Guymer and Julie Wells,' called out Nick, pushing the door open further. He called her name again. But there was no reply.

'She must be out,' said Julie. 'God, look at the state of the place.'

The door opened onto a hallway off which was the living room on the left, kitchen straight on and bedroom to the right. It was littered with junk, old newspapers, crisp packets, beer cans and assorted crap. The cheap green nylon carpet was pitted with fag burns and dark stains which could have been made by anything up to and including blood. Food was trodden in, some of it had gone mouldy. The place stank of stale cannabis smoke, cigarettes and decomposition.

'Tracy! Are you in?' She obviously wasn't.

'You know what? We should check that she's not left the bairn on its own. She's probably gone out to score,' said Julie.

'Yeah, good idea.'

He walked into the living room and looked around. The sofa was a 1970s thing made out of torn olive green vinyl and burgundy nylon cushions. An old rusty hubcap was upturned on a wooden coffee table and was full of fag ends, roaches from joints and ash. Like everything else it was filthy. Two corners of the room were black with mould from damp. The whole place smelled of decay.

'This place just isn't habitable,' said Julie. 'I've never seen anything like it in my life. I'm reporting it to social services on Monday morning. There's no way a child should be in an environment like this for any length of time, let alone live in it.'

Nick went into the small kitchen. The small sink was full of dirty plates and cups.

'No kid in here,' he said and then pushed open the bedroom door and took a quick look.

The ragged curtains were drawn, so it was quite dark. No-one there. He turned away and faced Julie, but as he did, what he'd actually seen registered in his synapses. It was so unbelievable, it was as though his mind refused to understand it for a few seconds.

'Tracy!' he yelled, flinging the door open.

She was naked and lying on her back, across the bed, hanging over the far side. Her hip bones protruded through the pale, ghostly flesh.

Julie followed and let out a small yelp of shock.

Nick ran around the single bed.

'Oh, my god.' A surge of fear and disgust rose in his gullet.

Her throat had been cut almost from ear to ear. A large pool of congealed blood had poured from the gaping wound, all around her neck and the sides of her face. Naked and lifeless, she lay there, butchered like a farm animal.

'Don't touch anything. Call the police,' said Julie. 'Let's get out of here. The child's not here.'

They went outside, closed the door and stood looking at each other in shock. Words didn't seem appropriate. Nick felt numb and ice cold.

'Come on, I'll ring the police from outside.'

They negotiated their way past all the filth and litter and shit. Once outside Julie pulled on his arm. 'Call Mandy first. It's Sunday, she'll be off duty, but she'd want to know first. Let her take control.'

He called her number and she answered quickly.

'Eh up, Nick. How's thee?'

'Mandy, I'm outside the Zetland flats and in Flat 6 is Tracy Berryman. She's had her throat cut and Katie, her one-year-old, is gone.'

Mandy was as world weary as anyone alive. You could tell her literally anything, no matter how vile or weird, and she wouldn't be shocked. As Nick spoke she made little deep grunts.

'Is that right? A bloody punter has probably done it. Right, stay there, I'll be down asap.'

As she spoke Blobby came to the window again, but no-one else seemed to be around. Nick gestured to him to come down.

'Christ, that's just brutal in there,' said Julie. 'The poor, poor girl. Just the most dreadful thing I think I've ever seen in my whole sodding life.'

Nick tried to not to let the facts engage with his emotions. There didn't seem much point. It wouldn't achieve anything to get upset.

'Where's her kid, though? She was only a year old. Not even walking. Has the killer taken her?'

Blobby emerged onto the pavement, hitching up a grubby pair of grey trackie bottoms, his fat belly protruding out from under a stained polo shirt. He stank of booze so strongly that it was almost overpowering, especially when mixed in with acrid, cumin-stinking sweat.

'Why are you 'ere?' he said, indignant and obviously very drunk.

'We came to see Tracy,' said Julie.

'Oh, aye? That dirty little scrubber.' He slurred his words.

'Have you seen her today?' said Nick.

'I dunno. I don't think so. She'll have gone to get heroin if she's not in.

Dirty fucking junkie.'

'No, she's in. The problem is, she's not alive,' said Nick.

'What? Has she carked it?' He was neither surprised nor sympathetic, but merely shrugged, an ugly look in his eyes. 'Well - junkie y'see - what do youse expect, like? That's how they all end up. It's no loss.' He said it as though he wasn't an obese alcoholic and didn't use drugs himself. His lack of respect or empathy towards his fellow degenerates had been noticeable in court.

'No. She's actually been viciously murdered,' said Julie. 'So shut your mouth and pay her some respect, mate!'

Blobby staggered a little to one side. 'Eh? Murdered? Oh, fuck.' A look of cold fear crashed across his fat pink head. 'She's told you about Danny, hasn't she? That's why she's been killed. You fucking crazy bastard, this is down to you!' He staggered again, as though the ground was undulating under his feet.

'Calm down and shut up for moment,' said Julie, scowling.

'Eh? Calm down? Who the fuck are you to tell us that? Fuck off, you stuck-up bitch.'

Julie slapped him hard on the left cheek with a powerful right hand, making his cheeks and neck judder like jelly being turned out of a mold.

'Do not speak to me like that! Shut your filthy mouth, you stinking drunk! Do not open your mouth, do not say anything else or I'll be the one to hurt you, right?' she yelled in his face, furious and indignant. 'Now, stand there and wait for the police to come.' She pointed to the door. Blobby took a step back, for a moment it looked like he was going to lash out at her, but seemed to decide better of it, and made grumbling noises but did as he was told. He was in no fit state to even walk away. In fact, standing up seemed to be a bit of a problem, he was so full of drink. One push and he'd have fallen over.

A car screeched around the bend on Bishopton Lane and headed towards them. It was Mandy in her Renault hatchback. She emerged from it, brown hair unruly, her face flushed pink. She was wearing a large pair of jeans and what looked like one of Jeff's denim shirts.

'Right, you can go back in your flat, Blobby. I'll get you when I need you. Don't give me any grief and don't go anywhere or I'll nick you. Who else is in the Zet?'

'I don't bloody know. No-one, I don't reckon. It's been quiet,' said the drunk, his eyes closing.

'Bloody hell, You're pissed as fart, Blobby, and it's not even one o'clock. Where's Kev Berryman?' She peered into Berryman's window.

'Not seen him since that vicar were slashed. Good riddance.'

'Right. Get inside.' She pointed to his flat, like he was a small boy.

Mandy had innate authority. She was just very good at telling people what to do and not allowing them a choice in the matter. Blobby did as he was told and was surely due to become unconscious very soon.

Approaching sirens blared out.

'Right. Quick, before my mob and the ambulance arrive. Tell me where she is, what's happened and why you were even here.'

It didn't take long to do that. She just stared unblinking at Nick as he explained, then she turned and went inside to take a look for herself, coming back within a minute.

'Well, it's a sodding horrible murder that, a right bloody vicious sod has done that. The place is a fucking disgrace. Fuck me. I'm going to get this place closed down. Fuck me...it's worse than I thought.' She shook her head in disgust, shock and anger.

'Her little girl has disappeared, Mandy,' said Julie.

'Killer must've taken her,' she said, turning her head to see the approaching police cars.

Nick found the photo Kev had sent him and showed Mandy the phone.

'This was taken yesterday afternoon in Benidorm. Is it Danny Ross?'

Mandy glanced at it and looked back at him, and glanced at it again. Quite visibly, the colour drained from her pink face.

'Yes. Yes, it sodding well is.' She threw her head back in surprise. 'What in god's name has been going on here, eh?' She rolled her eyes in anger as she asked the rhetorical question.

Two officers came towards her as four more cars pulled up in a screech of tyres. Mandy gestured for the crowd of police to gather around. She addressed them the way a major in an army might address their troops.

'Right. Listen up. We've got a really nasty murder. A throat cutting. Ear to ear. You all know her, it's Tracy Berryman. She's in Flat 6, in the bedroom, naked. She's cold so it happened a few hours ago. Her one-year-old girl, Katie, is missing. First things first, let's get the crime scene sealed off. Rob, Harry, get up there and do it. Watch the pile of shit on the stairs, I want SOCO to get me DNA off that, in case it's human.'

The two men, armed with reels of yellow-and-black tape, went into the Zetland flats.

'Now, the early number-one suspect, in my view, is the little girl's father, Danny Ross.'

'Ross is dead, boss,' said one of the officers, flatly.

She held Nick's phone towards them. 'This was supposedly taken yesterday in Benidorm. It's Danny. Now, it might be a hoax or a mistake, but if he's here, if he's come back today for his kid and he's murdered Trace, I want him nicked, even if he's a bloody zombie, back from the sodding dead.'

'But he really was murdered,' said a female PC. 'He were found dead in that doorway, weren't he?'

'I know that Janey, thank you. Let's not worry about that now. Weird shit happens, we all know that. Now, second, we had that slashing here a few days ago of Don Preston, as you'll recall. We collared Steve Hunter for it. He's a little scrote of a drug dealer, but he's not been violent like that before, and in the brief moments of lucidity he's had since, it seems he was told someone was after him and was going to kill him. Maybe he was scared of the perp what's done for Tracy.'

'He was scared of Kev Berryman, if you ask me,' said Nick. 'He and Don were dressed very similar that day, at least to someone who was stoned.'

'Right. So let's pull Berry in. I don't care what you pull him in for, just find 'im and pull 'im in. I want to kneel on his throat until he coughs.'

'He said he was going to stay with his brother-in-law somewhere up Durham Road,' said Nick. 'But I don't think he's been back here since that day.'

Mandy dismissed this with a shake of her head and a sneer. 'Nah, 'e's not. He were lying if he told you that. Doesn't have anyone he knows living up there. Right, you two can go home. No need for you to wade through the muck and nettles with me. I'll come round to yours later. Paul and Roger, get in there and drag out anyone who is alive. I don't care what state they're in. Start taking statements. Blobby looks barely compos mentis, he says it's been quiet so I'm guessing everyone is doped up to the eyeballs.'

Nick interrupted her.

'Before you speak to him, you should know that a couple of days ago, I met up with Tracy and afterwards he collared me in the street and wanted to know what she'd told me - which was nothing - but he was scared she'd told me who really killed Daniel Ross. He said that they would all be killed if any of them revealed that fact. He said they all knew who'd really done it, but no-one could say, under pain of death, and if I found out, it would mean they'd die. I wasn't sure if he was bullshitting me, or it was true. He seemed to believe it, but you never know with that lot.'

Mandy just nodded. 'Blobby is a pissed nutter. I mean, he's some shade of insane. He's made shite up all his life. But you heard that, didn't you, Paul and Roger? So you know what to do. Get it out of him what this is all about, by any means you've got to use. Right? But don't 'urt 'im where it'll show. I'm not having this shit going on any longer on my watch. If he's just off on one, nick him for wasting police time and for 'avin a head like a cock. Do 'im first 'cos he'll be passed out soon enough.'

She was bitter, fierce and angry. The two officers, both big, thick-set Northerners with forearms like a pit pony's leg, just nodded. This was Mandy Beale in full flow. Aggressive, hard-faced, dictatorial and the absolute boss of a situation. There was never humming or haa-ing about her. No stumbling over words or pauses for thought. She took control of events by the scruff of the neck, not least because she took any major crime like this as a personal insult and she would have her revenge on the perp, whatever it took. Somehow, the fact that she gave licence to her officers to maybe bend or even break a few laws of procedure in order to get a swift result was actually comforting. Sometimes you had to fight evil with a bit of your own evil. She knew that and wasn't afraid of it in the slightest.

She turned to Nick and held him by the arm just as they were walking off.

'Do me a favour, will you? When you get home, write up everything you can remember about the trial and anything said to you about it since.'

'I've already made notes.'

'Good lad.' She hit him on the back, quite hard. 'I'll see you later, eh?'

'I can't get the image out of my mind of that girl just lying there, cut open like so much human meat,' said Julie, filling the kettle as they got home. 'We've had service users at TW murdered, but seeing it really brings it home to you what it means. How can anyone do something like that?'

'The human race has a long reputation for acts of barbaric brutality. If you can think it up, it'll have been done, no matter how sick or violent. It's something our species has specialised in since we got on our hind legs. Any knowledge of history shows you the depths of depravity humans can sink to. So, in a way, it just doesn't surprise me.'

'I just hope it was quick, and she didn't suffer.'

'She'd been suffering for years, Jules. She was miserable to her core. Her life was completely shit; a living death. I think she even expected to die and die soon, one way or another.'

'Well it's disgusting from top to bottom; her life, that flat, the Zet, the people in there, the murder. Disgusting. Is it really possible that what that vile creature Blobby said was true about them being murdered?'

'I don't see how. He's got a notion in his head and has convinced himself it's true, that's all. In court he was like that. He went off on these long rambling stories, which were mostly made up or elaborations on a basic truth. I thought at the time he might have the first stages of Alzheimer's. If it was true, why didn't whoever was threatening them just simply kill them anyway? It'd be much safer. No chance of any information leaking out, then. And let's face it, everyone who lives or stays there, would have been, at some point, out of their mind on drugs or drink and so totally defenceless. The place is insecure, you can pretty much walk into any flat at any time. So why wait until Tracy might have told someone the truth? Makes no sense. If they're a ruthless murderer already, a few more bodies is no extra burden on their conscience.'

'Yeah, you're right.'

They hugged for a moment to comfort each other.

'If Danny Ross *is* alive, there has been a massive conspiracy. You know what it feels like? It feels like his murder was just the tip of a very big iceberg and that there's something huge underneath it,' said Nick, pouring them some Sencha green tea.

'But it's not like any of those people in the Zet are important in any way.'

'No. I just can't work out what has really happened, let alone why. I even had a stupid thought that if Danny isn't dead, maybe Tracy isn't dead either.'

Julie looked at him incredulously.

'But she was dead. She had bled everywhere. We both saw it.'

'I know. But I saw Danny's wounds in the photos in court, and it seems like he's alive, at least according to Mandy. Maybe her death was faked.'

'No, it wasn't fake. It just wasn't. That's ridiculous. She wasn't just lying there on the off chance we or Mandy or someone else might come along and think she'd been killed, not least because the paramedics will have gone there, looked at her and found she was alive.'

'I know it's insane, but who's to say she won't turn up in Benidorm with Danny, the supposed father of her daughter? I mean, why would someone murder Tracy?'

That annoyed Julie. She snapped at him.

'Don't be naive! Men have been killing prostitutes since the dawn of time. In case you think otherwise, we've had two service users murdered in this year alone. Both drug addicts and both sold themselves to pay for their habit. Sex workers are very, very vulnerable.'

He sat drinking tea. As he did so, his phone buzzed. It was a text from Helen Preston.

'I thought you'd like to know Don is much better today. He's sitting up and chatting. I think it's because they've topped his blood up.'

Nick read it out. 'That's great news. Shall we pay him a short visit this afternoon?'

'Well, he's your pal, isn't he? I don't really know him. You go, but give him my love.'

Don was sitting up in bed drinking tea when Nick walked in. He looked like his old self, ruddy of cheek and bright eyed.

'Now then, Holy Man, you're back with us, I see.'

'Hello, you. I'm feeling much better, Nick. Thanks for coming to see me.'

'No problem. They initially told me you'd died, you know. They got the paperwork wrong.'

'Yes, Helen said. But as you can see, I am resurrected! Roll away the stone, sha-la-la-la push push, as Mott the Hoople once sang.'

Nick laughed and sat down beside the bed. 'Man, it's good to hear you in good form. You gave me a helluva shock.'

'I owe you my life, Nick.'

'No, you don't.'

'Well, I beg to differ. I've been told that it was your compressing of the wound that saved my life. Without it I'd have suffered even greater blood loss, followed by deprivation of oxygen to my brain. At best, if I'd survived at all, I'd have been brain damaged. So God bless you and your easily ripped t-shirt.'

'Well I couldn't have blood spurting everywhere and I knew what to do because a similar thing once happened to Jules.'

'It was very impressive. I wish I could have spent a little time appreciating it, but sadly I was a bit woozy.'

Nick looked at the dressing on the side of Don's neck.

'How big a wound is it?' he said.

'You wouldn't believe how small it is for the damage it did. When the nurse dressed it this morning I insisted on taking a look. It's an inch-long slash but it dug right into my jugular vein. So it's only got about 10 stitches in. They say it'll heal quickly enough. I got lucky, thank the Lord.'

'No, you were unlucky to be taken there by me. I'm really sorry, Don. I didn't think anything like that would happen.'

'We walk in the valley of the shadow of death every day. Don't fret yourself about it. You were trying to be a good man and help someone. There's no need to apologise.'

Don reached out his hand to Nick with a smile on his lips. Nick leaned over and gripped his damp, soft hand.

'Everyone needs someone to help them sometimes, I know that better than most people,' said Nick. 'We're all in this together and we can't survive it on our own. That much I have learned.'

'Well, yes, and I got lucky to have a man who was as quick thinking as you.'

'Aye, but I was hanging around for ages afterwards, half naked. Very embarrassing. One of the police even thought I was a nutter out of the Zet who walked around without his shirt on.' He laughed a bit awkwardly. 'Have they told you much about Steve Hunter?'

'The man arrested? Not much. An officer came and took a statement from me but I had almost literally nothing to say. I was standing there, a lad came out of the flats, took one look at me and lashed out with a small knife. That's all there was to say.'

'We couldn't believe it. It took a couple of seconds for it to register in mine and Kev's brains, it was so shocking.'

'The odd thing was I knew exactly what had happened and just after he caught me, but before it had begun to really hurt, I thought to myself, why did he do that?'

'Was there nothing else you remember? Nothing he said or did?'

'He never said anything. Did he live there?'

'It seems like he was one of many who dossed there from time to time, but he is also a small-time drug dealer. Is there anything you can remember from the moment you were attacked?'

'All I recall is facing the blue communal door with the bells on the right.' Don closed his eyes to better remember. 'He opened that door, looked directly at me and lunged out immediately.'

'Was anyone else watching from the flat window?'

'I didn't see anyone.'

'Any other details you might have observed?'

Don closed his eyes again.

'That's about it, I'm afraid.'

'OK. So when are they letting you go home?'

'A day or so, I think.'

'Cool, well, if anything else occurs to you, let me know.'

'Are you still trying to prove Glenn Vokes's innocence?'

'I don't know. Not really. It's got so weird, Don. A lot has happened, but I won't trouble you with it. I can't work any of it out, really.'

'Well, God be with you.'

It was 8.30pm before Mandy Beale arrived at their house. Nick gave her photocopies of his notes from the trial. As she'd finished for the day, they went over the road to the Highland Lad because Mandy liked to drink lager and Nick and Julie didn't have any in the house. They sat outside in the warm evening air.

'Cheers, Jules,' said Mandy, as she placed a pint of Stella in front of her. She necked nearly half of it in a few swallows and let out a groan. 'Christ, I needed that.' She shook her head. 'That place, the Zet, it's bloody evil, I swear it is. It's like a horror house in a movie. Evil soaked in the bricks.'

'I don't know how it's even legal,' said Julie, sipping at a glass of white wine. 'It's an insanitary slum.'

Mandy nodded. 'It's a breeding ground for scumbags as well. If we tore the place down, we'd be able to disperse them a bit.'

'Wouldn't that make your life more difficult? At least you know where they all are,' said Nick.

'Yeah, but trouble makes trouble. If you can put them into nicer areas they tend get better, rather than shit the place up. Not guaranteed, mind. There's always them what just can't change their ways.' She took another drink.

'How many did you find in there?' said Julie.

Mandy looked at her. 'You know how many? Ten.'

'Ten?! How?'

'There was seven in Flat 5, opposite where Tracy was. All of them passed out asleep on skunk, valium and god knows what else. Seven! None of them official tenants. I thought they were all dead when I first saw them. Then there was Blobby passed out pissed sitting in his chair, surrounded by empty cans of Carlsberg Special, and Sid Smith, who supposedly lives in 5, but was in number 4 watching TV while smoking dope with a comatose woman who he said was a "guest".' She put the word in inverted commas with her fingers. 'Or a prostitute, as we'd normally call her.'

'Let me guess. No-one heard anything or saw anything.'

'Of course not,' said Mandy, rubbing at her forehead. 'Though in fairness, most of them were unconscious. Only Smithy was awake and he was stoned out of his bloody box, just staring without blinking.'

Nick ran his hands through his hair. 'Mandy, what the hell is going on there? How is Danny Ross alive?' said Nick. 'I thought the case against Glenn Vokes was unproven...'

'...aye, Jeff said you were the one gainsayer...'

'...because there was no hard evidence he'd killed Danny. And now it seems like he wasn't even killed at all. How can that be? How?'

She didn't speak for a bit, then took another big drink, smacking her lips as she drained the pint.

'Give me a look at that photo on your phone,' she said.

Nick handed it to her. She stared at it. 'You know what? 'E looks exactly like he did the day 'e supposedly died. I saw him earlier that week.'

'So it is definitely him?' said Julie.

'Mandy, I'm just going to say this straight out...' said Nick.

But she interrupted him. '...have the police done some sort of cover-up, or summat like that?'

'Exactly, yeah.'

She leaned back, arms folded across her large bosom. 'I'll be ordering an independent review of how we handled the case, for a start.'

'Do you remember the case?'

She nodded. 'We don't get so many murders that they all blur into one. I didn't work on it myself, George Dunne was the SIO.'

'Yeah, I remember him from the trial,' said Nick, also recalling that Dunne was one of those coppers who speaks in a strange jargon - saying 'proceeding' instead of 'going' and generally conducting himself in a stiff, awkward manner that had put Nick in mind of himself trying not to say the wrong thing in polite, posh company; self-conscious and unnatural.

'It seemed to be an open-and-shut case, as I recall. They found the knife in Vokes's flat along with a bloody top and he had no alibi. Given those facts there was no way the CPS wouldn't agree to it going to trial. I 'ear what you say about hard evidence, but that's often the case in court. Most crimes of violence only get to court if there is some doubt about the evidence, some wriggle room a lawyer can use to plant doubt in the jury's mind.' She went on. 'Obviously, if we've got 'im on tape doing the deed, it's never even going to end up in court, is it? He'll just plead guilty."

'Were there no other suspects?' said Julie.

Mandy shook her head in silence.

'No doubts about anything?' said Nick, getting up to go to the bar.

'Nothing at all. George says Vokes always maintained his innocence, but had several different stories from his arrest to the courtroom, which is typical for that lot 'cos their brains are fried.'

'Have you seen someone murdered like Tracy was before?' asked Julie.

'Throat cut?' She nodded. 'More than once. I've had a couple of beheadings to deal with before now an' all. Messy.'

'How do you deal with it?' said Julie. 'It's so horrible.'

'I deal with it by nicking the bastard what's done it. It's happened. There's no point in getting your knickers in twist about a bit of blood. What matters is making sure there's no more blood. My guess is that some psychotic punter has done it, which means he's out there somewhere and will, almost certainly, try and do it again. We've got word out to all the streetwalkers on Teesside to watch their backs.'

Nick walked to the bar in deep thought. If Mandy was lying to them, in the full knowledge that the police were in some measure corrupt or incompetent, it wasn't obvious to him. She seemed as confused as he was.

'Hello, Nick,' said Jason, a regular barman in the pub.

'Hey, Jase. Pint of Stella, a large white wine and double vodka and tonic, please.'

'No worries.' He started to pour the lager.

'So what've you been up to, then?'

'Me? I was in court for a couple of weeks, Jase.'

The barman laughed. 'I knew they'd nick you for something eventually. Was it the old trouble bothering goats?' He put the pint on the bar and turned to the fridge to get the wine out.

'Yeah, I'm mad for the goats. Only the nannies, though. I'm not a pervert.'

Jason laughed as he poured Chardonnay into a glass.

'So what was it all about?'

'I was on a murder trial jury.'

'Wow. I'd love to do that.'

'It was interesting, like.'

'Where was that, then?'

'Teesside Crown Court in the Boro.'

The barman put the wine on the bar, turned and put a glass under the vodka optic.

'Oh, aye, I read about that in the *Gazette*. The big murder trial. What was his name now...err...Glenn Vokes...he got put away for 25 years, didn't he?'

'That's right.'

'The boy he killed used to drink in here, y'know.'

'Danny Ross?'

He put the vodka on the bar, opened a bottle of tonic and poured it into the glass along with ice.

'Aye, Danny Ross, that's it. What a cocky sod he was. Used to come in here with a wad of notes so thick you could choke a donkey with it.'

Nick took a sip of his drink and passed him a £20 note.

'Really? Are you sure? He lived in the Zetland flats, which are basically a filthy slum. You wouldn't live there if you had any money.'

'Nah, he didn't, man. Or he might have done later, but when he drank in here, he didn't.' Jason shook his head. 'I talked to him a few of times. His parents had a massive property portfolio - they own loads of those posh new houses on the Wynyard estate. That was where he lived at the time, in one of their houses.'

'But that's some of the most expensive housing on Teesside.'

'Aye. Soulless bloody place, if you ask me. Though they reckon there's a lot of swingers' parties there, for some reason.'

'Really, I thought they'd all be too worried it lowered their house prices, Jase.'

The bar man handed him his change and laughed. 'Might raise the prices! So what was he doing at those flats?'

'He was a druggie, man. A smack head. He spent time there, holed up, getting wrecked.'

'Yeah? Bloody hell. I'd not seen him in here for a long while.'

'And he had a kid with a prostitute who stayed there with him

144

sometimes.'

Jason frowned and leaned on the bar.

'Oh, aye? Was she a nice looker? A really pretty lass, like? Smallish, straight brown hair, nice little body, like?'

'Why do you ask?'

'Well he used to come in here with a girl on his arm. I used to think she was a really sexy lass. Just my type, y'see.'

'Was she called Tracy Berryman?'

'Trace - that's what he called her, yeah. She was the prozzie? Bloody hell, Nick man, you'd not have known, she was class, her like. If I'd known, I might have saved up me money!'

'It'd only have cost 20 quid recently. Maybe she wasn't a hooker back then, but that's drugs for you, you've got to get money for your hit somehow. When was he in here with her?'

He stood and thought. 'Last time I saw them must have been a year ago. Back end of the summer, maybe. He was a regular until then.' He stopped and thought again. 'You know his dad is Ronald Ross, right?'

Nick shook his head. 'Who's he?'

'He used to be the Tory MP for Yarm, didn't he? He's in the House of Lords now. He was in the government in the 80s.'

Nick was shocked. Why hadn't this been mentioned in court?

'So Danny's father has got money and power?'

'Yeah, totally. Probably why Danny was such an obnoxious twat. Often goes like that. They think they've earned it, but they're just poncing off their parents, really.'

Nick scooped up the drinks and carried them back to Julie and Mandy.

'Cheers, Nick,' said Mandy as he put her pint down.

'What more do you know about Danny Ross, Mandy?'

'Off the top of my head, nowt much.'

'I've just discovered that he's got rich, powerful parents. That a year ago he lived in a house on the Wynyard estate, drank in here with Tracy, and that his dad was the Tory MP for Yarm and is now in the House of Lords. Did know any of that?'

She didn't flinch. 'Yeah. Of course I knew that. Didn't you, then?'

'No, I didn't. And it wasn't mentioned in court. Nothing of his background was mentioned. His father was only referred to as being the man who identified the body in the morgue and even then, his name wasn't mentioned.'

Mandy looked at him with a stern glare. 'What? It must have been, surely.'

Nick shook his head. 'Nope. Not once. We only learned Danny'd been to college. That's all.'

Mandy tapped the table with her finger. 'Are you sure, though? Maybe you just forgot?'

'He wouldn't forget that,' said Julie. 'He just wouldn't. He's got a great memory for names. It comes from remembering all those bands and discographies over the years.'

Mandy looked into the distance, drinking lager as she did so. Nick raised his eyebrows at Julie. She glanced at Mandy.

'Is this an unusual thing, Mand?' said Julie.

'Yeah. Background is usually mentioned, if only for context. Very odd. Don't like it. Don't like it one bit. Feels dodgy.'

'It was as if it didn't matter. In fact, very little was said about Danny.'

'I'll get onto Dunny about that. What was he playing at, not introducing his background?'

'Maybe they thought a kid who goes off the rails from a good home is an unsympathetic character,' said Nick. 'Maybe the defence feared the jury would think he was a useless posh kid, and by contrast, Vokes was a poor bloke with no privileges in life, and thus not convict him.'

Mandy puffed out her pink cheeks. 'Yeah, that's not the worst idea you've ever had, Nick. He wouldn't be the first kid from a good home to go off the rails, and some do take against them for it.'

'What bothers me is his father sounds like he could be quite a powerful rich man...' Nick stopped mid-sentence, realising he was heading towards saying he'd used his money and power to pervert the course of justice, in collusion with the police.

But Mandy Beale was too experienced and perceptive not to realise that.

'...so between him, Danny and Cleveland police, we faked Danny's murder. Is that what you're saying?'

'No, that's not what he said, Mandy,' said Julie, a little defensively.

'Why not? You bloody should be saying that. That's the way it looks to me. Summat's gone on, it has to have. Summat that I don't know nowt about, and to say I'm pissed off about it would be the sodding understatement of the century.' She scowled into the middle distance again.

'Much was made in court of the fact that not long after the murder, two officers let Davey Foster into the Zet unaccompanied to get a tracksuit of his, that he said was in Danny's flat,' said Nick. 'He had to step over Danny's body - or whoever it actually was - to go in. That was a corruption of the crime scene. Now, I think he was given the knife and sweatshirt with blood on it by Kev Berryman and he went straight to Glenn's flat...'

'...and planted it. Aye, I see where you're going. That was a bad bit of coppering.' She scratched her cheek and looked out at Norton High Street as cars passed. 'Half the grunt labour doesn't even know the law. If you don't tell 'em in block caps five miles high, they'd walk over valuable evidence all the time.' She spoke, half under her breath.

'Yeah, but they didn't even admit their mistake in court. They said they didn't know it was Ross and none of the flats had yet been declared a crime scene, so they hadn't done anything wrong. That was true, they hadn't been...'

'...but you don't need to be a genius to work out that you shouldn't be letting anyone step over a body. I know. The thing is kids, we're not perfect by a long way, but it's usually not corruption, just crapulence.'

'Well, it still all comes down to evidence, at the end of the day,' said Julie. 'And by the looks of it, Vokes has been jailed for killing a man who is still alive. That can't be allowed to stand.'

Mandy finished her pint. 'Well, someone was murdered that day. There's no faking a body from a crime scene, to the morgue, to the funeral parlour. That's just not possible. Even if I wanted to do that, I couldn't. You can't create a fictional murder. It's not a matter of just saying someone is dead. There are a lot of procedures to go through. For it to even have a chance, you'd need a conspiracy between the SIO, his officers, the pathologist, probably the coroner and maybe even the funeral directors. It isn't realistically possible.'

'Jeff says it's all to do with crash test dummies and dead pigs,' said Nick.

'Jeff would.'

'But if those people all did conspire, it would be possible,' said Nick, rubbing the stubble on his chin.

'Yeah, it'd be literally possible to do it, but it would be - or *should* be, anyway - revealed as soon as anyone put a magnifying glass to it.'

Julie spoke up. 'Nick and I talked about this in Durham last weekend. It'd be a great way to hide who you really killed.'

Mandy frowned heavily. 'Go on, Jules,' she said, gesturing for her to

147

expound further. Julie pushed her hair behind her ears, took a drink and told Mandy about their theory.

'You, lady, are a bloody genius,' said Mandy, pointing a thick forefinger at her. 'Do you fancy a change of career? I could use some brains on my team.'

She looked pleased. 'Well, I'll have another glass of chardo, then.'

'My shout. Can you text Jeff and tell him to come and pick me up?' said Mandy.

She went to the bar as Nick tapped out a short text. When she got back with the drinks, Jeff had already replied to say he'd be there in 15 minutes.

'Y'see, I remember one time, many years ago now, we had a body on the Portrack estate. He'd been whacked on the head. We were told he was called Charlie Worth by a couple of locals. We couldn't find any family or next of kin. Nothing on him to identify him. He was cremated as Charlie Worth, only for the real Charlie Worth to come back from working away a few weeks later.'

'So who was the body?' said Julie.

Mandy shrugged. 'Well, proving your idea correct, we never found out and by then he was ashes scattered in Acklam crem gardens. We went back to the two who'd said it was him and all they had to say was "Well, we thought it was him", and I believe they did. They weren't being malicious. There was nothing for them to gain by lying.'

'Yeah, but our case is different because Danny's family are known. They'd have been asked to identify the body and obviously would know it wasn't him.'

Mandy nodded vigorously. 'Exactly. And that's where the con kicks in. We find that phone number on him. It's Danny's dad's mobile. We call him, then go and knock on his door. So sorry your son's snuffed it blah blah blah, take him down to the slab. Can you identify him, please? If he says, yup that's our lad, then it's case closed, isn't it? We never question someone's intent at that point. If they say it's him, then it's him, unless other evidence proves otherwise. Danny Ross hasn't been seen since - until this photo - and it all goes to trial on the basis that it was Danny who was murdered.'

'OK, but that means that his father lied, took someone else's body and had it cremated,' said Julie. 'That is very spooky and weird.'

'It is macabre. And very sodding illegal.' She looked up. 'Aye aye, 'ere's big Jeffrey.'

Jeff had parked up the van down the road.

'Now then. By the sounds of it, you lot have a had a busy day at the coalface of Low Life-on-Tees.' He sat down next to Mandy with a grin and rubbed her back a bit. She grinned back at him. 'I see medicine is being taken for the stresses of the day.'

'How's Argie doing?' Mandy said.

'He's running a temperature. Poor lad's not well. I left him with Maggie next door. He's sleeping. I loaded him on Kalpol.'

'Aw, poor little lad,' said Nick.

'Jules and Nick have come up with a brilliant idea, I'll fill you in later,' said Mandy. She turned back to Nick and Julie. 'My problem with this case is, we can go and speak to Ronald Ross - Danny's mother died a while ago - but unless he fesses up for it, I'll never be able to prove anything, will I? All I'll succeed in doing is making him aware that I'm onto him. So first things first, we need to establish that it really is Danny in Spain, because if it isn't then this is a whole different ball game. Which is where you two come in, actually, and you, too, Jeff.'

'Me? I never dun nuffink, boss,' said Jeff, hands raised.

She took another big gulp of lager.

'How do you three fancy a trip to Benidorm on Cleveland Police's tab? You might want to take Kev Wells with you an' all.'

'Are we being parachuted behind enemy lines to work for Queen and country?' said Jeff.

'Sort of. It'd be your job to find out if Danny Ross really is Danny Ross, so to speak. If I send my mob out there and he gets wind, he'll just offski and we'll never see him again. Let's make sure it is him, and not an unknown twin, and then we can get him nicked and extradited and kneel on his throat until he coughs.'

'Is it actually illegal to pretend to be dead?' said Nick.

Mandy bulged out her pink cheeks and blew out air. 'Good question. He might not have broke the law actually, but his dad has by falsely identifying him and behind the reason to do that, there must be a cesspool of crime up to and including murder. But I don't want to move on Ross the Elder until I've got a case against him watertight. You don't mess with a rich Lord who will have posh lawyers coming out of his gills until you've got him provably banged to rights. So, are you up for this?'

Nick looked at Julie and Jeff. 'What do you reckon?'

'I could get a couple of days off work - but no more than that at short notice,' said Julie. 'Surely you could go on your own, you don't need the two of us in tow.'

'You need to look like regular tourists. No-one is there on their own, are they? And also, to be fair, as a team you're well balanced,' said Mandy, looking at each of them in turn.

'As a team? What do you mean?' said Jeff.

'I mean you've got brains, brawn and beauty. Perfect. I should put you on the force's undercover team.'

'Is there an undercover team?' asked Jeff.

'Yeah. And on many different levels. There's the undercover we know about, and then there's the undercover we don't know about, unless we have to know about it. Even as Chief of Police you wouldn't believe how much I don't know. There's so much I don't know, that I don't know how much there is that I don't know.'

'Well, to be fair, Mand, you can't know how much you don't know, because you don't know what you don't know. You might not, not know nothing. In other words, you might know everything. Or you might know almost nothing,' said Jeff conspiratorially, right index finger raised.

Mandy made a face and tutted, jutting her thumb in Jeff's direction. 'Thinks 'e's clever, y'know.'

'Well, I'm up for a Spanish jaunt,' said Nick. 'Two days of sunshine is always nice. I'll pack my budgie smugglers.'

Mandy laughed. 'More like cockatoo smugglers in your case, lad.'

'Well, I'm up for it. The Spain thing, I mean, and a cock or two!' said Julie, leaning into Nick.

'Can I park Lord Argie with you in the evenings?' said Jeff. 'Maggie will look after him during the day. She's mad about the boy.'

'Yeah, of course.'

'I'm in, then. Guru can run the shop.'

Mandy nodded. 'Right, let's get you out there on Tuesday then. I'll sort a flight and hotel. You'll have 48 hours to find out if it's our man or not. I can't cough out for longer than that without incurring several shades of brown wrath from the men on high - and I do mean men.'

The four of them high-fived like a basketball team after a score.

CHAPTER 7

'I love being on the public money gravy train,' said Nick, as he put their bags down and pulled back the curtains in their room at a huge budget beachside resort hotel in Benidorm. Outside it was 88 degrees, the sky an azure blue, the sea an intense turquoise. Around a huge central, circular swimming pool were hundred and hundreds of mostly Brits on holiday, almost all of them between 18 and 30 years old, a radioactive shade of pink, with pints and bottles of beer on tables next to rows and rows and rows of loungers, laid out in serried ranks on a huge terrace. The pool itself was standing-room only, with so many people in it that swimming would be impossible. Almost all the women were in bikinis, almost all the men bare-chested and in shorts.

Jeff stood alongside him. 'This is like being at an open-air social club for the working class of the North. Look at all the beer guts getting sunburnt. All the accents I heard on the way in were Geordie, South Yorkshire, Mancunian, Scouse and Scottish. I sort of love it because it's so unpretentious; two weeks of drinking lager and eating chips in the sunshine, but I also sort of bloody hate it and suspect a lot of them are some shade of moron. They go to English pubs and eat in McDonald's and let's be honest, they're hardly a svelte crowd, are they? As an ex-fat man, I feel liberated to call 'em bloaters. Am I being too harsh?'

'You missed out their predilection for shagging anything with a pulse,' said Julie, dressed in baseball boots, white crop top, white linen jeans and baseball cap. 'And some of the bikinis the lasses are wearing barely cover their bits. Dear me, look at her down there.'

She pointed below to a girl, no more than 18, in a bikini that was so small it just looked like a small piece of white paper had stuck to her crotch.

'I'm actually starting to feel prudish,' said Jeff. 'Nudity would offer more modesty than what she's wearing. Gynaecologists dream that. You can't exactly see up the valley, but all the contours are well-defined on the map.'

They all laughed. 'Look at me, I've got a fanny, must be the point she's making, though,' said Julie. 'God, look at those two over there under the palm tree. They're virtually doing it. Oh, god, they should have to test you for chlamydia before you're allowed home from this place, and they should dish out penicillin at the breakfast buffet.'

'I've never been to a place like this. It is quite shocking, actually,' said

Nick, vaguely horrified by the scene before him. 'When I was 20-odd like most of this lot, this was the last place I'd have thought of going. I'd rather have had a week at a Marske B & B.'

'I went to a place like this once in my 20s,' said Julie. God knows why. It was a nightmare. People just jumped up and down in the pool chanting, "You what? You what? You what you what you what?" I never found out why, but it seemed to keep people happy. I had a skimpy bikini on for half a day and was virtually sexually assaulted every 20 minutes by the pool. It was vile. I don't know what I was thinking going to a place like that with three lasses from Middlesbrough.'

'Did they like it?' said Nick.

'Well, they spent seven days on their back, either passed out pissed, or having it off; mostly both. They said it was great, but then people always say that about holidays. I spent most of it reading a book on the beach with my legs crossed.'

Nick turned to look at her. 'Your eyes are the same colour as the sea, Jules.'

'That's because you're a mermaid, isn't it?' said Jeff.

She opened her eyes wide. 'Aye, that's why I smell of fish an' all.'

Nick laughed and sniffed at her.

'Talking of smelling of fish, I hate to break this to you, but the bar that Ricky and his mate took the photo of Danny Ross in is called, somewhat predictably, the Cock and Pussy, and is just over there,' said Jeff, looking at his phone, pointing to a building set on the edge of the complex. 'Its website says it plays, and I quote, "bangin' tunes for bangin' to". That sounds very ominous. No chance of grooving to any Peanut Butter Conspiracy records, I suspect.'

'Oh, my god. That sounds like pure hell,' said Julie. 'It'll be painfully loud, as well. I think I hate any music that the word "bangin'" might be applied to.'

Nick looked at his watch. 'Well, we're going to have to brave it. Kev said he'll be in there in the next hour with Ricky. It's 3.30pm so Ricky will be five pints in and just getting over his hangover.'

Jeff tied his hair back into a ponytail and put on a white beanie hat, on which was embroidered the words 'not from here'. He looked at them with a manic grin.

'Right, just in case our man is there, let's go over our strategy. Obviously, Ross isn't going to give up his identity just like that and he's already been quizzed on it once, so will be uber defensive,' said Nick.

'What we want is his passport. That's our best bet. OK, he might have assumed a new identity, but my guess is he was driven through the channel tunnel to Europe, so he didn't show up on a flight, or on the train, and made his way down here.'

'Daddy Ross is a major dude, he might have paid for a whole new identity,' said Jeff, wafting his garish green, red and yellow Hawaiian shirt.

'Maybe, and if he has, we're knackered,' said Nick. 'There's no way he's going to confess what he's done to a total stranger.'

Julie crossed her arms over her chest and stared at the two of them with arched eyebrows.

'You underestimate the power of a woman. Ever was it thus, boys.'

'Have I accidentally committed a sexist faux pas?' said Jeff, holding up the palms of his hands towards her. 'If so, I apologise and can only blame the patriarchal culture that raised me, the lyrics of David Coverdale, and the fact there's so much quality fanny here.'

She roared with laughter. 'Hey, you leave my beloved Cov out of this. He's not sexist, he just sings about sex - there's a difference.'

'If you say so, but you do know that "Slide It In" was allegedly going to be called "I Won't Come in Your Mouth", don't you?' said Jeff. 'Just sayin', like.'

She wobbled her head in a silly manner. 'Nowt sexist about that. It's just good manners,' she said, flippantly, 'and where would we be as a species without sliding it in? It's worth celebrating. Especially sliding it in "right to the top". Now listen up, a lot of people carry their passport on them because they don't want to risk it getting nicked from the hotel. Back pocket is traditional. If chummy is in there, I'll chat him up a bit, one of youse two comes over and walks into him, spills his pint, and the other lifts the passport in the furore. How's that sound?'

'Like something off the telly and it relies on him having his passport on him. You make that sound so easy, like we're an expert con team out of a movie,' said Nick, already feeling rather out of his depth. 'We're not Ocean's 11.'

'No, we're more the Stockton Baths 3. Hasn't Kev got a fingersmith down here? The place is surely crawling with crims on the lam from Blighty,' said Jeff.

Julie pointed at him and nodded. 'Good point. We'll ask him.' She rubbed her hands together and grinned. 'I'm actually really looking forward to this, for some reason. It's exciting.'

'He might be a no show for the 48 hours we're here for,' said Nick.

'Nah. Blokes are creatures of habit. If he's usually in by 4pm, he'll be in today,' she said, confidently.

'Well, as long as I don't have to end up hitting someone in the face,' said Nick. 'I always seem to have to hit someone in the face.'

Jeff looked at his watch. 'It's a quarter to four. Time to rock 'n' roll. We are allowed to drink on this caper, aren't we?'

'It's not a caper, Jeff,' said Nick. 'This is serious shit and has involved two murders, so far.'

'Take a chill pill, daddio. I do know that. But abstaining from a cold beer will not bring back the dead.'

'Well, I'm up for an ice-cold double voddy and Red Bull,' said Julie, panting, with her tongue hanging out. 'C'mon, we're here for 48 hours, let's get this job done and then get down to the serious business of finding somewhere that plays proper rock music and serves cold drink.'

Even as they approached the bar, garishly covered in neon signs and a huge Union Jack, Nick's heart sank. The noise coming out of it was ridiculous. Some sort of drum and bass abomination was testing the solidity of the walls. A few tables were set on the patio outside so patrons who wanted to could converse without screaming.

'I'm really going to hate this,' he said to Jeff, as Jules walked in front.

'Of course you are. But just think of how much writing you'll get out of it. It's all inspiration, old son.' Jeff put his big hand on Nick's shoulder and squeezed it, affectionately. 'Come on, lad. We've been through worse than this. Remember, we had to sit through Ed Banger and the Nosebleeds at Redcar Coatham Bowl just because we had a brief and ill-advised lust for punk girls. This'll be nowt compared to that noise abomination and I promise not to dance this time.'

Inside, the very molecules of the air seemed to throb with the music being played by a DJ on a raised platform in one corner, peering at a laptop. It was impossible to talk, which was maybe why people went in there. Being freed from the obligation to communicate took the pressure off social situations.

Drinks were served in plastic glasses, and beer bottles were similarly non-glass. There seemed a tacit acceptance that everyone would get shit-faced and end up punching each other.

'This music could actually drive me to violence,' said Nick into Jeff's ear as the big man handed him and Julie a double vodka and Red Bull.

The photo of Danny Ross had been taken pretty much from where they were standing at the side of the bar. He'd been sat at a table under a red neon Budweiser sign, drinking a pint of lager. No-one was there yet. The bar was busy, but far from packed. Nick looked around the dark room but couldn't see the man in the photo.

'Shall I, in the traditional style, go and ask him if he's got any Quo?' shouted Jeff, nodding at the DJ.

'I would kill to hear some Quo, right now,' shouted Julie, sipping at her drink. 'This isn't music, it's just a beat and some ugly noise. I swear it makes you stupid. It destroys your brain! And why has the DJ got a laptop?! That's wrong!'

Talking was too-hard work for the vocal cords, so they stood and drank and waited. And waited. And waited.

And then, just after 4pm, there he was. Short, fair hair, tanned, skinny, wearing a white v-neck t-shirt and blue jeans. For a dead man, he was good looking, with narrow, shapely hips and broad shoulders. And for a junkie, he looked suspiciously healthy. A long, long way from being a wasted Zet loser strung out on heroin. Then again, if they were right, he'd left the Zet eight months ago for Spanish sun, so maybe he'd kicked the habit and got well. He came into the bar with another man of the same sort of age and wandered towards them, digging into his pocket for change.

As he approached, Julie turned around, looked at him and smiled and mouthed 'hello' as the music pounded in their ears.

He did a double take, raised his eyebrows, as though acknowledging her, but walked to the bar and got two bottles of lager.

Nick took a drink and assessed him. Tight jeans, skinny arse, he had something in his right back pocket. Was it his phone? Or was it his passport, or just a piece of paper? It was hard to tell in the half-light of the bar.

Julie leaned into his ear. 'Passport back right pocket.'

'Are you sure?'

'Deffo. Exactly the right size and shape. And he dresses to the right. Most unusual.' She flashed her eyes at him.

Danny Ross got his beer, glanced at Julie again, smiled, and walked away from the bar with his mate, heading towards the table under the neon Budweiser sign. That was obviously their regular table.

Julie stood alongside Nick and spoke into his ear.

'I'm going to go over there and say I think we met before. I'll flirt with him a bit, just to get him off his guard. Obviously, he'll just think I'm a right old slapper, 'cos I'm old enough to be his mother, like. I'm going to use the old passport photo ruse. Get him to show me his if I show him mine. If it doesn't look like that's working, come over and say hello and...we'll...improvise and rob his passport. You two go sit at one of the outside tables where you're out of the way but can still see me.'

Before he could say anything she'd left, walking towards the table with a swing of her hips that she didn't normally deploy, but which seemed to come naturally to her all the same. The tight white lightweight jeans showed off the curve of her hips and firm, round backside.

'Has Jules got a special lever that she pulls to deploy being a sex bomb?' said Jeff. 'I never saw a woman who could just transform herself like that. It's amazing.'

'She's always been very in touch with that side of herself.' Julie reached the table, rested her weight on one hip and opened her arms wide as though to give Danny a hug. Nick and Jeff walked outside and sat at a table near the open door, where they could watch Julie and Danny.

'She's brilliant at this,' said Jeff, watching her chatting with open, touchy body language.

'She says she's often got sex on her mind, one way or another.'

'Like a bloke, then,' said Jeff.

'Don't ever say that to her. You'll get the Hardwick Death Stare. To her it's just all part of being a woman, but a part that has always been frowned on, as though women shouldn't be sexual and certainly shouldn't enjoy the fact.'

'Fair enough. She's right. She usually is.'

They sat silent for a minute. Nick took a big drink, already feeling a little drunk due to having an empty stomach. He spoke again. 'It's not going to kick off with this bloke, is it?' he said, half an eye on Julie, who was still chatting into Danny Ross's ear as the music vibrated.

'He doesn't look the fighty sort to me, nor does his mate. Though by the look in his eye, he thinks he's pulled.'

'Yeah? How do you know that?'

Jeff shrugged. 'Instinct, innit?'

'Not for me it isn't. I could never tell if a lass liked me. I always needed them to virtually sit on my face.'

Jeff laughed. 'Yeah, I had to act as your interpreter, even back at school.'

'That's true. Even Sue Thomas had to ask me if I'd like to see her naked!'

Jeff laughed uproariously. 'God bless Sue. And remember Wendy from Harrogate? There's another woman you went out with who loved the nookie.'

'Oh, god, yeah. I'd forgotten about her. She was weird, though. Wanted to do pervy stuff which I had no interest in.' He shuddered. 'I totally lost interest in her as soon as she suggested all that.'

'Ha ha. You were terrified. I remember you came round my flat with a wild look in your eye.'

'It's so not my thing, all of that. I genuinely don't understand why anyone wants tying up, spanking or being pissed on. All I want is Jules bending over a Corby trouser press.'

Jeff gave him a wide-eyed look, cocked an index finger and said, 'And you claim not to be a pervert!'

They watched as Julie took her passport from the back pocket of her jeans, opened it and pointed to the photo. She seemed to be saying what an embarrassing photo it was. Danny shook his head and seemed to say the word 'beautiful'.

'Aye, aye, he's going for his back pocket,' said Jeff. 'He's putty in her hands. The boy didn't stand a chance.'

He stood up, took out the burgundy booklet and opened it up, turning the photo page towards her. She took it from him and looked at it closely, a hand on his bare arm, then held it up to his face, laughing as she did so. He pulled a face, trying to amuse her. She said something else, he nodded, and then she pointed at Nick and Jeff and came over to them.

'It's Daniel Ross, alright. His passport proves it.'

'Good work, Jules. We thought you were all over him like a rash.'

'Men are so easy to seduce. It's almost pathetic...no actually, not almost, it is pathetic.'

'So who did you say we are?' said Nick.

'Friends of my dad who has a flat out here, that I'm staying in. The question now is, do we just tell Mandy and then back off or do we try to find out what's been going on?'

'You mean, you cop off with him and try to pump him for info,' said Nick.

'Exactly. He thinks he's going to pump me, but I know I'm going to pump him.'

'That's dangerous, Jules. You can't just go off into the Benidorm night with him. He's not going to tell you anything, anyway, is he? Why would he?'

'Why? Because he wants to get it off his chest.'

'You don't know that.'

She spoke quickly and clearly. 'Listen, he's a youngish bloke, only 25. He's not the boorish Teesside piss-artist I thought he might be. He's a bit of a smoothy who fancies himself because he's good looking. He can't know what's happened to Tracy and the fact that whoever killed her has almost certainly taken his little girl. If I can find a way to feed him that info, he might trust me enough to say what's happened and I can also use the fact that he probably thinks he's going to get his end away as a way to persuade him to cough. I'm pretty sure, putting my work head on, that he's not dangerous. Also, I find it hard to believe he was a heroin addict eight months ago; even if he quit the day he left the Zet, he's made a hell of a recovery. There's something not right about all of this and I want to know what it is.'

Jeff looked at Nick, then at Julie. 'You should milk him as much as you can, Jules. In my view, anyway. What do you reckon, Nick?'

It didn't really make any difference what he thought. He knew Julie had already made up her mind. All he wanted to do was make sure she was safe. He reached for her hand.

'Do what you've got to do, but we'll not be far away. Text me.'

She nodded. 'Right. We'll just go to the nearest quiet bar. I'll text you once we're there so you know where I am.'

'What about his mate?' said Jeff.

'He's not going to play gooseberry, is he? Tell Kev what's going on, when he gets here,'

They watched as she returned to Danny Ross. Nick chewed on his bottom lip, half an eye on Julie, worrying for her. They had no idea what sort of man Danny Ross really was. He'd been a heavy drug user, though it didn't look like he was any more. Maybe life in Spain was so much better, he didn't feel the need to get out of his brain any more, the way Kev had also found. She made a gesture to the door, which suggested they were leaving. Danny's mate got up and wandered over to the DJ, leaving Julie and Danny to walk out together.

Even though he knew what was going on, it was still a horrible feeling to see her walking out with another man. One side of his brain knew it was all pretence on her part, but the other side knew that physically, she was attracted to him. It felt like witnessing someone being unfaithful, even though she wasn't. When the woman you love is really attractive to a lot of men, there's a constant dynamic that you have to deal with. Sometimes, it was like she was public property. Quite often, when they were walking down the street and passed a man, Nick would see them turning to look at her arse. As men walked towards them, you could see them looking her up and down. He was used to it after all these years, but still didn't like it. It felt invasive. Julie had told him that, as it had happened to her since she was about 14, she barely noticed it any more. But then, he was a terrible hypocrite because, in common with most men, he had done the exact same thing to attractive women most of his life. As soon as they'd left, Nick and Jeff walked up the street.

'Christ, it's good to get away from that noise,' said Nick, as they stood in the hot afternoon sunshine.

'They're just down the road. It's so weird, this. Watching Jules getting off with a bloke,' said Jeff.

Nick pushed at him. 'Fuck off, don't say it like that. She's not.'

'I know, I know, but that's what it looks like and that's what Danny thinks is happening.'

They watched the couple walking away from them. Julie had her hands in her jeans pockets, Danny was making a gesture with his hand, as though pointing to somewhere specific, perhaps indicating where he was living. They took a right and were out of view.

'They've gone in a British pub,' said Jeff as they followed them briskly.

Nick's phone buzzed. 'Yeah, she's texted me. It's called Union Jax.'

'Urgh. It bloody would be.'

'C'mon, let's go and get a drink in that bar beyond it. We can sit outside and keep an eye on things,' said Nick, now feeling nervous and a bit strange.

He sat down under an umbrella at a table and looked out across the palm tree-lined road to the beach beyond.

Jeff brought them out two bottles of ice-cold beer. 'I know you don't usually drink this stuff, but you can't not have one in this heat. Any news?'

'Nah. You know what I've just been thinking? The whole trial and the story that unfolded in it was about something which hadn't happened. It's all been made up. Danny hadn't been murdered. It's a sham; an illusion. It's an entire picture that's been painted to put in front of the actual reality. It's been created to hide something. And Danny doesn't look like a junkie, so maybe that's a sham and an illusion, too.'

'And Jason in the Highland Lad said Danny had money and lived on the Wynyard Estate,' said Jeff. 'Maybe he didn't live in the Zet at all. Maybe he's nothing to do with the place at all.'

'I don't trust anything that we think is a fact. Nothing. I'm even doubting we saw Tracy dead with her throat cut.'

'Oh, come on, Nick. Mandy saw her, too.'

Nick groaned and closed his eyes, his mood sinking. 'There's something evil about all of this. Really, really evil.'

'Talking of which, here comes Kev Wells,' said Jeff.

Nick stood up and waved. 'Kev! Kev! Over here.'

Kev Wells was walking on the other side of the road on his way to the Cock and Pussy. Dressed in khaki shorts and a pink polo shirt, he was on his own. He looked over and waved.

'Now then, lads. Bit different from Stockton, this, isn't it?'

'Not that different. It's full of English pubs selling English beer and full English breakfasts,' said Jeff.

Kev laughed. 'True. What are youse two drinking?'

'Can I have a double vodka and tonic?' said Nick, handing his bottle to Jeff. 'I hate beer.'

'Another of these bottles of yellow piss-fizz,' said Jeff, holding it up.

'Right. Oh, by the way, Ricky isn't coming down due to being pissed out his brains and passing out by the pool.' He shook his head in disgust. 'Where's Jules?'

Nick explained. Kev sat down next to him and grinned. 'So it is him? Bloody hell, that didn't take youse long to find out. Poor sod. He doesn't stand a chance. Jules will get him to spill his guts, alright.'

'Why are you so sure?' said Nick.

Kev gave him an 'are you stupid or what?' look. 'No man can resist her when she turns those baby blues on them. You know what she's like. She's got a way about her that, if she wants, she can make anyone think they've got a chance of copping off with her. Men are putty in her hands. She's always been like that, even when she was a teenager.'

'Seriously, I tell you why that is,' said Jeff. 'It's 'cos she understands the male psyche. Knows exactly what to say and do, in order to achieve certain results. And that's also why she's so good at her job, I reckon. She knows how men are likely to think and behave.'

'This might sound weird, 'cos I'm her brother, but it doesn't harm that she's always had a cracking body on her, either. No tits, like, but the rest of it is all 100 per cent.'

'Hey, fuckin' shut it!' said Nick, a fury rising in his throat. He pushed Kev on the shoulder and stared him down. 'That's my wife you're talking about, I don't care if she is your sister.'

Kev raised his hands up in surrender. 'Alright, alright. Don't get your panties in a wad.'

Jeff leaned over the table and got hold of his arm.

'Settle down, old lad. It's alright. We all know Jules is a great woman.'

Nick flinched, sucked in some air, but didn't say anything. He knew what Jeff and Kev said was true, and he was as much putty in her hands as any man, but neither of them really knew how she was underneath that veneer. The public side that everyone saw was only one aspect of a very complex and layered personality.

'Aye, well, the promise of some fanny makes blokes go soft in the head. Always has, always will,' said Kev, as he went to the bar.

As soon as he'd gone, Jeff spoke up. 'Are you alright, fella? I'm worried about you.'

'I just hate Julie being talked about like that.'

'I know. I get that totally. But Kev's not lying, is he? Everything he said was right.'

'I don't care. Julie's a person, not just a body and the person is the most important thing.'

'Aye, aye, obviously. But Kev's not a feminist intellectual, is he? There's no point in picking on him like that, he won't get it. He'll just think you're weird.'

'I don't care. Fuck him.'

'OK OK, look, you're just stressed out.'

Nick felt a dark rage rising in him.

'Of course I am! My wife is in that bar schmoozing with a young bloke. I don't fucking like it, Jeff.'

'You've got nothing to worry about. You know that.'

Nick pinched the corners of his eyes. 'I know, it's not that.'

'What then?'

He rubbed at his forehead.

'It's horrible when loads of men fancy your missus. It really is. Look, man I'm not stupid, I know how the world is and what the world finds attractive and I know almost everyone lusts after Jules. But I get so fucking tired of it. I really do. Hell, man, most blokes who lust after her would hate her as soon as she opened her mouth. Jules could be a massive blob of porridge and I'd still love her. What I love is her, not her body. Even though I do love her body. Do you get me?'

Jeff licked his lips and nodded. 'Yeah, I do get that.'

'I'm sorry, Jeff. I don't want to kick off or be some prissy PC prick, but me and Jules...we're like that.' He crossed his index finger and middle finger of his right hand. 'And I won't have people talking about her like she's just some sort of tart. I'm fucking sick of it. I wish now Julie hadn't had this idea.'

'Understood. Yeah. I can see what you're saying. I'll slap Kev down if he goes off on one about her.'

Nick nodded and rubbed his forehead again, knowing already that the black dog had been circling the house for a couple of weeks and had now found a way in. This wasn't good. Not good at all. It meant he couldn't talk or be with people. He didn't even have any Phenibut on him.

'Jeff, look, I'm not feeling good. I'm feeling...I'm feeling bad. I've got a mood on. I've got to have some time on my own.'

He got up and walked away from the pub and towards the beach.

In moments like this, it was as though his brain was on fire. His head felt actually hot. Being with people only made him feel more isolated. All he wanted to do was be on his own with the quiet of his own mind. It was obviously some sort of insanity, but it was what it was.

But this was no good. He had to be there for Julie. Shit.

The darkness was on him; heavy, black and airless. Like being suffocated by pulling a polythene bag over your head and breathing in deeply. He sat down on a low wall beside the sand and sucked in a deep breath. When he was younger, he just thought he suffered from bad moods when he'd felt like this, as though a bad mood was somehow natural and not even that serious, even though it was mentally crippling for as long as it lasted. But now that he knew his depression better, he knew this crushing feeling was all part of his dopamine roller-coaster ride, a ride that his body couldn't regulate successfully all of the time. These were the moments when you need your good memories, your good thoughts of happier times.

It was the booze, the lack of food and that fucking drum and bass music, coupled with the stress of the whole situation, it was all too much for him to bear. But he was letting Julie down by not being there, in case she needed him. He wasn't good enough for her anyway. Never had been, never would be. And as he sat there in the sunshine, sweating in the heat, he couldn't even really remember what on earth he was doing there. His brain was utterly fried and it was all he could do to not just break down in a flood of tears. He began digging his nails into the palm of his right hand, wanting the pain to release the foulness within him.

'You look fed up. Are you alright?' said a small, light voice.

He looked up and standing in front of him was small boy. Maybe seven or eight years old, with big brown eyes and a pink face.

'Not really.'

'I thought so. What's the matter, then?' said the boy in that gauche, forward way that some kids have.

'I'm just a bit fed up.'

'Why?'

'I don't really know. I get like this sometimes.'

'I get really fed up as well.'

'Do you?'

The boy nodded his head in an exaggerated manner.

'Why's that?'

The kid shrugged. 'Just do.'

'Can't you help it?'

He shook his head and squinted at Nick with eyes that seemed much older than his body. 'That's why I knew you were fed up. People who get fed up all look the same.'

'Yeah, maybe we do. What should I do?'

The boy shrugged again. 'Just pretend it's alright. That's what I do.'

'And does that make it go away?'

'Sometimes pretending makes things real. There's nothing else to do, so you might as well.'

A woman in a one-piece swimsuit came over to them. She was obviously his mother. 'Come on, Joe. Don't bother the man.' She smiled at him. 'Sorry. He's a bit of a talker.'

'It's no problem. He's a clever lad. Perceptive.'

She smiled again and took the boy's hand. 'You're not the first to say that and you'll not be the last.' She led the lad away and back to where his family was camped out on the beach. As he went he turned around and made an open-close-open-close wave of his hand to him.

He'd often felt, just as little Joe had said, that everyone who struggles with depression as a way of life can see it in other people. Quite how or why, wasn't clear; it's not like people shake your hand and say, 'Hello, I suffer from depression', but even so, there is something. A look which says I've seen the dark side.

He sighed. Maybe faking it was the best way to deal with it. Try and put on a happy face. He knew, from all of his therapy over recent years, that dwelling on the black dog only made its bite worse. The more you sat around thinking about it, the more closed down and internalised you became. Sometimes he'd found distraction techniques helped, and maybe just pretending you were alright was the best distraction technique of all. Just pretending wouldn't stop it happening and wouldn't take it away, you needed other help or medication for that. But as a short-term way to deal with it, he decided to give it a go. He rubbed his eyes, let out a groan, stood up and went back to Union Jax.

'I was just texting you,' said Jeff, standing up. 'Are you OK? I was worried about you. You just vamoosed.'

'Sorry. I...well...you know how it is. I'll be alright.' He looked at his watch. 'I've only been gone 15 minutes. No need to send out a search party. Where's Kev gone?' He was still digging his nails into his palm. Jeff noticed him doing it, but said nothing.

'Bogs.'

Nick looked at his phone. 'Still nothing from Jules.'

'They've not left, so she must be still working on him.'

'Ah, you're back,' said Kev, whacking Nick on the back as he returned from the toilet. 'Everything alright?'

'Not really, but going on about it won't help.'

'I don't know what we're waiting to happen, really,' said Kev. 'Now you've only got to text Big Mandy to tell her he really is Danny Ross. She'll extradite him if he won't go home. They'll haul him down the station and knock out of him whatever's happened.'

'Nah, it's not that simple. First, he could go awol to avoid being nicked, in fact, that's almost certain. Second, there's no guarantee he'll fess up the truth. I mean, he's been involved in a murder in some way or other. He might be too scared to say anything, especially once he hears that Tracy is dead,' said Jeff. 'Or he might have too much to hide.'

'Yeah, but that's the thing. Once he hears his daughter has disappeared and his ex-girlfriend is dead, it might actually persuade him to help the police nick the people responsible, and it seems certain he knows who the killer is and who was killed,' said Nick. 'Then again, maybe he's the killer.'

'Well, I'll tell you this for nowt,' said Kev. 'If Berryman is involved in this, he'll have someone out here watching our boy Danny. He's a scheming little shit and will want to keep an eye on him.'

Nick checked his phone, still forcing himself to be talkative. 'Still nothing yet from Jules.'

Jeff raised an index finger. 'You know, the more I think about this, it's quite brilliant. I mean, it's evil, but brilliant evil. Whoever did the murder at the Zet committed the perfect crime, so perfect that no-one even knows who the person that was murdered really was, nor who really killed him, because Vokes is in jail for it; case closed. And it was all set to be locked down, before you got wind of the whole thing being iffy and Vokes being not guilty.'

'Aye, it's a cracker, you've got to hand it to whoever is behind it. But there was always one weak spot in the plan, and our Jules is in there with him,' said Kev, pointing over his shoulder. 'Now that the murder victim is alive, it'll all begin to unravel unless someone jumps on all of us and shuts it down and only the police could do that.'

They sat in the sun for another half an hour, chatting and drinking a little. Nothing too stressful. Nick began to feel his internal torment decrease. He'd long since documented the fact that his biggest troughs came after heavy drinking sessions. The cruel trick nature played on him was that this was by no means inevitable and most times after a few drinks he'd be fine. He'd resolved to trade the black dog shitting on the carpet every so often, against enjoying alcohol. Whether it was a good deal or not, was less clear.

He went to the bar to buy another round. He'd just put his order in when his phone vibrated in his pocket. The barman pushed his vodka and tonic towards him. Taking a big hit, he looked at the text, a sixth sense telling him in advance that it was from Julie.

'*Sorry this is taking so long. I've got lots of info. He's intelligent. Not like a normal druggie. He trusts me now and I've let him believe he's a good chance of getting in my knickers. He's just gone for a piss. When he gets back I'm going to tell him I've heard about Tracy and Katie, which will change everything. Not sure how he'll react. So, be on your toes.*'

He texted back immediately. '*OK. Good luck. We're still next door to you. Stay safe. I love you.*'

She replied instantly. '*Love you so much. You're so gorgeous. Can't wait to feel you in me tonight.*'

The words made his heart leap. He was really shocked, so much that he had to read them twice and then three times. Had she psychically known he'd felt depressed and said that to make him feel nice? Whatever, in those few words, he felt the dark evil begin to properly leave him. It was literally like being exorcised of a possession. It was there one minute, and then gone. He could feel it depart, like it was an oppressive fog evaporated by the warm glow of love and affection. He could feel himself coming back to himself, like she'd resurrected a fire that had almost gone out.

As he paid for the drinks, he felt his eyes glaze over as his emotions shifted. Man, he was so very, very fucked up. This had been a quick black episode, over and done in half an afternoon. And thank god for that. He sank his drink, and ordered another immediately, taking time to straighten himself out before returning to Jeff and Kev, pondering, not for the first time, how not just her love, but also her raw lust could thaw him out when he felt frozen inside. And the thought of being with her later, skin on skin, face to face, breathing each other's breath, laughing together, made him feel more alive. It was something to look forward to and something to live for. And everyone needs both of those.

'Here you go,' he said, putting the glasses down in front of Jeff and Kev. 'Jules just texted me. She's about to tell our boy Danny about Tracy and the bairn. So get ready for kick off.'

Jeff held up his phone and pointed to it. 'You know, I've just been swotting up on Lord Ross. He was Minister for Town Planning in the Thatcher government. Still sits on various committees to do with that side of things: where to put up new houses, when to pull old ones down, that sort of thing. He's been in a primo position to be able to influence the awarding of public building works contracts pretty much his whole working life, and we know that Mike Cavani has used cash incentives in brown paper envelopes to get contracts. Old man Ross could easily be involved in all of that.'

Kev rubbed his thumb and forefinger together. 'Classic way to line your pockets. Building trade is as bent as a banana. Or it used to be. Con will tell you that and he's worked on sites his whole life. It was all cash in back pockets and you scratch my back, I'll scratch yours. I bet old man Ross coined it, someone's got wind of it all and was blackmailing him. If you ask me, he set up the killing, man. It's his son who's had to disappear, so daddy Ross has to be involved. He probably said, OK you can have your money, meet me at the Zetland flats. When he gets there, Ross's henchman does the knifey and, with the help of Berryman, who he's paid off, the plan swings into action and they set up Vokes.'

'So why hasn't the murdered person been reported missing?' said Nick.

'Probably has been, but there are thousands of people missing at any

166

one time. No-one knows where they are. A lot go abroad or change their names or whatever. Going missing is a piece of piss, if you know what you're doing,' said Kev. 'So the fact he's not turned up isn't unusual and there's no body to be found because he's been cremated. Like Jeff reckons, it is sort of brilliant, really.'

Jeff raised his eyebrows and pointed over Nick's shoulder as Danny Ross came out of the pub and sprinted away from them. Kev was up first and after him. Nick followed as Julie came out. She shouted something, but he couldn't make out what it was. By now Kev was five yards ahead of him. Nick got into his stride, switched up a gear and sprinted past him, gaining ground on Danny as he turned up an old, narrow side road which was partially uphill. Nick knew that he could catch him quickly.

'Danny! Danny!' shouted Nick, as he got alongside him. 'It's alright. We're on your side.'

'Leave me alone!'

But he was losing breath as the street went uphill. Clearly, he was knackered. Kev caught them both up and went on Danny's other side, grabbed his arm and tugged him back, making Danny stumble to a halt, hands on knees, gasping for breath. People walked around them as they all got their breath back.

'Just leave me be, please,' said Danny, sweat running down his tanned face. 'I don't want anything to do with any of it.'

'Sorry, Danny, we can't do that,' said Nick.

'Do just piss off and leave me alone, please. I have nothing to say to you, right?'

It was odd. Throughout the trial, because of the descriptions of his lifestyle, because magically, his father hadn't even been mentioned, let alone appeared to give evidence, he'd imagined Daniel Ross was an underclass loser, like the rest of the Zet. He'd imagined him as like Glenn Vokes, gaunt, with a hunted look and a broad Teesside accent, rough enough to cut steel. But he was anything but. He was, in fact, very upper-middle class. Posh, even.

Julie trotted up, her face pink with the exertion in the heat.

'I've not told him much yet,' she said, panting a little. 'I just said we knew about what happened at the Zet and he just legged it.'

'Owee, Danny boy, let's get out of this heat,' said Kev, slapping him on the back of his white v-neck t-shirt.

'Do I have a choice?' he said.

Kev laughed and patted him on the back again. 'Of course you do. We can go into that nice air-conditioned bar there and have a drink, or we can take you somewhere quiet and hurt you.'

'I thought that might be the choice. I can't believe I fell for all your bullshit, Julie. You bitch.'

Nick tapped him on the cheek with the flat of his hand. 'Hey. Have some respect, son. I'll let that word go, but only once. Get me?' With one harder tap, he made his point.

'Sorry...sorry...' he looked down in a defeated way.

'Don't feel bad, you're a bloke and thus easily conned with a flutter of the eyelashes and a touch of the hand. You're all the same, you lot,' said Julie, wiping the sweat from her brow.

'Easy for a lady as attractive as you, maybe, and on a man as lonely as I am.' He looked at the four of them in turn. 'Are you all the police, then?' he asked.

'Owee, let's go in the bar. All will be explained,' said Nick, waving at Jeff, as he ambled up the street, not even breaking into a sweat. It was deliciously air-conned cool inside the small bar. Nick bought them three bottles of beer, and gin and tonics for himself and Julie. Jeff put his head around the door and grinned.

'Ah, you've filled my anti-heat prescription. Nice one. Hello, Danny, I'm Jeff, I'm the slowest member of the group.' He held out his big hand towards the miserable-looking man, who just looked at it. Jeff turned his hand towards his own eyes and inspected it. 'Yeah, well, I don't blame you, you don't know where it's been.' He leaned into Danny's face, gave him his classic, intimidating manic grin, all teeth and eyebrows and beanie hat.

'Who the hell are you bloody weirdos?' said Danny, recoiling from Jeff, who, to be fair, did look quite weird.

'Right, I'm going to tell you everything, Danny. Cards on the table,' said Nick. 'We came here to find you. Here's why...' he proceeded to explain everything, starting with the trial. Danny listened to him without expression, sipping at the beer.

'Now, I've got some bad news to tell you. Me and Jules went to the Zet a couple of days ago and we found Tracy there in your old flat. She was dead. She'd had her throat cut. Baby Katie was gone.'

He sat back and took a drink. Danny just stared at him, though not really seeing him. Then he took a long drink. As he did so, Julie put a hand on his arm, sympathetically.

'I don't know how close you were to her, but I don't think she suffered.'

Danny didn't say anything, his eyes betraying very little.

'We think she might have been killed because she knew what had happened to you. Had you spoken to her recently?' said Nick.

Again he said nothing. He just finished his beer. It looked like he was weighing things up in his own mind. Kev was getting frustrated at his silence.

'Alright son, alright. You're doing a good moody on us. But start talking, eh, if you don't, the hurting will begin. Right?' He leaned into his face. But Danny didn't look scared.

'Shut up,' hissed Julie to her brother. 'I'm not 'avin that. Ignore him, Danny. He's my brother and he's an idiot. There'll be no violence. I guarantee it. You're not in danger from us. We just want to know what's happened. People have died, it's not right. Vokes has gone to jail for a crime he didn't commit. We're just trying to sort it out and do right by everyone.'

'Is Katie alright?'

'We don't know. We don't know where she is,' said Nick. 'She's your girl, isn't she?'

He didn't say anything, just nodded.

'Had you spoken to Tracy recently? Because if you did, you could be in serious danger,' said Julie, her voice still calm.

'I rang her a few days ago.' He pulled at his lip.

'Was she the only person there who knew what had happened to you? That you'd gone away?'

He rubbed his ear, looked nervous and took a drink. 'Yeah.'

'Really? No-one else at all?' said Nick.

He shook his head.

'So what did happen, Dan?' said Jeff, getting up to buy more drinks. 'Why did you leave? How come everyone thinks you're dead?'

'You won't believe me.'

'Try us,' said Nick.

He cleared his throat. 'Look, I don't know anything. I was in the Zet, strung out on smack on 18th October, my father arrived with the keys to an apartment here, gave...gave me a debit card for an account in my name and told me there would be 50 grand a year in it. One of his men drove me here. He said I should go away and never return because if I did I'd be killed.'

'Didn't you ask questions?'

'Yeah. But he didn't tell me anything. All he said was if I came back home, I'd be killed.'

CHAPTER 8

'And do you have good reason to believe that's true?' said Julie. 'I mean, most fathers don't say that sort of thing, obviously.'

Jeff put another round of drinks onto the table. Danny picked up the bottle and drank at it with gusto, then shook his head.

'I can see you're trying to do the right thing. I understand why. It's noble. But you have no idea what you're up against.' He drank again. 'I kid you not, my father is one of the most evil men in Britain.' He took another drink, belched and looked at each of them. 'If he knows that you know what has happened, he'll hunt you down and he will, and I mean *will*, have you killed.'

'Yer bollocks, he will,' said Kev, his reflex to any threat. 'He's just a posh old fart. I'll fucking hunt him down and twat 'im!'

Danny Ross looked at him with a withering sneer. 'You're soooo stupid.'

'He is stupid,' said Julie, 'and he's not going to say anything else, or he'll feel the back of my hand.' She glared at her brother with hard eyes, suddenly looking a lot like Jackie, her mother.

Jeff raised his index finger. 'OK, Danny, let's just sum this up. Have we got everything right? You're supposed to be dead. Your dad has, somehow, conspired to have someone killed and passed off that body as you?'

He nodded. 'Well, that's what Tracy told me had happened. But I know nothing about any of it. I don't know who died or who killed him. I just told Tracy why I'd gone away. She told me everyone was saying I'd been killed, but she said she'd keep it quiet and not tell anyone.'

'And you were a junkie?' said Jeff.

'Yeah. But I came out here and scoring was hard. I didn't know who to get it off. So I went cold turkey and kicked it. '

'You do look well,' said Julie. 'A bit thin, you need to eat more.'

'That shit ruins your appetite and it just hasn't come back. I could live off fresh air.'

'How come you even ended up living in the Zet?' said Nick. 'You surely could have done better for yourself? We've been in there and it's disgusting.'

'I was a junkie with no money. That's where the council put me. I was so out of it a lot of the time, I just stopped caring. It does that to you, or it did it to me, anyway. All you care about is drugs.'

'So your dad wouldn't help you?'

'Well, he brought me drugs. Or rather he had people bring me drugs. Free smack. I wasn't complaining. He used it as a way to control me. To get me to do what he wanted. I was an embarrassment to him. I was a junkie for years. He cut me adrift a long time ago but when the bags of heroin turned up I knew he was planning something. I knew he was using me somehow. He's an absolute bastard and I've no other family.'

'No mother?' asked Julie.

'She committed suicide a couple of years ago. That was the coroner's verdict, anyway. She'd been depressed and had stopped taking her medication. Personally, I always thought my father had her killed and made it look like suicide.' He said it very matter-of-factly.

'What? Why would he do that?'

'She probably knew what he was doing and wasn't prepared to shut up any longer.'

Julie's her face set in a heavy frown. 'How did she die?'

'She drowned in the River Tees, Julie. That's as much as I know.' He opened his arms out wide.

Nick looked at her, certain he was thinking the same as she was thinking. Ruth Small had died in similar circumstances. Her husband was Harry Small, who'd worked with Kev Berryman, who in turn worked for Ronald Ross and helped set up Danny's 'murder'.

'Did your mother know a woman called Ruth Small?' said Nick.

'Small? Was she the copper's, Harry Small's wife?'

Nick nodded.

'Yes, she did. They were old school friends. Both went to Grangefield Grammar back in the day.'

'Ruth died recently. Suicide, drowned in the Tees,' said Julie. 'That seems very coincidental.'

Danny took a drink, closed his eyes and looked weary. 'If they knew each other, it will be down to him. I guarantee it. Small and my father go way back.'

'So how come you're alive, Dan?' said Jeff. 'No disrespect, like. I'm not saying you shouldn't be. It's just that if he kills off anyone who gets close to the truth, why hasn't he done for you?'

'The drugs. He thinks I'm so doped up that I know nothing. And I think he expected me to OD. And it seems I was very useful to cover up one of his crimes. But, you're right. He'll come for me, sooner or later. Especially when he knows I'm off the junk. One day, there'll be a knock at the door, a gun will be put to my head and I will have my brains blown out. I expect it every day.'

'Christ, doesn't that worry you?' said Nick, who couldn't imagine the sort of stress that would put on you.

Danny shook his head. 'I live one day at a time. I'm an addict. I've looked death in the face more than once. I don't want it to happen, but I'm not afraid.'

'Is anyone keeping an eye on you out here? I mean, someone your dad's sent?' said Kev. 'I mean, is there anyone checking up on you?'

'I don't know. I don't think so. I've been out here for eight months now.'

'Well, don't look now, but the bloke in the far corner has been very interested in us. And if he's not English, I'm a Dutchman. He's been on his phone since we came in.' He made a move, to suggest he was going to have it out with him.

Danny glanced quickly. 'Don't recognise him.'

Nick took a look. He was definitely English. He had the defining beer-bellied, apple shape and wore the style-free, three-quarter length sports pants, flip-flops and football shirt that only a certain sort of Englishman on holiday wears.

'Don't you say anything to him,' said Julie, jabbing a finger and hissing at her brother.

'Alright, Jules. I've turned over a new leaf. I wasn't going to beat him up. Just find out what he's doing.'

'Don't be dumb, Kev. He'd just say he's on holiday, even if he was keeping an eye on us for Ronald Ross,' she said in a whisper.

'Suppose so, aye.'

'So what am I supposed to do?' said Danny. 'I can't go home and give evidence. I'll be killed, sure as day follows night. I want my father to pay for whatever it is he's done. So how do we make that happen?'

No-one said anything for over a minute. It was an impossible question to answer.

Jeff cleared his throat. 'Couldn't you give evidence via videotape, rather than have to go back home?'

'Don't make no difference if he does,' said Kev. 'His old man will just send someone out to whack him anyway, won't he? As soon as he opens his mouth, he's a dead man. Sorry mate, but if what you say is right about the old sod, that's true, innit?'

'All too true, I'm afraid. Yes,' said Danny, politely. 'One could portray it as a confrontation between truth and consequence. I have no desire to see Glenn Vokes in jail for a crime he didn't commit, but have no desire to have my throat cut like Trace. I'd rather Dad was dead, in fact. That'd be my preferred option.'

Nick pulled at his stubble with thumb and forefinger.

'How well did you really know Tracy?' he said.

He didn't directly answer the question. 'She was just in the Zet from time to time. If I had any money at all, we'd sleep together. I liked her company but she wasn't well, really and neither was I. I was under the control of my father and Harry Small.'

'Was that a regular thing between you and Tracy?' said Julie, leaning her chin on her upturned palm.

'Infrequent. I liked her. But not only does heroin take all your money and self respect, it absorbs your sex drive too, if you understand me. But I liked Tracy. Her father had abused her with other men when she was in her teens. We shared that. That's what set her on the path to drug addiction.'

'How long did you go out together?' said Nick.

'We didn't. Not in the normal way.'

'Yeah, you did. You used to drink together in the Highland Lad over a year ago. You were living in Wynyard at the time.'

'Oh, yeah, that was when I was going through a clean phase. I say clean, but I was coked up a lot. I just laid off the smack for a while but coke made me into a total prick, so I went back to the H.'

That would account for his arrogance. Nick stared at him, weighing up his response. Jason in the pub had said Danny was an arrogant rich kid

'And your dad let you use one of his houses?' said Julie.

'Yeah. Didn't last long. I couldn't stay off the smack. Trace probably didn't ever stop using. He kicked me out and put me in the Zet. Or the council did on his suggestion, which was just more of his controlling behaviour. She was a damaged soul, like me. But our relationship was all about drugs and very little about sex or anything else. We went down the toilet together. We both loved the drug and it destroyed us. I've spent my time out here getting well, getting more fit and trying to recover. But it's hard and there are still days when I want the drug more than anything.'

'So how do you know Katie was your baby?' said Nick.

He shrugged. 'She just told me it was.'

'And you believed her?' said Nick.

'I had no reason not to.'

'But surely, it could've been any auld gadgee, if she was on the game,' said Kev. 'She was probably trying to get some your old man's money off of you.'

Danny flinched and held up his hand. 'No. She never once asked for money. Not that I had any. In fact, she told me she wanted to bring Katie up on her own. That she didn't need any man's help to do it. And she meant it. She didn't like men. She used to say how she hated how men smelt, how she hated their bodies, their minds, their genitals. Understandably so, given the abuse she'd suffered from an early age.'

Nick looked at him as he spoke. He didn't seem overly upset at her death, even though he spoke clearly and sensitively. Maybe the heroin had hardened his heart to emotional traumas such as Tracy's murder. It seemed to have done its job, the job so many take it for - to hide away from, or suppress the pain of existence. And though now sober, the same ice was still in his veins.

'Tell me about Glenn Vokes, Danny. How long had you known him?' said Nick.

'Glenn? I didn't know him, really. I'd met him on the stairs or around the place, or cadged a fag off him, or whatever. You've got to remember, that place is a slum. People drifted in and out of it all the time. Glenn was just another drifter, like me. I was only in there six weeks or so. I think he went there to buy drugs from whoever was selling, usually Berry.'

'In court Vokes said he hardly knew you.'

'He's right. There's *knew* and *know*, isn't there? I knew of him, but I didn't know him.'

'Vokes said that Tracy was his girlfriend.'

He shook his head. 'No-one was going out with Tracy. She was no-one's girlfriend. Despite what Berry might have said, he never walked in on us in bed. We never had a fight.'

Nick chewed on his lip and looked around the four of them. 'You know what? Most of what Vokes said in court seems to actually have been true. He said he didn't kill Danny - well, we know that's true. He said he didn't find Danny and Tracy in bed, which is what was alleged by the prosecution. He said he wasn't even there when the murder happened and there's still no proof he was.'

Jeff raised an index finger. 'Ah, if I remember what you told me correctly, when the verdict was passed, at the moment of maximum stress, a time when your sense was that he was telling the truth, he said,

"I never killed him" - is that right?'

Nick nodded. 'Yeah, he was pleading with the judge and us on the jury, even though it was far too late.'

Jeff raised his eyebrows and kept his finger aloft. 'Alright, so let's assume you're right - dangerous assumption, I know, but go let's go with it - now, there's a big difference between saying "I never killed him" and "I never *killed* him" and "I never killed *him*", isn't there? Same four words, but three different meanings. The first is a flat statement of innocence, the second suggests an assault, but one which didn't result in death, the third is an admittance that he killed someone but just not Danny, here.'

'Bloody hell, you've lost me there, Jeff. I'm the one here what never went to university, remember,' said Kev.

Jeff ignored him and looked at Nick. 'Can you recall the emphasis he used?'

'I've thought about this before. I think he emphasised "him" but that could just be false memory.'

They all drank in silence for a minute, trying to work out a path through this. Finally, Kev puffed out his cheeks and blew out air. 'Well, this is how I see it. You're no use to Mandy Beale, really. Now she knows it's you, here, she can dig into it all. You've nowt more to tell her, have you?'

'Nothing. I literally know nothing other than what I've told you. Even if I wanted to help the police, I have nothing more to offer them, and what my father has done for me isn't illegal, is it?'

'Not as such,' said Julie. 'Threatening you with death if you go home is a bit dodgy, but would just be your word against his in court. A good lawyer would paint the situation as a father successfully helping his junkie son get off drugs, by getting him to sunnier climes. Tougher to get away with misidentifying a body, though.'

'And he'll have made sure he's covered his tracks so that even if they found the person who did the actual butchering, he'll not be tainted by it, just as he did with mother's suicide and Ruth Small too, in all probability,' said Danny. 'When you've got money and power, you can get away with quite literally almost anything,'

Nick folded his arms across his chest. 'There'll be a way to get him.'

'You seem very sure,' said Danny.

'I don't know what it is yet, but there will be and when we find out what that is, we'll have him. Like we said, he misidentified a body as you. That's some sort of crime.'

The man Kev had been concerned about got up and went to the toilet. Kev watched him go, then turned back to the table to be met with his sister's glare.

'I told you, didn't I?' she said.

'I'm doing nowt, Jules. Let's have one last drink eh? I'll get them in.'

He stood up, and reached in his pocket for money, timing his walk to the bar to coincide with the man, who had come out of the toilet and was also heading there, colliding with him apparently accidentally.

'Sorry pal, I wasn't looking where I was going,' said Kev.

'No worries,' said the other man, ordering himself a beer, then sitting back down.

Kev bought the round and took it back to the table.

'What was that about?' said Julie, knowing he was up to something.

'Nowt. I feel quite pissed and lost my balance. Not used to drinking, like.' Her eyes narrowed at her brother.

After they'd finished their drinks, they walked back down the street.

'Right, we're going this way back to our hotel,' said Nick, a hand on Danny's shoulder. 'Have you got a phone number so we can get in touch with you if we need to?'

'No. Sorry. That was another of father's conditions. No phone or computer.'

'But he wouldn't know if you had a secret phone,' said Julie.

After a pause, Danny smiled slowly, impishly. 'Yeah, you got me. I did buy one when I arrived here.' He gave them the number, and put theirs into his phone. 'But please don't use it unless it's an emergency. I'm paranoid that Dad would somehow know if you did. I don't want to risk it. Him and Small made me fearful and paranoid.' He began to walk away, shoulders hunched. 'Good luck with everything.'

'You too, Danny' said Julie. 'Stay safe.'

He turned, 'I'll try.' As he was leaving, Nick took a quick photo of him with his phone. At least they'd be able to show Mandy they'd found him.

Back in Nick and Julie's hotel room, the four of them sat on the balcony in the early evening sun.

'Right. Now that we're not in public, I can get a good look at this,' said Kev, pulling something out of his pocket.

'What's that, man?' said Jeff. 'Ah, a passport.' He pointed at him. 'You lifted it from that bloke's back pocket, didn't you?'

'Me? I'd never do something so dishonest, Jeff. It must have just fallen out of his pocket and into mine. I'll pop back round the pub and drop it on the floor later.'

'I knew you were up to something. He was always a good pickpocket, even as a boy he could steal a nipple right off your tit, without anyone noticing,' said Julie. 'So who is he?'

Kev looked inside the burgundy passport. 'Gary Simmonds. Well, what a surprise, he was born in Middlesbrough 14th July 1979. No way is that a coincidence. I'll get my network on to him. We'll find out who he is and who he's working for - pound to a penny it's Ronald Ross. We'll get this shit broke wide open sooner or later.'

He took a photo of the passport photo and then began tapping at his phone, sending text messages and emails to the Teesside-wide web of people he liked to call his network. Mostly it was low-level criminals and dodgy people who mysteriously lived off thin air.

Jeff rolled his eyes. 'It's like watching someone from *Mission Impossible*. Feels like there should be some theme music playing while you do that.'

Nick closed his eyes and sat back to enjoy the sun.

'Well, we did what we came out here to do. We found Danny. The rest of this has to be up to Mandy's mob to sort out. It can't be our responsibility, can it?'

'I know what you mean, but if he ends up dead, I will feel responsible. I was the one who got him to reveal his identity,' said Julie putting sunglasses on and pulling her hair into a ponytail.

'But that's crazy. The guilty one is the one who kills him, not you,' said Nick.

He was interrupted by Kev. 'Got 'im!! One-nil! Gary Simmonds worked for Kev Berryman as part of his extortion team. They both did six months in Holme House 10 years back. That's where they met. Might have known. It all comes back to Berry, does this. All of it. He's at the centre of everything. I said that the day we got him on the street, didn't I? It's like he's the spider in the middle of the web.'

'No, it's not Berryman. It's Harry Small,' said Nick. 'Berryman worked with Small, Small and Ronald Ross go back years, Danny said. Small connects everything. His wife and Ross's wife both died the same way and were old school friends. It's all Small, if you ask me.'

Kev had been absorbed in his phone, then looked up from it. 'I reckon I've got summat on Ronald Ross. According to my sources, he's a big fan of the prozzy. Would rather pay for it than work for it. Mate of mine who knows a lot of ladies of the night says he likes to pay extra for bareback riding.'

Nick turned to Kev. 'What's that?' Everyone groaned. 'What?' said Nick.

'It's sex without wearing a condom,' said Julie.

'Oh, right. Sorry for not being a man of the world.'

'Sex is a commodity to some men. That's the only way they can understand it and they use it to confirm their sense of power over people,' said Julie. 'He sounds a right piece of work.'

Her brother looked over to her. 'You're missing the point, Jules. He likes shagging prozzies, Tracy was a proz, she's been murdered and the kid has gone. To me that says it's Ross's kid, not Danny but dirty Ronnie,' said Kev. 'He's a sicko, isn't he? He's screwing his son's friend without protection.'

'So why didn't she tell Danny that?' said Jeff.

'I don't know. I'm not a psychologist. Maybe she didn't know either way. How could she? She'd have shagged loads of blokes in the week she fell pregnant; without a DNA test, you'd never know which one it was,' said Kev. 'All I'm saying is Ross knows that bairn is his.'

'She would know who the father was if he was the only punter not to wear a condom,' said Julie, arched eyebrows raised.

'Christ, that's disgusting,' said Nick, appalled.

'Hang on though, she'd be on the pill,' said Kev, far less squeamish about the seedy side of life than Nick. 'She'd only make punters wear a johnny to stop her getting AIDs or the pox. She'd still be on the pill even if he didn't wear one.'

Julie shook her head. 'Kev man, think about it. She was strung out on heroin or god knows what. She wouldn't know if she'd taken her pill or not half the time. Her life was chaotic and reckless. There's a good chance she wasn't protected by it on a regular basis.'

'It still doesn't explain why she'd lie to Danny about him being the father,' said Jeff. 'I can understand her not wanting to tell him it was his father's, but why tell him he's the dad? She didn't want anyone's help bringing her up.'

Nick chewed at his cheek again making it sore.

'I think I might know why. I think we're barking up the wrong tree to say old man Ross is the father. Like you said Jules, she was reckless. She was probably vulnerable to getting pregnant a lot, she *wouldn't* know who the father was, not least because her short-term memory was absolutely shot by the drugs. She was shooting her mouth off about the murder when I met her, and I liked her because she had attitude, but she wasn't stupid, she knew it might get her into trouble. She probably half expected to be murdered by a punter. I mean, she intimated that it was really dangerous doing what she was doing. By telling Danny it was his kid, even if it wasn't, she was trying to protect Katie's future. I wouldn't mind betting she told old man Ross it was Danny's too, so that if anything happened to her, he'd do exactly what's happened and take Katie.'

'I don't understand. Why would he do that? He doesn't give a shit about family. He's already cut off his son and probably killed his wife,' said Kev.

'True. But these posh aristocratic families are always big on family. They'll cut someone adrift if they think they're a bad egg, but blood is blood. He's no other kids. Now he's got a girl.'

Kev winced. 'Nah, you're overthinking it, man. And you're totally giving him more credit than he deserves. This is what he's doing - he's selling the kid to some paedos. You heard Danny, he said he was one of the most evil men on earth. He's not saying that for no reason, is he? And a few of the lads that have already messaged me reckon he's a notorious dirt bag.'

'I'm inclined to agree,' said Julie. 'Though he doesn't need the money, so I don't know if it's quite right, Kev. I do think there's something in what you're saying about Tracy trying to look after the little girl's interests if anything happened to her, Nick. She might have lived a chaotic life, but she wasn't stupid.'

Jeff looked up from his phone. 'Well, I've texted Mandy your photo of him, Nick, and all the info we have, including the fact that Danny is vulnerable to getting whacked, especially as Gary Simmonds will be reporting back to Berryman, who in turn is reporting to Ross senior. We'll just have to see what she does next.'

'There's still a lot of questions the cops need to answer, if you ask me,' said Nick. 'In fact, right now I think we have more questions than answers.'

CHAPTER 9

Julie came home from work the following Friday and threw a copy of the *Gazette* onto the kitchen table, as Nick was stuffing two chicken breasts with goat's cheese and pesto; slicing them open, putting in the filling and then tying them together to keep as much of it in as possible. He rubbed the skin with some olive oil, sprinkled salt and black pepper on and put them into his new portable halogen oven - essentially a large round glass bowl with an element in the lid.

'They're big breasts...' he said, as he lowered them into it on a Pyrex dish.

'It's nice of you to say so, luv, but they're really not.' He turned to look at her. She was pushing her breasts together and juggling them up and down.

'Do you want goat's cheese and pesto on those as well?'

'Only if you'll lick it off.'

'I've never fancied the whole sex and food or confectionary combo, have you?'

'I once put squirty cream on your doo-dah. As I recall, you rather enjoyed me licking it off.'

'That's true, but not due to the cream. Note, I'm not even making a squirty cream joke at this point. That's how mature I am these days.'

She rolled a laugh around the back of her throat. 'Boo. Don't go getting mature on me, not after all these years.'

She slumped onto a chair and groaned. 'Get us a glass of something cold, will you luv? I'm knackered.'

He set about fixing her a gin and tonic.

'Have you seen the *Gazette*?' she said.

'No.'

'Front-page story is about the Zetland flats. After two murders being committed there, there was an emergency meeting of the council planning committee and they've passed a motion to pull them down and build new social housing on the same site.'

'Really? Should've happened years ago. Shouldn't have taken two murders to persuade them the place was uninhabitable.' He pushed the large tumbler across the table. 'There you go gorgeous, one triple G & T.'

She took a big drink and released a breathy groan. 'Oh, god, I needed that. Thanks, luv. Aye, but the story doesn't stop there.' She opened the paper and read from it. ' "North Tees Demolition Ltd has been awarded the contract to demolish the existing property once current tenants have been rehoused. Firms have already been invited to tender for the contract to build the new property".'

'Why does North Tees Demolition sound familiar to me?'

'Because it's one of Mike Cavani's businesses.'

'Shit, yeah, I forgot about him. Con says he's got a stranglehold on the construction and demolition business all over the northeast.'

'Well he's a gangster, isn't he? He probably launders money through these places. Anyway, when I first read this on my lunch hour, having remembered it was a Cavani company, on a whim I looked up the NTD website. And you know who is on their board of directors?'

'No, who?'

'One Ronald Ross.'

'Bloody hell.' He thought for a moment. 'Yeah, it makes sense, doesn't it? Cavani would be bound to get into the pocket of a Head of Town Planning. He's probably been giving him back handers for years. Then when he retired, he put him on the board of one of his companies, just like how companies do with retired government ministers.'

'Yeah, and that means Ross is hand in hand with organised crime, which means he'd have easy access to someone who would be prepared to knife someone in the heart and slit a woman's throat.'

'Exactly, and what's more, the company he's on the board of stands to benefit from public money to take down the flats. Chances are the company that wins the building contract will also be a Cavani outfit, one way or another.'

Nick fixed himself a vodka with fizzy water and lime juice.

'That can't be why the murders happened, though. To get the contracts, I mean. They were over eight months apart.'

'Probably not, but they've certainly capitalised quickly on them.' He sat down opposite her and took a drink. 'I wonder what Mike Cavani's relationship is with him.'

'Cavani is simply an amoral bastard,' she said. 'He'd use anyone who was useful to him in some way, and then stab them in the back.'

He tugged at his lip. 'Yeah, yeah, you're right. Ross is actually up to his neck in a river of shit. Jeff's already said that Mandy is just waiting for the right moment to interview him about the whole business. He misidentified the dead body as his son. She could nick him for that alone, I'm sure.'

'I don't get why she's not done that already,' said Julie, clinking the ice in her glass.

'As soon as she does that, she gives away her hand. Jeff said she wants to root out everything. I imagine saying a body is your son when it's not isn't even a custodial offence. She wants to get him for everything he's done. As soon as they interview him, he starts to get an idea of what they do or don't know. And he'll have top-notch lawyers on his payroll ready to fight his corner, so Mandy probably just wants to find out exactly what he's been doing, and get hard evidence in place before they go in mob-handed. It sounds easy, but it won't be. He'll have covered his tracks very well.'

Julie nodded. 'And how does she get that hard evidence? Danny's word would be easily dismissed in court as the ramblings of an ex-drug addict. His dad would be painted as a doting father helping his son start a new life in Spain. They might even say his father was so upset at the state of his son, the balance of his mind was disturbed when he saw the body. We've seen the "he's gone mad" defence by rich aristocrats before, to get them out of jail, and then they miraculously recover.'

'The thing also is, Ross knows that Mandy knows about Danny being alive because Gary Simmonds will have reported back to Berryman, who presumably will have passed on the info. He knows he's going to have to answer those questions soon, so he'll be getting his defence together.'

Julie stared into her glass. 'Do we know Berryman worked for Ronald Ross? We don't, do we? We know he used Harry Small, and we know Small and Ross go way back, but that doesn't mean Berryman is in cahoots with Ross. And if he isn't, he might have kept the info about Danny to himself in order to somehow exploit the situation for money in the future. So Bad Ronnie might not know that we found Danny.'

'Good thinking, Jules. Berry is a schemer, so that sounds more than likely.'

Nick mulled things over, looking at his notepad, doodling in contemplation.

'On the Wednesday night during the trial, there was an old episode of *Columbo* on TV. You were out with the women from TW at the Penny Black doing your karaoke.'

'The old 1970s *Columbo*?'

'Yeah, and in it, the murderer made an alibi for himself by substituting the CCTV film in his house that showed he wasn't at home, for one he'd filmed earlier which showed him being there. Because he'd time-stamped the film to show the time he was actually going to kill the bloke, the film apparently "proved" he couldn't have done it because he was at home. I thought that was really clever. You create a false reality which proves you're the innocent party.'

'Who had CCTV in their house the 70s?'

'Oh, he was a film star and had it as a security measure.'

'So how did Columbo catch him?'

'The fake film showed him in his living room. He had a watch on. Columbo spotted this, had it blown up and discovered it was an hour earlier than the film purported to be.'

'Ah, good old Columbo. Why on earth did he need a raincoat in LA, though?'

'Anyway, that was in my mind in court the next day. Not that there was any videotape of Vokes...but even so...'

'Yeah, but you said that was odd because whether he was at the Zet, or was walking the streets as he claimed, he should still have been caught on film at some point that afternoon.'

'And that was why I thought of Columbo and was wondering if the reality we were being sold wasn't just a fiction. Because when you've no incontrovertible proof of anything, you can create any fiction you like and pass it off as reality, as long as it sounds feasible. And it was then that I wondered if the police had made the CCTV that proved he wasn't at the Zet, disappear. He said he walked down Durham Road to go to the Zet at 5pm. There should have been CCTV at least of that, but there wasn't. And they couldn't show film of him on the way there at 3pm to do the killing, because he wasn't there, he was at home, as he said in one of his accounts.'

'But he also said he was walking around town on speed.'

'That was the story he settled on and stuck to. And it did seem credible. But when first arrested he said he'd been in his flat all afternoon. But then he realised that meant no-one saw him, so he changed his story, maybe just hoping that someone would say they thought they'd seen him around when the murder happened. It's not like he thinks straight or could work out a plan, so it might have made sense in his doped-up head.'

She scratched her armpit and took a drink. 'You've made a good case but again, you've no proof. At least legal proceedings to get Glenn Vokes released from jail are already underway behind the scenes, now that the man he's supposed to have murdered is alive. Obviously, you can't be convicted for murdering someone who is alive, even if someone else was murdered there that day. The press is going to have a field day with this when it all comes out. Wish you could sell it as an exclusive, but then I suppose you set out to get Vokes released and that is what'll happen.'

'True. There's a story in that, at the very least. I want to get that five grand for your course fees. This isn't over.'

He took the chicken breasts out of the oven and served them on a bed of dressed wild rocket.

'These look good, you've got the skin all crispy,' said Julie, slicing into one, releasing the melted cheese and pesto. 'Oooh, lush,' she said, biting into the tender meat.

'Yeah, this organic free-range bird tastes like chicken tasted when we were little.'

'It's bloody gorgeous.'

As they ate, Nick turned over the whole case in his mind.

'You know what I'm going to do?' he said.

'What?'

'I'm going to follow the route from Vokes's flat in Roseworth to the Zet. I talked with Kev about it. Vokes said he wandered around for hours and must've walked for miles, but no matter what route he took, he had to wind up on CCTV somewhere toward the end, around the time he got down Durham Road to Bishopton Road. I'm going to look for every CCTV camera at both ends of the route. Make a note of where they are and see if there's any way to tell if they're working or not.'

'How many will there be?'

'Not a lot - mostly on the major junctions and outside any rows of shops. Do you want to come with me?'

'I can't. I've got work to do preparing some case notes for a meeting tomorrow.'

She cleaned the last of the pesto off her plate with the last piece of chicken. 'That was stonking, luv. I'll be interested to find out what you learn. Good luck.'

'Right, I'll get off now. Leave the dishes, I'll do them when I get back.'

'Don't worry, I wasn't going to do anything with them! That's your job, ladyboy.'

It was a grey, overcast and still evening, as he walked from their house on Norton High Street down to Norton Avenue, onto the A1027, then taking Darlington Lane to Ragpath Lane which led up into Roseworth and Redhill Road where Vokes's flat was.

Soon he was standing outside of the flat. The CCTV camera outside the off licence was still there and would have filmed anyone going in and out of the flat. He looked at the oblong black metal box mounted on a bracket. Was it on? There was no way to tell. No red light or anything. It looked old and very weathered and was in a fixed position.

Nick marked it on a printout of a map of the area he'd got from Google Maps. There were two ways to go to the Zet from there, the less direct way back down Ragpath Lane, or Durham Road into town. The obvious way was the latter, as it was the most direct, but both routes ended up on Bishopton Road. With a final glance at the camera he walked down Redhill Road past the branch library. As he did so, he noticed it also had a camera mounted on the wall to one side of the entrance.

As he got close, it was obviously the same sort of one as outside the off licence, and looked just as old. Just below the bracket, on the wall, was a blue chalk X. Frowning, he ran back to the first camera and looked at it again. At just the same height was also the remains of a blue chalk X, though it was almost washed away, as it hadn't had any shelter from rain. Did the X mean it wasn't working, in the same way that dead trees in a park get a X put on them to mark which have to be felled?

He headed to the roundabout, off which led Durham Road, but had only gone a few strides when he came to traffic lights and a crossing. On top of the lights was a small camera to monitor the traffic, but which would also have to film anyone on the pavement. He looked on the traffic lights for a blue cross, but there was nothing. Then again, it was exposed to the elements so wouldn't survive long, even if there had been. Further down the road there was another crossing and again, a camera on it. He inspected it and this time found traces of a blue line on a poster, advertising a long-gone jumble sale. The next camera was at the Mile House junction. No sign of an X there, though. He walked on, but there were no more cameras until he was nearly in town. But there, on the side of a second-hand car garage which had once been a petrol station, was a battered-looking one monitoring the small forecourt, mounted on the top corner of the old petrol station canopy. It'd easily also capture the pavement and road. It was at just the right angle. He walked right up to it. And there, innocuously enough, on the concrete support column, was a blue cross, protected from the weather.

This was Something. It had to be.

'Can I help, you mate?' said a youngish fat-bellied man eating a Mars Bar, emerging from the garage office, his grey slacks hanging off his backside. 'Looking for a motor, like?'

Nick dropped into his lying mode, one he always rather enjoyed, possibly because it freed him up from being himself to some extent. 'Alright there. No. I'm a private investigator.'

That made the man suspicious. 'Oh, aye? All our cars are clean, mate. There's nothing robbed here.'

'No no. Of course not. It's not the cars I'm interested in. It's that camera. Does it work?'

The man looked up at it. 'Yeah, it's on a small black-and-white monitor in the office.'

'Do you record it all?'

'Yeah. Well, it gets binned at the end of every week. It's just there to catch kids who coin the cars, that sort of thing. Why?'

'Ah, that's a shame. I think it filmed someone important last October. Someone on his way to commit a crime. But if you've binned it all, I'll not be able to prove it. Thanks anyway.'

'Was it that fella what murdered that lad in the Zetland flats?' he said. 'That were last October.'

'Yeah, that's him.'

'Read about that trial in the *Gazette*, like. He got sent down, didn't he?'

'Yeah, 25 years.'

'They must have found him on that DVD they took, then.'

'Who found him?'

'The police.'

Nick paused. 'There wasn't any video shown in the trial.' The man bit into the bar and chewed, melted chocolate at the corner of his mouth. 'Did the police come and see you?'

'Yeah. They took the DVD from the camera. Never gave us it back, like. Thieving gets.'

'Can you remember when they came? The date, I mean?'

'Same day the lad were knifed, whenever that was.'

'18th October. Do you happen to recall what time of day they came?'

'Aye, it were just before three in the afternoon.'

'Are you totally sure that's when it was and not half an hour later?'

'Nah. Deffo just before three. I know 'cos I had a tenner on a horse in the three o'clock at Kempton Park and I wanted to watch the race.'

Bloody hell. They'd taken the DVD probably just before the murder had been committed, before they'd even been called to the crime scene, before Vokes could have even appeared on the recording.

'So how come you're investigating it if the bloke's been sent down?'

'There are a few inconsistencies in how the police dealt with it,' said Nick.

This seemed to please the man. 'Well, I hope you can stick it up the coppers. I bloody hate them, me, like.'

'When they came to get the DVD, how many officers was there?'

'Just one. Harry Small, the bloody get. Always up my arse that one, going on about me cars being cut and shunts which they're not. He really gets under your skin, him, and you end up just wanting to twat 'im one, and that's just what he wants so he can nick you. He puts The Fear in you so that even when he's not around, you can feel his presence, looking at you. Such a bloody creep.'

'He's retired now, you know.'

'Aye, I was told that. Wouldn't have trusted him as far as I could shit him. Something evil about that one.'

Nick thanked him for his time and completed the walk into town, turning up Bishopton Lane and walking to the Zet. There were no more cameras. There was no way one of those six cameras wouldn't have filmed Vokes if he'd walked that route, and surely no way they were all broken. They were all accessible to the police, but Harry Small had got the only privately held footage. Each camera had been marked, presumably by someone indicating which camera's footage to acquire. Even if he'd taken the most obvious alternative route, he'd still have ended up walking past that garage. The DVD had to have evidence that Harry Small, and by extension, Ronald Ross, didn't want revealed.

Reaching the Zetland flats, he stood looking at the awful block, covered in graffiti. Danny's old flat now had a broken window. The place looked deserted, not even Blobby was looking out the window anymore. Maybe it was full of passed-out stoners, but it seemed more likely it had now been abandoned altogether. It had a ghostly, sick quality to it, as though it was a physical manifestation of the worst aspects of humanity. The fact that there was still a dark stain on the pavement outside the communal entrance where, whoever it had been, had breathed his last, and further over, Don's bloodstains too, all turned Nick's stomach. This was all so sodding sick and corrupt.

Wandering around to the back of the property, there was a broken green wheelie bin next to a back door. That had to have been where Berryman had kept his stash bag. Black bin bags and carrier bags of decomposing rubbish littered the enclosed area, three or four feet deep in places. By the look of it, the bin wagon had stopped collecting there a long time ago. In the far corner, a sheet of rusting corrugated iron lay on top of something. What a stinking mess. Whatever was under the sheet of metal was coloured yellow and blue. A tyre poked out. It was a bike. He pulled a few of the bags out of the way, and began tugging at the bike wheel. Avoiding piles of dog shit and the rank bags of rubbish, he pulled the bike out from under the metal. It had a badly twisted wheel and had obviously been run over. He took a closer look and hauled it up and away from the rotting mess.

It had probably been quite smart when new, with a nice yellow and blue paint job. Not cheap. Now, though, it was badly scuffed, rusting and bent out of shape and clearly had been for a long time. Someone could fix it up, though. It wasn't beyond repair. Seemed a real waste just to leave it there. It had obviously been dumped ages ago. He knew someone who worked in a bike shop in Yarm, he'd be able to repair it and make it good again and he fancied doing some cycling, so he stood it up and tried wheeling it along. It was impossible because the front wheel was so badly buckled. He'd have to return in the car to pick it up. Giving it a final inspection, he noticed there was a black metal clip on the back of the frame and one on the handlebars, too. They both had a three-letter logo etched into them: TBC.

Taking out his phone, he typed 'TBC bike logo' into Google. The top result was for a small mounted camera made by a company called Top Bike Camera. Scanning their catalogue, he found the right model to match the clips. It was about the size of a fat marker pen. You mounted one on the bike, or attached it to your helmet and it could record up to an hour of fairly high-resolution footage onto a small micro-SD card. Incredible. Modern technology still amazed him.

A thought suddenly popped into his brain. What if this bike had belonged to the man that was killed that afternoon on 18th October? It was too posh for anyone in the Zet to have owned it, and they can't have even known it was back here, or they'd probably have sold it for scrap for drug money. It had just been dumped and then effectively hidden under the cast-aside metal sheet. Rubbish was just hoyed out the back and left for the rats, so the bike had been all but buried and then ignored.

The cameras must have been stolen, whoever's bike it was. Not that they were expensive. Only £90, but even so. Taking a last look around he set off home.

'Well, where has Harry Small gone? Why doesn't Mandy just nick him?' said Julie, handing him a cup of green tea, after he'd explained about the cameras and blue chalk marks. 'It sounds like everyone knew he was bent. For whatever reason, he's clearly perverted the course of justice by taking that DVD maybe even before the murder even happened. He could go down for years for that.'

'I reckon he's gone to ground along with Kev Berryman. Neither have been seen since me and Kev let Berryman go. They've clearly conspired together, but to do what?'

'To get Vokes nicked for a murder he didn't do, clearly.'

Nick shook his head, frustrated. 'But that doesn't make sense. The video footage from those cameras would have helped prove Vokes's guilt, they'd prove he was on his way to the Zet to do the crime, if he was on them. If he wasn't on them, why would Small take the one from the garage and get rid of it? Why say there was no footage of him if there was, or why remove proof that there wasn't?'

She pursed her lips together and sat in deep thought, feet up on the sofa.

'Tell me again what was said about the CCTV in court.'

Nick crossed his legs and drummed his fingers on the armchair, then picked up his notes and flicked through them.

'The prosecution asked George Dunne, the senior officer in charge of the investigation, if he'd looked for Vokes on CCTV. He said yes they had but that he wasn't on any in that area, but also said that several cameras that might have filmed him were out of action. At the time I thought it was weird he'd not been filmed, but also that so many cameras were out of action - but apparently it's quite typical for them to be knackered. The thing was, the court and the defence barrister just accepted his evidence as gospel on day one of the trial. Shouldn't the defence have requested to see it?'

She put her mug down on the coffee table and tucked her legs back under herself.

'Vokes will have had a public defender employed by Legal Aid, because he had no money. When I worked at Carlisle's in the Boro and in London, there were some great PDs but some really shite ones as well. And even the good ones can't commit the same time and resources as a well-paid barrister can.'

'His barrister was wooly, I thought, and a lot of prosecution evidence went unchallenged when it really needed forensically picking apart.'

'Yeah, but to do that, he'd have to have his own team to look into it. He'd need to send out people to get evidence to prove innocence, and on a Legal Aid budget that's never likely to happen to any extent. It's disgusting that the rich get better legal defence than the poor, but it's true.'

'Yeah, I suppose so.'

'So tell me about this bike you found at the Zet.'

He went over everything. She listened, eyes narrowed and fiddling with her hair.

'It's probably nothing. But it seems odd to me that someone chucked away an expensive bike there. Even if you'd had it run over and knackered whilst...I don't know...whilst buying dope there...you wouldn't just dump it. You'd take it home and get it fixed, wouldn't you?'

'Maybe it was stolen by a doper, ridden there and then dumped. Bikes are nicked all the time,' she said.

'Yeah, yeah, maybe. Or - and I know this is a bit out there - the man that was killed there arrived on it. When the police arrived, then the ambulance, it gets run over. There were five police cars that attended in total. It's then just hoyed around the back with all the other crap.'

'OK, so you think the cameras on the bike could have filmed his murder? Is that what you're saying?' Suddenly, out of nowhere, she sneezed loudly, three times. 'Oh, god. That hurt. I nearly let some wee out.' She pressed at her bladder and winced. 'I hope I'm not getting that snotty bloody cold you had.' Clearing her throat, she went on. 'If that was true, surely the police would have spotted the cameras on the bike. Mind, just because there was a clip for a camera doesn't mean there was one on there, either.'

'Maybe they did and maybe they were made to disappear along with anything else which proved that Vokes didn't kill anyone.' She gave him a disbelieving look. 'I know, I know...but this whole thing is a massive conspiracy, so don't get cynical on me. Everyone thought Danny was dead, don't forget!'

She held her hands up. 'True. Sorry. You're right. There's been a stitch-up from the start on this, obviously. '

'Instigated by Ronald Ross. It surely has to be him behind all of it.'

'What does he look like? Any idea?' She sneezed again, twice, and let out a groan. 'Bugger, I feel so snotty. You and your sodding cold. Fuck it. I hate being ill!'

He typed the name into his laptop, got a photo from the *Gazette* website and turned it towards her.

She raised her eyebrows in surprise, sniffed and said, 'Oh, he's better looking than I thought. For some reason I imagined him as a posh, tweedy, fat old man. He's...what...early 60s? And very handsome, but in that heinous alpha male, v-neck jumper, jacket 'n' chinos, rugby club sort of way. All forehead and shoulders. Awful.' She mimed putting her finger down her throat to make herself sick.

'Yeah, he was the youngest minister in the last Thatcher government. Had Danny with Linda Collins. The now Lady Linda. Not the one the Beach Boys wrote a song about, though.'

'Now that would be weird.' She looked at the photo. 'He looks a bit like Oliver Reed, but without the roguish charm.'

'Danny said he was the most evil man alive. He doesn't look evil, does he?'

'No he doesn't. Was Danny exaggerating?'

'Hard to know.'

'How is the film stored from those cameras?'

'Just one of those micro-SD cards.'

'Did anyone mention a bike in court?' asked Julie.

'No. I don't recall that being said, but it's hard to remember everything. Sometimes I missed what a witness was saying because I was noting something down.'

They both sat, arms folded, in silent contemplation.

'I think I'll call Jeff, see if he's any ideas. He's usually good for a bit of creative thinking.' Nick hit Jeff's number. He answered right away.

'Now, then.'

'Alright, man. Where are you? At home?'

'I'm in the kids' hospital at James Cook in the Boro.'

'Why? Is Argie alright?'

'Not really. He had that cold, that turned into the flu and today he's really poorly and having trouble breathing. I've just brought him down here. They think it might be pneumonia.'

There was obvious worry in his voice.

'God, so what's happening?'

'They're doing tests and keeping an eye on him. I'm sleeping here overnight, just so I can be near him if he needs me.'

'Is he really that bad?'

'Yeah. Kids are often very vulnerable to pneumonia, apparently.'

'Bloody hell. He's not been ill before now, has he?'

'No, nothing.'

'Well, I'm sure they'll get the little lad sorted out. Do you want us to come down and sit with you?'

'Thanks, but no. Mandy is coming over when she comes off her shift. There's nothing you can do. Nothing I can do. That's the worst bloody thing about it. I'm absolutely bricking meself. He's got to be alright. Mandy said all parents go through sort of thing when their kids get ill, but I'm just not prepared for it. Anyway, what were you calling for?'

'Oh, it's not important.'

'No, go on. I need to have my mind taken off fretting over Argie.'

'OK, then...' he explained about the bike and where he'd found it. Jeff listened in silence. 'Am I being crazy thinking it was involved in the murder scene?'

'I reckon Jules's idea about it being a robbed bike that was dumped is the most likely. I agree, it is odd that it's there, though. You know, you said the bike was under a mound of bags of rubbish as well as the sheet of corrugated metal? Was there anything else under the bike or was it lying on the concrete?'

Nick closed his eyes to try and recall.

'It was on the ground.'

'OK, so that means it was put there before everything else, doesn't it? It must have been clear of rubbish or anything else for it to be on the concrete. So if you could find out when the council stopped collecting their bins, you'd have an idea what's the latest it could have been dumped there. If it was last summer, say, then you'll know the bike was there long before the murder and can be discounted.'

'Yeah, that's good logical thinking. Brilliant.'

'And something else...if you find it could have been there on the 18th, you might want to go and look where it was again. I've seen those cameras and they're often designed for easy clip on and off, so you can take them with you when you've parked your bike. They could easily have come off when it was thrown down there and skidded into a corner or gutter. They just look like a fat old Biro, really. Easily ignored. But no point in going there and risk getting savaged by rats unless you have to.'

'That's brilliant, man.'

'Just call me Sherlock.'

'Has Mandy said anything about arresting Ronald Ross yet?'

'Nope. I get the impression she's extremely wary of nicking him until she feels she's got a watertight case, and she's a long way from that, right now. She doesn't want to rely solely on the misidentification of the body. We've all seen various police forces getting a kicking for going after famous people without enough evidence. She has to avoid that situation happening, because as soon as he's arrested you know it's going to be front-page news. And he's probably got God as a lawyer, ready to pick apart the legals, if at all possible.'

Nick quickly recapped the CCTV situation and asked Jeff if he had any idea why Harry Small had made the recordings disappear when, if Vokes was on them, it'd have helped prove his guilt.

Jeff cleared his throat and said something to someone, probably a doctor.

'I've got to go. They're ready to see Argie.'

'OK. We'll be thinking of him.'

'Just quickly, though - it's not in order to hide Vokes they made the recordings disappear, it's because someone else is on them. Think on it.'

The next morning, after he'd cooked breakfast and seen Julie off to work, he called the council and was put through to the section that dealt with Environmental Health.

'Hi, there. I'd like to report a health hazard.'

A man with a light, slightly camp Durham accent, replied.

'OK, I'll just take the details. What is it and where is it?'

'At the back of the Zetland flats in Stockton. There is a mountain of rubbish in carrier and bin bags and it's attracting rats. I saw one there yesterday.'

'Ooh, nasty filthy things, rats.'

'I think it's built up because the bin men are not collecting from the flats for some reason. I don't know how long for. Must be quite a while, judging by the amount.'

'I'll look into that.' He paused and was presumably looking at a computer screen. 'Oh, the Zetland flats, yes, of course. They've been embargoed because of bin abuse.'

'Bin abuse? What's bin abuse?' said Nick, half laughing at the very idea.

'Basically it means setting fire to your bins or destroying them in some other way. They'd had three sets and ruined them all. And we have a policy of not collecting refuse which isn't in a wheelie bin.'

'Oh, OK, I see. When did the ban start?'

'Let's see. 16th October last year was their last collection. Ironically, of course, we will take away material that is hazardous. And by the sounds of it, it is a health hazard now. So we might as well have kept collecting it, really. Silly.'

Nick wrote the date down with a big tick beside it. The place could have been clear of rubbish on the 18th. If the bike had been dumped earlier, while rubbish was still being collected, the bin men would have taken it away either for themselves as perks of the trade, or just put it in with the rest of the trash. Within a week of the bins not being emptied rubbish would have started piling up on top of the bike, so the bike was there around the time of the murder. It had to have been.

After texting Jeff to find out how Argie was, he drove to the flats and with trepidation, looked at the big pile of bin bags and rubbish. First, he put the bike into the boot of his car, then pulled on neoprene gloves which Julie wore when colouring her hair, so as not to stain her fingers.

Putting one bag of stinking crap after another to one side, he steadily cleared a pathway to the corner and the sheet of corrugated iron, looking for the small pen-like cameras as he did so. As he lifted one sack up, a large brown rat made a run for it, leaping up and over some bags and scuttling under more of the fetid bags. Nick let out a high-pitched yelp as it emerged. Nasty rats! He shivered and swallowed hard, then moved another bag, but underneath it was yet another rat. This one didn't move. It seemed to have decided to try and out-stare Nick, its black beady eyes fixed on his.

'Go on then, get yourself fucked off,' said Nick, out loud. What did you do to shift a reluctant rat? Didn't they leap at your throat when cornered? He retreated to the car, keeping an eye on it, giving it a chance to get away. Once he was a few feet back, with something of a swagger, it clambered up and over the biggest pile of rubbish and disappeared into it. Christ knows how many of the evil beasts lived off this crap. His heart was beating fast. Bloody horrible things.

At least he now had a clear path to the corner where the bike had been, so he walked back, looking closely at the ground. The pointing on the back wall of the building was washed away and there were deep damp grooves at the base of the house as a result. He got down onto his hunkers and looked around closely. Nothing at all. He moved more bags around; thankfully, no more rats emerged. Still no sign of anything that might be a camera.

He searched for another 15 minutes but still couldn't see anything at all. Maybe there hadn't even been a camera. Oh, Christ, everything stank so badly that he was feeling distinctly queasy. As he shifted one last bag, it revealed a small square drain, into which an outflow pipe drained. The gaps between the bars of the drain were blocked with grit and muck and all around that area was damp. He kicked at it with his foot and scudded off the top layer of filth. And there, wedged into the muck, was a small black pen-like thing, a little bigger than a betting-shop Biro. He prized it out and peered closely at it. Yup, this was the same as the one he'd looked up online. No wonder no-one had found it. Now, was this one of a pair, front and back, or was it the only one? He cleaned out the rest of the drain but there was no other camera there and nowhere else for one to be. Well, one would have to do.

There was a small flap on the base, which once pressed opened up and the micro-SD card popped up. Sliding it out, he inspected it. It looked OK but it must have been wet over the last months, so whether it would still operate properly had to be in doubt. Even so, he felt a thrill that he'd actually found it.

Taking the camera back to the car, he cleaned it with a wet wipe. It was probably covered in rat piss and needed disinfecting, if he wasn't to catch Lyme disease or some other heinous lurgy.

He took off the gloves and was about to drive away when his phone buzzed with a text from Jeff. He'd sent it to Julie as well.

'Argie much worse. Not breathing well. Doctors very worried. Looks bad. Come and see him asap.'

Given Jeff's habit of understating almost everything, Nick knew immediately that this was serious to the point of being life-threatening. Bloody hell. He texted back, *'On my way now'*, and sent it. As he did so, he saw Julie's response: *'Will be with you in half an hour-ish'*.

Nick did a three-point turn outside of the Zet and accelerated towards Bishopton Lane. As he turned the corner, he passed a parked silver and black BMW Z4 sports car. As he drove away he looked in his rearview mirror, surprised to see such an expensive car there.

Making his way to the hospital on the A66, turning off onto Marton Road, his stomach churned with worry. As came off the roundabout, he noticed a silver BMW Z4 a few cars back. Was it the same one? They were quite unusual but not unique. He shook his head, dismissing the thought as witless paranoia.

He pulled into the car park, cursing out loud, as he always did, as he put money into the parking ticket machine. Sticking the ticket on the window, he strode into the hospital and followed the signs to the children's ward. Jeff was sitting reading a newspaper in a waiting room area.

'Hey, Jeff.'

Jeff looked up and gave him a half grimace, half smile and stood up, putting the paper to one side.

'Alright, man. Thanks for coming.' He patted Nick on his shoulder.

'How's the wee man?'

Jeff was pale and drawn. The bags under his eyes betrayed the fact he'd not slept properly for a couple of days.

'He's not good. He's really ill, Nick. He's got really bad pneumonia and, look...I'm not going to sugar coat this, loads of kids die of it. Their lungs get full of fluid and they can't breathe. That's our Argie's problem. They've got him hooked up to an IV drip and are giving him antibiotics through it.'

'Oh, god. Poor lad.'

Jeff pushed at his forehead, 'All I want to do is to be able to help him, but there's nothing I can do...I wish I could suck the germs out of him.'

Nick grabbed him into an embrace.

'Please don't let him die,' said Jeff, trying not to cry. 'I can't be without him. Life will have no meaning without him. He's my everything.'

Nick gripped him hard. They'd grown up together. They knew each other better than they knew themselves. And this was the heaviest of heavy shit.

'It'll be alright, man. It will,' said Nick out of hope rather than belief.

Jeff pushed him away and sat back down. Nick sat alongside.

'You know what, man? In other parts of the world, millions of kids die just like that.' Jeff clicked his fingers. 'We were the first generation that had proper healthcare for kids. Before that, death was always at the door. You pretty much knew if you had two or three kids, one or two of them wouldn't make it to adulthood.'

'Yeah, dying was sort of expected wasn't it? Maybe we were less afraid of death back then because we saw it close at hand.'

Jeff cleared his throat and rubbed his eyes. 'This is bloody torture because you feel so helpless, when your only job in life for your kid is to help them and be there for them. You feel like you're letting them down. He's an innocent little boy. Why is this even happening?'

'It's nobody's fault, man. It's just life. We're animals and we get sick. But he's a strong little fella. I'm sure they'll sort him out. Where is he?'

'He's just down the hall in his own little room. Can't have him near other kids as he might be infectious and kids who are in here already have low immune systems, so...you know...'

'Can we go and see him?'

Jeff nodded.

It was heartbreaking to see the lad in a bed asleep, hooked up to the drip. He was such a noisy, bubbly little boy normally, but here he was, becalmed by a bacterial infection. His breathing was shallow and rattled, the way old miners' lungs used to rattle. He looked hot.

The door opened and Julie stuck her head around.

'Ah, there you are. Aw, bless 'im. The poor little mite.'

'Thanks for coming down, Jules,' said Jeff. 'He's not responding to the antibiotics, not yet anyway.'

She leaned over the bed and took the boy's small hand.

'He sounds really congested.'

'He's been having coughing fits. His lungs fill up with fluid.'

She bit her lip in worry. It was almost unbearably sad. Nick put his hands together, closed his eyes and said a silent prayer for Argie.

'If there was a God, he'd not have even let this happen, so it's no use praying,' said Jeff, flatly.

A nurse came in.

'Now then, how is the little chap?' she said, checking his pulse.

Nick couldn't bear seeing the boy like this. It was he who had given Argie the cold, almost certainly. Alright, no-one owns a virus, but even so, it felt very like he'd made the boy ill.

'I'll just find a toilet,' he said, slipping out the room. He leaned against a wall and took a couple of deep breaths. It all seemed so unfair, so unjust that Argie was having to fight for his life at such a young age. Jeff was right, it was the powerlessness that hurt the most. You were utterly impotent to effect change.

Walking down the corridor, he found a toilet and used it. After washing his hands, he stood looking out the window down to the car park where he'd had to pay. Right by the entrance was a silver BMW Z4 again. Three in one afternoon. That was one too many for it to be a mere coincidence. Someone had been sitting in the driver's side on the corner of Bishopton Lane and they'd begun to turn around after he drove past.

It couldn't be Berryman in a pricey car like that, but it could be Ronald Ross, or even Harry Small, who'd have got paid off with a decent pension. But why would he be following him? From his angle he couldn't see if there was anyone in the car. The micro-SD card was in the boot along with the crumpled bike. Bloody hell. He might have seen him with the bike and wanted to get hold of the cameras. The top of his old BMW was visible and he couldn't see anyone around but all the same, he had the urge to check it was safe.

He ran down the stairs and out into the large parking area, weaving through cars until he reached his own. It was fine. The boot hadn't been popped. Looking around to see if anyone was watching and being satisfied they weren't, he opened it up, took the card out of the camera and put it in the money pocket of his jeans, then slammed the boot shut.

'Do you have any change, by any chance?' The voice came from behind him, He spun around to see a middle-aged man with swept-back brown hair give him a smile and raise his eyebrows. 'I forgot they make you pay. Seems wrong.' He held out a fiver.

Nick reached into his pocket and produced four pound coins and two 50p.

'Yeah, I think it's totally wrong, as well,' he said, as they exchanged money.

'Indeed. Well, thanks.' He half bowed, half nodded and strode away.

Was he familiar? Maybe. On Teesside you often see people who look familiar, for some reason. Maybe there's a genetic similarity that's commonplace, born out of the region's mix of Irish and Viking ancestry.

Nick walked away, back towards the hospital and turned to watch the man walk briskly towards the car park entrance, straight to the Z4, unlock it, get in and drive away, heading for the exit.

Then suddenly, he knew exactly who that was.

Exactly.

The fucker.

Ronald Ross. He looked him up on his phone, just to make sure. And there on the *Gazette* website was the picture he'd shown Julie, from a recent report about housing policy. The same man.

What the hell was that all about?

Walking back to Argie's room, he tried to work it all out. He'd followed him from the Zet. Did he know about the micro-SD card? No, he couldn't do. If he did, he'd have found them himself. It wasn't that hard, as long as you were prepared to brave a few rats. He must have been there for some other reason, then seen him leaving and followed. He'd already know who Nick Guymer was and what he looked like. His picture was all over the internet for one reason or another, as was Julie's and Jeff's, too, for that matter. Hellfire, there was even a video of him and Julie having sex out there somewhere, courtesy of Sean O'Connor's band of evil twats. The thought still made him shudder.

What was his game? What did Daddy Ross know about what he, Nick, knew? Was he going to try and shut him up? Was he going to try and kill him, even?

As he got back to Argie's corridor, there was a commotion with people shouting and nurses running past him and from the opposite direction. What was going on? A panic pounded into his heart with painful electricity as he realised they were running to Argie's room. Oh no. Oh, please no. No. Don't let it be true. Please god, keep him alive. Please.

Julie came out of the room as he got level with it, clearly getting out of the way of the medical people.

'What's going on?' he said.

She looked at him with tears in her eyes.

'He stopped breathing. Just like that. We both heard it. It was like he was holding his breath. But he wasn't. He'd just stopped. He couldn't get a breath. We hit the alarm and they've all just piled in.'

'Oh, god...no...' tears burst out of his eyes. 'Has he...has he...has he died?'

Her mouth turned down as her bottom lip quivered. 'I think he has, yeah,' she broke down, holding her head in her hands, weeping.

'Oh, god. He's not dead. Oh god...no...no...he's such a nice little boy. Oh, god...please no no...please no...please...'

They hung onto each other, sobbing for the short life of Argie Evans. He had been taken from them when he had all of his life ahead of him. One moment alive, the next, gone.

'He said my name. The only word he ever said was Nick and I was the one who gave him the cold!'

It was too much to bear. The pain in his heart was vicious and deep. All he wanted was to be able to change the truth. Change reality. Where was lovely Argie now? That laughing silly little boy. Where had he gone? How had this happened? How and why? No!!!! His soul screamed in pain at the loss of a life he had so loved.

Julie was crying in big heaving sobs, eyes red and swollen and desperate. They sat down on the seats in the waiting area.

When reality comes off its hinges and delivers a horrible shock, it's hard to know what to even think. Everything about existence seems pointless if something so plainly wrong can happen. All seems chaos and nothing makes sense.

Nick cleared his throat. 'Where's Jeff?'

'He was by Argie's bed. Holding his hand while they worked on him, to try to get him breathing again. He was just this little floppy thing...poor poor Argie...oh, god, you never saw anything so tragic as that small, defenceless little bairn.' She rubbed at her temples with both hands. 'I don't know how to deal with this. It was horrible enough when we lost Joni, but nothing like this has ever happened to me. You hear about children dying, but it's all so abstract. This is all too real.'

Nick got up and went in search of Jeff. He had to be by his side to help him through this.

Argie's room now had six nurses and two doctors in. All of them surrounded the bed. Jeff had been relegated to being a spectator at the back of the room. Nick raised his eyebrows and shuffled up to him, taking hold of his big leathery hand - something he'd never done before in his whole life. There was nothing to do or say. All you could do was watch the medical people work on the small life-form that had been Argie.

Jeff was a stone wall. No tears. Nothing. He just stared.

'They're trying to clear his lungs so he can breathe. Emergency measures, like.'

Nick nodded.

'How long can someone go without breathing?'

Jeff raised his eyebrows, in the way he did when answering some silly rock trivia question.

'Surprisingly long. Everything ticks over for a few minutes. It's the lack of oxygen to the brain that you've got to be careful of. I looked it up.'

'Yeah, I remember the paramedics told me that when I found Emily last year.'

Jeff nodded and tugged at his long beard.

They watched as a doctor with a stethoscope held it to Argie's chest, as a nurse administered an injection to Argie's arm.

One second.

Two seconds.

Three seconds.

Then it happened.

Argie coughed and then, weirdly, sneezed loudly and a long string of snot fired out his nose.

Jeff leapt forward, knocking people out of the way, and knelt beside the bed.

'Argie! You're back! Oh, Argie, son...' now his tears came.

The doctor said some words, though what they were Nick couldn't hear. He walked out of the room, emotionally shredded, needing to find Julie to tell her the news.

She had got a plastic cup of coffee from the machine was sitting, elbows resting on her knees, sipping at it.

'Jules. He's alive. They got him back.'

She looked somewhere between astonished and ecstatic, put the cup down, and hugged him.

'Really? But he was lifeless.'

'They injected him with something, Probably adrenaline. He coughed and sneezed and just came back to life.'

She sighed deeply and looked exhausted at him.

'Thank god. But will he be OK? I mean, he wasn't breathing for minutes.'

'That's a question we won't know the answer to for a while, I suppose. I'm just glad he's alive.'

She paused and looked into the middle distance, then blew her nose on a tissue. 'Christ almighty, I feel totally drained.'

As things quieted down and staff got back to their normal duties, Jeff emerged from the room, tying his hair back and collapsing onto a chair, rubbing his face.

'He's breathing a lot easier now.'

'Is he alright?'

'They'll test him in the next couple of days to see if he's got any brain damage from oxygen deprivation. The doc said his heart hadn't stopped throughout and that's a good sign, apparently.'

'So does that means everything was still kind of working?' said Nick.

'Sort of. You've got a certain amount of fuel in your tank, so 'cos we were there when he stopped breathing, he was able to function on that for the short time it took for them to get him going again. He seems a bit confused but then, he's been half alive and half dead, so that's natural.'

He turned and gave them both a huge grin. 'But he's alive and that's the only thing that matters.'

'I feel like someone ripped my heart out of my chest and used it as a football,' said Nick.

'Me, too,' said Julie.

'Yeah, I've had better afternoons, meslef, like. You know what? They should have a bar in this place. I could use a big single malt.'

'A chip shop would be good, as well. I'm bloody starving,' said Julie. 'My belly is touching my spine.'

'Youse two can get off. They'll be taking him down to intensive care in bit. I'll just stay on to make sure he's settled.'

'OK, if you're sure,' said Nick.

'Yeah, yeah. I just wanted you here because I thought the boy was a goner. I really did. But it turns out he's a bit of a fighter, thank god.' Tears fell from his eyes again. He wiped them away.

Nick took Julie's hand as they stood up. 'Oh, by the way, I got the SD card from the bike camera.'

'Really? Amazing,' said Jeff. 'I wonder what's on it?'

'I'm going to go home and find out. And another thing happened. I met Ronald Ross in the car park. He followed me all the way from the Zet, which is where I was when you texted me.'

'What?' said Julie, frowning so heavily, it made deep lines on her forehead. 'Are you sure?'

'Totally. He's driving a BMW Z4. He came up to me and asked for change. I didn't know it was him in that moment. I gave him the change but he didn't use it. He just went back to the car and drove off. It's like he was sussing me out or something. It was a weird thing to do.'

'What was he like?' said Jeff.

'Well-spoken. Polite. Didn't look like the most evil man you've ever seen.'

'The most evil men rarely do,' said Julie, 'Which reminds me, I must get back to work. I'll be in late because I'll be making up this missed time. Text me when you've looked at the SD card.'

All the way home, Nick kept his eyes peeled for the Z4 again, but didn't see one anywhere. Once back home in Norton, he took a shower to wash the mix of rat-scared, death-fear sweat off himself, put on his oldest, worn-out, washed-out jeans and a grey v-neck t-shirt and sat down with his laptop and a cup of Sencha green tea. What a bloody day it had been so far.

He loaded the card. The computer seemed to pause and think about whether it was going to work or not, as though its processing power was breaking through the skin of mank and dissolute that oozed from every pore of the Zet. It then opened up and showed another file icon titled with a random selection of letters and numbers. It was a 2Gb card and it was full.

Taking a sip of tea, he clicked on it. It took a few seconds before his media player loaded and the file began to play. It was clear that this camera had been mounted on the front of the bike and had been turned on as the bike was travelling down a road. It was sharp and well-focused, the resolution high enough to see most details. Nick stopped the playback and tried to work out where it was. It was on a vaguely familiar domestic street of suburban semi-detached houses. It shook as the bike went over bumps in the road and then stopped at a junction and turned left. Suddenly he recognised it. Of course. The bike had turned onto Fairfield Road and was going past the distinctive Dutch barn-style houses that had once been part of the council stock. It must have started in Wellburn Road where his old school friend Stewart Young had lived.

It was taking a familiar route from his childhood as it reached the Rimswell pub and took a right down Bishopton Road West. Picking up speed, it went past the Avenue on the right, but then slowed to let out a car from the Elm Tree Social Club on the left. Amazing that place had survived all these years. It had all been fields around it when Nick had been a boy, but now it was a sprawling housing estate. On it went past his old 6th-form college, across to Bishopton Road. There was only one way this was going. It was heading into town, and was on a direct route to Bishopton Lane and the Zet.

He sat back, hand over his mouth and watched the action unfold. It was a bright day. But which day? It came to a halt at the junction where Bishopton Road and Durham Road intersect, waited for traffic and then rode off under the railway bridge and up the gradual slope, off which, on the left, was Bishopton Lane.

Sure enough, it slowed and turned sharp left, rode towards the station, then took a right. There in focus was the Zet. Nick's hands were sweating, his heart beating hard. Who the hell was this and what were they doing?

The bike braked to a halt. The camera juddered as the cyclist dismounted, and then settled down. It must have been parked by jamming the right-side pedal against the curb so it was upright.

No-one was around at all.

With a sense of mounting horror, as the rider walked away from the bike towards the Zet, he knew with certainty it was the man whose body was passed off as Daniel Ross. This man was going to be murdered. It was like being God, watching. With his back to the camera, he held his phone to his ear. It had to be a drug deal, didn't it?

The lack of sound gave proceedings an unreal, almost fictional quality; as though this was all being acted out for the camera. The man stopped at the Zet's communal entrance and put the phone in his pocket. The angle of the camera meant it couldn't capture if anyone was at any of the windows. He turned and looked back to the bike. Nick hit the pause button to take a long look at the man.

Oh, god, he was no age really. Thin, like Danny, early 20s, like Danny. Wearing a grey hoodie with the hood pulled up, like Danny. He wasn't a lookalike for him, but could've been his cousin, easily. Nick's stomach churned as the camera kept filming. Did this man buy drugs at the Zet? He was obviously waiting for someone, but not someone who lived there, because they'd already have come out.

Then it all happened. And quickly.

The man turned and looked towards the camera but over the top of it. Clearly someone was approaching. This was his deal arriving. He must have filmed the encounter on purpose. A lot of cyclists filmed themselves in order to protect themselves legally if a car knocked them over, and he'd parked the bike in the perfect position to film himself.

A car didn't appear in the shot. But suddenly Ronald Ross was there, wearing gloves. Nick hit 'pause' and looked at him. It was definitely the man he'd met earlier, the same man he'd seen on the *Gazette* website. He clicked 'play' again. His heart leapt as Glenn Vokes walked into view.

Ross stood close to Vokes, talking into his ear. The cyclist looked from one to the other. In his left hand, Ross had a heavy-duty clear plastic bag, in which, Nick realised immediately, was a knife. The murder weapon.

Oh, shit. This was it. The murder. It was going to happen and happen now.

Ross gave Vokes the knife. He took it and stared at it. Ross nodded but kept talking. A lip reader could probably discern what he was saying.

Vokes took the knife out of the bag, handed the bag back to Ross, felt the weight of the steel in his hand, jogging it on his palm twice, then said something to the cyclist who was remarkably calm. Maybe he was so shocked that he was rooted to the spot with fear. He didn't seem to be in fear of his life at all. He looked at Ross and then...

Bile rose in Nick's throat and he had to turn away from the screen.

Ross really was evil, just as Danny had said. Clearly, to Nick, Ross had told Vokes to kill the man with the knife.

And he'd done it.

Murdered him. Just like that. Seven knife wounds in an arc from the middle of his back around to his side. Wounds one and two had penetrated his heart. Nick could still see the photos of them in his mind's eye.

It was hard to think that it was real. Like when he'd first seen a newsreel of someone getting shot in the Vietnam war, when he was a boy, it was hard to comprehend that it was an actual thing that had happened, that the bullet to the man's head had killed him.

He'd thought Vokes was too physically slight to have done it, but Vokes had pulled the man towards him and stuck the knife in, killing him, perhaps thankfully, almost immediately.

Nick steeled himself, rewound it a little and watched it again. It was all over in less than five seconds. The man just slumped to the ground, blood oozing through the grey hoodie, already dead. The pathologist said he would have died very quickly as soon as the knife tore into his heart. Ross took the knife off Vokes, returned it to the bag and then thrust it towards Vokes, who took it off him and ran.

The video continued. The body was still and lifeless. Ross took out a phone and walked off camera. He had to be calling the taxi that would find the body. After just a few more seconds the bike was clearly knocked over with some force. That's how it had got its bent back wheel, obviously. A car had to have hit it. Nick paused the video and drew out where the bike was, where the body was and where Ross had to have parked. He'd have to have done a three-point turn and that's when he hit the bike.

The force of the collision had released the camera and in a blur of light it came to rest somewhere around the back of the building. Yeah, that was what happened. No doubt about it. While it was still filming, there was nothing to record. It was pointed at the concrete wall and recorded nothing except changes in light as clouds came and went.

He got up and went to the toilet, feeling emotionally drained by seeing a murder, and by the fact that all along, he'd been totally conned by Vokes in court, the bastard lying toe-rag. He had been certain that he was not guilty, totally certain, but he *was* guilty. But then, he had also told the truth. He said he didn't stab Danny, and he didn't. It wasn't Danny, even though his father had told the police at the morgue that it was. So who was it really?

Ronald Ross must have a hell of a hold over him to be able to coerce him into murder. He must have been so afraid for his own safety to not even mention Ross's name in court, not even when he was being sent down. He was forced to kill a man, probably under pain of his own death. There'd have been a good chance that if he'd confessed to that, he'd have got a very reduced sentence. He might even have got off on a manslaughter charge. There's no way he'd have got 25 years. Then again, 25 years in jail meant he'd be out aged 50 and that was preferable to being dead. It showed the power Ronald Ross had. Why hadn't anyone else even mentioned his name in the eight days of the trial? Not the prosecution, the defence barristers or any of the witnesses. Daniel Ross's background wasn't raised or discussed. It was as though his father had been airbrushed out of his life. Somehow, Ronald Ross must have influenced the trial - but how? Via the judge? And if he could do that, the reach of his influence was to be rightly feared, and it surely extended to elements within the police.

After voiding his bladder and washing his hands, he paused to think about the course of action to take now. This was conclusive proof of Ross's guilt of conspiracy to murder and Ross didn't even know it existed. Even so, it would be sensible to make copies. So he went back to his computer and uploaded it to his Cloud. Then he texted Emily.

'*I need a secure, unhackable place to put an important video. Can you help?*'

She soon replied.

'*Is it another naked raunchy sex tape of you and Jules?!!*' She'd added an emoticon of an erect penis, a vagina, and another of a dog with its tongue hanging out. It made him smile a little, even though this was all very heavy shit. She followed it with a link to a server, with password and log-in code. '*I'll lock this down as soon as you've uploaded. Can I watch it?*'

'*Thanks, Em. You're a star. It's your choice. It's a film of a brutal murder.*'

'*Oh god. No thanks. Luv U. Be careful.*'

He uploaded the video to the secure server, then made a copy to a DVD.

Right, that was the evidence secured. Now what? Text Jules.

'*SD card shows Vokes did murder whoever it was, but Ronald Ross was with him and gave him the knife. He seemed to be urging Vokes to do it. Should I send it to Mandy?'*

While he waited for her to reply, he went into the kitchen, took two lamb chops out of the fridge and put them into a hot frying pan, then tossed some broccoli into a pan and put a flame under it. He cooked the chops to medium rare and spooned some homemade pesto over them. As he ate, the phone vibrated with a text from Julie.

'Yes. Send it now. Take her the card too, for evidence. Shocked. Are you OK?'

He replied. *'I'm fine. Feel strong. Am worried he's so well connected he can get off a conspiracy to murder charge and then come for us.'*

She came right back. *'Mandy will arrest him immediately. He can't get off when there's film evidence, can he?'*

He thought about it and texted Julie again.

'I'm worried Mandy is bent or compromised somehow, and if she is, we're dead as soon as we show her the video.'

She came back. *'Why do think that?'*

'1. Harry Smalls was given a free pass for years. Why? Everyone knew he was corrupt. 2. Ross's money and influence is huge. 3. The police have been suspiciously shit throughout this.'

'I'll be home at 8pm. Don't do anything yet.'

He texted Jeff. *'How's the big A?'*

'Much better. They think he's responding to the drugs at last. No coughing for an hour or two. He looks brighter.'

Nick replied. *'Fantastic! Video shows Vokes killed the man, but Ross made him, I think. Don't tell Mandy yet. Am worried police are bent and under Ross's money and influence. He wasn't mentioned in court at all, not by anyone. Suspicious of that.'*

Jeff texted back. *'Wow. Wouldn't surprise me. Almost certain Mandy is fairly clean. She bends rules, breaks a few, probably. But wouldn't be bought off. But how many of them are bent? I won't say anything until I hear from you.'*

Julie got home at 8.15pm, by which time Nick had cooked her some liver, onions and bacon, along with some thick gravy, peas and a sweet potato and celeriac mash.

'Phwoarr, that smells fantastic, I'm starving.' She went to the sink to wash her hands. 'Have you eaten?'

'Yeah, I had chops earlier.' He served up the food. 'I think this is OK. It might be a bit over.'

'I don't like it too pink, anyway.' She sat down and cut into the thick piece of liver. 'Oh, it's lovely. Still very tender. Not like the rubber liver we had at Ian Ramsey, do you remember?'

'I actually liked that. I remember going back for seconds, even though it was all hard and crusty around the edges. Always loved liver since I was little.'

'Delish onion gravy. Thanks for this. It's so nice to come home to a proper dinner. I'm so lucky.'

He put the kettle on as she ate.

'So this video, then. I'm not sure that I want to see it,' she said, scooping up some peas with her fork. 'I've had enough emotional trauma for one day.'

'It's not nice. Well...obviously it's not nice. One thing the camera shows is that the victim lived on or around Welburn Road, off Fairfield Road. That's where it was turned on, anyway.'

'In that case, there'll be a record of someone who's gone missing from around there.'

'Not necessarily. They might have been a loner who no-one would miss.'

'True. But wherever he lived, he'll not have paid the rent or mortgage. The mail would pile up. There'll be signs that he's not there any more. I'm sure the police could find out who he was. I just wonder why he had to be murdered? He must have had something on Ronald Ross.'

'Yeah, but he doesn't seem frightened of Ross. He had plenty of chance to run off when Ross produced the knife, but he didn't. He didn't make any effort to get away.'

She frowned as she mopped up the last bit of gravy with the last piece of liver. 'Yeah, that is strange. What about the sweatshirt? Was Vokes wearing that?'

Nick paused and thought. 'No, he's not.'

She pushed the plate away and took a drink of water. 'It doesn't make any sense, though, does it?'

'Why not?'

'They didn't need to frame Vokes for the murder with the bloody sweatshirt, because he'd actually done the murder.'

'They weren't framing him, they were just making sure he was arrested for it. I thought he'd been framed, didn't I? But he hadn't. He's clearly the killer.'

Nick poured some green tea for them both.

She nodded and sat thoughtfully for a couple of minutes.

'I'd better watch it then, just to see what it is you're talking about.'

'You don't have to. It's a bit gruesome.'

'I once saw a kid stab another kid on the Hardwick estate when I was about 13. He used a Swiss army knife. Thankfully, he didn't kill him.'

'Do you want to do it now? There's only a few minutes of action to watch.'

'Yeah, go on.'

He put his laptop in front of her and loaded the video, clicked 'play' and then began to load the dishwasher as she watched, sipping at her mug.

'Here we go,' she said. 'He's parked the bike and is standing outside the Zet...and...Ross and Vokes have arrived...' her eyes were fixed to the screen in an unblinking stare. 'He's stabbed him...hmm...' She paused it and then rewound the last 15 seconds, leaning forward to be nearer the screen, a deep frown on her forehead.

'Have you seen something?' said Nick.

She shook her head. 'No. But this is all wrong, somehow.' She watched the rest of the action then looked up at him. 'I...I...I'm going to say something that you'll think is weird.'

'What, like?'

She looked back at the screen and pointed to it. 'That's not real.'

'What? How is it not real? You mean it's been Photoshopped?'

'No no no...I mean that's not what a violent assault looks like.'

He scrunched his face up in puzzlement. 'I'm still not getting you. He sticks the knife in him. That's pretty violent.'

'Oh, Vokes is violent, yes. But everything else is wrong. It looks like Ross and the man don't mean it. There's no tension or escalating emotion. Ross hands him the knife as though it's not even a knife. Like it's a wooden spoon and couldn't harm anyone.'

'But it is a knife.'

'I know. Oh, bugger it. I can't explain what I mean. Look, I grew up around plenty of acts of violence, didn't I? Kev and Ricky kicking off on some poor sod. I know what it looks like and whoever is involved, it follows similar patterns of escalation. The victim isn't even scared. This looks fake to me.'

Nick just didn't understand what she meant. It looked real enough to him.

'Is the blood fake?' he said.

'No, that's not what I mean. It's the atmosphere of the situation that's wrong. It's like they're acting the part, not really doing it.' She took out her phone and dialled a number.

'Hiya, Kev. Have you got a spare half an hour? Yeah? Come over to our house and take a look at this video. It's of a murder. Yeah, a real murder. I need your advice.'

She put the phone onto the table. 'He's coming over now. I want to know if he agrees with me.'

Nick loaded up the dishwasher, set it going and wiped down the surfaces, while Julie went for a quick shower, returning in loose-fitting green army trousers and a white t-shirt, hair tied up into a colourful scarf.

'Thanks for that delish dinner, luv,' she said, gently patting him on the crotch and giving him a quick kiss before going to the fridge for a bottle of Chablis.

'You look like Goldie Hawn in *Private Benjamin* in those pants and t-shirt. This is a very good thing.'

They went through to the living room, each with a glass of wine. Nick hooked the laptop up to the flat widescreen TV so they could all view the film of the murder.

Kev wasn't long in arriving.

'Now then, sis. What's this about?' he said, as he came into the room.

'It's the murder at the Zet.'

'What about it?'

'We've got a video of it.'

Kev's blonde eyebrows shot up. ' 'Ave you now? Top work!'

'Do you want a drink?' said Nick, pointing to their wine.

'Nah. I'm still off the pop, me, like.'

'Right. I'm just going to show you this without comment. Don't say anything until it's over. Then tell me what you think about it,' said Julie, pressing 'play'.

Kev sat with his chin on his hand, in just same way Julie sometimes did. Funny how these things are passed down through families. It got to the part where Vokes and Ross appeared, and Ross gave Vokes the knife. Kev raised both eyebrows, then frowned as Vokes murdered the man, leaning forward, elbows on his knees.

After it was over, Julie paused it.

'If you had to sum that up in a sentence, what would it be?' she asked.

Kev rubbed his tanned bare arms. 'It looked like a scene from a bad movie. Like it was badly acted. Vokes is for real, the other two...I dunno, it looks weird.'

'Yes! See?' said Julie, to Nick.

'Is that what you thought, Jules?'

'Yeah. It's as though Vokes is playing it for real but the other two are just standing there. Why would the lad who was murdered just stand there and take it? He doesn't fight. Doesn't even flinch or pull back, or anything.'

Kev nodded. 'This is mad, but it's like the lad wanted to get stabbed. His body language is relaxed and open. No-one would be like that when a twat like Vokes is in front of you with a big fuck-off knife.'

'Do you think Ronald Ross wanted Vokes to kill him? When I first saw it I thought he was coercing Vokes. He seems to be in his ear. It looked to me like Vokes was reluctant to take the knife,' said Nick.

Kev looked at him like he was mad.

'No chance. Vokes was bossing that. Ross was carrying the blade, for a start,' said Kev.

'Why is that significant?' said Nick.

'It means if they got pulled over on their way there, Ross takes the rap for carrying a weapon.'

'And the...I don't know what you call him...the lesser of the two carries the knife?'

'Yeah, of course. He's the one who's doing what he's told, either that or he's the one getting the biggest payout and therefore taking the biggest risk. Could be that.'

Nick wasn't sure that was right, at all. Vokes might have *thought* he was bossing it, but Ross was the mastermind. He rewound it again to the moment before Vokes pulled the man towards him. Vokes was turned slightly towards the camera so for a brief moment, his face and expression were well captured.

'Now, that's a psycho,' said Kev. 'The fella 'as totally lost it. Y'see this in fights. There's lads who can just flip their switch and go into batter mode, just like that. It's like they can bring the rage up in them whenever they want. He's one of them. But look at Ross's expression.' Kev stood up and went to the TV screen, pointing with his right index finger at Ronald Ross's face. 'He's smiling. Look.'

'It's not a smile, Kev. It's a smirk. But good spot,' said Julie. 'It's like Vokes is doing what he wanted. You're right, Nick. Ross is in charge.'

'Yeah. And chummy, who is about to be knifed, he's not even set himself. You do that instinctively. When someone comes at you, you tense up, usually you take one step back, unless you're our Ricky, and then you take one step forward. Vokes has pulled him into him with his left arm and stabbed him with the right, one, two, three, four, five, six times. That's all pro work. Not the first time Vokes has done it, I'd say. He seems very sure how to do it. That way you get him in the heart a couple of times and even slice a kidney if you're lucky. Everyone thinks you stab someone in the heart from the front, but it's all bone that side, isn't it...you've got to get up and through the ribs. Much easier to do it from the back.'

Kev seemed to be in his element discussing this, like it was his specialist subject, but Nick interrupted him. 'Hang on, hang on...you said there was six stabs...you must have counted wrongly. There were seven wounds in the photos we saw in court.'

'Deffo six. I'll show you.' Kev got the video back to the first stabbing and moved it through one second at a time. 'There's the first one - and that's the really big one. That's the one he's really trying to kill him with, and the second as well, another big one. Look how far he pulls his hand back to do it. Wham. Then the third, fourth, fifth and sixth are all done really quickly, but he knows he's got him with those first two. The rest is decoration and probably didn't do him much harm.'

There really were only six stabs. Six. Not seven.

Nick sat back on the sofa, pulling at his stubble as Julie and Kev talked. They'd been given the pictures of all of the puncture wounds, which they'd been told had been taken in the morgue. One man had even felt faint at seeing them and they'd had to adjourn for half an hour while he got himself together. Clearly, Vokes had only stabbed him six times, there was no doubt about that. None. So that meant the evidence in court was wrong. But how do you get that wrong? That body had seven, this body would have had only six.

This had to be a different killing.

'You know what? I think this whole thing is a sham,' he said, waving an arm to dismiss it. 'It's all bollocks from start to finish. Nothing about it is true.'

'Eh? How come?' said Kev.

'I'm still working it out. Hold on...' he rubbed at his temples, letting his thought coalesce. 'Right, first up, it's not Danny who was murdered. That's the first and biggest lie. Danny doesn't look like he was ever a drug addict, no matter what he says. The pathologist said there were seven stab wounds and she showed us the photos. There's no way she got that wrong. So those photos are not of this body.' He pointed to the bleeding man on the screen. 'We were told the identity of the body was only finally confirmed by his father at the mortuary at North Tees, but we know Daddy Ross lied. You both think the fight is fake, somehow. Why was it being filmed by the man who was murdered? Why didn't he fight back or even struggle? Why didn't he run? He could have. Why did Harry Small take the DVD from the garage?' He paused again, trying to hold it all together in his brain.

Julie twirled a strand of blonde hair around her index finger. 'Can you remember the name of the judge on the trial?'

'Oh, yeah. It was Quentin McQueen.'

Kev laughed. 'Fucking hell. Quentin! Posh queer, was he?'

'Hey, watch your language,' said Julie, getting up to fetch her laptop.

'What have I done, like?' said Kev, indignantly.

'We don't tolerate homophobic language in this house.'

Kev shrugged and looked at Nick for help.

'She's right. We don't,' said Nick. 'Also being called Quentin isn't a marker for the nature of your sexuality, just for being a posh sod.'

'I have no fucking idea what the fuck you're talking about. I've nowt against benders, anyway. Get your kicks any way you can, I say. Was just 'avin a laugh.'

'Don't push your luck, you,' said Julie, jabbing a finger in her brother's face.

She typed the judge's name into Google.

'Hmm. Here we go. Born in Darlington. From 1972 to 1982, he was educated first at Eton and then Cambridge. What a surprise that is. Then became a lawyer working in Newcastle and then back in Darlington. OK, so let's just see what Ronald Ross's vital statistics are.' She tapped at her keyboard. 'Yes!' she punched the air and held her fist aloft.

'What is it, Jules?' said Kev. Nick had already guessed.

'Ronald Ross, born in Darlington, went to Eton in 1971 and then Cambridge, graduating with a degree in law in 1981. He was the youngest minister in the 1987 Thatcher government.'

'So they knew each other,' said Nick.

'And what was the name of the pathologist?' said Julie.

Nick went to the music room where he sat and wrote everything. Picked up his folder of notes and returned to the living room.

'She was called Carolyn Parkin.'

Julie typed that into Google along with '+ pathologist'. 'Got her. Born in Wolviston in 1960. Went to Cambridge University in 1979 to study medicine. That gives her every opportunity of also knowing Ronald Ross. That's simply not a coincidence.' She looked from Kev to Nick. 'The judge has guided the jury to pass a guilty verdict and has instructed the barristers to keep his name out of it. He's pulled a favour in.'

Kev wasn't surprised. 'And they'll have had to have the SIO onboard as well. Who was that again?'

'George Dunne,' said Nick.

'Oh aye, Dunny. He's alright, him. Never heard that he's bent, but there's no way you can scam something like this if the SIO isn't allowing it, just because it has to be knitted together.'

'Could Mandy know about this?' said Nick. 'It's bothered me all along that she is, in some way, dodgy.'

'Not necessarily, or not if she wasn't at the scene,' said Kev.

'She wasn't. She also said she was launching an independent enquiry into how the case was handled.'

'Well, that will expose the conspiracy, surely,' said Julie, drinking her wine.

'Depends on if she wants it to, or not,' said Kev.

They sat in silence for a minute. There were so many elements to this conspiracy that it was impossible to keep them all in your head at one time.

'I think my brain is going to melt,' said Julie.

'I thought you were supposed to be the brainy one, Jules,' said Kev.

'I just feel like such a mug,' said Nick. 'I fell hook line and sinker for Vokes's sob story. I was sure he'd told the truth about being on speed and not even being there. I hate that all the stuck-up people on the jury like Tina Harris were right. '

Their front door bell rang. Nick jumped up to answer it.

'Jeff! What are you doing here? Is Argie alright?'

Jeff grinned and put both thumbs up. 'The wee man gets better every hour.'

Nick sighed. 'Thank god for that. Owee in...Kev's here as well.'

'Ah, right. Cool.'

They went into the room.

'Now then, Jeff,' said Kev, getting up and shaking his hand. 'The fucking state of your hair. You look like a wizard.'

'I'll take that as a compliment. I come with news. First, that they've found the right antibiotic to treat Argie. Gave it to him in intensive care and he bucked up within an hour or two. He's out of danger, anyway.

They reckon he'll be fighting fit in a week or less. Early signs are no brain damage.'

'That's so good to hear,' said Julie. 'God, I'm so relieved.'

'Also, Mandy called me about half an hour ago to tell me to cancel the restaurant because she's working late due to the fact that they've just arrested and charged someone for the murder of Tracy Berryman in the Zet.'

'Really? Who is it, did she say?'

'No-one we know. She said it was a crazy punter. Tried it again in Redcar, but the woman got away, and called the police. They nicked him and he confessed to killing Tracy.'

'But where's the little girl?' said Julie. 'What did he do with her?'

Jeff shook his head. 'Again, I don't know the details, but he took her and sold her to someone for £100 apparently. I know...what a world we live in, eh.'

'Told you, didn't I?' said Kev, looking smug.

'Is the bairn alright?' said Julie.

'As far as they know. They'll go and get her. Those wheels are in motion right now.' He puffed out his cheeks. 'Heavy shit, isn't it? Still, at least we now know that killing was nothing to do with old man Ross, or anyone else shutting her up. We got that totally wrong.'

'Well, the Vokes murder is less clear cut,' said Nick. 'You want a drink?'

'Aye, go on. I've had one of the most draining days ever. I'll risk getting pulled over on the drive home.'

Nick went and poured him a large single malt. When he returned with it, Jeff was in full flow.

'Mandy won't be in on this. And I'll tell you why,' said Jeff. He took the glass. 'Cheers, man. She's been in the force for over 35 years. She's always wanted to be top dog, or top bitch, as she likes to call it. There's no way she'd risk everything she's worked for just to fit up some toe-rag criminal like Vokes. Look, I suggest you give this to Mandy. In fact, not to do so is probably some shade of illegal. We don't have a choice but to trust her. I assume you've made copies, so if it goes missing in strange circumstances you've still got proof. I mean, if you don't give it to her, what are you going to do? Vokes will get let out of jail and given he's a knifey psycho, that wouldn't be a good idea, would it?'

Jeff was right. The whole point had been to get evidence of Vokes's innocence. But he wasn't innocent, so sod him. Nick took the DVD out of the computer and handed it and the SD card to Jeff. 'Will you do the honours?'

He looked at his watch. 'I'll drop it into her office now. She'll still be there. Do you need a lift, Kev?'

'Aye. Cheers, Jeff.'

When they were on their own, Nick turned off the TV and computer and flopped down onto the sofa.

'Christ, I feel so drained by everything today. And I feel like a fool. How could I have got Vokes 100 per cent wrong?'

'Because you're nice.'

'I'm not that nice. I'm not nice at all, in fact.'

She laughed a little. 'Not in the conventional way, like. I just mean, you wanted to give someone the benefit of the doubt, knowing that life deals rubbish cards to some people. Doesn't make you stupid to think well of someone who didn't deserve it.'

Nick mulled it over, still feeling annoyed with himself, feeling like he'd really shown himself up as easily duped. All those nice respectable people on the jury, the people he'd really disliked, the people he thought were vaguely despicable, and at the very least, not fit to judge a man like Vokes. Those people had all been right. He had been wrong. What lesson was that going to teach him in life? He hated that a haughty, snooty woman like Tina Harris had been right. But her instincts had been better than his.

'The thing is, Jules, how do you cope with people you loathe being right?'

She shook her head wearily and closed her eyes. 'Don't overthink this, man. For fuck's sake, please don't make this about you being shit. You wanted to do the right thing, you tried to do the right thing. Leave it at that. No-one is perfect. Stop dwelling on it!'

Her intolerance and the raised tone made him pull back. She wouldn't admonish him if it wasn't justified. She was right. He was far too obsessed with how he dealt with life. Normal people don't do that. Normal people shrug off the imperfections of being human.

He rubbed his face and went to fix them both a drink, returning to find her stretched out on the sofa, TV on.

'It's an England game,' she said, pointing at the screen.

'Oh, yeah, it's a pre-tournament friendly against Norway.'

'Thrilling. We're winning 1-0. Ashley Young goal.'

'Ashley bloody Young,' grumbled Nick, half under his breath. 'You know what'll happen, don't you?'

'At the Euros? Yeah we'll get through the group stage and then get knocked out on penalties to the first good side we play, probably Italy.'

'I'd be amazed if anything other than that happened.'

They watched the game in near silence. Nick's mind kept wandering back to the Zetland flats. They had assumed Tracy's murder was related to the other murder, but it hadn't been. That had been a total red herring. When he'd met Ronald Ross in the hospital car park, he'd seemed quite normal and certainly very polite. Not evil at all. But then, his judgement of people was poor, as he'd proven over Glenn Vokes.

'Is it possible that Ronald Ross is actually the good guy in all of this?' he said.

She looked over at him and frowned. 'I told you, stop thinking about it. It's none of your business any more, whether he is or isn't.'

'You were with us when Danny said he was the most evil man in the country. I took him at his word on that, did you?'

'No, of course not. I didn't disbelieve him, but he could easily have been exaggerating. People get very strong views of their parents. He blames him for his mother's suicide, I remember that. But you can't take people's words at face value all the time, not when you don't know them...and even then. I mean, I'm not objective in my view of my own mother. Not everyone thinks she's an auld shitehawk, but then not everyone was brought up by her. Christ, this is a terrible game of football. I hate watching England, they're so tedious.'

Nick's phone buzzed with a text.

'It's from Jeff.'

'What's he saying?'

Nick read it out. ' "Mandy is raging. She watched the recording. Has called in all the top brass to haul George Dunne over the coals and get to the bottom of it all. Thinks there's been something either very dodgy, or very crap going on. Watch this space..." '

'Mandy is scary when she gets a proper cob on,' said Julie.

As Nick was reading the text, another came in. Once he'd read Jeff's, he flicked the screen and looked at the new one. It was from Hair Bear.

Something weird has happened. You were talking to me about Danny Ross. The dead Danny Ross. He's not dead. He came to me today to score some grass. I told him I don't deal anymore. I told him who to see to get sorted and he said he'd already been there for his heroin, but the man didn't have any grass. He even showed me it, man. A huge wrap of smack. It's all a bit Zombieland, Arizona. Thought you'd like to know.'

Nick read it out to Julie.

'He's back in the UK?' she said, sitting up and turning to him. 'Why's he come back?'

'God knows. He said he was too scared of his father to come back.'

'And the first thing he's done is buy drugs. I thought he was clean.'

'Maybe he was lying about that as well. Lying about his father, lying about everything. That's what you do when you're from the Zet, remember? You lie and you lie and you lie about stuff you've not even got any reason to lie about. You lie even when it won't gain you anything. It's just an instinct to cover your tracks and muddy the waters all the time.'

She sat, arms folded, looking at their old Persian rug, not saying anything, musing over their trip to Spain.

'You know what I've done? I've been taken in totally by him, just like you were by Vokes. When I was chatting him up, I thought I had the upper hand because I knew who he was and knew his history. I also knew he fancied me and that he thought I was giving him the come on, which to be fair, I was. That also gave me the illusion of power and as a result, I stopped thinking. Because I thought I had the whip hand, I had assumed he was, by and large, telling me the truth, when he wasn't. He said he was sent away by his abusive father. He said he'd kicked a drug habit. But we've no proof that either of those things was true. How do we know his story about his father was true? We don't. How do we know he was sober, or even ever an addict? We can't. But since we came back from Spain we've totally assumed those were facts. We've seen him as an innocent party, almost. That was sloppy of me.'

'And you also fancied him, that didn't help.'

'I did not!' She spoke with indignation.

'Yes, you did. I could tell. And that distracted you. It made you want to believe him.'

She looked away from him and pursed her lips together then jabbed a finger at him.

'Stop being perceptive. You're supposed to be the socially dysfunctional loony.'

'Well, you don't buy heroin if you've not got a drug habit, do you?' said Nick.

Julie took a drink and shook her head. 'Mandy will get to the bottom of all this. There's the video evidence, Ronald Ross will have to answer for his actions and so will the police officers involved, and the pathologist. I mean, you got Vokes wrong, but your instinct that something wasn't right about the whole thing was on the money. Albeit via a strange route, you did uncover something very weird.'

The morning dawned rainy and windy, and it was the sort of persistent, extra wet, heavy, fine rain that Teesside specialised in, one which came on a cool, brisk northeasterly and made a mockery of any dreams of early summer. Nick put the radio on in the kitchen as he set about making Julie's breakfast, one of his favourite jobs of the day. He loved feeding her, feeling that the woman he loved so deeply was constructed, at least in part, from the food he unromantically put in her face.

He tried not to do the same meal twice in a week. Taking some uncooked king prawns out of the freezer, he put some coconut oil in his wok, got it smoking hot and fried the grey chunks of protein until they were a lovely peachy-pink. Once they were done, he put them to one side, added ginger and spring onion into the fat and fried it off for a minute, while he beat two eggs. He chopped some chestnut mushrooms and added them. Once they were cooked, he threw in the cabbage along with mirin and tamari sauce, whacked up the heat for 30 seconds and slung the whole lot onto the prawns. Working quickly, he poured the beaten egg into a bit of melted butter and made a small omelette, seasoning it with salt, black pepper and five-spice powder. Once it was set, he tipped it out onto his wooden chopping board and shredded it into strips.

'Brekkie is ready, Jules!' he called up the stairs. She called out an affirmative response.

Back in the kitchen, he put a flame under the wok, got it hot and tipped in the prawns, egg and vegetables again, adding some fine glass noodles that he'd soaked in hot water. As they got hot, he chopped some fresh coriander, throwing it into the pan, stirring it twice and turning off the heat just as Julie walked in, sniffing the air.

'Chinese food? Excellent! Hang on, you've not put garlic in, have you? I don't want to fry some poor service user's face with garlic breath.'

'I thought of that. No garlic.'

She put her hands on his hips as he stood at the cooker and mimed humping him up the backside.

'Aw, what a sex god you are. It smells great.' She looked over his shoulder and kissed him on his neck as he tipped the contents of the wok into a blue-and-white china bowl.

'Do you want chopsticks or a fork?'

'Fork, obviously. A fork beats two bits of wood every time.'

She sat down at the kitchen table and tucked into the food while he made coffee.

'Is it any good? I always worry about overcooking frozen prawns.'

'It's bloody delicious. Y'know, the first time I went to Las Vegas, I was staying at Caesar's Palace and I signed up for the eat-until-you're-dead breakfast buffet...' she sucked some noodles into her mouth '...and for the first few days I was all bacon and eggs. But then I got into the Chinese food and had it for the best part of two weeks. My friends thought I was mad.'

'I dunno why. Ah, breakfast is a funny meal. Some people have this strict idea of what you can and can't eat in a morning.'

'When did the whole sugary cereal thing get going? It's bonkers.'

'After the war, I think. You might as well eat biscuits as eat cornflakes. Mad. When I was at college you know what my breakfast always was?'

She gave him a look. 'Was it a nubile student's panties? You shag monster.'

'Obviously, yes. But when they were not available, I had Ryvita and Marmite.'

She gave him a sneering look. 'That's rubbish.'

'I know. It was easy, though. No wonder I was skinny. If it wasn't for the beer, I'd have had no nutrition at all.'

'But you *could* cook. You used your cooking skills to win the affections of girls.'

'I did, but the bar was set very low. I could cook steak and chips and spaghetti bolognaise. I did a brilliant spag bog. But anything else was pretty much beyond me.'

'Well, this is ace. The five-spice powder in the egg is especially magic.'

'The key is to have more protein than anything else and not pad it all out with vegetables or noodles.'

She nodded, head bowed down to the bowl as she hoovered in more noodles, then spoke again.

'When I first moved to London, sushi was a big thing. I had no idea how to use chopsticks but if you couldn't, it was frowned upon, as though you were a real hick. So I sat in my flat trying to learn how to use them, so that I looked sophisticated. I got quite good at it but then thought, nah, a fork works better than chopsticks for almost anything. Sod 'em. Hate that sort of snobbery.'

As Nick took their tub of coffee out of the fridge, BBC Tees, the local BBC radio station, moved to a news story.

'Mandy Beale, Chief of Cleveland Police, held a press conference at 7am this morning. She announced an independent investigation into the murder of Daniel Ross last October.'

It switched to a recording of Mandy. 'Evidence has come to light of a miscarriage of justice in regard to the apparent murder of Daniel Ross at the Zetland flats in Stockton, last October. It has transpired that Daniel Ross was not in fact murdered that day. I will give you more details when I have them. Members of the public should rest assured that no stone will be left unturned and if there is corruption to be found, we will find it. If there is malpractice we will find it, if there's bad practice, we will find it. I am determined to get to the bottom of why a man was declared to be murdered, when he was actually alive. I ask for the public's patience while we get to the bottom of this. To say I am unhappy would be something of an understatement, and I won't rest until we've sorted this highly unusual situation out. Thank you.'

Nick turned to Julie, eyebrows raised. 'Sounds like the shit is well and truly hitting the fan. I'm sure Ronald Ross will be getting a visit from Mandy today. She can't put it off any longer, surely.'

'Well, she's got the film of him at the crime scene. He's got some explaining to do about that and about the body, too.'

'What a mess.' Nick ran his hand through his hair.

'But you know what? All of this would have gone undiscovered if you hadn't felt that the verdict was wrong.'

'But I still don't know what it is we've discovered. Is it a murder? Is it a set up? A fake? It's all swirling around in my brain like so many leaves blowing around in a gale.'

'Who knows? Mandy will get it sorted out, I'm sure, and I'll be sodding glad when she has.'

After she'd gone to work, Nick wrote a piece on the upcoming European football tournament. In the middle of doing that, his phone rang. He didn't recognise the number.

'Hello?'

'Hello, is that Nick Guymer?' said a nice sing-song female Geordie voice. He'd always thought some Geordie accents were very sexy. On women, anyway. The sort of accent that suggested a good time was not out of the question.

'Yeah, it's me.'

'Great. I got your number from Sarah Simmons. She edited your novel, *Kidda*, I think.'

'That's right.'

'Lovely. Sorry, I should've said who I am. Debbie Healey, I'm a producer on *Look North*. We do an arts feature today. I was wondering if you could come in and talk about your novel?'

'To be broadcast this evening?'

'Yeah. I know it's short notice, but short notice is how we do everything. It's a book about a lad from Stockton who hits the big time and then falls apart, isn't it? I'm sorry, I've not read it. I'll be honest, I really hate football.' She laughed, the sort of dirty Northern laugh that he loved.

'Weirdly, I don't really like football, either. Not anymore. The money has ruined it for me. I've been phoning my passion in for years. But yes, I'd love to come in.'

'Eee, that's great. We film most things in the afternoon. Can you get into the Newcastle studio for filming at about 3pm?'

'I can. Thanks, Debbie. This means a lot to me. Getting publicity for your book is such hard work.'

'Aye, I can imagine. No bother, Nick. Mike Wallace is the presenter, he'll look after you, if you can get here about 2.30pm.'

'I will. No problem.'

'Great. Eee, well, it's been nice talkin' to you.'

He rang off and sat with a smile on his face, feeling like something had gone right, for a change. So while the stars were aligned he called Trevor Daley at the *Mirror* in Canary Wharf.

'Now then, Nick.'

'Hi, Trev. How's tricks in the smoke?'

'Crazy. Sometimes I still I miss Darlo, you know. I was saying to the missus last night, when I worked with you on the *Northern Echo*, life was real. Down here everything seems phoney. Phoney and expensive. Anyway, you didn't ring me to listen to moaning on about living around Cockneys. What have you got for me?'

Nick knew he'd have to talk this up in order get as much money as possible.

'You remember the story I put to you the other week. Well, it's got bigger since then.'

'That's what I like to hear. Give me an outline.'

Nick did exactly that. When he told him about the video he'd found, Trevor let out an incredulous gasp.

'What? He filmed it?! Bloody hell. So we've got a Peer of the Realm being an accessory to murder and on film? That is fantastic. What was his name, again? Have they nicked him yet?'

'Not yet, but the wheels are turning. Mandy Beale, who is...'

'...I know Mandy from way back. Helluva shagger, y'know, if I recall the Christmas party in 1989 correctly.'

'You didn't, did you?'

'I did, aye.' He said it with mock fear in his voice. 'I couldn't keep up with her. She was voracious.'

Nick grinned to himself. 'I've heard that, like. Someone told me you've got to go into training if you're going to keep her properly serviced. Well well well, I never knew that. You never said anything at the time, Trev.'

'She was too much for me to handle, man. I was so rubbish with her, I thought it best not to mention it the next day. Didn't make me look good. Aye, good old big Mandy. I heard she'd got the top job. Yeah, so back to the story, has she arrested this Lord yet - what was his name?'

'Ronald Ross. No, not yet. But she'll be having him in for questioning. It's still not quite clear yet what has happened.' He went on to say how Ross and the other man's behaviour was oddly unconvincing.

'So was it some sort of fake killing or a joke thing?'

'No. Well...everyone thinks Vokes was for real.'

'I don't get how two can fake it and one be real. Are they setting him up?'

'I think so. Still some work to do on that. But there's a junkie son, a murdered prostitute and a missing baby girl to tell you about as well.'

When he'd gone over everything in his notes. Trevor whistled. 'This is a tabloid jackpot, Nick. Kids, aristocracy, drugs, sex, police corruption: the perfect quintet.'

'Can you use it now or will you wait until someone has been charged?'

He made a clicking noise with his tongue. 'I'll have to be careful. Need the lawyers in on it. Can you write up everything you've got? We can always add to it as things develop. Has anyone else got this?'

'Nope. I found the video. I've got copies of it, if you want it.'

'Yeah, deffo. Send it to me.'

'Before I do that, we need to talk money, man. I need 20 grand.'

Trevor exclaimed loudly. 'Twenty, Nick? Bloody hell.'

'C'mon, Trev. This has got everything. That's not big money for an exclusive like this.'

'I'll have to get someone upstairs to approve it. I'll ring you in an hour.'

Nick hated having to be pushy about money, it just wasn't in his nature, but when you worked for yourself it was so easy to devalue what you did, and not to charge properly for it. These days, everyone wanted everything for almost nothing. He doubted he'd get anything like 20 grand, but one thing was for sure; if you didn't ask, you'd never get it.

He began writing the piece. It was harder than it often seemed to write for a tabloid. Things had to be kept brief, simple and straightforward.

When Trevor called back he sounded weary. 'Bloody hell, that was like getting blood out of a stone. I've just spent 75 minutes arguing with my boss over your money. How does 10 sound?'

'About half as a good as 20. To help you out, I'll come down to 15.'

Trevor exhaled into the phone, making it distort. 'I'll get my arse kicked for this. But if you can get that video to me right away, it'll help keep them on board.'

'OK. Will do. I'll get the piece done as far as I can, and over to you in the morning. Then as there are developments, I can re-edit and add to it.'

'Good. Let's hope Lord Ross is arrested for conspiracy to murder. I love bringing down a Tory Lord. Exactly the sort of thing the paper should be doing. Last year we had a freelancer who came to us saying he was preparing an exposé about someone in the Lords but nothing came of it.'

'Oh, yeah? Who was the freelance?'

'Can't remember off hand. Not a contact we'd used before. I didn't get anything off him and after couple of phone calls, I never heard from him again.' He put his hand over the phone and shouted something at a colleague, then came back on the line. 'Kyle Campbell, that was his name.' Someone shouted something else across to him. 'He was from the northeast, apparently.'

'That's interesting. Very interesting. I'm going to try and find him. I'll be in touch.'

He made himself fresh coffee and did a search on Facebook for Kyle Campbell, but couldn't find anyone from the northeast. He then looked on Google, and found a photo and a brief notice from when Campbell worked for a small local newspaper.

His phone buzzed.

'Hello, Kev. What can I do for you?'

'I've had the boys look at a screenshot of the bloke who was stabbed in the video and we've come up with a name.'

'The boys? Your network of dodgy blokes, you mean?'

'Basically, yeah. Teesside is too small a place for someone not to recognise you, eventually.'

'So who is he?'

'Rory Tyreman.'

'And who is Rory Tyreman? What's his story?'

'Ah, that's where it gets interesting. He is the son of Harold Tyreman, who...'

'...was a minister in the same Thatcher government as Ronald Ross.'

'That's it, aye. And then he was on Stockton council planning committee, alongside Ross.'

'Is Rory a criminal?'

'Nope. He's not. But he's got his problems.'

'Which are...?'

'...gambling debts. He's a regular in the Boro at that casino which Big Fish opened. Ever been in there? Bloody great.'

'No, I haven't. So the lad has gambling debts, therefore he does this faking a death thing for Ross, in order to get him to pay them off?'

'That'd be my guess. But I've been thinking. He doesn't trust Ross, does he?'

'Doesn't he?'

'He's filmed it, hasn't he? Filmed it. He wanted it on record for a reason. He parked that bike where he parked it, so it'd film everything. He wasn't to know the bike would get run over, was he? That was a small camera, smallest one you can get, so he was being clever. Probably went back at some point to try and find it but couldn't.'

Nick doodled on a pad as Kev talked. 'Any idea where he lives?'

'Not yet. But I'll get it sorted and then we'll kneel on his throat and find out what the hell Lord Ronnie has been up to.'

'Good work, man. I'm selling the story to the *Mirror*. I'll give you some of the money for all your help.'

'Nah, man. I don't want your money. You and Jules need it. I'm alright. Thanks, though.'

Nick blew out air and put his hands behind his head.

His phone buzzed again. He rolled his eyes. Now what? He looked at the phone. It was Hair Bear.

'Hey, man. How are you?' he said.

'Like Jimi said, "existing, nuthin' but existing". Thought you'd like to know, Danny Ross has been buying a lot more smack. I got the word from my contacts.'

'Bloody hell. When you say a lot, how much does that mean?'

Hair Bear didn't speak for a few seconds. 'If you ask me, the dude is going to bite the big one.'

'Bite the big one?'

'Kill himself. He's going down with two huge wraps. No coming back from that.'

'Bloody hell. OK, thanks, HB. Let me know where you end up in Darlington.'

'OK, man.'

Whatever Danny Ross was thinking of doing, Nick was in no position to do anything about it, so he went back to writing the newspaper piece, absorbing himself in words. Words were his thing; the instruments of communication. How you could use one word to provoke approval and another to provoke contempt was, for him, a source of endless fascination.

After an hour, he had a break and rewatched the stabbing video, concentrating on Ronald Ross. Ross was in Vokes's ear the whole time, not shouting, but he was saying something and Vokes went from being quite expressionless to quickly getting an ugly violent face on, a face which was so familiar to anyone who went to football in the 80s. Vokes surely wasn't trying to be the hard man, as Kev had said, he was being agitated into doing the knifing. He wondered if Mandy Beale would get a lip reader in to find out what he was saying. It seemed the obvious thing to do.

Writing the piece helped coalesce his thoughts and draw lines of logic between incidents and it allowed him to see it all more clearly. But there was one element he couldn't explain; why did Ross specifically want Vokes to knife someone? Why Vokes? Did he have vendetta against him for some reason?

He found a note of Julie's idea about hiding a murder by

misidentifying the body. He began scribbling down ideas and as he did so, it all began to make sense. It was complex, but as he stared at his left-handed scrawl he knew he'd got to the truth, finally. The key to it all was to stop doing what everyone in the courtroom had been guilty of doing, including himself; prejudging everyone by who he thought they were, and by where and how they lived.

'Oh, my god,' he said out loud. 'That's what really happened. That's how he's done it.'

He went into town and met Jeff in the shop.

'Now then, sexy,' said Jeff, from behind the counter, cleaning records with a soft anti-static cloth.

'Jeff man, I've worked it all out.' He put his arms out wide.

'Worked it out? What? Life, the universe and everything? I've told you often enough the answer is 42.'

'Thank you, Douglas Adams. I mean the Vokes murder. I'm writing an exclusive for the *Mirror* and now it's obvious. Well not obvious, it's the opposite of obvious, but it was Jules's theory about a perfect way to hide a murder that made it all drop into place. That's what Ronald Ross has done.'

'Run me through it, then.'

Nick gathered his thoughts. 'OK, here we go. He planned all this out meticulously, probably along with Harry Small. Ross probably knew Vokes through Danny. He knew Vokes was unstable, maybe even psychotic, and could fly off the handle. I mean, I saw that with my own eyes in court. He went from a sorry, pleading man to a raging, spitting crazy man, just like that. Ross probably saw him do that at the Zet when visiting Danny, or on some other occasion when with PC Harry Small, who we know he knew well.'

Nick went on. 'So Ross gets Vokes all wound up and persuades him to murder a freelance reporter called Kyle Campbell, who was digging into Ross's affairs. Murders him probably around 2.15pm to 2.30pm at the Zet. He was wearing the green and blue sweatshirt when he did it. That's how it got the corpse's blood on it. Now he's got a body on his hands, but doesn't want it identified because Kyle's research might get unearthed. A dead reporter gets everyone's interest. So he says he'll pay this kid Rory Tyreman's gambling debts in return for Tyreman's performance as a dead man. Julie and Kev both said the stabbing was fake and it was. Tyreman wasn't scared because he knew he wouldn't be killed. So he didn't behave like a normal person in those circumstances.'

Jeff had his mouth open. 'I think I know where you're going with this. It's an amazing conspiracy.'

Nick went on. 'Now, as Kev told me, Tyreman rightly doesn't trust Ross, so he secretly films everything, in case he needs some leverage later. Tyreman wears a stab vest and a couple of blood capsules which burst when Vokes pulls him in close to do the stabby, just to convince Vokes that he's been successful. Ross has picked up some psychological techniques from Harry Small who, through work, has known Vokes for a long time. Harry knows what presses Vokes's buttons and Ross uses it to wind him up for the murder. In fact, I think Harry walked Vokes from his flat to the Zet, winding him up as he went, getting him ready to kill two people. Telling him all sorts of lies, promising him money. I bet you anything, though he's not on the film, Harry Small was present throughout both the real and so-called murders. Vokes is so wound up that he does both knifings within minutes of each other. As soon as the second stabby happens, Vokes gets into Ross's car, now driven by Harry Small, thinking he's killed two men. The bike gets totalled and the camera knocked off by Small's clumsy, 3-point turn. He then drives Vokes back to his flat. He gets there just past 3.15. That's when Vokes's legs are caught on the Co-Op camera. But he doesn't go to his flat. He walks off in the opposite direction. That's when Davey Foster breaks in and plants the evidence. Meanwhile back at the Zet, unbeknown to Vokes, Tyreman has got up and left the scene. His bike has been wrecked and he can't quickly find the camera. Ross has then put Kyle's body in the doorway and called the cab. The cabbie arrives and finds Kyle, then it all follows the story I was told in court. We'd have seen all of that if the bike hadn't been reversed into and the camera dislodged and lost. A couple of hours later Vokes goes back to the Zet to score drugs thinking there's nothing to worry about, unaware that in the subsequent two hours he's been fitted up. He's arrested for the murder of Danny Ross. He says "it wasn't Danny" and maintains that all along. And he's right, it wasn't.'

'Bloody hell, this is complex, my brain needs an extra battery fitted. So what part does Berryman play in this?'

'OK, hold on to your trousers. This is what I reckon. Though he's a horrible bloke, I think Berryman is innocent in all of this. I think Berryman saw it all happen from his flat, sitting in his chair, looking into his positioned mirror, as block boss. Now, Berry can't grass on Ross for fear of repercussions. And he wouldn't tell the police anything about anything, almost on principle. But he's not guilty of anything, other than that, at least in this instance.'

'Yes, yes...this brilliant - and that's why he had his stash bag ready to go,' said Jeff. 'We thought he was working with Ross, but actually, he was scared of him and of Small too. Then somehow, Ross discovered he'd seen it go down. That's why he's gone to ground.'

'Exactly. Gone to ground, or maybe gone in the river. If he's dragged out the Tees, it's just another Zet doper who no-one cares about.'

'Yup yup yup. I love this. Well, I don't love it, it's sick, but you know what? Danny's mother and Harry Small's wife both met a watery end. Pound to a penny, that's what has happened to Berry. And I reckon it's Harry Small who does it. He's got a little modus operandi. Maybe he's killed others this way.'

'It makes a lot of sense. Now, the next crucial thing is identifying the actual dead body. Ross put the note with his own phone number on it in Kyle's pocket. The police found that. Called him up. He goes to the morgue and says yup, it's Danny. I Googled Kyle, he was a similar age and build. There's no-one to contradict Ronald Ross and no-one would suspect he was lying about such a thing. Thus he's then cremated and Kyle Campbell has literally disappeared and, as far as Ross knows, there can be no proof of any crime. Danny is in Spain, Kyle is ashes and Vokes is in jail for Danny's 'murder'. All stitched up tight. Harry Small sorted out all the CCTV which would have had himself on with Vokes either by wiping it, or losing it. He took out the camera in Nolan House so nothing would be recorded and seen remotely in Thornaby.'

'This was meticulously planned, man. It's incredible.'

'Oh, yeah. They plotted it all out and it all went perfectly until I got a feeling Vokes was innocent. It was me who fucked it all up, even though I had no idea what I was doing.'

'...that's the weirdest thing, though. You thought he was innocent, but he knew he wasn't. He was lying all along, but in fact, he hadn't killed either Danny or that ringer, but he *had* just butchered Kyle.'

'When he proclaimed "I didn't kill him. I've been set up", he was actually telling the literal truth. He knew it wasn't Danny, and he had been set up, even though he thought he was a double murderer, when the reality was he was just a single murderer.'

Jeff got two mugs of coffee from Alisha and put them on the counter and then held his index finger aloft. 'But tell me this, Batman. Why didn't Vokes even mention Ronald Ross in court? Why didn't he just say what happened?'

'They probably promised him a payout, got a message to him in Holme House, saying shut it or you get no money and a visit in the night. Don't forget, Vokes *had* killed someone - he thought he'd killed twice - so even if he tried to argue that Small and Ross talked him into it, or that he knew it wasn't Danny, it wouldn't have meant he'd get off. As far as he knew, he'd go down for murder, anyway. So keeping quiet about them was his only option, apart from death. They'd trapped him. The fact he was only getting sent down for one murder was, in his twisted mind, a bit of a win.'

Jeff shook his head. 'Bloody hell. What a sodding scam. To go to these lengths, Ross must have had a lot to hide. A lot of corruption.'

'Enough to send him to jail for the rest of his life and to be stripped of his peerage. And like Kev said, his sort are very protective of their reputations, ironically enough. Being humiliated in the court of public opinion would be unacceptable to him.'

'You've got to get all of this to Mandy,' said Jeff. 'She's barely slept. I've never heard anyone swear as much and for so long. Having a body passed off as someone who was still alive will be a major black mark against her force.'

'It's all to do with assumptions, man. A death at the Zet wasn't treated that seriously. Certainly not as seriously as if it had happened in a nice part of Ingleby Barwick or Yarm. So I reckon everyone just took their eye off the ball, and were less than rigorous, because they knew a Zet death wouldn't be scrutinised overmuch. Just get it cleared up and out of the way and move on.'

'Yeah, I think you're right.'

'I'll write it all out for Mandy. Has she arrested Ronald Ross yet?'

'That's going to happen today at some point. She's paranoid about getting it all played by the book, so he's got no wriggle room.'

'What does she arrest him for? Accessory to murder?'

Jeff shook his head. 'That was the idea. But now what you're saying is, there was no murder on the video. It was a mock murder. Can you be an accessory to a mock murder? When she gets all your info, she might hold off for a day or two to get more evidence against him. There's no hurry. The thing she's got in her favour is that Ross doesn't know that video exists. I'm not even sure he knows that we know Danny is alive, unless Gary Simmonds was reporting back to him or Harry Small rather than, as we assumed, Kev Berryman. And I don't think that's likely.'

'I have a strong feeling Berryman, like his daughter, is dead. If he is, no-one will weep. She told me he abused her when she was a girl. I think she had that in common with Danny. They were both on the H for the same reason, in some ways.'

'Christ. The depravity of the human race still shocks me. But one person it doesn't shock is Mandy, and she will get to the bottom of it all. Now she's got her teeth into it, she's relentless. She'll be all over Harry Small like a rash, as well. At least he's was in the Durham force and not Cleveland. That helps with local politics. '

Nick nodded, pulling at his stubble. 'It's a sick business. Oh, I forgot to tell you, I've got to go up to Newcastle, I'm on *Look North* tonight talking about *Kidda*. Sarah got me a media gig.'

'Brilliant. Is that your editor Sarah?'

'Yeah. She's good for contacts.'

'I remember meeting her at some event with you. She was a lovely blonde lass with well-proportioned and quite delicious breasts.'

'Yeah, superb breasts, but more importantly, an even nicer person.'

'So you're driving up there?'

'Up her breasts?'

'Boom!' Jeff hi-fived him.

'Aye. I think they record all the interviews in the afternoon and then broadcast them in the evening. I'm booked in for 2.30pm.'

Jeff looked at his watch. 'It's already after half one. You better get a shift on, lad.'

Before setting off, he texted Julie to tell her about his interview, in case he was late back, and that he'd prepared a sea bass for her, that it was in the fridge, and how long to cook it in the Halogen oven.

She texted back. '*Good luck on the telly. What a nice fella for thinking of feeding me. I shall reward you later with my velvet glove.*' He grinned at the screen, a welcome mental image immediately dropping into his synapses.

The BBC's home on Barrack Road in Newcastle was a largely featureless building that looked like it was made out of Lego and assembled like so much flat-pack furniture. Nick arrived just before half past two and was greeted by Debbie Healey.

'Hello, Nick. Thanks for coming up at such short notice,' she said, shaking his hand firmly and grinning at him with an open, heart-shaped face and mottled grey-blue eyes. About 40 years old, with expensive-looking hair, orange tan, big hips and a flabby belly, she just looked very

Geordie, somehow. 'Can I get you a coffee?'

'No, I'm fine, thanks.'

'Smashing. We're running a bit late, but we'll get Mike to interview you in about 20 minutes or so. We've just got to record another guest first. Politician.' She raised an eyebrow and made a yawning gesture, then made her nice smile at him again. He thought, for about the millionth time in his life, that there was so often something fantastic about women from the north of Britain; something innately open and generous.

'No problem, Debbie.'

He sat in the green room, took out his laptop and began to write down all of his ideas for Mandy. It'd be her job to get evidence to prove them correct, but as he typed, it was clear that it all locked together to make a perfect picture. There was going to be serious difficulty proving that Harry Small was involved in murdering both his own wife and Danny's mother, but hopefully some close scrutiny of his career would bring up enough criminality to get him sent down. His early pensioning off surely meant someone in Durham police already knew he was a very bad apple. He told her he was at the BBC in Newcastle right now, but would be home in the evening if she needed to talk to him. He'd no sooner sent the email to Mandy's personal address, when surprisingly, she replied.

'Ronald Ross is due to speak to *Look North* this afternoon about town planning. I'm following his every move. He might be in the building. If you see him, don't on any account tell him anything about anything, especially about the video. If you do see him, just blank him. And watch your back. He's dangerous.'

Nick closed the laptop and exhaled heavily. Debbie had said they were interviewing a politician, she must have meant Ross. He hadn't noticed his Z4 in the car park, though. Then again, he had to have a bigger car in order to have put Kyle Campbell's body in the boot and so comprehensively crushed the pushbike.

Nick sat, arms crossed in contemplation, staring at the carpet. Danny had said his father was evil; for a while he'd thought he was exaggerating but it now seemed pretty close to the truth. The door opened. He half-expected it to be the tall, dark-haired Ronald Ross standing there with a knife in his hand. But it was just Debbie again.

'Right, we're all ready for you, Nick. Have you got a copy of the book to hold up to camera?'

'Yeah, I've got a couple with me. How long will this be?'

'It's a five-minute slot. I know it's not long, you just need to give a quick idea of the story. Mike will ask you a couple of questions about being a writer. And that'll be you done. Don't worry about getting all your words right, we can always do a retake if you mess up and swear or forget to put your pants on.' She laughed a little.

He shook the interviewer's hand and wished he had some better social skills in order to make small talk.

'I've read this, actually. Really enjoyed it. Got it on Kindle when I heard it was a local author,' said Mike, as they sat down opposite each other.

'Oh, that's good to hear.'

'It's always nice to read about places you know.'

Nick nodded, not knowing what else to say.

'We just had someone else up from Teesside, actually,' said Mike.

'Was it Ronald Ross, by any chance?'

The presenter, a middle-aged man with a heavy tan and a curiously fashioned moustache, looked surprised. 'That was a good guess!'

'Oh, I just heard that he was going to be on. I don't know him. He's in the House of Lords, isn't he?'

'Yeah. He was talking about how they're going to improve the quality and amount of housing stock on Teesside. An important issue, but all a bit dry, to be honest.' He spoke the sentence in a half whisper.

'Unlike some of the housing stock,' said Nick, with a raised eyebrow. Wallace laughed.

'Right, let's get down to business. This will be quite painless, Nick.'

But Nick was distracted. At the far side of the studio were the doors he'd entered through. Standing in front of them, dressed in a smart dark suit, was Ronald Ross. He wasn't doing anything, just standing there, looking at him. His presence made Nick nervous. Was he going to say or do anything? What could he do or say? Hopefully nothing before Mandy arrested him.

Seeing he was distracted, Mike turned and looked in the direction of Nick's gaze. As soon as he did, Ross pushed open the doors and left.

'Sorry, Mike. That was Ronald Ross, wasn't it?'

'Yup, that was him. Right, down to business...'

The interview was soon done. Debbie met him at the doors and shook his hand again and thanked him for coming. Nick walked through the reception lobby to the glass-fronted entrance, feeling like he had to get away as quickly as possible, just hoping that he wasn't going to be confronted by a crazy knifey man. He'd not had to hit anyone in the face for eight months and he didn't want to have to do so again now.

Outside it was cloudy and about to rain. He stood and looked from side to side for Ross. No-one. His car wasn't far away. He sprinted from the door to the old BMW, fumbled the lock with a shaking hand, pulled the door open and got in, slamming it shut and hitting the central locking, heart racing, expecting Ross to appear from somewhere. It had been a horrible coincidence that they were booked to have interviews recorded on the same afternoon.

But everything was cool. He must have gone already. Drops of rain began splattering onto the windscreen. He started the engine and flicked the windscreen wipers. It was only then that he noticed it.

A note.

A note was anchored under a wiper. His heart leapt into his throat and sank heavily. This wasn't good. He got out, took hold of it, got back in and locked the doors once more. On the small piece of paper in neat block capitals was simply, 'Say nothing, or Jeff Evans's son will die.'

Fucking hell. He felt hot and cold all at once.

Ross really was evil.

He rang Jeff, his hand shaking as he hit the 'call' button.

'Yo, crazy dude,' said Jeff.

'Jeff, where are you?'

'I'm with Argie at the hospital. They've put him on a regular ward now.'

'Thank god for that. So he's with you?'

'Yeah, he's sitting up in bed, eating a banana and colouring in photos of people in the newspaper. I'm sure he's going to be an artist.'

Nick told him about the note. 'Ross has to have left it. There's nothing to identify it but he was there. It's a clear threat. Don't let the boy out of your sight.' Nick heard him talking to Argie, who was chattering away in his almost-language-but-not-quite.

'I'm calling Mandy. They've got to take Ross down. He's dangerous. Bloody hell, to think I thought the Zet mob were scumbags, he's a million times worse,' said Jeff. He rang off.

Nick drove back down the A19 to Teesside and got caught in rush-hour traffic, crawling along at 10mph for what seemed like miles. As he came to a halt north of Dalton Piercy, he texted Julie to let her know where he was and to say he'd probably be home in half an hour. She finished work early on a Friday so would already be home. She messaged him back right away.

'*OK luv. I've had your delish fish and am now lying on the sofa with a glass of wine and a hand down my pants having a bit of a fiddle while thinking about you giving me a proper seeing to.*'

He laughed out loud, knowing that was almost certainly true.

'*Leave something in the tank for when I get back.*'

She replied. '*I'm just saving you the trouble of foreplay!*'

He laughed again and let out a sigh. Although they'd not discussed it, in the last couple of years, one of her ongoing strategies to help his mood was to flirt with him by text, writing him dirty little messages and putting him on a promise. And for him, it so often worked. Maybe it raised his dopamine, or maybe it was the promise of the excitement and pleasure of sex. Someone expressing physical desire for you is a life-enhancing thing and Nick never tired of it. And the truth was, she probably enjoyed it as much as he did.

Eventually, he arrived at the turn off for the A1027, then took a left off the roundabout for Norton High Street and parked up outside their house. As he walked in, his phone vibrated with a text message.

'Hey, Jules!' he called out, kicking off his brown leather boots.

She came out of the living room, dressed in a long black t-shirt and red jogging bottoms and grinned at him. 'Now, then. Traffic bad?'

'Terrible.'

'Did the interview go alright? It should be on in a bit.'

'Yeah, it was easy enough. Everyone was nice.'

'Good. You'll be getting quite a few orders in for it tonight, I should think.'

'You should take up writing erotic fiction, Jules. Your texts are works of art.'

They went into the kitchen.

'I could do the dirty bits, it's everything else I'd be rubbish at.'

'Well, if I ever have any dirty bits in my books, I'll ask you to write them. Might as well get an expert in.'

She let out her dirty laugh. 'Do you want a drink?'

'Need tea, please,' he said, sitting down at the kitchen table and taking out his phone while she filled the kettle. 'Here's the weird thing, right? They were interviewing Ronald Ross before me.'

'Getaway, that's an incredible coincidence.'

'Well, sort of. He's often on, from what I could tell, due to his influence in town planning. It's all classic local news stuff. I didn't actually meet him, thank god. Just saw him at a distance. But he left this on my windscreen.'

He passed the note to her. Her eyebrows shot up as she read it.

'Are you sure this is from him?'

'Of course. I'm going to give it to Mandy for her forensic team to analyse. They have our fingerprints on file. If they can get some DNA from it or anything that can be connected to Ross, that'll be another nail in his coffin.'

'That man is a stinking pig. I can't wait to see him get arrested and put away. Though I worry that he's got too much power and influence and money for that to happen. I mean, Danny said that himself when we were in Spain.'

Nick nodded. 'Speaking of Danny. He's just texted me. Bloody hell...'

'What is it?'

Nick licked his lips and read it out. 'He's copied in Jeff and your Kev as well. It says, "I've decided I'm going to take my father down. He's ruined too many lives. Be at the Zet at 6.30pm, bring the police." What does that mean? Hair Bear said he'd bought a lot of heroin.'

'Maybe he's going to try and fit his dad up with enough dope to get him sent down for a long time?'

'I hope not. No court would believe he was a dealer.'

'So what's he thinking of?'

'I don't know, but we better get over to those flats and find out.'

She ran upstairs and changed into a pair of blue jeans, pulled on some trainers and threw the keys to the Porsche to him.

'You'd better drive. I've had a large wine.'

'OK. Jeff's texted me. He's not leaving Argie on his own in the hospital in case Ross has sent someone over there but he's called Mandy and told her about Danny's text, so there should be some police presence. Kev's said he's walking down. He said, "this should be a bit of fun", but I very much doubt that.'

As he drove up Bishopton Road and turned left onto Bishopton Lane to park the car outside the station, he had a churn of nerves and fear in his stomach.

'I don't think there's anyone around,' said Julie, getting out of the car and peering towards the Zet.

They walked around the corner and stood for a moment taking in the scene. Everything was quiet. Nick looked at his watch, 6.28pm. There was a voice behind them. Nick turned. It was Kev Wells.

'What's going on?' he said ambling up.

'Nothing. No-one here.'

'The police should be here soon,' said Julie.

'Them flats look totally fucked, now,' said Kev, nodding to the derelict building. All the windows had been smashed and there was no sign of anyone being inside.

'They're going to knock them down,' said Nick.

Kev snorted derisively. 'They'll need to disinfect the whole area after that. Christ knows what germs will be released into the atmosphere; anthrax, probably.' He stopped and turned his head, listening to something in the distance. 'Hear that?'

'What?' said Nick.

'Two cars, one is chasing the other. Cops after our boy Danny, I should think.'

'How the hell do you know that?' said Nick.

'He's got a sixth sense for anything involving the police or crime,' said Julie, only half-joking.

He was right. The screech of tyres got louder and a car came roaring around the bend. It was a silver Z4 and hot on its heels was a police car. Shit, was it Ronald Ross?

They backed away off the road as the Z4 braked hard and skidded a full 20 feet, leaving a trail of smoking rubber as it came to a stop right outside the Zetland flats. Danny Ross jumped out of the driver's side, ran around the front of the car, yanked open the passenger-side door.

'Get out!' he yelled.

The police car parked up and two officers got out. Nick recognised them from his last visit to this death hole. They spoke into phones, clearly waiting for backup before doing anything.

Danny yelled into the car again and began pulling at an arm. He turned to Nick. 'Nick! Give us a hand to get this twat out!'

Nick sprinted to the car, leaned in and saw Ronald Ross. 'Leave it to me. I'll get him out.'

Ross sat rigid, looking straight ahead as though pretending none of this was happening.

'Don't ignore me, son,' said Nick, growling out the words, letting the anger and fear that the note Ross had left earlier that afternoon drive his strength of purpose. 'Get out the car or I'll hit you so hard in the face, you'll wish you were dead. Don't think I won't do it.'

But he didn't flinch, or look, or make a move. Nick stood up and looked down the road. Another police car arrived. Knowing that Ross would briefly have relaxed, at speed he bent down again, leaned in, grabbed Ross's arm with his right hand and his hair with his left and with one almighty yank, flung him off the seat so he was hanging head first out the door. He screamed at the pain of having his hair pulled. Amazingly, none of it came out. Must have good follicles. Now half prone, he was unable to do anything as Nick pulled him by the shoulders, out of the car and onto the road.

'There you go, Danny. One scumbag father.' He jabbed an index finger into Ross's neck and hissed 'You're in so much trouble, prick.'

The police still hadn't approached them but were monitoring what was going on. They had to be waiting for Mandy to arrive before they did anything. After the disastrous policing in the past, she probably didn't trust them to do things properly.

Danny kicked at his father. 'Stand up!'

This time, Ronald Ross did as he was told. He had a kind of stiff back, chest out, military bearing. He wouldn't look anyone in the eye, though. He was cornered, there was no way out of this; in effect, all he could do was keep quiet and wait for it to be over.

Kev, totally in his element when there was confrontation or anger, wandered up, hands in his jeans pockets. 'Do we need a random act of violence, like, just to oil the wheels of justice? If so, I'll have a pop at him for you, Danny. I could mash him with a couple of right handers, easy. And by the way, pal, if you're thinking you might run away from us, I'm as fit as fuck and I will take pleasure in hunting you down and hurting you. Right?'

Still no response from Ronald Ross.

'Do me a favour, Kev. Film this for me on this phone. I want a permanent record of it,' said Danny, handing him an iPhone.

'Right, over there,' Danny pushed his father and pointed to the Zet. 'Walk, or I'll get both of these men to break you into a thousand pieces.'

Again, without comment, Ross walked towards the block of flats, two strides ahead of Danny and Kev, who had started to film it on the phone.

Nick walked back to Julie.

'What's going on?'

'I don't really know, Jules. It's a bit weird. Danny seems to have a plan but I don't get what it is. His father is shutting it all down. I think he's scared but giving it the officer-class stiff upper lip. He's so out of his depth.'

She put her hand on his chest and looked into his eyes. 'Don't forget how evil that man is. He's not ordinary. He's dangerous.'

He looked to the four police officers standing in a huddle.

'Ah, here's Mandy,' he said, pointing to the car that was just parking up.

'Thank god for that,' said Julie. 'Be careful, right?'

'He's not a problem, Jules.'

She jabbed him in the belly. 'Don't say that, he is, he's an evil shit and evil shits are always a problem.'

The warm June breeze blew his hair across his eyes. He pushed it to one side and looked at Mandy Beale, who was advancing towards them. She stopped briefly to speak to her officers, and then strode on, looking at Kev, Danny and Ross as she did so.

'What the hell is going on?' she said, her tone indignant.

'I don't know. He wants to say something about his father, I think,' said Nick.

She turned to Danny Ross and began to walk towards him. 'Danny! Danny! What's this about? Talk to me, lad!'

Danny turned around and looked at her, then began gesturing for them all to come close.

'Kev, keep filming, right.'

Now Ronald Ross was getting edgy and was looking around himself, as though trying to find an escape route. There wasn't any. It was a dead end and his escape route was blocked by police. He held his hands up in surrender.

'Ah, Mizz Beale. I'm glad you've come. My son, here, he's really not well. I've gone along with his wishes so far, but quite clearly he is delusional, poor boy, no doubt caused by the drugs he's addicted to. I think we really need to get him to hospital. And I'd like to press charges against Mr Guymer here for common assault.'

Mandy turned to Nick and raised her dark brown eyebrows quizzically.

'I pulled him out of the car, that's all.'

Mandy turned back to Ross. 'You look alright to me. If Nick had hit you, you'd know about it.'

Ross was indignant. 'He threatened me and he pulled my hair! Now I really must insist...'

'Shut it. You'll live,' said Mandy, scowling. She turned to Danny, only to hear Ross blustering again about his mistreatment.

'...this is outrageous!'

She stood right in front of him, staring into his eyes. 'Mister Ross, I suggest you stand there and keep quiet. There will be plenty of time for you to talk, because believe me, you have got some explaining to do. I'll tell you what is outrageous; identifying a body as your son when you know it's not him. I'll tell you what's outrageous; talking a man into committing murder.'

On hearing that, Ross took a phone out his jacket pocket. 'I am calling my lawyer,' he said, as though that somehow trumped the power of the police. And that was the noticeable thing about Ross, like a lot of privileged, wealthy people, they don't believe the law really applies to them the way it does to everyone else and to suggest it should is a total insult to them. The look in his eye said he had nothing but contempt for Mandy Beale, this big, brusque Yorkshire woman. But the power of the state lay with her, not with him. He could use his influence and power later, but here and now, it was Mandy who was in charge. She simply grabbed the phone from him and tossed it to one of her men.

'You'll have plenty of time to do that later. I won't tell you again, Mister Ross. Stand there and keep quiet.'

'You...you...you harridan!' he exclaimed, cheeks pink with indignation. Who even used the word *harridan* in the 21st century?

He was so posh that it was almost comical. He actually sounded quite like Prince Charles.

'Aye, whatever. I've been called much worse, by much better people than you, Ronnie,' said Mandy, sneering at him with magnificent contempt as she turned to Danny.

'So, Danny. Why have you brought your father here like this? I hope I'm not going to have to arrest you, Danny. C'mon, let's 'ave it. What's going on?' She could have arrested him there and then, but her old copper's instinct knew when to let someone talk and when to cuff them. She waited, arms folded.

Danny ignored her, and began addressing the iPhone Kev Wells held, speaking quickly.

'My father is such an evil man. He and Harry Small conspired to have Glenn Vokes think he'd murdered someone in order to hide the murder of a reporter called Kyle Campbell, who was about to expose his corruption. But Vokes didn't do that murder...'

Nick looked at him as he spoke, and suddenly, without warning, the penny dropped. He'd been wrong! His logic had brought him so close to the truth, but at the last second had swerved and settled on the wrong culprit. He realized that even though he knew better, he'd still been guilty of prejudging people by where and how they lived, because it appeared to fit the facts. This was what his subconscious had been working on for so long.

'Oh, my god, Danny,' he said. 'It was you who killed Kyle Campbell! Vokes didn't do it, *you* did! And your father used Vokes to cover it up perfectly! This whole thing was set up to get you out of the country to avoid a murder charge! The whole sordid tale was all to hide what you did.'

Mandy and the others looked at him with surprise. Danny raised an eyebrow.

'Well done, Nick. Surprised it took you so long to work it out. So tell me the rest. Why did I do it? Answer Mandy's question. Why are we here tonight?'

Kev turned the iPhone camera towards Nick. Everyone's gaze followed him. Ronald Ross seemed frozen in fear for a moment.

Nick's brain spun as the pieces of the puzzle whirled around and dropped into place. It seemed so obvious now. It all fitted. All eyes were on him as he spoke.

'You were *never* a junkie,' he said. 'You looked too healthy when we saw you in Spain. You weren't a junkie, you just *sold* drugs from your flat here at the Zet! That's why Vokes said in court that you always had a big bag of gear up there.' More pieces began to fit, and he spoke again with increasing confidence. 'Berryman's main job was to be a sort of bodyguard for you. And he was working for your father here, who was your supplier! And when Campbell came round asking questions...'

'...Oh, my god, it all makes sense...' began Julie. 'Berryman saw the murder. He knew what had really happened. He was the only one in the Zet who did. And now I bet he's dead.'

Danny cut her off. 'Kyle was looking for dirt on him, and he was about to expose him and that meant I'd be exposed as a dealer as well. I got messed up. I should have admitted it all to the police and took a drugs charge, but I was scared. Scared of my father and what he'd do to me if I did that. He'd have had me killed. I know he would. So I went along with what he wanted, and what he wanted was for me to kill Campbell and then send me to Spain. He knew that between Harry and himself, they could control me. So I did it. It was, in effect, kill or be killed.'

Ronald Ross rolled his eyes and appeared to be ready to make a run for it and take his chances. But nothing got past Mandy and she just clicked her fingers and pointed. This was her silent gesture to indicate one of her officers should handcuff Ronald Ross. Ross scowled at her as one of her men did exactly that.

'Nonsense, absolute rubbish. Fantasy!' yelled Ronald Ross.

'Quiet!' barked Mandy. 'Go on, Nick.'

'They did the body switch and sent you to Spain, called the cops, fitted Vokes up with the knife. It was bleached to make sure there was none of your or his DNA on it, and then planted with the sweatshirt with the victim's blood on; the sweatshirt you had worn when you killed Kyle. He passed Kyle's body off as you, in the morgue. He used all his Establishment connections with the court to pull in favours and get himself airbrushed out of the picture.'

Mandy puffed out her pink cheeks. 'This is quite a bloody story. You're a one you, aren't you?' she said to Ross.

'Shut up!' said Ross, looking down his nose at her. 'This will end badly for you, Beale.'

Mandy scrunched up her fleshy face and shook her head. 'Somehow, I doubt that, sir.' She managed to use the word *sir* as an insult. 'Right, are we done here then, Danny?'

'No, not yet. Just a moment. I want this filmed. Nick's got it all right,' said Danny. 'Except for one thing. I really *was* a user. I wasn't lying about that. What I told you in Spain was all true. Smack helped me cope with life after being abused as a teenager, by some of this monster's associates. They gave me it to soften me up and make me pliable and helpless. They planned it all for weeks.'

'Oh, really!' blustered his father.

Danny went on. 'But the drug sucked me down into a massive hole along with Trace. Ironically, getting to Spain was the saving of me. In effect, killing Kyle kept me alive. I know the Zet is a bloody hell hole, but for a few weeks it was my home and you know what, being around other people who are fucked up makes life much easier. Not having to have standards takes the pressure off. But I was just working for him. Making drug money for him and taking the stuff myself. I was scared of him and I knew it meant free dope. It was an easy life for a while, really, but all along I knew this twat here and Harry Small were evil bastards. Small was always in my ear about shit. He grinds you down and makes you feel worthless. He puts The Fear in you. Ask anyone. I swear I wouldn't have killed that bloke without Small getting into my mind for those weeks, telling me it was the right thing to do and how it'd protect the family reputation and all of that. I can see it all now. They controlled me while I was there. I was their puppet. I did what they said and what they wanted. I just lost it that afternoon and...and...I don't even really remember doing it. It feels like a dream that I can only half remember. I was some sort of insane. But they had it all planned and they'd been working up to it all happening that afternoon of the 18th. They had Campbell and Vokes all lined up and ready to go. They even gave me that sweatshirt to wear. They got Campbell down there on some false pretence, wound me up and I did what I was told to do. I deserve to go to jail. I did a terrible thing. I've been hiding from the truth in Spain, but I'm not hiding any more.'

Ross senior began blustering again. 'How much longer do we have to stand here and listen to these people talking to each other? These are all the ridiculous ramblings of a deranged man! Do not listen to him. It's clearly all lies. I am a pillar of the community. These are monstrous and unprovable allegations which I will fight in court should you ever be stupid enough to arrest me for them. I will ruin your career. Do not doubt that!' He directed his comments squarely at Mandy. She just stared back unmoved, made a yapping sign in his face with her right hand, then turned away from him with contempt.

'Well this is all very enlightening. I appreciate you bringing it all to my attention, Danny. I think we've got to wrap this up now and get on with the legals, right?'

Danny nodded. 'I know I'm going to jail. But I will at least have made some of the wrongs right.'

'Daniel Ross, I'm arresting you for the murder of Kyle Campbell. You do not have to say anything, but it may harm your defence if you do not mention when questioned something which you later rely on in court. Anything you do say may be given in evidence.'

She turned to his father.

'Ronald Ross, I'm arresting you for conspiracy to murder and obstructing the course of justice. You do not have to say anything...' but he interrupted her.

'Outrageous! You'll be sorry you ever did this, you fat bitch!!!'

Mandy shrugged. 'Yeah yeah, they all say that and you know what, son? I never, ever, ever am.'

'But he's right, you will,' said Danny to Mandy. 'Whatever you charge

244

him with, he'll get away with it. He's too powerful, too rich and too evil. Just consider what Nick said about how he influenced the trial through his legal connections, to make sure his name was kept out of it. That tells you everything you need to know, Mandy. He's so evil, he even had unprotected sex with Tracy until she eventually fell pregnant just to show me who was boss! Just to own something I cared about. It's been like that my whole life. The sick bastard. And he is guilty of conspiracy to murder more than once. He had my mother killed by Harry Small, who then killed his own wife, to keep her from talking about what she knew of his ever more evil life. And I loved my mother.' His body language relaxed and he let out a huge sigh. A huge sigh that Nick recognised as some sort of final acceptance. 'That's why it's all got to end now!'

In an instant, he took a large plastic syringe from his denim jacket inside pocket and in one swift overarm move, jabbed it into Ronald Ross's neck and pressed down hard and fast. A needle isn't much to look at. As an instrument of death, it's an unassuming assassin. But it worked.

The look on his father's face was one of surprise, but nothing more.

'What was in that?' shouted Mandy.

'Enough smack to kill an elephant.' He pushed at his father, turned him to face the Zet and then yelled in his face. 'Look at it, look at that stinking place. That's you! That's the embodiment of your evil. You created it, you exploited it and now it's going to be the last thing you see before you fucking die!'

His father was biting the big one, not him. But he didn't seem to realise, even as a trickle of dark blood ran down his neck from the needle's puncture wound.

He tried to maintain his innocence to the last. 'Look, this is ridiculous, I'm an innocent man, my son has problems...he's...' then the drug mainlined into his bloodstream. And it hit him like a train. His eyes rolled up into his head as his body closed down, his whole frame seemed to shudder in a brief seizure and he keeled forward onto his face, hands still cuffed behind his back, his head striking the concrete with a sickening wooden-sounding crack, face down on the stain that Don Preston's blood had made.

He was dead, almost in an instant.

Mandy looked at Danny and shook her head. 'Well, you've saved us a lot of trouble, there Danny, so thanks for that. But now I'm going to have to also nick you for a second murder, due to killing people with drugs being just as illegal as stabbing them with a knife.' She gestured for one of her officers to handcuff him, then turned and took the iPhone from Kev's hand.

'I don't care. Someone had to do it. He would have got off,' said Danny, eyes blankly staring at his dead father.

Nick spoke. 'He wouldn't have. I found video evidence of what happened here with Vokes. There's no way he could have claimed he was innocent, even if Vokes didn't kill anyone. And your existence is proof that he lied at the morgue.'

'I don't believe that. The Establishment are brilliant at buying off and covering up. The law doesn't apply to them like it does to regular people. And even if he'd been put in prison, he would still have existed. And now he doesn't. And that's a good thing for the world.' He looked at his father's corpse and then at the Zet, his bottom lip quivering with emotion. 'I hope they blow this bloody place up. It's soaked in Teesside despair, soaked in Teesside evil and soaked in Teesside blood.'

CHAPTER 10

Kevin Berryman's lifeless, bloated, drowned body was fished out of the Tees two days later, alongside the Riverside Stadium. He'd apparently been in there for a quite a while, probably since the day Nick and Kev had confronted him. A week later, Harry Small was arrested for murdering Ruth Small, Danny's mother, Sally Ross and Berryman, though Mandy Beale thought the chances of conviction were 50/50 at best and would mostly rely on the jury's dislike of a bent copper, and the fact that there was a lot of undocumented cash in his house in Roseworth. Where had it come from? What was it payment for? Small had said he did car boots and bought and sold antiques, but it all looked very dodgy. There were plenty of people prepared to testify to his bullying, not least Danny Ross. The fact that Small had killed his former partner, simply because he'd found out that he knew what had really happened outside the Zet that fateful day, showed just what a stinking amoral bunch of people these were.

The police soon tracked down where Kyle Campbell had lived, in the lovely market town of Barnard Castle. He'd been single and tragically had seemingly not been missed by anyone. The rental company, as no rent had been paid, had taken possession of the flat and got rid of all his stuff. It had been noted by his neighbours that he seemed to have left. But no-one could have suspected what had really happened.

Rory Tyreman gave a full account of the mock stabbing and how meticulously Ronald Ross and Harry Small had planned out that bloody afternoon. He was scared and totally out of his depth, unaware of the cesspool he'd jumped into.

Danny Ross was charged with the murder of Kyle Campbell and of his father, and would inevitably be found guilty and sent down. How long for, would depend on the weight given to his mitigating circumstances, but it would be unlikely if he was out in less than 25 years.

Glenn Vokes, surprised and pleased that he'd not actually killed anyone after all, was officially declared innocent of the murder of Danny Ross and although everyone thought he should be provably guilty of something, no-one could quite decide what, as he'd hurt no-one. So he walked free. It would surely only be a matter of time before he was back inside for something. He wasn't one for changing.

Nick rewrote the whole story for the *Mirror*, who somewhat

grudgingly paid him the promised £15,000 for the exclusive. It was never easy, working for the tabloids but he felt vindicated. He and he alone had come to the right conclusion in the end.

A few weeks later, Jeff invited Nick and Julie around to his house in Hartburn Village on a Saturday night for a beef curry, cheesecake and lots of drink. Mandy was already there when they arrived just after 6pm.

'Phwoarr, that smells good, man,' said Nick as they walked into the house. 'I've not had a decent curry for ages.'

Jeff emerged from the kitchen wearing a Motörhead apron. 'It's a stonker and it's not even finished cooking yet. I've got the bog roll in the freezer, just in case.'

Mandy came out of the room holding Argie and hooted a laugh. 'I love a proper 'ot curry as long as I'm not on stake out or more than 10 seconds away from a bog.'

'I'm as bad,' said Julie. 'I'll be raising the sheets tonight.'

'After a curry, I could light her farts and cook on a wok over her bum hole,' said Nick. 'But enough of my sexual fantasies, which I don't have. Here, give us Argie.' He held out his arms and Mandy passed him to him. 'Now then, little fella, how are you? I like your tie-dye t-shirt. You look like a little hippy.'

'Aye, 'e does, doesn 'e. I hope I'm not busting him for possession of magic mushrooms in 18 years,' said Mandy, combing her fingers through the boy's messy hair, then kissing him on the top of his head. Her way of quite naturally and affectionately fussing over him was very striking. She wasn't the boy's mother, but you'd never have known that as a dispassionate observer. She behaved towards him exactly as if she was.

'Have you learned any more words, Arg?' said Nick.

'Ayo Nick,' said the boy, then pointed at Julie. 'Ayo Joooolz. Ayo Mannnndz.' They laughed delightedly.

'He's started to almost walk,' said Jeff. 'He's at that drunk-a-bottle-of-tequila stagger stage. He sets off, gets a few feet and then falls on his face. It's brilliant, he looks pissed as fart.'

'Pisssst,' said Argie, laughing.

'Hey, no rude words, Argie. Not until you're 18. C'mon, young fella-me-lad, it's time you went bye byes.' Jeff took him from Nick and went upstairs to get him into bed.

'Right. Drinkeepoohs,' said Mandy, rubbing her hands together. 'What are you 'avin, kids?'

'V A T for me,' said Nick.

'Me, too,' said Julie.

'Rightyho, follow me.'

She led them into the kitchen where a large pan of curry was simmering. A large lemon cheesecake sat on the bench.

'Two vodka and tonics coming up. Small, medium or Mandy-sized?'

'I'll have a double Mandy, please,' said Julie.

She fixed the drinks and poured herself a Stella from a can. They sat down at the big circular pine kitchen table.

'Cheers!' said Mandy, raising her glass to them and downing half a pint in four gulps. 'Ooof, I needed that. It's been sodding long week. One of those weeks where you feel you've achieved nothing, but it's knackered you all the same. All I've done is sit in meetings.'

'I hate meetings. I'd do almost anything to avoid a meeting,' said Nick. 'Whenever I have to have one, I go to it hoping it'll be cancelled at the last minute.'

'Well, this was unavoidable. We got in the preliminary report into how we handled the Kyle Campbell murder - the one we thought was Danny Ross.' She puffed out her pink cheeks.

'Good news?' said Julie.

'You must be joking. One bloody bollock dropped after another.'

'Who did the enquiry?' said Nick.

'Bristol and Avon force. I bloody hate these sorts of investigations. Always feels like other forces are taking the piss out of us.'

'Was there any actual corruption in the force, Mand?' said Julie.

She cleared her throat. 'Well, there was only one thing I still think smells bad. '

'What's that?' said Nick.

'The fact our patrol car showed up before the cabbie had even finished his 999 call.'

'I thought that was odd in court. But it wasn't followed up.'

Mandy sneered a little. 'The explanation offered by the two officers first on the scene was that someone in Nolan House had anonymously called to say there was a fight outside the Zet and they arrived just as the cabbie was making his call. So it was a fortuitous coincidence.'

'Well that's plausible,' said Julie.

'Hmm. Maybe. I sense the hand of Harry Small in it somewhere. But it made no material difference to the case, so outside of Harry Small in the Durham force, there was no corruption. It has to be said his bosses in

Durham knew fine well something was iffy about him when they pensioned him off. Cleveland came out of it looking useless but clean. Dunny got a severe reprimand from top brass. His crap work made it easier for Ross to pull off the scam. He had been put under pressure by the judge not to bring Ronald Ross into his reporting. The judge, cleverly, had suggested it would likely harm the chances of a conviction because no-one likes a rich kid who's gone off the rails after having all the privileges of money. So he pulled back on that, thinking it was a good idea, never guessing the old boys' network was in operation.'

She yawned and put her hands behind her head. 'An old pro like him should never have fallen for that. In a way, I wish there had been corruption. As it is, it just makes us look shite. The problem from the start was we didn't take it seriously enough because it was a Zet death. It shouldn't be the case that when a junkie has been killed, that it doesn't matter as much as a respectable member of society, but the truth is, it doesn't. Dunny just thought, bloody Zetters again, I'm sick of them. Shovel them up and get rid. Everyone's brains went into neutral. They didn't secure the crime scene properly. The fact he had a phone number on him but no other ID should have rang alarm bells, but it didn't. They should have looked into Danny Ross's history more, but no-one did. They should have been far more thorough when they discovered there was no CCTV camera footage. Harry Small should not have gotten away with taking those DVDs, even if we got lucky and it ended up not mattering. The fact the pathologist had given such a big window of time for when Danny died didn't help us either. I'm still of a mind to say she'd been squeezed by Ross in some way to fudge her judgement on time of death, but I can't prove it. Oh, and just to let you know, Nick, it was a coincidence those cameras were missing from Nolan House. They busted a group of neighborhood kids recently for property damage and during questioning they admitted stealing them.' She growled. 'It was shite, really. The whole investigative team just wanted rid of the body and the paperwork. Then, when it got to court, as I say, the old boys' - and girls' - network kicked in and kept Ronald R's name out of it. That's what that lot do. They cover each other's arses, like they're all in the same family. "Just a word in your ear, old boy." That sort of thing.'

'Poor Kyle Campbell,' said Julie. 'He died and no-one knew or cared.'

'There's a lot of people in that situation,' said Mandy. 'We've stopped looking after each other, in favour of looking at our phones. That's what I reckon and it's wrong. When I was a lass in Castleford, everyone looked after everyone else. No-one, and I mean, no-one, could have died and it not be noticed by anyone. It just couldn't happen.'

'Exactly. It was the same on the Hardwick estate,' said Julie.

'But it was certainly possible in Fairfield, where I grew up,' said Nick. 'There was little sense of community and my parents didn't want anyone knowing their business. That was part of the back-to-back terraced-houses upbringing that they wanted to get away from. What you both describe was what they wanted to put behind them. In that respect, they were inventing the future.'

'Yeah, well, I think we need to 'ave a good look at ourselves. And Lord knows how we're going to prosecute Harry Small, though. I mean, he's on remand in Durham jail, but when that comes to court, we've got zilch on him, really. A lot of circumstantial. The autopsy on Kev Berryman was inconclusive. He'd been in the water so long. You know what? I reckon, for what it's worth, Small drugged his wife, Ross's wife and Berry to immobilize them, gave them a little shove into the river, so that all of them were unable to save themselves by swimming, but because of the length of time they were all in the Tees, the drug didn't show up in the post mortems. I just wish I could prove it.'

'He had no history of physical violence, but he is a very cruel man. A little shove into the water sounds like his sort of thing,' said Julie.

Jeff came in. 'The lad was asleep before his head touched the pillow. Ah, I see you're refuelling. I shall have a tequila on the rocks, I think.'

He poured himself a large measure over ice and sat down with a groan. 'I see the paper is reporting the Zetland flats are getting pulled down next month. Long overdue. Let's hope some decent housing is built in its place.'

'What's happened to Blobby and that other bloke, Smithy?' said Nick.

'Smithy is dossing in some place in Southbank,' said Mandy. 'Blobby carked it about two weeks ago. Didn't you hear?'

'No. Really? It doesn't really surprise me,' said Julie. 'He was a horrible mess.'

'Aye. He had a heart attack while drinking by the river. When they did the post mortem, guess how much alcohol he had in his blood?'

'I don't know how you measure that,' said Jeff.

'Let's do it by equivalent pints of Stella,' said Mandy. 'How many pints?'

'10,' said Nick.

'15,' said Julie.

'I'm going against the trend here, I think he'd just had two,' said Jeff.

'You got one number right, Jeff. He'd had the alcoholic equivalent of 32 pints of Stella in his bloodstream. Yes, 32!'

They looked at each other in astonishment.

'How can anyone drink so much?' said Nick.

'I never knew a man drink as much as Blobby. He's been like that for years. He probably drank 3 or 4 bottles of cheapo voddy and then 10 or 12 beers every day. But that's still basically only about 60 quid's worth of booze. It costs nowt to kill yourself on a bender these days. He had rotted his brain with it, hence all that paranoia he came at you with. He didn't know who had killed or who had been killed. He made it all up in his head. I think he had a notion that Tracy knew something and from there, he'd made up a story and then forgot he'd made it up and thought it was truth.'

Nick took a big drink. 'You know, when I was in court on the jury, I really did feel sorry for all the low life who gave evidence. I didn't like any of them but I could empathise to a degree. But now, I realise that was totally misplaced. You had it right, Jeff. You told me they were scumbags. Berryman was scum, Vokes a nut job, Blobby a massive pisshead. Only Tracy was alright.'

'Yeah, I knew what they were like. But then, I'd have put Tracy and Danny in that group as well and that wasn't right,' said Jeff.

'I don't feel sorry for Danny, either,' said Julie. 'He had me believing he was just a nice kid with an evil father, when here he was a drug dealer and murderer all along!'

'I do feel for him, though,' said Nick. 'He was abused as a teenager, he was an addict because of that and he was used like a puppet by his father and Small. And in the end, Jules, he did the right thing. He came back and put his hand up for the crime.'

'And killed his father. Which I wholeheartedly condone,' said Jeff. 'The sodding evil swine.'

Julie nodded. 'I was wondering if that Gary Simmonds fella who was eavesdropping in the bar in Spain, the man we thought was reporting back to Berryman, was actually just a Boro bloke on holiday who had known Berryman in jail, but that was it.'

'My view is neither Ross nor Small knew you'd found Danny out there. If they had, they'd have taken evasive action immediately, and they didn't,' said Mandy. 'So your Simmonds bloke is probably a coincidence. Was probably drawn to you because of your accents and that you were talking about a man he knew. He was being nosy, not spying,' said Mandy.

'Aye, there were a lot from the northeast in that place,' said Jeff. 'Most of them almost totally naked.'

'You did a good job out in Spain finding Danny, though,' said Mandy. 'Which brings me to a little idea that I've had put to me.'

She looked at each of them in turn.

'How do you three fancy being an undercover team?'

Jeff laughed. 'I'm happy to dress as the Milk Tray bloke in black pants and roll neck in return for free boxes of chocolates.'

'I'm serious,' said Mandy.

'You're not,' said Julie, half laughing.

But Nick could tell she was 100 per cent serious.

'When you say "undercover team", what does that really mean, Mandy?' he asked.

She drained her pint, went to fridge and got another, pulling the ring on it as she sat down.

'Look, I've not even talked to Jeffrey about this but a week or three ago, I got a visit from MI6, specifically to talk about you. You're on their radar, y'see.'

Nick looked at Julie and then Jeff. They each had an expression of frowning surprise.

'I'm on MI6's radar?' said Jeff. 'Why? Do they want a good source of early albums on the pink Island label?'

Mandy smiled at him and patted his hairy arm. 'Yes dear, the safety of the country relies on such things.' She turned to Julie and Nick. 'You're on both MI5 and MI6's radar, actually. It started with how you dealt with the terrorists who wanted to destroy MIMA. You can't fight for your town the way you lot did without attracting the attention of the security forces. I mean, you were prepared to lay down your lives to try and stop something terrible happening, and that's what they're looking for. Ricky and Kev also. Now, there's no way Ricky and Kev are of interest to the state due to being severe piss artists and with criminal pasts, but they've had their eyes on you three ever since. There are substantial files on all three of you.' She held up her hands. 'Nothing bad, so don't panic.'

'You say nothing bad, but there's a film of us shagging somewhere on the internet,' said Julie.

Mandy waved that away. 'They don't care about that sort of stuff. That was covertly done. It's not like you were showing off or doing it for money. Nor does it matter that you smoked dope, Jeff, or that you suffer from depressions, Nick. They're interested in things like bravery, creative thinking, intelligence, loyalty, strength of mind, as well as the ability to dispense someone with a stiff right-hander and discharge a weapon without shooting yourself in the foot.' She'd counted the assets off on her fingers.

'I don't much like the idea that we've been spied on,' said Nick. 'Even if it's complimentary.'

'Understandable. But you've been impressing important people for a while now. The fella you called Shadow Man wrote you all into his report in very glowing terms and he is one of their top agents. And, basically, that was how I was able to give you a safe house in Great Ayton last year, remember? We don't actually have safe houses, that was a joint MI5-MI6 gig. They wanted you to be safe, Julie, that's how highly they value you.'

'I'm sorry, Mandy, this is all a mind blow for me,' said Julie. 'I'm just a lass off the Hardwick estate. I'm not exactly Mata Hari or Jane Bond.'

'I had it put to me that you three and Kev should go to Spain to dig out Danny Ross, and what did you do?'

'We dug out Danny Ross,' said Jeff.

'Exactly. And you impressed people in doing so. They were looking into Ronald Ross for most of this year, apparently, but only you guys found where Danny was. Didn't I say you were a good team?'

'Bloody hell. We didn't do much,' said Julie. 'I just chatted him up and then we chased him and got him to talk.'

'That's a talent, lass. When I said you were a good team, I meant it. Brains, brawn and beauty. And all three of you have got all three.'

Jeff put his hand up in the air. 'Please miss, in no universe do I have beauty. These two, yeah, I can see that; me, no.'

'You're beautiful to me, Jeff.'

'You're wearing the infamous Stella beer glasses then,' said Jeff.

Mandy turned back to Nick and Julie. 'Don't worry, this isn't a pitch for you to become spies. That isn't what this is about at all.'

'So what is it, then?' said Nick.

'There are certain situations, specific instances when both MI5 and MI6 need men and women who are ordinary members of the public, but who are working to their agenda. All they're asking is that you be ready and available to do work for them, when they need it. It'll all come through me and you will always have the right to decline any job. Now, it's not going to be exciting stuff. It won't be gun running in the Middle East, or chasing bank robbers across Switzerland in your Porsche, it'll more likely be hanging around a bar to keep an eye on someone they're interested in. Getting into conversation with someone. It might be following someone, or finding someone, the way you did with Danny, and possibly gaining their trust in order to get them to tell us something we need to know. I know this is all very vague. But if you accept, you could be paid a significant amount of money. Fees will vary depending on what you're being asked to do - the more dangerous, the more money. If you'd worked for them in foiling the terrorist attack they'd have paid you six figures for that, I reckon. I don't say this lightly. I've been a copper my whole adult life, but the three of you have really got something, both as individuals and as a team. You can be assets to your country, or at least to Teesside and North Yorkshire. Now, this might not even happen. Or if it does, maybe it won't be for a year or three. You don't have to make a decision now, but what are your feelings about it in principle?' She sank more lager. No-one knew what to say. It all seemed so extraordinary.

'Oh, I forgot!' Mandy got up, went to a brown leather briefcase, opened it and took out an envelope. 'A little reward for your Spanish jaunt.' She put it in the middle of the table. Nick picked it up. Inside was a cheque. He slid it out. It was for £5,000. He held it up to Jeff, who whistled, and then to Julie, who whooped.

'That's amazing. If it's alright with you, Jules...' said Nick.

'Aye, deffo, go for it,' she said, immediately understanding what Nick was suggesting.

'...this is yours, Jeff. Put it into Argie's savings account. The *Mirror*'s paid for Julie's course, and we'll be set up for a while.'

'Really? Bloody hell, that's great, man, thank you,' he said. 'And I'm not going turn it down. The wee man's future needs as much financial insulation as possible. ' He grinned widely.

Mandy beamed at them. 'Right, so anyone up for this?'

The three of them looked at each other.

'I'm in,' said Jeff, without hesitation.

'I'm in,' said Julie, immediately.

'I'm in,' said Nick, with a nod.

But even as he said it, he wondered what on earth they were getting themselves into.

THE END

Books in the Nick Guymer Series
Published by HEAD PUBLISHING

1. Teesside Steal (2013)
2. Queen of the Tees (2013)
3. Teesside Missed (2013)
4. DJ Tees (2014)
5. Teesside Blues (2014)
6. Tyne Tees (2014)
7. High Tees (2015)
8. Teesside Meat (2015)
9. Teesside Shadows (2015)
10. King Tees (2016)
11. Teesside Dreams (2016)
12. Blood on the Tees (2016)

A Nick Guymer Comic Short Novel
Published by HEAD PUBLISHING

Knickers Always Go Down Well (2016)

Kindle/Paperback

http://www.johnnicholsonwriter.co.uk

About John Nicholson

John is a well-known football writer whose work is read by tens of thousands of people every week. He's a columnist for Football365.com and has worked for the Daily Record, The Mirror, Sky and many other publications over the last 14 years.

Books in the Archie Taylor Series
Published by HEAD PUBLISHING

1. The Girl Can't Help It (2014)
2. Sugar Mama (2016)

Kindle/Paperback

http://www.johnnicholsonwriter.co.uk

Other John Nicholson Books
published by Biteback Publishing

We Ate All The Pies -
How Football Swallowed Britain Whole (2010)

The Meat Fix -
How 26 Years of Healthy Eating Nearly Killed Me (2012)